BENEATH BLA[CK]
[T]ID[ES] II

AGAINST DARK TIDES

CLARE SAGER

For the ones who find 'home' in books.
This home is for you.

To surviving the dark.

— TRADITIONAL ALBIONIC MIDWINTER
TOAST

THE VISCOUNTESS VILLIERS

Vice smiled sweetly across the card table, the expression making her muscles ache. She'd used this smile so often over the past two weeks, she thought she might've grown accustomed to it by now, but no. Some things she'd never get used to.

Knigh Blackwood kept his gaze on the cards already revealed on the green baize. Cool, calm, and collected as ever. He'd re-perfected his mask over their voyage so far, and every blank expression made Vice's insides ache and itch until she had to fidget. How easily he shut her out.

From their seats either side of Vice, Lord and Lady Pevensey exchanged a glance before both raising their eyebrows at her. Vice fought the urge to give them a triumphant grin and instead cocked her head at Knigh.

"*Darling,*" she said, voice over-bright, "remind me again, does a full house win?"

Does a full house win? She bit back a snort as she revealed her cards. Lady Pevensey had two of a kind, Knigh three of a kind, and Lord Pevensey had folded already. Obviously it won.

A flicker of a frown crossed Knigh's face and his lips flattened. He glanced at her cards, then back at her, his grey eyes narrowing a hair's breadth. For a man with such controlled expressions, he really should've been better at poker.

"Well, my *dearest* Verity, you appear to have won *again.*" But he didn't smile, and the way his eyebrows rose said he learned she'd cheated.

Of course she'd bloody cheated. She was a pirate. What did he expect?

It wasn't as though he was in any position to lecture her.

"Oh, you two," Lady Pevensey sighed. "Gazing adoringly at each other." She smiled and shook her head, hand resting on her chest. Another sigh. "Young love." She shared a meaningful look with her husband.

With her perfect plum-coloured gown and caramel-gold hair, Lucia Pevensey understood the importance of appearances. However, that understanding didn't extend to seeing what lay behind them. In the case of Viscount and Viscountess Villiers, it was less young love, more fake marriage of convenience between mortal enemies.

Vice gave Lucia a sweet smile, though, and scooped up her winnings. A few guineas. Some money of her own, and—

A warm grip, a little too hard, fastened around her hand, pressing the coins into her palm.

Knigh.

The hairs on her arms stood on end. She gritted her teeth. His touch had no effect on her. None whatsoever.

Urgh, why did I say he could help me find Drake's treasure? It had been a stupid, *stupid* moment of weakness, wanting to help his family... not wanting to say goodbye to him. The way he'd bathed her that night must've addled her brain—no one had treated her so gently since she was a child. After all the pain of the gibbet cage, was it any wonder it had messed with her mind and screwed up her judgement? Well, with any luck, he'd be only too happy to leave her to her own devices once they were back in Arawaké.

"Let me help you, *my love.*" He turned over her hand, exposing the spot up her sleeve where she'd been hiding cards all evening. As if it was a caress, he slipped his fingertips under the cuff and across the delicate skin of her inner wrist, no doubt checking for more illicit cards.

Well, he could check all he liked. She'd used the last one in that hand.

He gave her a pointed look.

So what if she'd cheated? It was his fault she had nothing of her own—or at least hadn't until she'd had such a mysteriously good run of luck at cards tonight. She couldn't keep relying on him and his money forever. Hells, he had so little of the stuff, she couldn't if she wanted to.

No way did she want to rely on Knigh Blackwood for anything.

Not after what he'd done.

Her chest tightened.

His hand was still on her, fingers on her pulse point. He'd

gone very still. So had the room. His eyes were doing that thing again—saying sorry without any words.

Well, sorry wouldn't cut it. Not when he'd betrayed her, arrested her, and left her at the mercy of a naval court.

Yes, she was *technically* guilty of the crimes. But that wasn't the point.

The *point* was, he'd shared her bed and said such pretty, *pretty* words when all the time he'd plotted with FitzRoy to capture her and claim the bounty on her head.

And it was a very sharp point—a lot like a dagger in the back.

Oh, he'd tried to explain. During this trip, he must have made at least half a dozen attempts. But every time he started, rage bubbled up in her, burning and unbearable.

At least, that's what she thought it was. If it wasn't rage stinging her eyes and blocking her throat, then it was something far worse.

Something unacceptable. Something powerless and pathetic and broken. Something she *would not* succumb to.

Anger was stronger.

Lord Pevensey cleared his throat.

Knigh flinched as if he'd forgotten they had company. Vice blinked and snatched her hand away, skin burning where he'd touched it.

"Are we going to play another hand," Pevensey said, his voice teasing as he raised one black eyebrow, "give us a chance to win back our money, or are you two going to do this all evening?"

Vice smirked. Another hand meant another chance for her to win. She stacked her coins. "Well, if you—"

"I'm afraid not," Knigh said with a stiff smile. "My wife grows tired. She's on the mend, but we mustn't keep her from her sleep. Isn't that right, darling?"

Vice's skin prickled, and her hand squeezed around a golden guinea until it bit into her skin. She was still weak from the iron gibbet cage, and she'd spent the first few days of the voyage sleeping, but she'd put on weight and had much more energy now.

Last night, she'd burned another candle low trying to work out FitzRoy's damn clue. When she'd opened his pouch, she'd found a page torn from what was perhaps a handwritten journal with lines from Drake's poetry written on one side. Whoever had copied it had broken the lines in strange places, leaving half the page empty. On the back were a few jagged lines, like someone's pen had meandered across the page. Was that a clue or an accident?

One thing was for certain—it was bloody infuriating and she'd made no progress on working out what it meant, despite not dropping into bed until eleven o'clock.

Still, if she could manage that, she could stay up later than —she glanced at the clock on the wall—than *nine*.

This wasn't his concern about her health.

Jaw clenched, she unleashed a first-rate glare at him. How bloody dare he? If she cheated, it was none of his business. Besides, the Pevenseys could afford to lose it.

"Indeed, you seem much improved, Lady Villiers." Pevensey gave her a small, pitying smile that turned her stomach. His wife's opposite in looks and character—dark where she was fair, arch where she was gentle—the expression was all wrong on him. "Though I'm sure your health wasn't helped by that terrible fright you had on your way to Portsmouth."

"Oh," Lucia exclaimed and fanned her face. "Do not mention it, darling! I cannot bear to hear of it." Swallowing, she turned her wide blue eyes to Vice. "You poor thing! Attacked by a highwayman—I don't know how you survived. It must have been so frightening." She bit her lip. "Tell me about him again."

For someone who couldn't bear to hear of it, Lucia asked about the fabricated attack a lot—every night they'd dined together, in fact.

Knigh had made the story up to explain Vice's—or rather, Lady Villiers' lack of jewels and limited wardrobe. After all, the wife of a viscount should have rings and necklaces and new gowns for her trip.

But she wasn't his wife. Verity, Lady Villiers didn't exist. She was Lady Vice, wanted pirate, and here solely out of necessity. Perhaps Knigh had forgotten that.

Fine, if he wanted to usher her away like a good fake-wife, he could. But it wouldn't be without consequences.

"Frightening doesn't cover it, Lucia." Vice made her voice grave, her chest heave, as if terrified at the thought. "He's quite the most vicious beast I've ever encountered."

She shot Knigh a small, cruel smile.

Just desserts.

She widened her eyes, the perfect mirror of Lucia's expression. "I rather think he played upon my sympathies, telling me how desperate his family's situation was, plying me with pretty manners and even prettier words. Why, I nearly cared for him" —only *nearly*—"but then he took *everything*."

Maybe Knigh hadn't taken it, exactly, but he'd made her lose it all and that was practically the same thing.

She raised an eyebrow at him, while Lucia gasped and fluttered about how terrible it was.

Knigh's face was a mask. Still. Solid. Only his chest moved, steady.

Then his nostrils flared, just once, the movement so small no one would have seen if they hadn't been paying attention.

But Vice *was* paying attention. And as far as Knigh Blackwood was concerned, that minuscule movement was a great victory.

"Now, darling," she drawled and rose, slipping the coins in her pocket, "let us retire, since I'm so *very* tired." She held out her hand as if she needed his help.

He had no one to blame but himself. She was only playing up to the role he'd made for her—the invalid wife who needed to get to bed so early. The poor weak thing.

Maybe it was cruel. But it wasn't as cruel as locking a fae-blooded woman in an iron cage. And it wasn't as cruel as sleeping with someone you planned to betray.

A breath later, Knigh rose and circled the table, his face a mask once more. "Of course," he murmured, offering his arm.

They wished the Pevenseys goodnight and left the cabin. No sign of Barnacle—probably off with the ship's tomcat again.

In silence, Vice and Knigh walked the corridor, gaits offsetting the ship's sway with ease.

She let out a long breath. That sway cooled her, pushed

away the anger. Not so long ago, she thought she'd never feel it again.

The sea.

Her beloved sea. Immense. Ancient. Ever-moving. It whispered to her gift, called her, sang to her.

It would never let her down.

Unlike Knigh Blackwood.

KEEPING UP WITH THE
PEVENSEYS

A s soon as their cabin door closed, Vee rounded on him, cheeks flushed, eyebrows drawn low.

"How bloody dare you?"

Knigh held his face stiff against the desire to wince. Stopping her cheating *was* the right thing to do and yet...

After what he'd done, perhaps he should let her do whatever she wished. It certainly didn't feel right to deny her anything.

But, gods, this cabin—it was too small for both of them *and* her anger. A double bunk against the bulkhead with a chest at its foot, a tiny desk and a dressing table, then a strip of deck down the middle. That was it.

Chest heaving, she shook her head. "You do understand you're the reason I have no money, don't you? All I wanted was some of my own."

He stood stock-still, but inside, his stomach twisted and his heart faltered. A chill snaked through his bones.

It *was* his fault.

Just like her skinny body was his fault, and her wasted muscles, too. She had put on weight but still didn't fill the clothes he'd bought her. Physically, she was a shadow of the woman he'd first met. And her gift wasn't in any better condition.

His fault.

His poor judgement. *Again.*

Bile touched the back of his throat.

Jaw clenched, he swallowed. "And how would we have explained it when they discovered you were cheating?"

"They wouldn't have found out." She huffed and turned her back on him, pacing as far away as she could in the cramped cabin. Scowling, she yanked pins from her hair, wincing and rubbing her scalp. She did that most nights—the weight of her hair coiled and pinned in place was yet another small torture he'd played a part in inflicting upon her.

She shot him a sharp glance and dropped the hair pins on the dressing table. "And there is no *we*. *I* could've explained it away just fine." She began to undress, shrugging off the top layer of her gown. "Thanks ever so much for your concern."

He sighed and untied his cravat. There was a *we* whether she liked it or not. It might have been necessity, but it was still there. If they were going to make it back to Arawaké safely, they needed the Pevenseys as well as Billy and his crew to believe that they were indeed husband and wife, rather than fugitives —she a pirate and he a Navy deserter.

Deserter.

He held still as his stomach twisted again. Deserters were cowards. They fled their duty to Queen, country, and comrades. Yes, he'd walked away from his post, but he'd done it out of a sense of duty to right the wrong he'd done Vee.

No matter how much he turned the thoughts around in his head, the two things didn't fit. Deserters were cowards.

He shook his head, running his hands over his face. However hard it was to reconcile, the outcome was the same—he was a deserter and the punishment for that was death.

At least he and Vee had that in common.

All stiff, jerky movements, she finished undressing and threw her clothes into the chest at the end of the bed, leaving just a chemise skimming her body.

He winced, first at the careless way she stowed her clothing, then at the lack of curves for that chemise to glide over. The hips he'd held on to, the breasts he'd worshipped, both diminished thanks to the torture of an iron cage.

His fault.

Breaths heaving, he turned away and hung up his jacket. His chest was hollow, his heartbeat echoing against his ribs.

"The Viscountess Villiers," she muttered with a snort. "Well, at least Papa would be happy to hear that, albeit three years too late."

He scrubbed his face again. Such a tangled web. Pretending to be married to his former fiancée... Lying about her name—Verity was the first name he'd come up with, easy to explain away if he slipped and called her Vee.

Plus the fact they'd ended up on Billy's ship, of all places. Hopelessly tangled.

Stuck at sea with the two people he'd most wronged in his twenty-three years of life. Perhaps the gods were even more angry at him than Vee was, and this was their way of punishing him.

He'd caused this. He had to endure it.

With a long breath, he squared his shoulders and faced her.

She stood at the dressing table, shawl tugged around her shoulders. She was often cold since her ordeal.

Another stab of guilt in his gut. He clenched his jaw against it.

A small teapot sat on the dressing table, steam rising from the spout. The cabin boy must've brought it while they'd been playing cards.

Vee poured the hot water into a cup, then stirred in a spoonful of herbs. An open jar stood beside it, the green, brown, and purple herbs familiar.

Why would she have the preventative? And where from? He hadn't presumed to pick the stuff up when he'd bought her supplies ahead of their escape.

Maybe it was a different tea. He cleared his throat. "Is that—"

"Yes. It is. It helps with our moons." The teapot's lid clattered off when she slammed it on the table, her shoulders square, back to him. "Get over yourself. I'm not about to jump on you. It's not all about sex."

Knigh winced. Two words. That's all it took to set her off, like ill-treated gunpowder.

And he was the one who'd done the ill treatment.

It wasn't as though he expected her to want him. Not after betraying her so badly. He'd hurt her too much. They'd so nearly had something, but now all that was left was this mangled wreckage.

He smoothed away the wince. Helping her get back to Arawaké wouldn't repair things between them, but it was the only way he knew to even attempt to make amends. He had to endure this.

Stay the course.

With all the timing of a ship-killing wave in a storm, an all-too-familiar creaking began from the cabin next door. Rhythmic. A woman's cry. A muffled grunt.

"Do they never stop?" Vee hissed.

The Pevenseys. Very happily married, by the sounds of it. Every night. A noisy, insistent reminder of what was missing from this cabin. From his life.

The air thickened.

Just a few months ago, he would have taken those two paces towards Vee, pulled the shawl away and replaced it with his own warmth. He'd have traced the lines of her back with his hands, lifted her into his arms, covered her mouth with his, and taken her to that bunk. Their cries would have put the Pevenseys to shame.

Now, those two paces may as well have been two leagues of rough sea for all he could walk across it.

She spun on her heel, eyes wide.

He froze, face hot. She couldn't know his dangerous thoughts. Did she somehow want—

Then he heard it, too: a shout. "Help!"

From above deck.

"Man overboard!"

BENEATH THE SURFACE

K nigh's stomach dropped, and he threw open the door. Vee sprung after, tea forgotten.

Frowning, he called over his shoulder, "Vee, you can't—"

"What have I told you about telling me what I can't do?"

He huffed through his nose, running for the companion-way. No time to argue, even if she was wrong.

If a sailor had fallen overboard, he'd be left behind in the darkness, floating on an endless ocean for cold or sea or creatures to snuff out. The only hope was to halt the ship as quickly as possible and send a swimmer or boat back.

But in the dark...

Legs pumping, Knigh took the steps two at a time.

Problem was, most sailors couldn't swim.

"Llyr!" The shouts were louder. Llyr was one of the younger apprentices, a cheerful boy of fifteen with a keen eye.

Other cabin doors thudded open. Vee's breaths huffed behind him. She was too weakened for this. If she exhausted herself, she could get ill again.

To aft, men clustered on the quarterdeck with lanterns. To fore, there was movement and the scrape and squeak of wood and metal—they were launching the ship's boat.

"Heave!" Beyond the common room skylight, men braced the main mast, readying the ship to heave to.

Vee could halt it quicker, but...

He paused at the base of the quarterdeck steps and turned to the companionway as Vee emerged. Breaths heavy, she leant on the skylight.

"We need to stop." Just saying it tightened his throat. She hadn't been able to use her gift since Portsmouth, but if they didn't reach Llyr, the boy would die.

Taking a deep breath, she nodded and clenched her jaw. "I —I can do it." Another inhale and she closed her eyes, a frown running dark lines between her brows.

Something in the air changed. Maybe the pressure, maybe the wind, but it made his ears pop, like diving at the reef had.

The ship drew to a halt and shouts of surprise came from the men working the lines.

Face tense with concentration, Vee nodded. "I've got it."

Torn between running to the quarterdeck and keeping an eye on her, Knigh started up the steps, constantly glancing between her and the lanterns raised over the stern.

When they reached the crowd searching over the rail, his muscles were thrumming with pent-up energy and she had paled a few shades.

"Llyr!" The cry went over and over. No response.

The sea was black and glinting like spilt ink. The night sky was lighter, spattered with a spray of stars, twinkling and serene despite the calamity playing out on the *Swallow*.

Hands tight on the rail, Knigh scanned the ever-shifting waves. At his side, Vee did the same. Out on the water, movement flickered, and he sucked in a breath to shout that he'd seen Llyr, but then a gleam of cold moonlight followed. It was only the shadows playing tricks.

The crew discussed who could swim—not many of them. And it didn't sound like they were confident in their skill.

"I need to"—Vee pulled the shawl from her shoulders—"if I get in there, I can—"

"No." His stomach lurched, and he yanked the shawl back into place. "Vee, no."

"Don't you—"

"I'm not telling you what you can't do," he hissed. "Yes, you'd be the best person to go in any normal circumstances, but"—he pushed the soft wool onto her shoulder, letting his hand rest there just a moment—"but you're not well enough. You're freezing and I can see how much it's taking out of you to hold us still. That boy needs you to keep the wind in check."

Was she always going to be like this—weakened, because of his betrayal?

Her jaw knotted, and she glanced out across the waves, nostrils flaring. "Gods damn it, Blackwood. I hate it when you're right."

"Sorry." He winced.

She was right about one thing—someone needed to get in the water and find him. It was the only way.

How must it feel out there? Cold. Alone in the dark. Unable to swim.

Teeth clenched, Knigh nodded to Vee before turning and threading through the crowd to Billy.

He leant against the stern rail, hand clenched upon it, pale in the lantern light. His usually bright expression had vanished and his round eyes squinted out over the water. A balding sailor beside him held a coil of rope in one hand and its end in the other as if ready to throw it out to Llyr.

"Billy." Knigh clapped him on the shoulder. "I can swim. I'll go." He nodded to the sailor, who blinked once before handing over the rope. Eyes on the sea, Knigh tied one end around his waist.

There was movement behind him. "Knigh"—Vee grabbed his hand—"no. What are you doing?"

Knigh? She hadn't called him that since Portsmouth. It was always Blackwood.

When he looked up from the knot, her expression made his guts twist. Eyes wide. Brows knotted more tightly than the rope at his waist. She was afraid.

She shook her head. "If you go in there I—I can't pull you back in." She squeezed his hand, gaze beseeching. "Please, Knigh, don't."

Turning his hand, he caught her chilly fingers. "I have to."

Alone in the dark and the cold, unable to swim...

Knigh shuddered. The poor boy could be dead already.

He grazed his thumb over her knuckles, then finished the

knot. "How do you think people manage when they don't have a sea witch on board?" He patted the rope and tried a reassuring smile.

She still wore the same stricken expression.

Seeing Vee afraid was frightening in itself. Seeing her afraid for him...

He shook his head and turned for the rail. No time to puzzle over that.

The soft hush of oars signalled the ship's boat was in the water. A moment later, it came into view, lanterns pooling across the sea's surface.

Beyond their light, the blackness stretched out, now punctuated by the occasional ripple reflecting golden light.

Nodding to Billy, Knigh climbed onto the rail, his balance effortless from a decade of working on ships. He threw the coil of rope to the burly bosun, Morholt, who piloted the ship's boat. An experienced sailor, he caught it deftly and nodded, understanding what Knigh meant to do.

Knigh took a long breath and dived.

DARK TIDES

T he air was chilly, whistling through his shirt. Then the sea was colder still. It closed around him, pressed on his ears, somehow made the darkness thicker. But, above, lamplight flickered.

Salt stung his eyes as he kicked his way up and broke the surface, drawing deep breaths. Now he was wet, the cold air nipped at his skin, sharp as broken glass. Down here, no longer cradled by the ship's hull, the swell felt far greater, lifting, lowering, pushing him wherever it willed.

He trod water and got his bearings. There, the *Swallow*. And directly astern—where Llyr should be.

The ship's boat pulled up alongside, the other end of his tether still in Morholt's sure grasp.

"Hold the oars." Knigh raised a hand, and they obeyed. "Listen."

His heart thudded. His breath gasped with the cold. Waves

25

lapped against the *Swallow* and the boat. But out there a different splash sounded...

He cocked his head.

A low, wordless cry.

His pulse leapt. Llyr was alive. There was still hope.

He surged in the direction of the sound. *Just hold on.*

His hands ached from the cold, but he kept them cupped, catching the water and pushing through it. The driving motion of his thighs gave some warmth, but the sea soon leached that away.

Something ahead, bobbing in the water. He called for the boat, and its comforting lanterns rose, illuminating the drawn faces of the crew.

Wood, not a person. The barrel they'd thrown overboard when Llyr had gone in to mark the spot. The boy wasn't hanging onto it, using it as a float, though. Knigh sighed. Hopefully, he wasn't far.

Knigh trod water again, the boat stopped, and he listened.

Heart. Breath. The lap of waves.

Nothing else.

Damnation.

He turned and scanned the gleaming, ever-shifting water.

Nothing.

He raised his eyebrows at Morholt. "Do you see any—"

"No." Brows set, his grim gaze searched, but he shook his head again. The rest of the crew did the same.

Only one thing for it.

A deep breath, then Knigh dived.

He kicked and pulled his way down, eyes burning from the

salt. However much he turned, all he could see was darkness below and all around, and lamplight rippling above, until he was forced to surface for breath.

The air was even colder in his lungs and on his face.

Surely the poor boy hadn't gone far from the float. Unless...

What creatures swam the seas at night? Predators?

A shudder rocked through him, all the harder because of the cold. Wild Hunt, why had he let himself think that?

He shook his head. Llyr was relying on Knigh. If he didn't find the boy, he'd join far too many others in Davy Jones' locker. And if Knigh was going to fail, it wouldn't be because he was afraid of nocturnal carnivores.

He shoved the idea from his mind, but a second dive gave the same result.

It was hard to catch his breath when he surfaced this time as his teeth chattered and the chill seeped into his bones until not an inch of him was warm.

"Ser," Morholt called, "we should turn back. He's lost."

Knigh shook his head. "One more." He could at least do that.

Despite inhaling the way Vee had shown him at the reef, this dive was harder than the others. His cold limbs were sluggish, and the darkness refused to part for the weak lamplight. What were a handful of lanterns against the vast night ocean?

Heartbeat pressing on his ears, he sculled his way through a turn... Maybe Llyr had drifted to port. The sea was pushing Knigh further from the ship's boat. It must have done the same to the boy. He'd been out here longer; maybe he wasn't quite on the course they'd expected.

Knigh kicked away from the longboat, away from the *Swallow*, staring into the blackness.

A shaft of lantern light shifted and hit a pale shape.

Muscles complaining at the cold, Knigh swam towards it.

It might not be Llyr. It might be one of those night hunters.

The light moved, leaving the shape, but Knigh pushed on. Stay the course. No time for fear. A life depended on it.

Just like his life had been in Vee's hands that day at the reef. He'd almost drowned—it was probably the closest he'd ever been to death. The world had gone black around the edges, leaving only a pinprick of turquoise light. Mama, Is, George, Aunt Tilda... He'd failed them. Billy had been next in his thoughts. Another failure. Then Vee had come to mind, and the tide had shifted.

When he'd felt her sure hands, albeit magical ones, he'd known he wasn't going to die. At least not that day.

But she wasn't here, and her gift was too weak to reel him back in. Or Llyr.

Knigh swallowed, ears popping, as he drew a few feet from where he'd seen the shape. If something was going to snatch him, it could lunge now, take him in huge jaws, crunch him in two...

The shaft of light shifted again and hit that pale shape—a hand.

Lungs burning, heart pounding, Knigh kicked once, twice more, and grabbed.

The fingers twitched and closed around his. Another hand found his forearm.

Still alive.

Grip sure, Knigh pulled Llyr up and up, until at last, blessed fresh air broke over their heads and they gasped it in. Knigh's head spun, from the cold or holding his breath, he couldn't say.

They were just outside the circle of lantern light, so the boy was nothing more than gleaming edges in the darkness. He coughed and spat out water, barely keeping his head above the surface, even with Knigh's help. But he was alive.

"I have him," Knigh called, fighting to keep them both afloat.

A cheer drifted over the waves, then the sound of oars, and within a minute, Morholt hauled Llyr from Knigh's hold and onto the boat. A moment later, he did the same to Knigh as if he weighed nothing more than the boy. Someone tugged a blanket around his shoulders, and several men slapped his back with smiles and nods.

Knigh shivered and gripped the blanket as tightly as he had Llyr. The boy panted, huddled up, but he looked back with bright eyes. He was alive.

Bending over the oars, the sailors took them back to the ship while the cold bit into Knigh's bones.

As they winched the ship's boat up the davits, faces appeared over the rail.

At the centre of the crowd, Vee, pale, eyes wide, hands clenched at her chest, strain drawn in the crease between her brows, the solid line of her jaw.

When they stepped on board, a cheer went up and sailors bustled to reach them, with claps on the shoulder and congratulations.

But that didn't matter. The ship was still becalmed, its sails slack. Vee was still spending her precious energy. With polite nods, he pushed through the crowd until he found that familiar dark hair.

"Knigh?" She stared up at him, chest heaving against her dressing robe. Her hands were clasped, the knuckles white.

"I'm here. I'm safe." He smiled, pulling the blanket closer. Better if it were her, but... He stifled a sigh. "Are you still holding the ship?" he whispered. "You—your energy—"

"I'm fine." But her hand trembled as she reached for his arm. When she touched it, she let out a long breath and nodded to herself. "You really are here."

Wind flowed back across the deck, filled the sails with a billowing sound, and the ship groaned into motion again. Cries of surprise rose from the crew.

Vee sagged and Knigh caught her elbow. Not as fine as she was pretending.

A shiver lanced through him. And neither was he.

"Come on," she murmured, "there's a brazier over there. You need to warm up."

"So do you." Yes, he was cold, but her skin didn't feel at all warm in comparison. She'd been standing on deck in chemise and robe, expending energy into her gift.

She shrugged and led the way past Billy and to the welcome glow of the brazier, steps heavy.

Billy nodded in thanks, but a confused line furrowed between his brows and he watched Vee far too closely.

Knigh nodded back and plastered on a smile, but it was tight on his lips. Damnation, Billy suspected something about Vee.

YULETIDE

Warm, solid at her back. She wriggled against it, trying to get closer, warmer. Steady breaths. Back to sleep...

Eyes screwed shut, Vice snuggled under the blankets. In the week since Llyr had gone overboard, she'd struggled to get warm, but this behind her finally staved off that chill. Besides, she was playing at being the useless wife of an aristocrat and today was Alban Arthan, Yule, Midwinter, and she didn't have a watch to get up for. She could stay here. She could—

That warmth. The weight over her waist. The slow breath on her neck.

Her eyes flew open. It was Knigh.

Gods bloody damn it.

She'd woken in his arms other mornings of their journey. She figured *he'd* come to *her*. No way would she do *this* with *him*, even if the crew said he was a hero for saving Llyr. Determined for it not to happen again, she'd gone to sleep with her back to the bulkhead.

She must have rolled over and shuffled closer to him in the night, seeking warmth... contact... him.

It was bad enough that her body had betrayed her by being so weak since the iron gibbet cage, but now this? Sheer treachery.

Even worse, Knigh's arm tightened, pulling her close with a soft sound, and something hard pressed against her backside.

Wild Hunt take her, but heat flared in her veins and her heart beat a little faster.

It was that cage's fault. A week without human touch. A week full of pain and nausea. A week of fading hope. It would do strange things to anyone.

And her in particular. She wasn't someone to hold back from physical contact. She hugged Perry, Saba, Aedan all the time, kissed them on the cheeks, worked near people all day long. Was it any wonder her body had dragged her closer to Knigh, even in sleep?

Traitor.

And the traitor was winning, because, Lords and Ladies, it would be so easy to arch her back, invite him in, press her breast into the hand now resting on her stomach. They'd done it before, back on *The Morrigan*. So many times she'd lost count.

And Wild Hunt it had been *good*. More than good. Glorious. Devastating.

But that was before.

Because her body wasn't the only traitor here.

I did warn you not to trust me.

Idiot that she was, she had.

He'd lured her in with that gorgeous face and dry humour, slipped the snare around her ankle while she was distracted by the devastating sex. And then he'd closed the trap and handed her over to the Royal Navy.

So... no. No arching her back. No invitations.

Besides, a dark corner of her mind whispered, *he wouldn't want you now, not after seeing you all skin and bones.*

She'd filled out a little since they'd left Albion, but he'd seen her wasted body at its worst—skinny limbs with knotted joints. Who'd want anyone after seeing them like that?

He didn't look at her with desire anymore—all he saw was a mistake and the guilt that went with it.

He just wanted someone, and she was here. That's all his arousal meant. It had been a long time for them both.

Probably. Her stomach twisted. For all she knew, he could have—

A sudden breath in her ear. A low grumble as his arm tightened around her waist again and that hardness pressed against her more insistently, separated by a couple of layers of fabric.

Oh, Lords. Her body throbbed, too hot, too breathless.

Then he tensed with a sharp breath. "Oh gods," he muttered. "Sorry, I..."

In an instant, he was out of the bed, leaving her back cold.

Hells, leaving *all* of her cold.

She screwed her eyes shut. The idea of contact with her was clearly too offensive to bear. Her chest clenched. How bloody humiliating.

He padded around their cabin, clearing his throat.

With a long breath, she rubbed her eyes and sat up as if she'd just woken.

The sight of him did *not* help. He bent over, pulling on breeches, the soft linen of his shirt outlining every detail of his shoulders and back, shadowing at the deep groove over his spine. The lean, powerful muscles of his legs soon disappeared beneath those breeches and then boots, but they were all too clearly etched in her mind.

Frowning, she stroked Barnacle, who lay at the foot of the bed. With a yawn, the little grey cat stretched and began a low purr.

Here Vice was, struggling to stay awake past ten o'clock or angle a current, while he stood there, just as strong as ever. And *he* was the one who'd committed the wrong. He'd betrayed her, but she was the one suffering.

She had to get her strength back. *Had to.* Relying on his help was insufferable. Being so powerless—she'd sooner die than carry on like this.

She clenched her jaw as he straightened and tied his cravat in place. He'd stopped wearing one back on *The Morrigan*, but now, although he was out of uniform, he'd reverted to full, formal attire. Breeches, boots, shirt, waistcoat, and jacket, complete with the cravat tied up right against his throat.

"How do you...?"

He raised his eyebrows at her in the mirror, adjusting the knot.

She pursed her lips and gestured at him. She hadn't meant to ask, but she'd started now and at least it might give her a way to pass the time, since she wasn't able to work and the clue she'd stolen from FitzRoy had become more a frustration than a help. She'd work it out, eventually, but it would be good to have something else to do, something simpler.

"Your body... it's still strong, even though you haven't been working the ship. Though I suppose an officer probably doesn't do the hard work on a naval ship." She shrugged. "So how do you keep it that way?" All broad and—*no, shut up!*

He shrugged and tucked the cravat's ends into his waist-coat front. "Oh, *that.* I do exercises when you're on deck—more space, and..." His gaze dropped from hers, and he cleared his throat.

Less of you in the way. That's what he meant but wouldn't say. She bit her lip. She was asking for his help, she couldn't snipe at him. A civilised question would be better. "Like what?"

"Sit-ups, press-ups, that sort of thing." He shrugged again and pulled on his dark blue coat, the armour complete. It wasn't a uniform, but it wasn't far off.

Press-ups. Yes, she could do those.

A couple of years ago, she'd challenged a particularly cocky new crewmate after he'd made some patronising comment about women needing help because they were so weak. If he could do more press-ups than her, she'd be his servant for the day. And no way was she losing that wager.

She'd matched him and when his arms had given out, she'd done another twenty, just to prove her point. Fae strength wasn't cheating—they'd mentioned nothing about that in the rules. Besides, Saba probably could have beaten him and she wasn't fae-blooded.

The crew had loved it, taking bets on who'd win, cheering, keeping count with bangs on the deck, mopping sweaty brows.

Her smile soon soured with the memory. Her crew. Her *friends*. Perry had cheered loudest of all. Where was she now? Had she also been arrested? Knigh said the plan hadn't included arresting her and the others on the *Covadonga*, but how could he know the authorities hadn't done it, anyway?

Vice gritted her teeth. Damn it. She needed to get to Nassau.

Knigh had paid Billy for their passage to Arawaké, but he'd have no business in a pirate haven like Nassau. She chewed the inside of her cheek. They didn't have much money left, but Nassau was non-negotiable. They *had* to get there. Somehow.

In the pirate world, everyone ended up there eventually, including Perry and the crew. Or else news of their fate.

If they'd been taken... Well, Vice would get a ship, sail to Albion, and take them back.

To do that, she'd need every ounce of power she could summon.

She shuffled off the bed and onto the floor.

Knigh cocked his head, a faint line between his brows. "What're you doing?"

"This." She placed her hands solidly on the floor and pushed.

Gods, her muscles groaned—her belly and thighs keeping her body in a straight line, her shoulders, her arms.

But she was up. She huffed out a breath, then lowered, arms trembling the whole way. And another—up, muscles burning, breath strained, down—

She thudded face-first on the floor, panting.

"Vee, are y—?"

"I'm fine," she growled. It didn't hurt much, just a faint sting to her cheek and forehead. She'd had far worse in weapons practice.

Wild Hunt, take me now.

Two press-ups. More humiliation.

Knigh's boots scuffed on the floor. If he was coming to help her up, she'd—

"Don't touch me."

"But... are you hurt?"

"I said I'm fine, didn't I?" She rolled into a sitting position and shook out her throbbing arms. Fine. Two press-ups. Tomorrow she'd do three. She scrubbed her face. And *tomorrow*, she'd do it while he wasn't here.

He crouched at her side. "Let me help you—"

"I said I'm fine," she bellowed, hands knotting into shaking fists.

His wide eyes, parted lips, raised brows, then the crumple of hurt. Each component of the expression cut her.

Because he *was* suffering. He'd given up his place in the Navy, his life as a free and law-abiding subject of Albion, even his family. And yet she couldn't stop lashing out at him.

But then the look disappeared behind his flat mask. "Very well. I'll leave you to it." He rose and strode from the cabin, closing the door softly.

No, Knigh Blackwood never slammed doors, however provoked.

Jaw clenched, she stared after him and shook her head.

This was impossible. This bloody ship. The ridiculous charade of playing his wife. Having to share this stupid cabin with him. Being around him all the damn time—it left her too raw, like a wound never allowed to heal.

"Bastard."

She needed to get hold of herself. Calm down, that's what Perry would say. This situation was unavoidable, so she needed to find a way to deal with it.

Taking a long breath, she closed her eyes. The sea would help. She was still too weak to work it, but she could feel it when she reached out and...

She opened her awareness.

The great expanse, wide and deep. Thick with life. Bright and warm, cold and dark. Surging... Churning... Whipped up by a hard wind. Peaks, powerful and swift. Almost black at the base, white-tipped. Nearby.

Somewhere else, she frowned.

Above that agitated water, she reached for the weather... Dark clouds—so many, blotting out the sun—heavy with rain, crackling with—

With a gasp, she was back in her body.

"A storm."

Not just a storm.

A ship-killer.

PASSENGERS

Vice burst onto the *Swallow's* deck. The air cooled as grey clouds engulfed the sky. A streak of smoky grey disappeared down the hatch—the ship's tomcat, a grey-black tabby. Seeking shelter belowdecks, no doubt. Smart kitty.

But where the hells was Knigh?

She couldn't go to the captain, Billy, directly—it would raise too many questions. And much as she was frustrated with this charade, they had to maintain it, as much for Billy's sake as for hers and Knigh's.

There, his blue coat, just the other side of the helm, talking to Billy. She'd have to get him away.

She hurried over. The sailors she passed smiled and nodded, touching their forelocks.

But her gaze was tugged unerringly to port where darker

clouds billowed. Bollocks, that was it. And fast-approaching. Aloft, men were at the yards, changing to storm sails. Good.

"Knigh, darling," she said, smile stiff as she nodded to Billy, "I need to speak to you. Now."

Knigh's jaw clenched. He probably didn't want another earful. "I'm in the middle of—"

"I'm sorry, but this isn't about..." She winced. No way was she going to talk about their argument in front of Billy. What else would make him understand? "Don't you think those clouds are a bit *ominous?*" She gave a pointed look to port, then back at Knigh.

"Ah, Lady Villiers," Billy said, smile bright, "we're aware of the storm and are changing canvas as appropriate. But that's only a precaution, as it's quite distant and nothing to worry about. We'll be out of its path long before it hits."

The back of her neck prickled, cold. "We won't." She touched Knigh's arm, staring at him, eyes wide. Gods, please let him understand. "It's fast-approaching. We can't outrun it."

Knigh searched her gaze, head cocking.

A flash of a frown covered Billy's face. "Madam, I appreciate your fears, but my men are seasoned—"

"Apologies, Billy"—Knigh kept his eyes on hers and cupped his hand around her elbow—"I need to speak to my wife on a matter of some urgency."

She huffed a relieved breath as he manoeuvred her to the rail. The deck was already pitching, requiring their years of experience to walk across evenly.

"What is it?"

"Can't you feel how strong it already is?" She nodded at the mizzenmast's lanterns swinging to and fro. "That storm is coming this way much faster than they realise and"—her stomach knotted—"and it's far bigger, far worse than he thinks. It's a ship-killer."

Knigh stiffened, eyes widening for a second, spoiling the controlled façade. "You're sure?"

Lips pursed, she frowned. "Are you seriously asking me that?"

He huffed a quick breath. "Sorry, yes. Of course." He shook his head. "Can you do anything about it?"

She winced. Was this how people without magic felt? Powerless? Like the world just happened at and around them and they could do nothing to affect it?

"I know you're... not at your best," he went on, "but can you—"

"No." She closed her eyes. "No, I... I can't get us past it. I can't speed us out of its path. I can't..." She folded her arms, brow sore from frowning so hard, head buzzing with the storm's threat. "I can't do anything."

When she brought herself to look at him, his mouth was set in a straight line. He nodded as if confident, but his throat bobbed in a long swallow. "Then we'll have to do this the old-fashioned way. I'll explain to him the danger, help make preparations." He took a breath and started towards Billy. "You need to get below with the other passengers."

Passengers. It turned her stomach. She was a sailor, a sea witch, a pirate. She wasn't cargo to be carried from Albion to Arawaké and dropped off in a warehouse.

She certainly couldn't huddle in her cabin while Knigh

stayed up here battling this thing, his life in danger.

But he was already off speaking to Billy, and she couldn't argue.

Gods, it burned in her.

Without her strength, she was useless.

Arms tightened around herself, she leant on the rail and glared at the storm.

The clouds loomed, just as she'd felt them when she'd reached out with her gift, tall and black, billowing across the sky.

She cocked her head. Yes, it moved a little too fast, a little too unerringly in their direction. Was this the work of another sea witch? If so, who? And why?

Lords and Ladies, she was losing her mind. Wishful thinking about her own diminished magic was making her believe the storm approached with unnatural speed when really it was just a gift from nature. A harsh gift, yes, but nature gave what it gave.

Beneath those huge clouds, wind blew the sea into jagged lines like a serrated edge, ready to saw a ship into splinters. As the peaks shifted, they revealed a small shape cutting through the water.

She blinked and scrubbed her eyes and stared again. She didn't have her spyglass anymore, but the waves parted again and—

Lightning streaked in the distance, lining the shape in harsh light and shadows. A ship.

Three masts and a long beak at the bow. The triangle of a lateen sail stood out at the mizzen mast, sharp against the water's curves. That built-up poop deck and forecastle, the crow's nests on the masts—something about it was familiar. Old-fashioned, but familiar.

Frowning, she leant out over the rail, fingers tight around it as spray spattered her face. She had seen that shape before but never moving, never in person, only in etched lines on paper.

Just like the illustrations from her book on Ser Francis Drake.

Drake's ship? But that was centuries old. Galleons like his had fallen out of favour so long ago, she'd never seen one on the water.

And was that smear a purple flag? What nation had a *purple* flag?

"Vee?" A hand closed on her arm and dragged her from the rail. "What the hells are you doing still on deck? You need to get below."

Knigh marched for the hatch, but she planted her feet, despite the way the ship rocked, harder than when she'd first come up the companionway. "Knigh, no. I"—she yanked and his grasp slipped, *almost* releasing her—"see, there's a ship out there. I think it's... Doesn't it look like a galleon?"

"What?" He glanced towards the storm—closer now—and shook his head. The rising wind whipped the white streak into his face. "What are you talking about?"

"There's a ship out there, look." She pointed and stared and wished for the waves to part again and reveal that familiar hull. But they didn't.

Wild Hunt, maybe she *was* going mad.

"Vee, look, come on, you need to get inside." His touch was

gentler this time and his expression, too, resting on her in a way that practically begged. "I'm not saying this to diminish you. I know you could tell this thing to piss off, if you were at full strength. I know you could sail *The Morrigan* through it without a care. But you're *not* at full strength, and I can't help sail if I'm worrying about you."

She glanced back at where the ghost ship had been. Maybe it was just some fractured figment of her imagination. "But—"

"Villiers," Billy bellowed, striding across the deck, his dark hair blown wild, "get your wife below. Now."

The sailors working lines and climbing down from aloft wore deep frowns. No more smiles, instead they set their mouths in grim lines. The saltwater now hitting the deck was heavier than a spray.

"Vee," Knigh murmured, breath warm in her ear, "come on. Captain's orders. I'm saying *please* this time, but I will put you over my shoulder and carry you down there if I have to."

She clenched her jaw and jerked away from him. Just let him bloody try. Not that her damn body would be able to resist right now.

Traitor.

She shrugged off his hand and huffed a sigh. "Not necessary."

When she strode for the hatch, the deck pitched, forcing her to grab the common room skylight to stay upright.

A cold rain began. Those billowing black clouds were almost upon them. The storm was here, ready to crush and drown and kill.

But there was nothing she could do about it. Stomach turning, she retreated to the common room belowdecks.

LEMON SHERBETS

Vice wasn't someone who waited. Especially not for other people to save her from a storm.

But here she was, sitting on one of the common room settees, stewing, while the Pevenseys chattered about *something* and gasped every time the cabin pitched or there was a bang.

Up there, men were aloft, their frigid hands furling some sails, reefing others, and bracing yards. More crew worked the pumps, flushing water from the bilge. Morholt was big and strong. He'd be at the helm, battling the wheel to move the rudder and ensure they weren't broached by a wave.

Maybe someone had been swept away. Maybe someone had lost his grip up in the shrouds and fallen into the sea or upon the deck with a sickening *thud* like Evered had all those years ago. She'd been too far away to hear him land, but she'd heard a body hit the deck since then, and it always chimed in her thoughts when she went back to that day.

For all she knew, *Knigh* had been swept away or fallen to his death...

And here she was, doing precisely nothing.

Her stomach roiled with the sea's same intensity.

With a shuddering creak, the common room tilted drunkenly. Lucia gasped, clutching her chest. Her husband fell silent, his face turning grey.

Vice gritted her teeth. That felt much stronger. Weren't they past the peak of the storm yet? She chewed her lip. There was one way to find out, even from down here...

She drew a deep breath and opened her awareness.

Chaos.

No up, no down, no large or small, no sea bed. Just churning.

The line between sea and sky was hopelessly blurred, with bubbles foaming through the water and spray peppering the air. Waves reached so high it was as if they wanted to join the rain clouds. Beyond, even higher peaks loomed.

And they were coming this way.

With a gasp, Vice jolted back to herself. It was bad now and with waves that large coming, it would get even worse. Bollocks.

"Oh, my dear," Lucia said, reaching over and squeezing Vice's hand. "It's understandable that you'd be concerned for your husband, but he's an experienced officer. I'm sure he's fine." She smiled, eyes kind, despite the pallor of her face.

Ha! Yes, Vice was just worried about Knigh, not *all* their lives. This thing could sink the whole ship.

Lucia cocked her head, keeping her hand on Vice's. "The bosun didn't seem overly worried when he asked us to keep below decks."

Lord Pevensey sat up straighter, as if buoyed by his wife's bravery. "Indeed, he assured me it was just a precaution," he said, but his smile was tremulous and his cheeks pale.

Of course Morholt wasn't worried—he didn't know this wasn't the worst of the storm. And it's not as if he'd want his passengers to panic.

Vice could warn them worse was yet to come, though. Hells, she *had* to. And she had some strength back. She could help. If she went up the main hatch, she'd come out on deck by the main mast, rather than the helm. That would give her a chance to use her gift before Billy spotted her. She might even find Knigh on his own.

Teeth clenched, she lifted the corners of her mouth. At least concern for her 'husband' could explain her interest. "Yes, I'm sure you're right." She patted Lucia's hand and nodded. "But I don't think my nerves can take it. I simply *must* check he's safe." She rose and grabbed a handful of the lemon sherbets Lucia had brought from their cabin. "You don't mind if I borrow these, do you?"

But she didn't give them any time to answer, sweeping from the room's aft doors and dropping the sweets in her pocket. With the extra energy, she might be able to use a little of her gift, even if it was only to deflect the worst waves.

SHIP KILLER

As soon as Vice opened the hatch, she got a face full of rain and spray, whipped up by the shrieking wind. She staggered to the mainmast as the deck pitched and bucked underfoot. She couldn't see much past that, with so much water veiling everything in slate grey.

Bloody hells, it was worse than she'd realised. Feeling a storm through her gift was different from experiencing it first-hand. Weather had no concept of the discomfort for living things of the cold and wet.

Fingers already chilled and aching, she clung to the mast and squinted into the lashing rain. No visible sign of any sailors, but shouts came from aloft and the quarterdeck—orders and wordless cries of shock and dismay. At least Knigh wouldn't be able to spot her and haul her back inside.

It was no comfort.

She gritted her teeth as a wave roared over the deck, up

past her knees, tugging at her feet. It was all she could do to hold on.

As soon as it had passed, she dared to release the mast to dip a hand in her pocket, unwrap a sherbet lemon, and throw it into her mouth. Sweet and sharp splintered through the cold, the citrus a teasing taste of warmer days.

With a deep breath and the sweet lodged firmly between her tongue and the roof of her mouth, she opened to the storm.

From up here, it was much easier to feel the weather. It was challenging to get a human scale when she used her gift. Like discomfort, weather and sea had no concept of miles, but, Lords, this thing was *big*. It blanketed an expanse of ocean, the edges so far away, her stomach plummeted.

But the shape... yes, she had a much better sense of that. And they weren't in the centre of it. The storm's edge was on the starboard bow. If they shifted course they'd reach it much sooner than if they continued on—

"Vee!" A hand closed around her arm, pulling her back from the sky with a gasp that nearly lodged the sherbet lemon in her throat.

Knigh stood over her, neck corded, hair plastered to his face, which was rigid with rage. "What the devil are you...? Get the hells back to our cabin. You're too weak to help, you—"

"We need to go that way," she shouted over the roaring waves. Teeth gritted, she tried to yank from his grasp, but he was right when he said she was weak. She could still help, though. She pointed, glowering back at him. "We need to go that way. That's the closest edge of the storm. We'll escape much quicker than if we carry on this course."

"But—"

Another wave broke, splashing their faces, pushing them. Vice's one-handed grip failed, but Knigh was there, his powerful frame pressing her against the mast, one hand on it, the other on her. Only a ghost of his usual warmth smouldered through their drenched clothes.

Chest heaving, he righted them as the wave drained from the deck. "Thanks for the tip," he bellowed against the howling wind. "Now get yourself back—"

"No"—she shook her head—"you need to get the course changed. I have enough strength to adjust the wind's direction to speed us in the right direction. If course and wind aren't aligned, the storm might take us aback and then we really will be screwed." If they were taken aback in this gale, with the wind against the front of the sails, they'd lose a mast—hells, maybe all three.

Jaw knotting, he looked from her to where she'd pointed, though that way was only grey rain and the ghosts of waves past it. His shoulders sank. "Fine, I'll get the course changed." He shook his head. "No idea how I'm going to explain it, but I will." He took a coil of thick rope from where it was stowed nearby and lashed it to the mast, then handed the other end to her. "Stay safe. And don't use too much energy. *Please.*"

She took the rope and nodded. But he was already fighting through rain and wind to return to the helm.

The deck dipped. Rain and waves battered her from head to toe. Her waterlogged gown was heavy, dragging at every movement. Clinging to the rope and mast, she waited for the crew to brace the sails.

Knigh was good to his word, and a few minutes later came the cry: "Heave!"

Above, the yards began to turn.

Vice let half her awareness fly, ready to shift the wind to work with their new course as soon as—

Ah, perfect. Sails aligned, she pushed with her gift and her muscles groaned like the mast and hull under stress, but the ship and wind turned. In this state, she wouldn't have been able to start a gale from still air or force it back on itself in a whole new direction, but she could shift its angle just enough.

Arms and legs shaking, she gritted her teeth, forcing her focus to stay out there on the weather and sea, rather than here with her weak body. She closed her eyes.

The *Swallow* sped through the water now, mounting one wave, then another. Not far from the edge of the storm, a matter of ten minutes, maybe twenty?

Not too much longer. She nodded, muscles burning, skin cold. The wind and sea bucked against her gift, twisting, powerful. It didn't so much fight her as simply want to be free.

Hold fast, like Aedan's tattoos.

Her chest heaved and her pulse pounded, as loud in her ears as the rolling thunder.

She staggered against the mast as the deck tilted. She still had the rope. She was fine.

Stay the course.

She didn't know if that was rain or spray on her face anymore, and maybe the gods didn't either. It was just wet and cold and stinging and constant.

Then a wall of water crashed over her. No air. No light. Who knew where the deck was anymore? Or up. Or down. There was only sea and blistering rope slipping through her hands as she hurtled through the wave.

With a bubbling yelp, she fought to regain her grip, even as the rope skinned her palms.

She kept a quarter of her awareness still on the wind— without it, they'd lose their course and possibly a mast—the rest she brought back. She stopped slipping along the rope.

Air broke over her head and she gasped in sharp breaths. Thank the gods.

As the sea level dropped, her feet didn't land on any deck, though. Hard timber against her front and for a moment she wondered why she couldn't get her feet under herself to stand on it.

She blinked away the saltwater.

That timber—the *Swallow's* rail. Below was only churning sea.

Her stomach flipped. She was hanging off the side of the ship. She'd been swept overboard.

Knuckles aching, she gripped the rope. *Lords and Ladies help me.*

HOLD FAST

Vice called for help, but another wave crashed over her, stealing air and words, choking, bashing her against the hull. A dozen points of pain pounded across her body, highlighting each strike, bruising hips and knees and elbows. Her lungs burned, but to inhale now would be death. There would be air soon.

Soon.

Arms shaking, she kept hold of her gift and that rope. At full health, she'd have been able to push the wave away and climb up but, right now, the thought alone was exhausting. The only tiny spark of comfort was that it had been tied by Knigh. He knew his knots: they would hold as long as she did. Probably longer.

Then there was air. She coughed out the saltwater, the tang dry on her tongue, nauseating.

The sea dragged and made her torn hands burn. But letting

go would be death. And stilling the surrounding waters would mean letting go of the wind, which could destroy the ship.

Another wave, and another. Her joints popped. Her muscles screamed. Her body begged her to give up.

Let go. Return to the sea.

If she did, this far out on the open ocean, she'd die, and with this storm so would everyone on board.

She'd spent her life not giving in. She wasn't about to start now.

But maybe it wouldn't be her choice.

The next wave slammed into her, harder than any blow from an enemy. It sucked at her feet, pulled on her skirts. It flung one hand from the rope.

When it subsided, she'd slipped another foot along the tether. Her other hand hung, bloodied and limp.

She huffed for breath and tried to reach the rope, but...

Eyes squeezed shut, she shook her head. *Come on.*

But her lungs burned. Her bones ached. And she was weak.

Come on!

Crying out, she put every ounce of energy not used by her gift into that dangling arm.

It rose an inch.

The sea roared.

Another wave was coming. She wouldn't be able to hold on one-handed.

The cry became a scream, lost in the crashing storm. Her hand rose another inch, then two, then three...

It was at her shoulder now.

Keep going. Keep going.

Lords, it burned, bright and harsh as Avalon's forge. But that forge had made Excalibur. The blade had survived its fire and come out all the stronger.

She could, too.

Half-blind from the salt-water streaming down her face, she pushed her hand up.

Eye-level, now.

Spray hit her—the herald of that coming wave.

And her hand closed on something warm, pliant, not rope.

Gasping, she looked up.

Knigh.

Brow knotted, jaw set, mouth in a grim line. His hand fastened on hers and hauled her over the rail the instant the wave struck.

He shielded her, the water breaking over his back and shoulders, and she buried her face against him, clinging on.

Then the wave was gone, leaving them huddled against the rail, panting.

Alive.

"Vee," he growled, back straightening from where he'd bowed over her, "what were you...? You should have..." He stood very close, every inch of him solid, fingers holding her arm in a death grip. A wild look haunted his eyes, even as he glowered at her.

She'd seen it before, when he'd come back from berserking on the deck of the *Covadonga* and thought he'd hurt her. But he hadn't then, and it had been her decision to stay on deck today. He didn't get to tell her what to do, damn it. She glared right back, chin lifted.

"Why the hells weren't you inside? I should've made you—gods, I thought you'd gone overboard." He shook his head, the glower breaking as he squeezed his eyes shut and dashed away the salt-water dripping from his hair. "I never should've—"

"Let me push us out of the storm?" She arched an eyebrow and nodded fore.

He started and looked to the bow, eyes wide.

Ahead, light broke through the clouds, casting a rainbow through the drizzle. The waves were already gentler, just coating the deck at their feet.

And when she reached out, her gift confirmed it—they'd reached the edge of the storm.

TRADITION

That evening, rum and wine flowed in the common room. Crew and passengers alike sat around a long table, brought together in celebration—both of Alban Arthan *and* surviving the storm. Over the laughter and chatter, one of the crew played his fiddle, the sound bright and lively. Another kept time on a tambour.

Knigh raised an eyebrow and resisted the urge to look at Vee, who sat beside him.

Dancing felt imminent.

He'd done it with Vee and *The Morrigan's* crew, but that was an exception. Although he was immune from Vee's fae charm, she could probably get him to do anything, eventually.

Like letting her stay on deck, weakened, in the middle of a ship-killer of a storm.

His throat closed, and he thudded his glass onto the table

harder than intended. When he'd turned and seen her no longer by the mast, the bottom had dropped from his world.

Terror. Sheer, unbridled terror. That was the only thing he'd been aware of as he'd battled his way to where he'd last seen her. The lack of her had shrieked inside him.

Gone. Gone. Gone.

It was only when he'd spotted the line trailing over the rail that he'd been able to think straight. And, thank the gods, the Lords, the Ladies, even the Wild Hunt, she'd still had a hand on that lifeline.

Seeing her fighting to climb back up hadn't only been a relief, it had warmed him with a ferocious pride. She did not give in. Hells, she'd still been directing the ship, despite what it added to her struggle.

He shook his head. Vee was certainly a force to be reckoned with.

Cheeks warm, he loosened his cravat, then finished the fruity red wine. It was no palm wine, but it would do. He eyed Vee sidelong.

She was giving the fiddle-player an odd look, brow creased. She had to be thinking of Perry.

Knigh bit his lip. That was his fault. Along with a myriad of other things. No surprise her thoughts were on her closest friend.

He leant over, touched the back of Vee's hand and murmured, "We will find her, you know."

With a wince, she returned her attention from the musician. "Sorry, we're meant to be celebrating, aren't we?" She smiled—a friendly smile, a sweet smile, a *warm* smile. No cruelty or sardonic edge.

It had been a long time since he'd seen that look from her. His throat tightened.

She raised her eyebrows, nodding decisively. "We survived the storm, and this is a feast day. Feels appropriate. Isn't Alban Arthan about getting through the darkest part of winter?"

The look she gave him carried a weight at odds with how lightly she spoke. The words crept across his skin, as affecting as a lover's fingers, lifting the hairs on the back of his neck. He took a long breath and nodded. "I think we've survived the worst." *And not just of winter.* But he bit his lip against those words. Maybe he was reading too much into her behaviour.

With a gentle scoff, she cocked her head. "I bloody hope we have." She sighed, peering into the glass of berry-dark wine. "And, yes, I do miss Perry, but we're on our way to Nassau and everyone ends up there, eventually. There's nothing to do but stay the course." She raised her glass, drained it, then discarded it on the table. It rang softly as it touched his.

She gave him a long look. The wine had left a rosy sheen on her lips.

He fought to keep his breathing even, despite the want—the *need* to—

At his shoulder, a man cleared his throat. "Blackwood."

He froze, heart pounding as though he'd been caught red-handed. Ridiculous—he'd only *thought* about kissing Vee, and there was no crime in that. Taking a deep breath, he looked up to find Billy at his side.

Despite the festivities, Billy's mouth and shoulders were

tight lines. "Could I have a moment?" He gestured to the far end of the room, away from everyone else.

Perhaps it was just as well—Lady Pevensey had refilled Knigh's glass too many times. Who knew if he'd be able to resist that dangerous urge to kiss Vee if he stayed at her side any longer?

He and Billy stalked away and the further he got from Vee, the more his heart rate slowed.

Billy squared his shoulders, eyebrows low. It had to be something bad.

Knigh's stomach lurched. Surely he wouldn't bring up the past—not now. Although if he did, Knigh had to take it. He owed the man that much. Hands at his side, he braced and gave Billy a small nod of encouragement.

"I wanted to thank you again for your help with the storm."

"Oh." He almost laughed. "As I said before, it's no problem. I'm only glad I could help." *That Vee could help.*

"But"—frowning, Billy sighed through his nose—"you should've told me your wife was a sea witch."

Knigh kept his breaths even, his stance relaxed. Damnation, it wasn't a huge leap from *She's a sea witch* to *She's Lady Vice.* Raising his eyebrows, he scoffed, even though it weighed on him to add to the lies he'd already told Billy. "Oh?"

The skin around Billy's eyes tensed. "Come on, Knigh. Why else would she be desperate to get on deck in that storm? And how the hells did my ship stop dead in the water the night Llyr went overboard?"

Wild Hunt take him, he couldn't keep this up—not with Billy. The man wasn't stupid, and Knigh owed him better. He bowed his head, sighing. "I'm sorry. I didn't want to put you on the wrong side of the law." True. "I figured if you didn't know, you wouldn't be implicated and wouldn't be tempted to lie to cover for us." Also true. He met Billy's gaze. More of the truth burned on his tongue.

She's Lady Vice, the pirate fugitive. I broke her out of a gibbet cage. We're on the run.

The hurt screwing up Billy's face pierced Knigh. "I know what the law says," Billy murmured, glancing over at Vee who was laughing at something Lady Pevensey said. "She should be Navy property. But, gods, Blackwood, you can trust me." He stared at Knigh, eyes wide.

"I do." More truth. "And I always have. I just—I was trying to protect you and I was desperate to get her away." His chest heaved at the thought of that night in Portsmouth.

"Desperate? I knew it!" With a snort, Billy shook his head, tension dissolving. "I *knew* there was something off when you were happy to leave so quickly." He flashed Knigh a smile of triumph. "At first, I assumed you were trying to smuggle someone out of the country who was merely posing as your wife. But seeing the two of you together—you're clearly mad about each other."

More like we drive each other mad. Knigh bit back a laugh. His feelings for Vee were, it was fair to say, complicated. Hers for him?

As his gaze sought her out, she looked up and raised her eyebrows at him, a glint of amusement flashing in her eyes.

Before tonight, he'd have said she hated him, but the way she was acting... Maybe *her* feelings were complicated too.

"Ah, it's enough to make a man jealous." Billy clapped him on the shoulder.

"There's someone out there for you." Knigh took a deep breath, chest suddenly full and warm as he dragged his attention back to Billy. "I'm sure of it."

"Well, I'm not going to—"

"Lord Villiers!" Lady Pevensey cried, closing in on them, a spilling pitcher of wine in her hand. She tutted, shaking her head. "This will never do!" Her pink cheeks suggested she'd filled her own glass a time or two. *Or four.*

"My apologies, madam," he said, glancing a question at Billy, who shook his head. "What won't do?"

"Come and see." She hooked her arm through his and half-dragged him across the room. He turned to mouth an apology to Billy, but he only waved, laughing.

She stopped in front of Vee and gestured at her, giving Knigh a pointed look. When he raised an eyebrow at Vee, she only lifted a shoulder, apparently as clueless as he was.

"Oh, for goodness' sake," Lady Pevensey huffed, rolling her eyes and pressing him into his seat. "You haven't put holly in your wife's hair. Are you *trying* to anger the fair folk?"

Oh yes, *that* tradition. He bit his lip, giving an apologetic smile.

Looking at Vee just now, with that reminder of their sham marriage fresh in the air, well it could be dangerous, so he watched Lady Pevensey bustle away. A moment later, she returned with a sprig of holly, the leaves dark and glossy, the berries even brighter than the wine. Little copper bells jingled, threaded between the berries.

Prickly and beautiful. Just like Vee. He swallowed a laugh. To tell her that—*ha,* it would be suicide. But... holly was prickly for a reason. He'd seen it keep livestock and deer at bay, even as neighbouring plants were stripped bare.

Lips pursed, Vee angled her head and let him clip the sprig in place. Once it was secured, he allowed himself to smooth a single displaced curl.

He could just sink his fingers into that thick, silky hair, stroke it, comb through it, throwing the clips all over the floor. His heart pounded so hard it was a wonder no one else could hear.

Lords. This was bad. He needed to maintain control. He needed to put this—this, whatever it was he felt for Vee behind him. He'd destroyed anything they might have had the moment he'd arrested her.

For something to do with his hands, he lifted his refilled glass in thanks and nodded to Lady Pevensey and the rest of the table. "The light in the night of the year. The sun returns. Winter is won. To surviving the dark."

"To surviving the dark," everyone echoed.

Vee gulped hers, not at all ladylike, and he snorted into his glass. He should have realised she was a pirate the first time they'd met at—

"And the rest of the tradition!" Lady Pevensey still stood over them, but now she held a sprig of mistletoe. The lamplight gilded its white berries, contrasting with still more of the little copper bells.

"Lord and Lady Villiers must have their Yule kiss."

FUN & GAMES

"Come along now." Lady Pevensey raised her eyebrows, dangling the mistletoe over Knigh and Vee's heads.

Knigh winced. Ah, yes. The rest of that tradition. Of course. He'd forgotten that bit. Being unmarried, he'd never had to think about it before.

Every man watched him and Vee, chuckling, leaning forward, waiting.

He dared to look at her.

Instead of a look of fury or discomfort, she scoffed, shaking her head at the crew with a dramatic roll of her eyes. "Come along, husband, let us satisfy these *voyeurs!*"

That won a peal of laughter from Lady Pevensey. The mistletoe bells rang in echo.

Despite himself, Knigh grinned and cocked his head at Vee. "If you insist, *wife.*"

He leant towards her and her gaze flicked to his mouth. A tease of a smile stayed at the corner of her lips.

This was just part of their sham marriage. That was all.

He took a long breath and closed the distance. She was soft, warm, firm. She smelled of wine and winter rain. His heart squeezed, and he had to clench his hands against the desire to hold her, to angle her head back and stroke his tongue against hers.

And then it was over. Just a chaste kiss, leaving the sweetness of that fruity wine on his lips.

A couple of good-natured *boos* sounded around the table as the crew members huffed and sat back. Evidently not what they'd been hoping for.

They weren't the only ones disappointed.

Knigh chanced a stiff smile at Vee.

Her chest rose and fell, and she pursed her lips. A small crease etched its way between her brows as she gave an absent-minded nod before reaching for her glass. She went to take a sip, but her frown deepened as she stared into it. Empty.

Despite Lady Pevensey insisting they play a game, the next hour dragged, utterly excruciating. Vee's every movement, even when she was out of his sight, marked its way through his awareness thanks to those damn bells in her hair.

Hells, who was he fooling? He'd have been aware of exactly where she was, even without the jingling.

Lady Pevensey kept topping up their glasses, and Vee kept glancing his way with another tinkle of bells, sounding as if the fair folk themselves were here. The more drinks, the more often Vee touched him—just little gestures. Her hand resting on his shoulder. A light stroke across the back of his hand when it sat on the table. Not moving her knee away when it ended up against his.

All of it ached in his chest. Dull and constant.

But she instigated it. *She* was the one touching *him*. And hadn't he sworn to provide her with whatever she wanted?

Maybe after all this, she'd forgiven him. Maybe he'd earned it. He didn't *feel* worthy of it, but who was he to judge? Anyone's judgement was better than his. If she'd forgiven him, then perhaps he could enjoy it.

He allowed himself a small smile as he finished yet another glass of wine. Gods knew which number it was.

When Lady Pevensey called for a game of musical chairs, Vee grabbed his hand and he was powerless to resist. With two dozen chairs lined up, the fiddle-player struck up his tune.

As Lady Pevensey and the mixed passengers and crew started up, skipping around the chairs, Knigh began a sedate stride—sensible and gentlemanly.

Vee set off at a romp, but soon turned and clicked her tongue at him. "Knigh," she huffed, shaking her head. Evidently his pace, although acceptable in Navy circles, was not acceptable to the Pirate Queen. She grabbed his hand and tugged him into one of the dances they'd done around the campfire after they'd snuck away from the Grays' ball all those months ago.

They wheeled through the crowd, hands linked, chaotic in their snaking path. She kept glancing back, grinning, and Knigh found himself grinning right back.

Maybe she *had* forgiven him.

When the music stopped, they both found chairs, collapsing onto them, laughing, breathless, as giddy as children. One-by-one the number of players dwindled until only he and Vee were left, one chair between them. Despite the drink, their fae speed gave them an advantage.

When the fiddler's spirited reel struck up for the last time, there was no more hand-holding. Vee continued her cavorting dance around the chair, but he wasn't foolish enough to think she wasn't on alert. There was a glint in her gaze like she had in battle.

Who'd've thought the flippant, casual Lady Vice had a competitive side?

Now she wasn't dragging him around, Knigh returned to his sedate stride but he couldn't keep his eyes off her and his heartbeat was anything but calm.

They circled, eyes locked until—

Quiet.

Knigh was closer to the chair's front, Vee almost behind it. As one, they burst into movement.

Knigh slid into place, Vee an instant behind. He grinned. He'd won, he'd—

Vee landed in his lap, breathless, hand on his shoulder. Somehow he was already holding her waist.

Their giddy laughter mingled, filling the air between them and spreading around the room until everyone was infected.

Lady Pevensey waved her glass, splashing her husband. He was apparently too busy laughing to notice or care. "Is it possible to call a draw in musical chairs?"

Even as he grinned, Knigh shook his head at Vee. Of course

she wouldn't give up. Damn the bloody woman. Equal measures infuriating and intriguing.

His fingers twitched against her waist, pulling her closer, and he had to bite his lip against the urge to kiss her—thoroughly this time.

Her grin softened and her laughter faded into heaving breaths. Her eyes were now almost the same deep blue as his Navy uniform, and they met his, dark and intense. She cupped his cheek as if she were about to pull his lips to hers as she'd done dozens of times before.

Before he'd arrested her.

It twisted in his belly.

But her soft smile stayed in place and her breaths brushed his lips, sweet with wine.

Please. He almost said it. In that moment, he'd have begged if she'd demanded it. Because that stupid chaste kiss earlier had been nowhere near enough. Better they hadn't shared it than be left with such an unquenched thirst.

The want throbbed through him, hot and hungry. He wanted her, in a base way that tensed low in his belly, yes, but also...

He wanted to add another method to those he'd used to show her how truly sorry he was. He wanted to hold her close, to whisper against her skin how wrong he'd been, how he'd do whatever it took to make it right. He would worship her with his body, prove how much he cared, how much she meant to him. Her willing servant.

He didn't mean to, but he leant towards her, just a fraction of an inch.

Her chest rose and fell deeply, and her gaze flicked to his mouth. Did she see all that in his eyes? Did she understand what he would do for her if she just said the word?

But instead of kissing him, she stood. Still watching him, she inclined her head. "I concede. Congratulations on your victory, *my Lord.*" With a smirk, she led the applause.

Oh yes. The rest of the room. That existed, and there were other people in it.

He shook his head, face hot. He'd completely forgotten—or hadn't cared. The outcome was the same. Rubbing his forehead, he rose with an awkward chuckle and gave a quick bow to acknowledge the audience.

"I think, perhaps," Vee murmured, bending close, "it's time to retire."

That low, private voice—did she mean...? He raised his eyebrows at her, but she just smiled at Lady Pevensey.

No, she was only tired. That was all. After the storm and then the energetic party games, it was no surprise.

"Of course," he murmured and offered his arm before making their excuses. He led the way back to their cabin, every sinew of his body burning to hold her.

No matter how comforting it would be to succumb, he had to resist.

THE LONGEST NIGHT

Vice stumbled into their cabin and laughed at herself. Lords, how many times had Lady Pevensey refilled her glass?

Knigh turned, chuckling as he raised an eyebrow at her. "How drunk *are* you?"

She leant against the door and grinned up at him. "Drunk enough. You look quite rosy-cheeked, yourself." And his skin had been hot under her hand a few minutes ago. She rubbed her thumb and fingertips together at the memory. It was that or reaching up and cupping his face again, which would only lead to kissing. And kissing would lead to a lot more.

But wasn't that why she'd suggested they retire—to catch him alone? To have their own private celebration? That damn kiss under the mistletoe had ghosted over her lips all evening, an irritatingly unsatisfying tease of what she knew they could have.

He stepped into her space and she held her breath. Maybe he had the same idea. His hand rose, came closer... and reached past her, landing on the door and pushing it the rest of the way shut.

She huffed out a breath, half-sigh, half-laugh, but when she met his gaze, any laughter died on her lips.

He fair smouldered, standing much too close to resist, hand on the door above her shoulder. After all this time in such close proximity, she thought she'd have stopped noticing his scent, but no, the teasing taste of cinnamon and soap and leather, warm and welcoming, still hung in the air.

She could just reach up, touch that gorgeous face of his, kiss him, and let the night lead the way. He was here, and willing in body and mind, if his demeanour was anything to go by. And it was a beautiful body at that. Powerful. Skilled.

Bloody hells, Vice, when did you start overthinking things?

An excellent point.

Besides, didn't they deserve some pleasure after all the horror of Portsmouth and the tension of escape and fake married life? And although he clearly didn't find her attractive anymore, not after seeing her in such a state from the iron cage, he still had needs that required fulfilment, the same as her. What would be the harm?

This could be just bodies. Comfort. Pleasure. A celebration of Alban Arthan and of survival and of *life*.

The only obstacle was if he wasn't as willing as his signals suggested. So, she would make an invitation.

She swallowed, then tilted her head and shook the bells still fastened in her hair with the holly. "Could you?"

He blinked as if waking, stared at the sprig for a few seconds, and finally nodded. "Of course." His voice came out low and throaty and he took half a step nearer, even though he was already close enough to reach with ease. He fiddled with the clip, sending echoes of sensation across her scalp as her hair moved.

She closed her eyes and let the simple pleasure of his smell and warmth and touch consume her attention.

Lords, please say he did want this.

"There," he said at last, and when she opened her eyes, he held up the sprig of holly. "A promise of summer, even on the darkest day of winter."

She smiled faintly. It was almost funny to think of it that way after spending so many years in Arawaké with its warm climate, and yet it rang with truth in her bones, in her blood. Pirate crews celebrated festivals from across Europa and Arawaké and even further afield, each member bringing their own traditions and stories. So even at such a distance, the feast days of Albion still stayed with her, and Alban Arthan was one of the most important.

She looked from the holly to him. "It's going to be a long night."

He lowered the holly and looked past it to her, his intensity making her gown far too warm. His brows rose fractionally. "The longest." He hadn't backed away, leaving those two words hanging in the narrow space between them, heavy with meaning.

He'd responded to the invitation so far, now to push it that little further. "Whatever will we do with ourselves?" She tried to say it lightly, but it came out husky and low.

Knigh had gone very still, but there was a flicker of something at the corner of his mouth—a glimpse of a reaction despite his usual mask. "We *could* sleep."

The way he emphasised 'could' suggested there might be another option.

She arched her eyebrows and nodded. "We *could.*"

His gaze drifted to her mouth. "Or..."

She swallowed, every fibre in her body tense at the unspoken suggestion. He was accepting the invitation, or at least turning it back on her, checking if she meant it. "Yes," she breathed, "I think we'd better."

The distance vanished and their lips met, melting together, warm and soft and delicious and right. She sighed against his mouth as he pressed her against the door.

They both needed this and her body was only too willing to comply, fitting with his. Their tongues met and her pulse pounded an urgent rhythm, almost loud enough to drown out the sound of their breaths and the creaking of the ship.

She made short work of his clothes, tossing them to the floor, which was sure to drive him mad, but he made no reaction, save for kissing her all the harder and working on her gown. His hands were sure as he removed all her layers, one-by-one, the delay delicious and frustrating at once, but at last they were both naked, lust staving off the cold.

His fingers combed through her hair, pushing out half the pins and clips, sending it spiralling over her shoulders in wild curls. When she moaned softly at that, he massaged her scalp, easing out all the soreness that came from the weight of hair and the tightness of the coils. A delicious kindness.

Gods, why hadn't they done this sooner? Why had it taken him diving into the black waters after a drowning sailor, a battle against a storm, and a midwinter festival to bring them together like this? Everywhere he touched whispered of rightness. Every inch of her throbbed with it.

Like that first time back in the glow-worm cave, they should have done this a long, long time ago.

Smiling against his lips, she planted her hands on his chest —still gloriously firm with that tickling touch of brown hair— and urged him towards the bunk. He sat, biting his lip in a way that made her want to jump on him.

Hells, there wasn't any reason to delay, was there? They had the longest night to tease things out, but for now...

She swallowed and climbed onto his lap, claiming his mouth in a kiss that stole her breath and sent shivers across her exposed flesh. His touch was everywhere—gliding up her hips to her waist, gripping her backside, then sliding up her back, across her shoulders, leaving a trail of fire in its wake.

She didn't need to check this time—he wanted this too.

Pulling away the barest inch from his lips, she met his gaze. His eyes were hooded, sparking with dark intensity. Hands on his shoulders, she slid onto him, not breaking eye contact. Their gasps mingled as he filled her.

Fool woman that she was, she'd resisted this all these weeks... They could have been doing this, enjoying each other all this time. She huffed a breath that was nearly a laugh.

A smile twitched at the edge of his lips, and as one arm wrapped around her, he gave her a brief, deep kiss.

"Vee," he breathed into the fractional space between them. He shook his head as if unsure what to say, slipping his other hand to her pearl and stroking slowly. He kissed her again, the touch of his lips and sweep of his tongue matching the rhythm of his strokes.

This angle, the sublime friction against his body.

She moaned against his mouth, forcing herself to ride at that same speed, even though she wanted to drive harder, faster. But all working together, every point of contact merged into one glorious cadence, like waves lapping at the shore.

"You are beautiful," he murmured and kissed her again, driving the waves higher. "Bewitching." And again. "Beguiling." Again. Higher still. "All the best B-words." Again, sending the waves over her head, drowning her in pleasure until there was only sparking white and black oblivion.

As she shuddered back to awareness, he tore his lips from hers and, their foreheads touching, he looked into her eyes —*really looked,* so intense it could have been a physical blow.

She faltered in her rhythm, even as he stoked fresh pleasure in her.

"Vee, I—"

She shook her head. No words. The way he looked at her was more than enough.

No, worse—it was far too much with that crease between his brows that said *sorry* and—and—

"I..." His fingers flexed against her back, pulling her even closer, driving her onto him harder.

"Quiet." The word burst out of her, forced by his insistent rhythm. If she said anything else, it would come out a cry, and if *he* said anything else, she might weep.

There was only one option. She kissed him to silence.

But it hurt.

Not her body—gods, that was so far from pain, she could die from it.

No, this pain was much harder to deal with. There were no fae gifts to heal it.

It twisted, choked, near physical in its ferocity.

Traitor.

No.

She squeezed her eyes shut. Her head spun, her thoughts too. It was just the drink bringing up unwelcome ideas.

No words. No pain. Enough of dark things.

She turned her back on them and instead, she rode towards bliss.

His lips on hers. His hold on her hip and shoulder. His glorious body under her hands, inside her, driving mounting pressure, unbearable pleasure through every fibre.

No words. No pain. This was beautiful.

This is broken.

Her eyes stung. The pressure surged, more than her body could contain.

So broken.

He breathed her name, and she fractured into a thousand pieces, her cries driving tears from her eyes.

She tried to cling to the moment of nothingness, but it was black sand between her fingers. Too soon she was back in this cabin, on this bunk, with *him*, and it was that simple and that horribly complicated.

Still holding her close, their rhythms one, he moaned against her shoulder and shuddered beneath her in climax. His exhalations blew cold across her skin, harsh and fast.

What a fool. What a damn fool.

This wasn't just bodies.

She sank into his lap, still straddling him, slumped, raw, her breaths sounding as ragged as her heart felt.

Not just bodies.

Her throat closed. She jerked away from him, staggering to her feet with a hiccoughing breath.

Still panting, he stared up at her.

Gods. What had she done?

He lifted his hand, reaching perilously close. "Are you—"

"That was a mistake," she blurted, shaking her head. She backed away until her heel slammed into the bulkhead.

His cheeks were still flushed, chest beaded with sweat, but where his eyes had been dark with desire, now they were bright with hurt. His face fell.

She shook her head, crossing her arms against her churning belly. "We shouldn't have—*I* shouldn't have..."

Why did he have to go and ruin it like that? Saying sweet words, *looking* at her like that? Why did he have to ruin good sex with *feelings?*

She swallowed, rubbing her tight throat. Was that entirely fair? Was it only *his* feelings? With a huff, she leant back against the bulkhead and stared at the ceiling. From the periphery of her vision, she saw him watching her, hands running through his hair. She couldn't bear looking directly at that. "I thought it was just... I thought this would be fun. But you had to go and confuse—and ruin everything."

Damn it, it *was* his fault. He was the one who'd started speaking.

She drew a quaking breath. "I—I thought that we could go back to doing this. I thought it would just be gratification."

"Just bodies," he murmured.

The words shook through her, forcing a mirthless laugh from her mouth. That was what she'd said to him back on *The Morrigan*, the day she'd almost screwed FitzRoy in an attempt to prove to herself that what she did with Knigh was nothing more than sex.

She nodded. "Just bodies." But that was a long time ago. *Before.* Bile coated the back of her tongue, blocking her throat. No, it wasn't bile, it was the bitterness of what he'd done.

"You betrayed me, Knigh." The words cracked. She hadn't said them out loud since they'd left Portsmouth, but now they were there and either voicing them or the drink meant she couldn't stop spewing it all out. "You bloody betrayed me. You almost got me killed."

"I'm sorry, Vee—I..." He sighed—the sound not angry or frustrated, but dejected. "I don't know what else to say. If you would just let me—"

"I nearly lost my gift." She couldn't listen to his explanation, not standing here naked, skin still burning from the touch of him, body still throbbing from the feel of him. She squeezed her arms, fingers digging in. "I was in that cage, in pain, slowly dying for *a week*. Do you really think 'sorry' can make that better?"

He raked his hair. "Vee, I—no. I just..." He shook his head, throat constricting in a tight swallow. "I'm sorry. I thought this meant you felt the same way I do. I thought—"

"You betrayed me," she spat, tension thrumming in her limbs—a horrible echo of the throbbing pleasure of minutes ago. "How the hells do you *think* I feel about you after that?"

He stiffened with a long breath, close to a gasp, but slower, lower, that touch more restrained. "I thought this meant you'd... The way you acted earlier—the touches, the fact you didn't murder me after we kissed—you kept looking at me, like..."

She managed to rasp out one word: "Like?"

His eyes were wide when he looked up at her, the grey warmed by lamplight. "Like perhaps you'd forgiven me."

A couple of hours ago she thought maybe she'd forgiven him too, but...

"I thought we were getting past it," he went on. "I thought that was why this happened."

"Getting past it?" She laughed again—it was that or crying — and threw her head back until it banged against the wall. The low pain was welcome—an antidote to her body's fading pleasure and counterpoint to the aching in her chest. "I am *not* past what you did. I have *not* forgiven you." How the hells could she? No battle wound had ever hurt like this, not even getting shot.

She looked back at the ceiling to avoid facing him and

traced the scar on her shoulder—the skin was unnaturally smooth and, right at the centre, numb. "And this…" Her voice crumpled—stupid, weak thing. "And this has opened it all back up again." She grinned, fierce and bitter. "On *The Morrigan*, back *before*, I—I thought…"

That this was something. But to say that? Impossible. What did it even mean?

"I thought maybe I felt *something* for you, but"—she closed her eyes—"but I was an idiot. It's just that you're good at this." She jutted her chin at the bed. "That's all. It addled my brain, and I thought it was special. So when you betrayed me, it hurt more than it should have." That made sense. It certainly explained a lot. She should never have let him get close—not then and certainly not tonight. "So, no, I can't go back to this—not with you."

A long breath in, then she hugged herself and braced for the inevitable argument. He was going to put forward his case for why she should forgive him. He'd probably mention the fact he'd saved her from the gibbet. He'd definitely remind her how he'd left the Navy and broken gods knew how many laws to free her.

She dared to look at him.

He was still on the bed, bent over, forearms resting on his thighs, head bowed. He'd run his hands through his hair so many times, it had become a hopeless mess, flopping into his face where it had grown too long. His only movement was the expansion and contraction of his ribcage and shoulders with long, heavy breaths.

The silence hung in the air, so thick it was hard to inhale.

He still said nothing. No defence. No argument. Just... acceptance?

Her stomach knotted, tight below the hollow soreness of her chest.

"I'm sorry, Vee," he said, voice barely crossing the few feet between them. "I truly am. I never would have... if I'd realised..."

She swallowed and scrubbed the heels of her hands across her face. He looked a state.

As a child, she'd once seen a wild sabrecat at her uncle Rufus's house. Or, rather, a taxidermy display of one. It had been posed rearing—at least that what she guessed the arrangement was meant to be. It was probably supposed to be impressive, but the thing was poorly stuffed and had these dead, glassy eyes. Its strange shape and eerie stillness had given her nightmares for a week.

Sabrecats were magnificent creatures—tall and muscular and lean, with coats that gleamed in the sunlight and rippled over their powerful shoulders and flanks. They were hunters. They drew carriages that weighed a ton or more for miles and miles. They carried warriors into battle. She'd even heard how, in the east, they revered a winged sabrecat as a god.

They were not made to be crumpled into odd poses and mounted in entrance halls to sit and gather dust.

And that was Knigh right now.

After all he'd done, hurting him should have been a victory, but it only left her sad, like that sabrecat had.

Maybe that was what made her open her mouth again. "I

thought it was just bodies." She stared at him, nostrils flaring as she shook her head. "But it can never be just that between us."

Unable to look at him any longer, she grabbed her chemise and tugged it on. She shook her head because what she'd said was true. It had never been just bodies. That was why she'd run away from Knigh to FitzRoy's cabin that day—fear of what was stirring for him. Perry had been right.

Bloody Perry. Why wasn't she here?

Vice sighed. Her limbs were so heavy. Her eyelids, too.

What she'd said that day was right. Some feelings weren't worth having. They were exhausting. Painful. Weak.

Arms folded, she focused on a point somewhere over his shoulder. "Let's just stay away from each other as much as possible." *Ha*—that would be easy when they shared this stupid cabin! She needed to keep him far, far away where he couldn't do her any more damage. "Get me back to Perry and I'll consider the debt paid and you can go on your way. You don't have to help me find Drake's treasure—there's no point in dragging this out further."

She flopped onto the bed, as far from him as possible, and crawled across it to the bulkhead. She burrowed under the blankets and curled up around the knotted pain in her belly. He'd betrayed her. She had to remember that one simple fact.

He'd betrayed her.

Her movement seemed to wake him from his stupor, because he pulled on his shirt and snuffed out the lamp before returning to the bed, nowhere near touching her.

With a deep breath, she blinked at the dark.

Alban Arthan. Yule. The longest night.

Too bloody right it was, and holly, mistletoe, and copper bells weren't going to change it.

HOLLOW

A week after Yule, Vice sat at the small table in their cabin, glaring at the unfathomable piece of paper.

Disturb us, Lords, when We are too well pleased
with ourselves, When our dreams have come
true Because we have dreamed too little,
When we arrived safely Because we
sailed too close to the shore.

Drake's poetry. She squeezed the jewelled pin hidden at her neckline, letting its hard edges bite into her fingertips.

Since the lines had been broken in strange places, she'd tried taking the last word of each line, but it hadn't spelled out a message. The last letter was no better. The first didn't help, either. Every other letter. Every capital letter. Drawing lines from top to bottom and reading along them.

All nonsense.

What the bloody hells did it mean? There had to be some hidden message, the way to an object or location. Otherwise what was the point?

Lips pursed, she stared at it. There had to be something she was missing, something she'd overlooked. *Something*.

Because if it wasn't a clue, this was all pointless. She was no closer to Drake's treasure or humiliating FitzRoy.

She should've killed him when she had the chance.

Behind her, the door swung open and, a few footsteps later, clicked shut.

Him.

She clenched her jaw, spine straightening, fingertips pressing into the tabletop.

Since Alban Arthan, they'd avoided each other as much as it was possible to avoid a person when you shared a cabin with them. Just as well, because she couldn't help but snap at him every time they were in the same room.

The avoidance had been easier than she'd expected. As a naval captain, which he still was as far as Billy and his crew were concerned, Knigh had all the excuse he needed to be up on deck.

She, on the other hand, had to slink around belowdecks, only venturing into the fresh air for a daily walk with Lady Pevensey.

In private, she'd managed to improve her press-up count and add in other exercises, but progress was irritatingly slow and being cooped up inside didn't help.

To have a man's freedom! She huffed. That was exactly why

she'd left Albion and its stuffy manners in the first place, but here she was having to play along with its stupid rules.

Teeth grinding, she pushed the clue away.

With any luck, he was only here to fetch something before pissing off back on deck or to the common room.

A soft sigh sounded from the doorway.

Her finger tapped on the table. Minutes ticked by. He made no other sound, as if he just stood there.

She cracked her neck where it ached with tension. Still nothing. What *was* he doing? Maybe he was looking at her. What the point in that would be, the gods only knew, but it was possible. Maybe he was gathering the courage to speak to her.

Gods, no. Please. Not that.

He'd tried to approach her once since Alban Arthan to *talk*. Needless to say, she'd cut him off mid-sentence. She'd said all she'd needed to say that night. There was nothing more.

Her chest still ached—no sense adding to it.

After she'd sniped at him a few times, he'd left her alone. Wise man.

The further away he stayed, the safer for him. And for her. No chance of stupid mistakes.

She just needed to hold on until they were in Arawaké and then she'd free him of his agreement to help her find the treasure. Somehow, she'd find a way to help his family directly, if that still bothered her. But the important thing was, she wouldn't have to see him ever again and have that constant reminder of what he'd done.

Wild Hunt, he was still silent.

She huffed and turned in her chair. "What is it?"

He was leaning against the door, head bowed—as broken as he'd been that night.

Bloody hells, he was going to try to apologise again, wasn't he?

"I've told you already," she said before he could, "I don't want to talk about it. I leave you alone, you leave me alone, and everything will be just wonderful."

Still nothing.

Piss off, already.

"Whatever it is you're doing, could you go and do it somewhere else? You know, up on deck, where you're free to come and go? I only have this cabin and the common room and it's bloody impossible to get anything done with the Pevenseys in there." Snuggling on the settee and smiling at each other all the time. She scowled, forehead aching with it. "At least you can—"

"Vee," he murmured, voice muffled where his head was bowed, "could you not?"

She blinked. *"Pardon?"* A tendril of fire snaked through her, like a burning rope dropping from the yardarm of a ship ablaze. "Can I not?" She scoffed, the anger making her hands tremble. "You don't get to say things like that to me. You don't get to—"

Her voice cracked, forcing her to pause and hold her breath —it was that or letting the stinging in her eyes become full-blown tears. And that was not an option.

She glared at him. *Go away, traitor.*

He didn't take the hint.

Fine. A few nasty words would do it. Her stomach turned,

but she swallowed and forced her lips to part. "You know, there's one thing I can't work out." Her belly spasmed again and bile burned her tongue—it was only the years at sea in even the roughest storms that stopped her throwing up. "I don't care that you screwed me"—*liar*—"I just can't fathom *why*. What part did it play in your twisted plan?" The chair shrieked as she rose, as shrill and sharp as the pain in her chest.

A few more words, then he'd go, and she'd be able to breathe properly again without it hurting. "Was it to twist the knife harder or simply for your own sick amusement?" Arms folded, she cocked her head as if it truly were a mystery for the ages.

Her throat narrowed to a reed's width—at least that's how it felt with each rasping breath. He wasn't leaving. She should say more... and yet no more words would come. Perhaps some part of her did want an answer to that question. *Why?*

But another part of her seethed and ached in answer. It couldn't stand to hear anything about it or any word from him. It itched to stride across the room, yank open the door and stride up on deck, away from him and any explanation he could give.

She had to push harder. Her heart throbbed, heavy and sore, but she drew a long breath and carried on.

"What was it you said in Nassau?" She narrowed her eyes as if she didn't remember every single word of that conversation. So long ago in the sun, in the days *before*, when they'd come far too close to kissing in Waters' book shop. She'd been a fool for him even back then, long before the sex had started. "Oh, yes: *whatever it takes to get the job done.* Isn't that what y—"

"Vee," he growled, straightening. His eyes were wild, red-rimmed, shadowed by a frown.

She stopped mid-word, staring at him. That look—just like on the *Covadonga* when he'd returned from his berserker rage, desperate and afraid.

His jaw knotted, as tense as his frown. "Do you think you could maybe—just *maybe* get through one day without attacking me? Is that too much to ask?" He stomped further into the cabin. "And what—Wild bloody Hunt!" He stopped in his tracks and bent over. "Would it kill you to put things away after yourself, too?" He straightened, brandishing a book that she'd thrown on the floor earlier.

He slammed it onto the dressing table and paused there, hand pressed into the cover, nostrils flared.

Vice blinked. This was *not* Mr Control.

She exhaled and eased against the desk. She'd pushed too hard. She'd been too harsh. Bloody hells, she'd only wanted to scare him off, not *hurt* him. At least not this much. He was so stiff, she'd forgotten he did actually feel under that mask of his.

A deep breath heaved through his chest. "I—I'm sorry." He cleared his throat, gaze dropping. "It's hard enough dealing with being around Billy, without you adding to it." He exhaled, shoulders sagging.

Billy? What in the world had Billy done to add to Knigh's distress?

She frowned, worrying her lip between her teeth. Knigh *had* been quiet since they'd set sail, which she'd put down to the obvious. But yes, now she thought of it, he was worse whenever he spent a significant amount of time *with Billy.*

Knigh hunched over, like that badly stuffed sabrecat—hollow, somehow. And although he was formally dressed, his jacket was rumpled around the shoulders and his cravat was wonky, as if he'd tugged at it absently. As for his hair...

She scrubbed her face. Gods damn it, she'd been so absorbed in herself and the clue, she hadn't realised he was suffering. And from the look of it, badly.

CONFESSION

"What's wrong?" Vice clenched her hands against the desire to reach out and touch his shoulder. "I thought Billy was your friend."

He stood there, still and solid, but a few seconds later, the tension trembled through him. When he blinked, his eyelashes glistened. "I—I can't. I..."

He shook his head, jaw flexing as if holding back a library's worth of words.

Vice's throat closed again and that pain in her chest flared afresh. Lords and Ladies, the poor man. "Here," she murmured. Gently, she pulled his hand off the book. "Come on." When she tugged him away from the dressing table, the tension dissolved and he followed. At her coaxing, he sat on the bed, and she took a seat beside him.

He bent over, staring at his hands, so like he had the night of Alban Arthan, it sent a shudder through her.

Was this like Mercia—something he couldn't bear to speak of? What had Billy done? She narrowed her eyes, watching his stillness. No, not something Billy had done—the way Knigh's pain had blended with the guilt he'd already expressed over betraying her... this was something else he felt guilty about—something *he* had done.

"Knigh." She took one of his hands. She wasn't like Perry—she couldn't talk a person down from a ledge with the right words, but she could *try* to comfort him. Perry had words and Vice had touch. As complicated as things were between her and Knigh, this was the tool she had. The other was humour, but this wasn't the time. "If you don't want to talk about—"

"How do you think Billy lost his hand?"

Her brows shot up at such a sudden and strange question. She shrugged. "An accident?"

His shoulders rose and fell with a long breath, and as his back straightened, he pulled his hand from hers. "No. And not to an enemy, either." His gaze levelled and met hers in the dressing table mirror opposite the bed. "It was me."

Him? She fought to keep her expression like his neutral mask, but she didn't have his practice—the shock showed in her open mouth and wide eyes. He couldn't mean—no, it was a misunderstanding. This man beside her—the one who, back in Portsmouth, had washed her hair so tenderly, it had brought tears to her eyes—he wouldn't hurt a friend like that. He had to mean something else. She kept quiet, waiting for him to explain.

"You remember on the *Covadonga* when I grabbed you? When you had to call me back to myself?"

She nodded, silent. It wasn't a sight she'd ever forget. Wild eyes that didn't seem to see. Breaths so harsh and hard, spittle flecked his lips. And this emptiness, like he wasn't there anymore, like the only thing left was rage. That man—was *he* capable of such a thing?

"It wasn't the first time I had one of those spells," he murmured. "The first time, Billy was the one who came between me and the fight and... and..."

And, still lost in that wild place, he'd reacted, all animal instinct.

On the *Covadonga* hadn't he grabbed her, his blade raised? And when he'd returned to himself, he'd snapped from ferocious to afraid. He'd even checked her over, asking whether he'd hurt her.

Stomach turning, she swallowed. No wonder he'd been so horrified.

And, gods, no wonder he kept such a tight rein on himself. She couldn't imagine the guilt, the fear of what he might do if he lost control. No doubt, it lingered with him as part of his normal life, but being here on Billy's ship—surely he was reminded of it every day.

A wince tightened her features, and she rubbed her face to hide it.

Because she'd spent the past month piling more guilt on top, together with a big dollop of cruelty.

With a shaking sigh, she bowed her head. "And yet you still took a place on his ship."

"It was the only option."

It had been the next passenger ship scheduled to leave. A

day later and the Navy would probably have recaptured her. And yet...

She cleared her throat. "Not true."

He frowned, head cocking.

"You could have forgotten about the whole stupid idea and got on with your life. But instead you decided to set sail across the ocean with the two people in the world you probably think you've wronged most." She scoffed softly, shaking her head. Stupid, noble man.

He lifted one shoulder, the corner of his mouth rising too, bitter with irony. "As I said, the only option."

Meaning it would've been impossible to turn his back on her and walk away. Her heart thudded hard. Yes, far too noble for his own good, that was Knigh.

But she gave him a small smile. "Noble fool."

He huffed, gaze falling away from hers.

"Look, Knigh, I..." Gods, was she really about to say this? Apparently so. "I'm sorry to have added to your suffering. I've been cruel."

"I'm sure I deserve it after what—"

"No, not this." She sighed and clasped her hands together, picking at her thumbnail. "I might be angry as all the hells at you, but that's not the only reason I've been so downright spiteful." She chewed the inside of her cheek. Apologising. Admitting to her own feelings. Perry would bloody love this. "It wasn't my intention to hurt you—at least not *very* much." She gave a half-smile. "Just a little sting, perhaps."

He scoffed but let her go on.

She pursed her lips and caught his eye in the mirror again.

"I didn't want to cause you this much pain, especially not on top of being around Billy, I just—after Yule, I wanted—*needed* to keep you at arm's length."

His face was mostly still again, but his eyebrows flickered— just a touch of surprise. "I—of course." He nodded slowly. "I understand. And... thank you." He flashed a brief, sad smile before looking away. "But I did a terrible thing. A few kind words won't heal my guilt or help Billy. I ruined his life, too, and, quite rightly, he hates me for it."

She studied him in that mirror—the lines between his brows, the flatness of his mouth, the tension in his jaw. Unmistakable anguish. Had his mask broken entirely? She rubbed her chest, but it didn't help the ache. "You know, I'm not sure you're right."

Billy had greeted her with warmth. The first time they'd eaten together, when she'd been well enough to leave their cabin, he'd bombarded her with eager questions, smiling at them both. He'd even clapped Knigh on the shoulder and congratulated him at least twice for making such an excellent match.

She shook her head. "No, I don't think Billy hates you."

Knigh straightened with a sharp inhale—probably about to argue.

She lifted her chin at him in the mirror, daring him to disagree. "He was genuine when he congratulated you. And he couldn't get enough details of how we'd met." She shook her head—it had been tricky, but they'd concocted a safe version of the meeting at deLacy's ball and used that as their cover story. Billy had hung onto their every word as they'd worked together to spin the tall tale. "I honestly don't think he bears you any ill-will."

Knigh's frown softened, turning thoughtful.

She lifted a shoulder. "Maybe you should talk to him if you feel this way?"

He scoffed. "I'm not sure I have the courage."

With a snort, she gave him a playful shove. "Oh, if you can come in here and face the hissing hellcat who's been stalking this cabin for the past week, you are certainly brave enough to face a whole ship full of Billys."

He cocked his head and stroked Barnacle who was curled up on his pillow. "Barnacle's not been that grumpy."

She raised an eyebrow. "I meant *me.*"

He froze, staring at her—face-on, no longer through the mirror. The corner of his mouth twitched.

She lifted one shoulder. "You can laugh—I won't bite."

"Hmm. I'm not so sure." But he chuckled, and she joined him. "I can't believe you of all people are encouraging me to talk about my feelings."

She raised her eyebrows. "Oh, the irony isn't lost on me. I've clearly spent too much time around Perry."

He laughed again, much more softly, and caught her eye. "We will find her, you know."

"Of course we will." She nodded as if she'd never doubted it, even though a trickle of worry ran through her.

They sat for a long while, just looking at each other. At one point, he lifted his hand as if to take hers but didn't.

Eventually, he raked his hair. "You're right, though. Not that Billy doesn't hate me, necessarily—I don't know about that. But his reaction—it hasn't been what I expected. What I deserve." He sighed, long and low. "I should go and speak to him—it's the least I can do, and perhaps I can get to the bottom of how he really feels." He winced. "I just can't shake the feeling he's putting on a brave face."

She waved to the door. "Well, you won't get your answers in here."

He rose and squared his shoulders, clearly steeling himself. In a few strides, he was at the door and pulling it open. "Vee," he said, pausing in the doorway and turning to her. He bit his lip, then smiled. "Thank you." Then he was gone.

She exhaled, the breath almost coming out as laughter.

Swallowing, she touched her chest—it no longer hurt.

A FULL LIFE

Knigh rubbed the back of his head. Now he stood in Billy's cabin, this felt like a terrible idea.

The cabin was nothing like FitzRoy's—there was no gilt, for starters. But it wasn't like a typical naval captain's quarters either. The etching secured to the bulkhead showed a frigate, sails full of wind, on a choppy sea. A modest selection of books stood in a glass-fronted cabinet. By the stern windows sat an armchair with a folded bottle-green tartan blanket. All little signs of comfort and homeliness—nothing like the spartan living accommodation encouraged by the Navy or the lavish excesses some captains and admirals got away with.

Billy sat on the edge of his desk, eyebrows raised. "Come on, man—out with it." He chuckled, shaking his head. "Or do you expect me to guess?"

Knigh winced. He was so jovial—all an act. "You don't have to do that, you know."

Billy squinted back, head cocking. "Do *what?*"

Biting his lip, Knigh looked away. He'd started it now—there was no turning back. He would've sworn there was something stuck in his throat, but he pushed the words past it: "Put on a brave face."

The room was suddenly very quiet, leaving only the constant creak of the ship and the faint rush of the sea.

The silence yawned on.

Knigh dragged in a deep breath. *Stay the course.* "I—I know you must..." He shook his head—he was starting in the wrong place. Arms by his sides, he pulled himself to attention and looked at a spot over Billy's shoulder. He might not be in the Royal Navy anymore, but he would take this like an officer. "Billy, I know it isn't enough and could never *be* enough, but please understand how sorry I am. I think of... what I did to you every day and I feel awful, but"—he swallowed but that thing in his throat was lodged in place—"but you're the one who lost a hand, so you must feel a hundred times worse.

"I can't stop thinking about how I ruined your life." There it was, the bald truth. That day, he'd cost Billy not only his hand, but his career and a chance at a normal life where people saw just a man, rather than a disability. "I know I don't deserve to even ask for it, but I can't quiet my mind and Vee—*Verity* suggested I come and speak with you." His breath shook as he forced his gaze to meet Billy's. "I just need to know if you think there's a chance you might ever forgive me. If there's anything I can do to even inch towards it."

Billy's jaw flexed, a muscle twitching. There it was—he was angry. Finally, showing his true feelings.

Well, good, he deserved it. Knigh braced, lifting his chin.

Billy folded his arms, raising one eyebrow. "Have you finished?"

Knigh tried to swallow, but his mouth was too dry. He nodded.

"Good. Then you can stop making such a damn fool of yourself." Billy huffed, irritation sparking in his hazel eyes as they caught the afternoon sun from the stern windows. "While I appreciate you coming and speaking to me, it was entirely unnecessary." He pursed his lips. "It appears too much time on deck in the Arawakéan sun has addled your brain—or perhaps it's too much rum with the locals?" He cocked his head, expression still cool. "Either way, I'm clearly going to have to spell out for you why your dramatic speech was, at best, misguided and, at worst, insulting."

Knigh gritted his teeth against the surprise that wanted to leap across his face. Insulting? He never meant—

"I don't need nor want your pity." Billy's mouth settled into a flat line and he raised one eyebrow, so close to Vee's best glare it might have made Knigh laugh in other circumstances. "In fact, I find it rather irritating—the idea that being as *you* are is the only way a man can be fulfilled, happy, *useful.*" His chin rose, and he gestured at himself. "Tell me, Knigh—when you look at me, do you see half a man? Someone broken? A useless waste of space?"

Knigh retreated a step. "No!" Was that what Billy thought? If so, he had every right to hate Knigh. "I never said—"

"Not in so many words, no, but your speech implied it. The way you look at me"—with a sardonic smile, Billy shook his head—"you don't see me as whole—you don't think my *life* can be whole. Well, allow me to disabuse you of such a ridiculous notion." His chest heaved, and he circled his desk.

Perhaps Billy was going to hit him. Knigh lifted his chin. It would be no less than he deserved. He stood, waiting.

But Billy went to the oak cabinet against the wall. With a clink, he pulled out two glasses and deposited them on the desk, soon followed by a decanter of honey-coloured liquid. *"Sit."*

Knigh raised his eyebrows. Not a fight, then, but a drink. Perhaps the punch would come after.

He obeyed the instruction while Billy returned to his seat, filled the glasses and shoved one across the desk. The alcohol and peat scent of a decent Alban whisky curled through Knigh's awareness. Watching Billy, he took the glass.

Beneath his guilt, did he really think Billy only half a man?

He had to admit it—he pitied Billy. The Navy had been Knigh's making—the best thing that had ever happened to him. It had stomped out his childish arrogance at being the son of a viscount (and a future viscount himself), and had given him a new confidence—a far truer confidence, born out of skill, capability, and learning.

Later, he'd realised the arrogance of his younger self had been nothing more than insecurity, hiding behind the strutting façade of a lordling. It was but a dim and quivering matchlight in comparison to his pride when he'd passed his lieutenant's exam with full numbers. A pride he'd earned, rather than tumbled into through pure luck of birth.

And in losing his hand, Billy had lost his place in the Navy. Of course Knigh pitied him for that.

But he schooled his face into stillness, hiding it.

Billy leaned back in his chair, sighing as his level gaze remained on Knigh. "Now, drink, and listen, rather than thinking you know best."

Thinking you know best. Maybe he was wrong—maybe what was best for him wasn't best for Billy. Knigh rubbed his brow and obeyed. The malty flavour and alcohol burn worked their way past the lump in his throat.

Billy raised the glass, examining its gleam as he swirled the liquid. "First off"—he took a gulp of whisky—"I admit, I was horrified when it happened. Hells, even *I* thought my life was ruined that day." He smiled stiffly. "I did, indeed, put a brave face on it, in part to make you feel better, though mostly it was to comfort myself. But, actually? I don't need to anymore. My life is good."

So it wasn't an act? Or at least wasn't anymore. Knigh sipped his drink to hide any reaction that might leak through his self-control. Other than that, he kept his mouth shut—this was his time to listen.

"This injury allowed me to escape the Navy." Billy snorted softly and met his gaze over the glass. "I know you've always loved it, so probably regard that as a tragedy in its own right, but I am not *you*. And now I'm a civilian, I don't have to fight and kill for a living any more. Life at sea is always a risk, but as a merchant I don't *tend* to have anyone shooting at me. When was the last time someone fired at you? Other than Llyr going overboard, when were you last in fear for your life or someone else's?"

Knigh dragged his gaze away and surveyed his own glass. The sunlight cast an amber glow on the whisky, sparkling on its surface. It was an easy question to answer—every minute of the night he'd taken Vee from the gibbet cage.

Before that, the day he'd arrested her—he'd been so sure she would resist and end up shot right in front of him.

And before that, it had been fighting the *Covadonga* and the handful of other ships they'd taken with *The Morrigan*. Then there was the *Veritas* and—

"Struggling to keep track?" Billy asked, a brow arched.

Touché. "Something like that," Knigh muttered into his glass and took another sip.

"*Exactly.*" Billy lifted his glass again, as if toasting. "Then I used the pension to start this business—sorry, correction—my *strangely generous* pension." His eyes narrowed.

Knigh went very still, not even daring to swallow. The whisky burned in his mouth. Did Billy suspect Knigh had contributed a good sum to the payout when he'd been honourably discharged from the Navy?

Billy sighed. "I know how much a missing hand is worth in the Royal Navy's books. I *mysteriously* received twice as much. It's quite obvious where that additional sum came from, and I don't mean Mercia."

The long years of discipline kept Knigh's reaction in check at the mention of that name, especially in relation to Billy and *that day*, but it pushed his pulse up a notch. Slowly, he swallowed and conceded by raising his shoulder.

Billy flashed a smile. "Which I thank you for. And, yes"—he held up his hand—"you'll try to protest at my thanks, but, really, you didn't need to do that. What you *do* need to do is understand. I have a great—a *full* life. All that's missing is a wife I love, as you have with Lady Villiers. And that's something I can wait a few more years for."

Knigh bit back a laugh at the irony. If Billy only knew. Instead, he took a deep breath and nodded.

Billy had a business, a ship, a good income if the quality of the furnishings and whisky was anything to go by.

But, of course, he hadn't seen that before now. He hadn't been able to see past the empty spot at the end of Billy's sleeve. Wild Hunt take him, he'd been exactly that person who stopped Billy from having a normal life by seeing only him as a disability and not a man.

Knigh ran a hand over his face. "You are entirely right. I've been a perfect fool. I must add *this* to my list of things to apologise to you for."

Billy rolled his eyes. "A fool, yes"—he downed the last of his drink then sighed—"but not one who owes me any more apologies or guilt. I forgave you long ago."

Knigh drew a sharp breath, almost a gasp. His throat burned with it. "You..." He swallowed, shaking his head again. Billy had forgiven him? But...

Eyebrows raised, Billy pursed his lips. "For a man who came here to beg my forgiveness, you don't look terribly relieved."

He was right. Billy had forgiven him, so why did it still weigh so heavily on his shoulders? These past two years, he'd dreamt of hearing those words from Billy, and just the dream had brought such a sense of relief, he'd almost cried from it when he'd woken. Of course, it always burned away with the morning mist. But that was how forgiveness was meant to feel, not like this.

Not still the same.

He clutched the glass so tightly, his knuckles whitened as his stomach lurched.

It was meant to change everything.

"Ah." Billy huffed softly and his glass clinked onto the desk. "Of course." The corners of his mouth rose, but it was a sad smile. "It's not my forgiveness you need." He leant closer, hand flat on the table. "It's your own."

The hairs on the back of Knigh's neck stood to attention.

Billy topped up their glasses as he continued, "For hurting me, for allowing yourself to lose control. For accepting that you're only human, not a perfect, unfeeling, automaton. You made a mistake and you need to move past that. No one else can do it for you."

A shiver crept through Knigh. It was the truth. All of it. If Billy had already forgiven him and yet it still dragged upon him, he was the only one standing in his own way.

The question was, how in the world did he forgive himself?

IMPLICATED

O ver the following weeks, the *Swallow* stopped off
in Port Royal and Ayïti for Billy's business. They
traded the Albionic goods in the hold and
dropped off passengers. The Pevenseys disembarked at Port
Royal. At each stop, Knigh checked whether there had been any
word of Lady Vice's escape from Albion. There had not. He still
insisted she stay hidden, out of caution.

Keeping belowdecks set Vicc's teeth on edge. It wasn't like
anyone would recognise the helpless Viscountess Villiers as the
Pirate Queen. Well, no one *else* would realise who she was. The
day Knigh had spoken to Billy about his hand, his old friend
had revealed that he'd worked out her identity. Thankfully,
he'd also agreed to help by dropping them off in Nassau.

Frustrating as it was, Vice had to play along for his sake. If
anyone saw her on his ship, it could get him in trouble, even if
he didn't admit to knowing the truth.

It felt like a lifetime before Nassau came into view. Vice stood at the ship's bow for the entire approach, gripping the rail as her heart leapt. The air was warm. Music drifted across the water. The island was its usual swampy green. And the port town huddled by the sea, all the shades of sun-beaten timber.

This place was beautiful.

Vice smiled. She might've been born in Albion and grown up there, but *this* was home.

She scanned the ships at port, tugging her lip. No sign of the *Covadonga*—she'd recognise its sail plan. On the plus side, there was no sign of Vane's *Maelstrom*, either. He'd just *love* to see her arrive on a civilian ship, disguised as a demure lady. He'd never let her live it down.

A short while later, the *Swallow* put in at the docks and she and Knigh gathered with the crew to say their goodbyes. Llyr gave Knigh a smart salute, eyes bright. Billy reassured them he had Knigh's messages for his family back in Albion and would make the delivery personally to stop the letters ending up in the wrong hands. Should they wish to send messages back, he'd direct them to his offices in Arawaké.

The crew eyed her, no doubt wondering why they were dropping a Viscount and his wife in a town known as a pirate haven and why she didn't look the slightest bit concerned by that fact.

But who cared? She was home. And chances were, if Perry wasn't already here, she'd arrive soon.

Knigh hefted two duffel bags over his shoulder, and together they stepped off the gangplank.

Her smile stiffened. This was all assuming Perry and the

others hadn't been arrested in Plymouth. She swallowed. She'd get information from friends in town—surely they'd have heard.

First things first—a place to stay and a shop to rid herself of Lady Villiers' clothes. They took a room at a waterfront inn—sharing to save money—and dropped off their bags before heading for the nearest place that sold second-hand clothes. They traded in the rich clothing to avoid spending any of their dwindling supply of cash, which got them several outfits. Vice changed immediately and heaved a sigh of relief. It was fun to wear gowns once in a while, but not every day.

Leaving Knigh outside to keep an eye out for friendly faces, Vice ducked into a couple of taverns. Her mood and eyebrows lowered with each stop.

"No one's heard from Perry," she muttered to Knigh as she left the third. The smell of stale beer and even staler sweat clung to her nostrils—unpleasant and yet comforting in its familiarity.

She glanced up at Knigh, at the harsh shadows cast below his tricorne hat and the darker ones below his drawn-together eyebrows. His eyes were little more than steely glints, scanning the road ahead, restless, watchful. But there was no sign of Perry or the others.

The taverns might have no information, but maybe Waters did. She owed him a visit—he'd been implicated in her trial, and she needed to warn him in case there would be repercussions. Speaking of which...

"How did they have Waters' name?" She hadn't stopped to think about it since the trial—she'd been too absorbed with recovering her strength, deciphering the clue, and not murdering Knigh.

He blinked and shot her a confused glance. "What? Who had his name?"

"At my trial. They named Waters as the one who'd forged our supposedly fake letter of marque. How did they know his name and that he was linked to me?"

After all, Knigh knew who Waters was and that they were friends. The ghost of anger itched down her back, and she bit her tongue to force herself to wait for his response.

It was one thing betraying her, but to drag an innocent—or mostly innocent—old man into it. If he had anything to do with that, any truce between them would be off. She'd turn around and walk away, right now, leave him in this pirate den to face his fate.

He exhaled, drawing a deep sound from his throat that was nearly a growl. "Did they, now?" He shook his head, muscle in his jaw ticking. "Maybe FitzRoy or Bricus? Someone else in the crew?"

He inclined his head, bringing their eyes level. His were wide, intense, edged with pain. "I've been an idiot and I've done some terrible things, but I never named Waters in my debrief or any report or—"

"All right"—she raised her hands and backed away—"I believe you." The vulnerability in his eyes was no lie.

Huffing a long sigh, she strode on. They walked in silence for a while, aiming for Waters' shop.

She folded her arms. "What if they were taken?" Her stomach twisted in a way that was growing familiar.

The feeling had found her a few times since she'd been in that iron gibbet cage. When she'd truly believed she would hang in a matter of hours. When they'd crept through Portsmouth. All the while she'd waited for Knigh to rescue Llyr from the night sea and while she'd sat belowdecks as he'd faced that ship-killer of a storm.

It was worry.

Worry! Since when did she, the Pirate Queen, the notorious and terrible Lady Vice, *worry?*

Since never.

She gritted her teeth and stared ahead at the sand-strewn streets. Perry or Saba or Aedan could step around that corner at any moment...

Her stomach still twisted.

"The plan..." he said suddenly, the sentence petering out as quickly as it had begun. His jaw knotted, shifting shadows beneath his hat. "It was only to capture you. That's why the others got away with such lenient sentences."

A day in the stocks. *Very* lenient for pirates. She chewed her lip and gave a noncommittal shrug.

He didn't look at her but went on, "We only had Perry dock in Plymouth to—to..." He gave a soft grunt as if in pain and his hands clenched at his sides. "The idea was that you'd be separated from your allies." His brows lowered further, extinguishing even the glint from his eyes.

It was the most he'd spoken about the plot against her. She'd always found some way of shutting him up before— usually by starting an argument or outright telling him to piss off.

If he tried to explain where shagging her fitted into his plan, she'd have to cut him off. She couldn't listen to that. Not when the mere thought of it blocked her throat.

She gripped her folded arms tighter and looked away. There had to be some irony to finally letting him tell her a little of his plan here of all places—where it had started and ended.

Separating her and her friends to make the arrest easier. She'd suspected, but this confirmed it. "Very clever of you," she said, voice hollow.

Whatever it takes to get the job done. That's what he'd said on these very streets.

"I can't take the credit, I'm afraid." From anyone else, it would have been a quip. But he said it so levelly, his voice so crisp, he sounded every inch the officer giving a formal report. "It was Bricus's idea."

"Of course it was." She should've known. Lords, the man really had hidden so much bitterness behind his jolly façade, hadn't he?

And now he was enjoying life as a landlubber with a parcel of land and a pocket full of gold.

Jolly bastard.

She shook her head, sighing. "That's all well and good, but what if someone went against your plan and betrayed you? What if the Navy captured them anyway?"

"They wouldn't."

"You seem to have a high opinion of your own influence." She raised an eyebrow, but pushed a half-smile onto her lips to try and soften the words. She was trying to be nicer to him. Or at least, less awful. *Must remember that.* "Well, we're here."

Waters' shop. The familiar sign, a red book on a green background, creaked overhead.

Except glass crunched underfoot, making her pause. The display windows had been smashed and the shop door hung open. An ugly scar of splintered wood marred the blue paint around the lock. Vice stared, heart jolting.

Knigh made a low sound. "Someone's—"

"I know."

Someone had broken in and not bothered to hide it.

THE BREAK-IN

"Waters," she called as they entered. "Waters?"

Books covered the floor, pages open, tumbled on top of each other as if someone had swept their arms across the shelves. Shards of pottery crunched under her feet—a mug or pot, perhaps. One bookcase leant drunkenly upon its neighbour—exactly across the spot where she and Knigh had hidden from Vane all those months ago.

A knot of worry in her belly tightened. What the hells had happened?

"Waters?"

Around the corner, the clink and scrub of tidying. She gave a sigh of relief and stooped, retrieving an armful of tomes from the floor. At least Waters was all right.

"It looks like the Wild Hunt's ridden through here," she said with a chuckle, picking her way through the debris and rounding the corner to the counter. "What've you been—"

A salt-and-pepper-haired woman looked up as she swept, her tanned face drawn.

"Vivienne?" Vice cocked her head. "What're you doing here?" She glanced around, stomach falling. "And where's Waters?"

"You're back, then." Vivienne gave a faint smile and nodded, leaning on her broom. She did a brisk trade in reworking silver treasures into jewellery pirates could use to show off their success and wealth. Her shop was nearby, so it was no surprise she knew Waters, but Vice had never seen her here before.

Around Vivienne, the floor was clear where she'd started the monumental task of cleaning. "Suppose the Wild Hunt themselves couldn't keep you away, eh?" Her lips pursed, and she glanced at Knigh as he rounded the corner.

He took it all in with his usual calm expression.

If Waters was in the back room, he'd have replied by now. A chill crept over Vice's shoulders. "What happened? Where is he?"

Vivienne's eyebrows contracted. "Best we can tell, he was attacked. Guy says..." Exhaling, she folded her arms, hugging the broom. "He's not going to wake up."

It was exactly like plunging into a lake at Midwinter. For a moment Vice was breathless, frozen in place.

He's not going to wake up.

She blinked, body creaking back into action. "No." She brushed past Vivienne to the back room and up the stairs.

Not wake up? She shook her head as she reached the landing. Vivienne had to be wrong. Waters was probably just—

She threw open the door to his bedroom.

He was probably just lying on his bed, senseless.

Heart in her throat, she stared from the doorway. He was horribly still, face pale except for purple-black bruises to his jaw and forehead. He looked small and... and *old*.

"Waters?"

No response.

The green curtains were drawn, letting in a sickly light. She glanced at the shelves and low chair—no sign of Guy. He hadn't even bothered to stay with his patient.

At least this room hadn't also been trashed. The shelves were neat as always, full of yet more books, plus trinkets from Waters' years of travel. He'd told her tall tales in the evenings they'd spent chatting and drinking in the small lounge next door. She'd seen this room before, thanks to the times he'd drunk too much and she'd needed to carry him to bed.

If Guy had only given Waters a cursory check before pissing off...

She hurried to the bed. Maybe if she gave him a gentle shake—that was it, Vivienne must not have tried waking him since Guy left.

That charlatan Guy didn't know what he was talking about, anyway. He'd been a Navy surgeon for a few years and they'd let him go. The Navy didn't just *let men go*—especially not skilled surgeons. They were worth their weight in gold. He was a crook—and that was saying something in a town full of pirates.

She grabbed Waters' hand and knelt. Cool, dry. It was only his chest moving, that assured her he wasn't—

"Waters," she said softly, giving his hand a shake. "Come on, you old goat, talk to me. You've got to tell me who I need to pay a short, sharp visit to."

Just that slow, shallow breathing. A faint rasp sounded each time his chest rose.

A death rattle? No, not possible.

She always joked about him being an old man, but he was hearty and hale. He didn't use a walking stick. He climbed his rickety little steps to reach books on the top shelves every bloody day.

Shaking her head, she squeezed his hand. "Waters, just"— she scoffed—"come on, this isn't funny anymore. Stop mucking about."

Any hint of laughter faded when she smoothed the hair back from the dark bruise above his temple. It disappeared into his hairline. Blackness crusted in his sideburns and the curve of his ear.

Guy hadn't even cleaned his wounds properly. Bastard.

"Please," she said, shaking Waters by the shoulders. Her sight blurred.

He still didn't move, and he wasn't going to. Guy might be a crook, but on this he was right.

She squeezed her eyes shut and pressed her brow against Waters' cold hand.

Wake up and tell me to stop being soppy. Any minute now, she would hear his gruff voice and peer up and feel very stupid. Which, for once, she'd be fine with.

A presence behind her—maybe it was warmth or a minute

movement of the floorboard that told her she wasn't alone. She looked up.

Knigh stood inches away, bent over Waters. His mask had slipped into a frown, lips pursed. Thoughtful or concerned?

With a light touch, he pushed back Waters' grey hair, the same as she had. "Hmm." He nodded, but the way his mouth was so flat, it was hard to tell if it was positive or just grim acknowledgement.

Acknowledgement of the inevitable?

Vice held her breath, chest thick with grief.

Everyone dies. Everyone leaves, somehow. Everyone lets you down, eventually.

"Give us some space," Knigh murmured, waving her off and kneeling by the bed.

She shuffled along, still gripping Waters' fingers. Her hand went to her ribs and the spot of smooth skin where a scar ought to be.

Knigh's gift. He'd used it to heal minor scrapes, burns, and, from the neatness of it, Billy's wrist, but a head injury? If they'd damaged Waters' brain...

She swallowed and scrubbed away the tears on her cheeks. "Do you think you can—is he strong enough?"

Lying here, he looked frail, old. Not like Waters.

Knigh didn't look at her, he just raised one shoulder. "I don't know. But he definitely won't wake from this without my help."

It was like when FitzRoy had threatened her with his hand around her throat, except this time it was ice in place of fingers.

She didn't trust Guy as far as she could throw him, but if Knigh said the same thing...

Knigh placed one hand over Waters' brow, the other on his crown. He paused there, gaze fixed on his patient, but he angled his face an inch towards her. "Do you want me to go ahead?"

That ice crept through her—down her shoulders, over her back and legs, all the way to her toes.

Such responsibility. But who else could take it? Waters couldn't speak for himself and he had no family that she knew of, certainly none in Nassau.

If Knigh didn't help, he would die. If Knigh did, he might still die from the force of the fae gift consuming his energy.

She stroked the back of Waters' papery hand. At least if they tried, he stood a chance. And if he died in the attempt, he'd have someone with him—someone who cared.

She nodded, voice uncooperative.

Knigh closed his eyes. The golden glow of his magic flared around his hands and Waters' head.

It warmed her face, like a pleasant summer's day in Albion. But soon the light grew unbearable, forcing her to look away.

Instead, she stared at the death grip she had on Waters. The hair on her forearms rose—she knew how Knigh's gift felt. Warm and glorious, burning and terrible.

With any luck, Waters' unconsciousness meant he would be blissfully unaware of it all.

Gods willing, he'd wake up with the pleasant aftermath.

Hells, she'd settle for him just waking up.

Eyes closed, she waited with nothing but the sound of their

breaths, the heat of Knigh's gift, and the smooth skin of Waters' hand.

Seconds ticked by. Did more time mean it was harder? That it was working? Or that he was struggling?

She bit her lip and waited.

The sound changed. Two deep sets of breathing became three.

Vice looked up in time to see Knigh lowering his hands. He kept still, watching Waters intently. Not triumphant.

Her throat closed. But—but Waters' breath had deepened. The rattle was gone. Surely that meant—

His eyelids fluttered open.

Vice sagged as Knigh sighed with what had to be relief.

Waters' mouth moved and a rasping sound came out, but no discernible words.

"Water," she muttered, staggering to her feet, "on it." She fetched a glass and poured from the pitcher of water Vivienne must have drawn earlier and left up here.

"Here." Vice held the glass as Knigh lifted his patient's head and helped him take a few sips.

"Not too much," Knigh said before taking the glass and stalking away to place it on a table.

She smiled at Waters. "Is that better?"

"Much better than your tears," he croaked, eyes bright as he managed a grin. "I didn't have you down as a crier." His finger-tips brushed her cheek and rose as if holding a trophy. "I'm touched."

A low growl sounded in her throat and she narrowed her eyes. "I was worried whoever took over the shop might charge even more ludicrous prices. Or, even worse, make it into yet another tavern."

They chuckled, and even Knigh gave a soft snort from where he'd settled by the shelves at the foot of the bed.

"Here," Waters said, patting her arm, "help me sit up. I'm both too old and not old enough to be receiving a lady lying down." He winked and waggled his eyebrows. "You're a bit young for me, and I'm not near death any time soon."

Scoffing, she moved him and his pillows. The bruises had gone and his cheeks had some colour. Knigh had done a good job.

She shot him a grateful look, but he fiddled with something on the shelves, apparently absorbed.

"So"—she dragged over a chair and plopped onto it—"are you going to tell me what happened?"

Waters shifted, gaze dropping from hers, eyebrows lowering. "Some young men took advantage of an old coot is what happened."

Vice's jaw clenched. "Who?"

"You're probably familiar with some of them."

Her back straightened, and she shared a glance with Knigh, who looked up from his fidgeting. "Go on."

Waters' blue eyes darkened. "They're FitzRoy's men."

"FitzRoy?" Pain sparked in her palms—her hands had tightened to fists. He'd come out of retirement? And was— "He's *here*?" She'd gladly pay him another visit. One with a more permanent ending—for him.

Or was getting Drake's treasure revenge enough? And even sweeter now he'd come back to witness it for himself.

Either way, she had all the more reason to destroy him now.

"I didn't see him—he sent others to do his dirty work."

Knigh leant on the end of the bed, frowning. "Which was?"

"They wanted something they thought I had." Waters gestured to the water and Vice fetched it. He took a long gulp and cleared his throat. "A book, unsurprisingly." He raised his eyebrows at Knigh over the glass. "An old one with a dragon on the cover."

Knigh sucked in a quick breath. "A dragon? Or a drake?"

Waters raised an eyebrow. *"Exactly."*

Vice looked from one to the other. What were they talking about? "Care to let me in on your weird code?"

"Your book." Waters's eyes widened at her, as if it were obvious.

"My Drake book? But Fitz has seen that a million times—he's had access to it for three years, surely it—"

"Not that one." Waters clicked his tongue and rolled his eyes. "The one our friend here gave you."

Vice squinted, shaking her head. "I suppose you *have* just had a blow to the head." She scoffed at Knigh to share the joke, but he didn't reciprocate.

Clearing his throat, Knigh raised his eyebrows at Waters. "I haven't—she doesn't have it."

She huffed. "Have *what?*"

It was Waters' turn to look from one to the other and back again. "I see." He sipped his water, watching Knigh over the rim.

Knigh pursed his lips. "Last time we were in Nassau, I bought you a book. You're right, by the way, he *is* a ruthless salesman." His eyes narrowed at Waters. "I was going to give it to you as a gift, but then..." He raised a shoulder.

But then she'd told him she'd killed Lady Avice Ferrers. And of course, noble but stupid Knigh Blackwood wouldn't gift a book—or *anything*—to a murderer. She gave a stiff smile and nodded in acknowledgement.

At least this explained what was in the brown-paper parcel.

"The cover is embossed with a copper dragon—it's quite beautiful, really. And, of course, we thought you'd be interested in it, because of Ser Francis Drake."

Not just a gift, but a thoughtful one.

Damn him.

She took a deep breath and nodded.

Waters winced—no doubt he felt the tension humming in the air. He cleared his throat, as if that would cut through it. "Do you still have it?"

Knigh inclined his head.

Vice exhaled through her nose. "Wild Hunt, will one of you tell me what's in this bloody book? Because FitzRoy wanted it enough to—well..." She gestured at Waters.

"I don't know," Knigh said.

"What?" She squinted at him. "What do you mean, you don't know? Surely you opened the thing when you bought it— otherwise, it could've been a cookbook for all you knew."

Knigh scuffed his boot on the floor and sighed. "It appears to be written in Ancient Hellenic—I recognise some of the alphabet, but couldn't make it out. I can read the modern form, so I'd expect to pick out a few words at least, but..." His mouth twisted.

Waters raised a hand as if fending her off. "And I fared no better, but I thought, with your penchant for languages, maybe you'd be able to work it out and read its stories."

A mysterious old book in an unreadable language with a dragon—or *drake*—on the cover. And FitzRoy wanted it. Badly.

The hairs on the back of her neck stood on end and her pulse sped. Could this be a lead? She had FitzRoy's clue already —did Knigh unwittingly have another?

"And where is this book now?" Her voice came out breathless. Lords and Ladies, please say it was somewhere safe.

Knigh stiffened, and his expression was grave. "At the inn."

RECOVERY FROM DESPAIR

Thankfully, their room hadn't been picked over by FitzRoy's men and when they slunk around the wharves, there was no sign of him. They bumped into one of Vice's friends on their circuit—turned out FitzRoy had shown up yesterday in a large frigate and left this morning. They'd missed him by a matter of hours.

As they walked, Knigh lifted one shoulder and haltingly explained, "I didn't give the book to you on the *Swallow*, because I didn't want you to think I was trying to buy your forgiveness or win you over with a gift."

Vice didn't know how to respond, so she distracted him with dinner and they said nothing more of it.

A week later, she stood at the window of their shared room, combing her wet hair. The dampness cooled her in the noon heat. Even with the windows open, it was stifling.

Barnacle lay on the bed, curled up fast asleep. She'd been

doing a lot of that lately. Maybe she was as bored of waiting as Vice was.

Knigh sat on the room's only chair, sharpening his sabre with the steady ringing of steel on whetstone.

Vice gritted her teeth and directed her scowl out the window so he wouldn't see it. She was still attempting to be nice to him—or not horrible—but it wasn't easy. Making their limited funds stretch as far as possible necessitated this shared room, which he spent his time tidying. That's when he wasn't shooting her reproachful looks whenever she dared to not return something to the chest at the end of the bed.

Good grief—anyone would think they were about to get inspected by one of his admirals.

And the book—the Copper Drake, as she'd dubbed it—hadn't eased her frustration, only added to it. As Knigh had surmised, it was the Ancient Hellenic alphabet, but the letters weren't in any order that made sense. Despite knowing the language, she couldn't make out a single word.

There were drawings and diagrams on the pages, too—buildings, symbols, figures, vignettes of tucked away beaches and caves. But aside from the fact the structures and symbols were broadly Arawakéan in style, they didn't tell her much and she didn't recognise them. A few had labels in Albionic, but they didn't make any sense or reveal anything useful. One had a list of vegetables!

How the hells was she meant to have revenge upon FitzRoy and help Knigh's family if she couldn't even decipher a single scrap of information about the damned treasure?

At least Waters was safe and well—that was the only silver lining in the storm cloud of her feelings right now.

A rap sounded at the door.

Vice spun from the window, and Knigh was already on his feet. They exchanged glances, and she swapped her comb for a pistol. Trouble didn't usually knock, but you could never be too careful—especially as a pair of fugitives. The bounty on her head must've gone up now—that would be enough to tempt some pirates.

Knigh crept to the door, and she flanked it, cocking the gun. If trouble had found them, he could open it and gut the person with his sabre, while she fired through the timber.

"What is it?" she called.

"Been told you'd pay for information." The disembodied voice sounded like a girl of ten or twelve—probably one of the kids who scrounged the docks for errands to earn a few coins. "And I've got some."

What trouble could a kid be? She nodded at Knigh and he opened the door. The girl was alone. With a shiny coin, they got their information: a ship had arrived and its captain was Berit Peregrina.

"They made it." Vice grinned, pulling on her boots once the girl had left.

"Or it could be a trap." Brows lowered, Knigh peered out. "FitzRoy already attacked Waters. If he realises you have the book, he won't hesitate."

She grunted and shrugged. "Fitz left and he won't even know we're back yet."

"And what about Vane?" He raised his eyebrows.

With a grimace, she stood. She wasn't exactly Vane's favourite person, true, but he wouldn't dare. Would he? "Come on."

She hurried out, Knigh at her side, advising caution that she ignored. It wasn't a trap—Perry was here, finally.

And with her—the future.

A ship, a crew, and Drake's treasure. There had to be something in the clues she was missing. Once she was back to normal life, she'd figure it out.

In the meantime, she would get Perry to agree to drop Knigh somewhere and then she'd be free of him forever. He could piss off and do whatever he wanted. No more guilt for him, no more reminders of treachery for her.

This time when she scanned the docks, she spotted a familiar set of sails—the *Covadonga*. She sucked in a breath and grinned over her shoulder at Knigh. *"See?"*

Laughing, she passed the bustling dockers and pirates, heart leaping and stride speeding up the closer she got to the former treasure ship.

On deck, familiar blonde hair shone in the midday sun as Perry pointed aft, directing the crew—Saba, Lizzy, and Aedan among them.

Her friends. The ones FitzRoy had to send away because they wouldn't have let his betrayal pass.

For a moment, Vice's chest was too full to call out. She managed a weak laugh, eyes stinging, before clearing her throat. "Perry," she shouted, drawing up to the *Covadonga's* berth.

Perry froze, then spun on her heel. Saba and Aedan's heads jerked in Vice's direction, eyes and mouths wide.

Perry's eyebrows shot up an instant before she smiled and broke into a run, hopping onto the gangway, then the docks, then into Vice's arms.

Laughing, Vice swept her into a spin, although it made her muscles groan. Still, the fact she was able to lift Perry at all was progress. Even if she was only five-foot-nothing.

But enough of that—it didn't matter right now. Vice screwed her eyes shut. All was well. Perry was here and safe and *alive*.

Perry huffed out a breath, patting Vice's back. "Too tight." She chuckled as Vice put her down, but her laugh faded as her gaze skimmed over Vice from head to toe.

The smile stiffened on Vice's face. Perry had to be thinking how thin she looked, how much her muscles had withered. And that was despite how much better and stronger she'd grown over the weeks at sea.

Vice squeezed Perry's shoulder, forcing the smile to stay in place. "How did you get back?" Obviously, they'd stolen the *Covadonga,* but anything—even a stupid question—to avoid addressing the lingering weakness of her body.

A flash of a frown crossed Perry's face, but she nodded. "It's a long story. But"—she took a shuddering breath, eyes brimming —"I can barely believe you're here." She grabbed Vice in another hug. "I despaired when I heard what had happened," she whispered, breath hot in Vice's ear. "I feared all was lost and we'd be too late to save you—that maybe you were already dead."

Vice opened her mouth. She wanted to joke: *I thought I was dead, too.* But the words wouldn't come out, and just the thought made her eyes sting. Perhaps it wasn't a joke.

"But then news came," Perry went on, squeezing so hard it was like she'd never let go, "you'd disappeared. You hadn't been hanged. And a young man, a naval officer no less—a much lauded pirate hunter, tipped to become an admiral before thirty... Well, he was implicated in your disappearance. And I knew"—her voice cracked—"I knew you were in safe hands, even if I didn't know where in the world you were. That was the moment I went from despair to hope." She pulled back and gestured at the gold lettering on the ship's hull, spelling out *Respair.* "It's an old word, meaning to recover from despair."

Despair. Hope. Respair. It all knotted Vice's throat, making words impossible. She shook her head and pulled Perry close again, hiding her face in the crook of her neck.

"I'm here," she managed to say at last. "I'm here." Maybe it was as much for herself as for Perry. Just saying it, she felt stronger.

No sooner had they pulled apart, nodding and smiling, than massive arms fastened around Vice, pulling her back against a warm, solid body. When she looked down, tattoos covered the knuckles of both hands wrapped around her waist, spelling out HOLD FAST. "Aedan."

He released her long enough to turn her, give her a good look, and gather her into his arms again, as though she were precious. "I can't believe it." He crushed the breath from her. "What the hells happened?"

Eyes shut, she sank against him. It was too hot to be this

close to someone, but she'd been away from them so long and he was safe to take comfort in. He hadn't betrayed her.

I missed you. She'd missed them all—it was a million years since they'd said farewell on the deck of *The Morrigan.* But again, the words wouldn't come.

Instead, she inhaled the scent of his salty skin and squeezed back as hard as she could. She didn't make a dent in his powerful muscles. Another reminder of what she'd lost and was working to regain.

He buried his face in her hair. "You're damp," he grumbled, but the soft breath that followed, brushing against her neck, felt like a chuckle. "I thought I'd never—we left as soon as we heard what happened. I can't—"

A low sound rumbled in his chest as his entire body stiffened.

"What's *he* doing here?" Aedan set Vice down and took a step forward.

He'd placed himself between her and Knigh, who stood ten feet away, still as death.

Smiling, eyes bright, Saba approached, but stopped when she followed Aedan's gaze.

Aedan lifted his hand, steel and polished wood gleaming.

Vice's stomach dropped and her hand went to her side where her pistol wasn't. Aedan had it pointed directly at Knigh.

STAND-OFF

Aedan's body trembled, but his aim was sure. Jaw knotted, he glared at Knigh as he cocked the pistol.

Vice couldn't move. Despite the Arawakéan heat, her blood whispered through her veins, as cold and sluggish as a glacier.

Aedan's finger slid onto the trigger.

Wild Hunt, he was not bluffing.

Her stomach turned.

A scrape of metal and Saba had her sword drawn. "He helped FitzRoy," she growled.

Her words rippled through the crew and across the wharf, muttered from one person to the next. The *Covadonga's* berth grew quiet as dockers and pirates backed off, watching, whispering.

Vice drew the slowest of breaths as though even inhaling

might make Aedan pull that trigger. Her gaze inched away from him.

Around them, the *Covadonga's* crew—Lizzy, Wynn, Effie, Clovis, and more—wielded makeshift weapons from belaying pins to marlinspikes. Tension thickened the air, unbearable in this heat.

Only Perry still had empty hands. She shot Vice a wide-eyed glance.

Vice could practically hear the words: *Stop this.*

"Look at her," Aedan said, voice raw as though getting it past his throat was an effort. His eyes bored into Knigh, and if looks could kill, Knigh would have been a dead man. "Look!" Aedan pointed at her, hand shaking. "What the hells did they do to her? No, what did *you* do to her?"

Some dark instinct whispered in Vice's ear. She could just step back, let him and the others do what they wanted to Knigh. No one else would ever know. She wouldn't have to look at him anymore. It would be easy. And would it really be her fault?

It's what the Royal Navy's version of Lady Vice would do.

But the Royal Navy had always been wrong about her.

She was no worse than any other pirate—hells, she was kinder than many. Most of what they said about her was a lie— torturer, murderer, sadist. One story claimed she'd made a bargain with a fae Lord, lying with him to gain power over the sea.

Yes, she was a pirate and a killer, but she'd never killed someone who wasn't fighting back, so how was that different to a marine cutting his way across a deck or a naval gunner firing a cannon?

Whatever Knigh had thought that day on *The Morrigan's* deck, when he'd bound her wrists and handed her over, she was not a monster. Even what he and the Navy had done to her in Portsmouth hadn't changed that. Despite the dark place it had opened in her heart, seething with hurt and anger, she was still herself.

Hells, if Saba had told her this story of a traitorous former lover, maybe she'd have egged her on, told her to call him out— make him pay for his treachery.

But turned out, it wasn't that simple.

She was still angry at him, still hurting. Her hand went to her chest. Her heart hammered against her ribs, hard, sore.

But her feelings were more complicated than that. The idea of the world without him...

Her lungs burned as though she couldn't draw in enough air.

Because he'd die if she left him to her friends. He'd still die if she cast him off now she'd found Perry.

With the Navy after him, the lawful world wasn't an option.

And without her protection, the lawless one was even more dangerous. Pirate crews would hunt him down—the pirate hunter who'd betrayed Lady Vice! They'd make a game of it. Gods, maybe they'd even bring her his head on a platter as some sick trophy.

Bile blocked her throat, and the world tilted.

Saba drew level with Aedan. "I thought you were on our side. I thought you—"

Aedan barked a laugh. "To think I almost called you 'friend'. You don't know the meaning of the word. And you took her—"

"Aedan," Vice burst out. She didn't need her dirty laundry airing in the middle of Nassau's wharves. At least it had broken the stillness blocking her throat. She swallowed, working her tongue around her mouth, reminding it how to work.

"Aedan," she said, voice steadier this time. "Enough. Put the gun down."

The pulse in his throat jumped, hard and fast, and a sheen of sweat coated his brow. His gaze and his aim didn't falter, as though Knigh consumed every scrap of his attention. As though he didn't hear her.

Buggeration. He truly meant to do this. He burned for it.

If she begged him not to, she'd lose all credibility with the crew, and it would be around Nassau before sunset. No one would ever take her seriously enough to vote as captain.

The way Aedan had held her, looked at her—he'd missed her. He cared, that much was obvious, though to what extent? Perhaps he'd been carrying a torch for her since they'd slept together. Was that why he was so eager to kill Knigh?

Lords, this was worse than she realised. And messy.

Explosive.

She winced. And it would take more than a few words to defuse.

Well, she knew one technique that had worked before...

She drew a deep breath and stepped in front of Aedan. "If you want to shoot him"—she grabbed the barrel of the gun and pressed it against her chest—"you'll have to go through me first."

His lips parted on a gasp. He'd been in Knigh's position last year, with FitzRoy threatening his life. He understood she meant it.

Aedan's finger flew off the trigger and he yanked at the gun, trying to drag it away from its new target.

Teeth gritted, she shook her head and gripped harder. "If you want to shoot him," she said again, each word clipped, "you'll have to go through me first."

He swallowed, blond brows knotted. "What the hells, Vice? Are"—he scoffed, shaking his head—"after all he's done, are you shagging him?"

She tried to laugh back, but it just came out as an abrupt breath. "No. Of course not."

No one could know she'd succumbed to his charms on the *Swallow*. What kind of pirate captain slept with the man who'd betrayed her? No, she'd never win a vote like that.

A denial wasn't enough: she needed to fix this. She lifted her chin. "Yes, I'm still fuming at him, but he's helping me, and I only made it back here because of him."

Aedan's jaw twitched and his gaze flicked over her shoulder —presumably to Knigh.

She scanned the crew, pausing on each person who met her eye. "If anyone has a right to be pissed off at Blackwood, it's me."

Grumbles and cocked heads. Perry gave the slightest nod. Saba's grip shifted on her sabre's hilt.

"And if I can get past that enough to work with him and *not* murder him"—Vice flashed a brief, fierce grin, which won a few laughs, easing the tension thrumming through the air—"then so can you."

With a slow blink, she returned her gaze to Aedan, her eyes narrow, mouth flat. A copy of one of Perry's best withering looks. Once he'd endured it for a few seconds, she raised one eyebrow in question.

He sucked in his lips and glared over her shoulder again. His chest heaved and Vice tensed her grip on the barrel, muscles coiled. If he tried to snatch it away and shoot Knigh...

He blasted a heavy sigh and his shoulders sagged. "Fine."

She let him lower the pistol, her stomach's roiling tension easing. A metallic ring signalled Saba sheathing her blade.

Vice held her open hand out to Aedan. "Now give me my damn gun."

He slapped it into her palm and backed away, arms folded.

Low murmurs spread through the crowd, and now there were no drawn weapons—and thus no show—it dissipated.

Back still to Knigh, Vice returned the pistol to her belt and waited for their audience to leave. She couldn't risk turning to him now, even if she itched to see for herself that he was safe. If she did, someone else would spot the softness—the *weakness* in her. They'd know she cared and that it wasn't purely transactional, that he'd saved her life and now she'd saved his.

Instead, she smiled at her crewmates while they stowed their makeshift weapons and let the crowd disperse.

Perry patted Saba's shoulder and gave Vice a meaningful nod, gratitude warming the slight curve of her lips.

Lizzy cleared her throat, hazel eyes narrowing. "Helping you with what?"

Vice cocked her head.

"You said Blackwood was helping you."

"Yes, what's your *friend* helping with?" Aedan muttered, throwing Knigh another glare.

Vice inhaled and kept her attention on Lizzy—the others probably hadn't heard him. "I'm glad you asked." She grinned and turned to eye her crewmates, leaning forward conspiratorially. She made sure her gaze skidded past Knigh. Looking at him too long would only draw their attention, and she was under no illusions—just because she'd talked them down now didn't mean he was safe.

Pirates weren't the forgiving type.

Speaking of which... "You see," she continued, "there's someone else we should *all* be much more pissed off at than Blackwood."

They looked back with raised eyebrows. Some glanced at each other.

Perry's face screwed up with thought. She cocked her head, as if asking what Vice was up to.

Vice flashed her eyebrows up at her, giving another second of quiet. *Let them wonder.* "FitzRoy himself." *The bastard.* He hadn't even had the good grace to try and save her after his treachery. At least Knigh had that on his side.

She lifted her chin, letting her voice carry. "He betrayed me, it's true." The mutters that rose suggested they knew what had happened. Hands on hips, she turned, letting them all get a taste of her fae charm. "But, even worse, he betrayed all of you."

Some tugged their beards or lips, others bared their teeth, many nodded. All of them glowered.

"FitzRoy owed you far more than Blackwood did—he was your captain and he left you at the mercy of Albionic law." She scowled, tutting. "He didn't care what happened to you, as long as we were separated so you couldn't come for me."

"We've come for you now," someone shouted.

She pointed at them, grinning. "And I'd have come back to Albion, if they'd taken you." She let the smile fade and narrowed her eyes again, sweeping to take in the whole crew.

"But that's not the end of FitzRoy's treachery." She paused, the seconds ticking by as she let the surprise give in to muttered queries between themselves, until they all looked back at her with a question in their eyes. "FitzRoy had a clue to Drake's treasure that he kept to himself. That he kept from *you.*"

They exploded in angry demands.

"The son of a bilge rat!"

"He did what?"

"How could he?"

"Where'd he get it from?"

"What clue?"

"Why keep it from us?"

"The scurvy bastard."

Perry's mouth dropped open. She must've realised where this was going.

Saba shook her head, sidling close. "Is that true?"

Vice nodded, lips pursed. "As true as me standing here now."

"Bloody bastard."

"Exactly." She gave a fierce grin and grabbed Saba into a hug now the madness of drawn weapons was over. "Don't worry, though, I have a plan."

Saba squeezed her back, shaking with a low chuckle. "Why am I not surprised?"

Patting her shoulder, Vice pulled back. She had her friends again. She'd been reunited with the crew. And she was back in Arawaké. Things were slotting back in place—everything as it should be.

Even better, that crew was exactly where she wanted them —demanding information, burning with injustice, brimming with the sense that they'd been cheated. Feelings she knew only too well.

"So, Lizzy"—she smiled at her friend—"you ask what Blackwood's helping with." She bared her teeth. "We have Fitz-Roy's clue."

The crew's questions and shouts fell silent.

"Which Blackwood is helping me decipher." Make him indispensable and none of them would be stupid enough to stick a dagger between his ribs while he was somewhere quiet and lonely away from her protection.

So much for her plan to be free of him.

She smiled sweetly at Aedan. "So, you see, he's no friend of mine, just a necessary evil."

He huffed, shoulders easing. Maybe that was enough to satisfy him.

"What's more," she went on, scanning the crew, "we've already outdone that traitor. *We* have a second clue."

They strained towards her on a collective held breath.

Perry exhaled through her nose, almost a laugh. She knew.

Vice raised her eyebrows in an unspoken question.

One shoulder lifting, Perry nodded.

Good, she had her approval.

"So." Vice held out her hands. "What do you say? Shall we find ourselves some treasure?"

They roared.

THE PROMISE

S cowling, Vice stuffed the folded sheets of paper in the back of the Copper Drake and shoved it in her pocket. With a huff, she leant on the newly renamed *Respair's* poop deck rail, letting her gaze drift fore. Deciphering the Copper Drake was nowhere near as easy as she'd made it sound to the crew. After a week on the former *Covadonga* examining the damned thing, she was no further than when they'd left Nassau.

And much as she'd claimed Knigh was here to help her, she was avoiding him—much easier now she had an entire ship to lose herself on, rather than a shared room.

Thank the gods.

But there was still the damned book.

It had frustrated her so much that she'd resorted to embroidery. She'd borrowed needles from Perry and scrounged together a few scraps of fabric and different shades of thread from friends in Nassau before they left.

As a child, she'd hated the task, but for Lady Avice Ferrers, it had been a required activity. Well, if she *had* to do it, she'd bloody well be good at it, so she'd fought to become skilful with her stitches. As her skill had improved, so too had her enjoyment.

Maybe it was the long familiarity or simply that it kept her hands occupied—whatever the reason, embroidery, like reading, calmed her mind.

Unlike the Copper Drake.

Everything came back to this bloody book. It had even started appearing in her dreams, mocking her with its indecipherable text.

She gritted her teeth and squinted fore at the sunlight sparkling off the sea, beyond her crewmates working. Amongst them was Knigh, every line of his body angled in tension, his brows low. He had to weave between the rest of the crew. No one would let him pass, even as he carried huge coils of rope for stowing.

With a slow blink, she forced her gaze away from him and to the sea ahead.

There had to be something about the book she was missing.

Now she'd had a thorough look, she was sure it was ciphered. The question was, what was the key to that cipher? She'd tried the simple answers—writing the Ancient Hellenic alphabet forwards and backwards, substituting the letters for each other.

Still nonsense. Still no closer to the truth.

"Thank the Lords and Ladies your gift isn't the ability to glare a person into oblivion," Perry said, appearing at her side, "or that poor young man would be dead."

Vice exhaled slowly and turned.

Perry's eyebrows shot up. "And now so would I."

"He's not a 'poor young man'. Traitor, remember?"

A thoughtful sound came from low in Perry's throat. The look she gave Vice—head cocked, eyes a little too intent—made her shift. "Can't a person be both? He is struggling, you know?"

Vice scoffed. "My heart bleeds."

"It should. You could make things a lot easier for him."

Arms folded, Vice looked at the sails overhead—anything to avoid that searching gaze. "Oh, could I? Lucky me!"

"Yes." Evidently Perry had lost all understanding of how sarcasm worked during their time apart. "You can. You just need to forgive him."

Air burst from Vice's lungs—if she'd been drinking, she'd have spat it over Perry at those words.

Evidently Perry had also lost her mind.

"Forgive him? You must be joking. He betrayed me, Perry. He nearly got me bloody killed."

One eyebrow arched, Perry cocked her head. "And you gave him no reason to do that, did you?"

Vice snatched her gaze away. Why did that feel like an accusation? She set her jaw, glowering fore. "What do you mean? I'm a pirate, we are all—"

"I heard you might have told him you'd murdered someone he cared about."

Well, of course. That explained it. Vice narrowed her eyes. "You 'heard'? Have you been talking to him?"

"Someone's got to. And since you won't, it may as well be me." In the periphery of her view, Perry shrugged. "Why did you tell him you'd killed, well, *you?*"

Vice huffed. "Oh, don't look at me like that—I didn't *mean* it. He—"

"You might not have meant it, but you didn't think it through, did you?" Perry edged closer, brushing Vice's clothes, voice low. "*Of course* he'd think you a monster—killing an eighteen-year-old girl. But you were too busy being flippant to even consider it."

Precisely, why was that her problem? He was the one who'd cast judgment and then acted upon it. "He didn't ask me, though, did he?"

"No. But then, you are so well known for your willingness to talk about your past, aren't you?"

"Bloody hells, Perry." Vice huffed and frowned at her. "Anyone would think *I* sold *him* down the river, the way you're going on. I might have said something silly, but I didn't plot with FitzRoy to get him hanged."

Perry's stern expression broke, replaced with a soft smile—a sad smile, perhaps. "No, you didn't." She pushed a windswept lock of hair from Vice's face and tucked it behind her ear. "But he is sorry for that. Horrified, in fact. Poor boy beats himself up over it more than you do, I'd say."

Vice stiffened. She pulled away, tucking ends of hair back

into her braid. No use, it was a mess. "Sorry is an easy word to say."

"He hasn't just said it, though, has he? He's done everything in his power to make things right."

The breeze stiffened, pushing through Vice's shirt, raising goosebumps over her arms. She crossed them, gripping her biceps. Turning and leaning against the rail, she looked aft. It put a little distance between herself and Perry.

"His life as it was is over," Perry went on. "He broke I don't know how many laws to save you. He's walked away from the Navy. He even endangered his friend to get you back to us, to safety." She shook her head, gesturing for the helm to adjust their course, before leaning next to Vice, mirroring her pose. "He's an outlaw now. I'm not sure he'll ever be able to go back and see his family." She frowned, eyes on their wake. "Think on that for a moment—the Royal Navy's star pirate hunter, a man who was made by his uniform, whose family relies on his wages. And he gave all that up when he realised the wrong he'd done you.

"He gave all that up in order to make it right and save your life. He gave it up *for you.*"

Vice pulled her arms tighter, shivering. She was trying to conserve her energy, so best not to change the wind, but it had whipped up and needled a chill through her.

Had Knigh put Perry up to this? He couldn't even come and ask for forgiveness himself.

But was Perry wrong? *A man who was made by his uniform—*that had to be an exaggeration. But he *had* done all those things. Lost all those things. Like she'd said to him on the *Swallow*, he could've just left her in that gibbet cage.

She sighed softly, and the wind snatched it away at once. "You two must've had a bloody long talk."

"Look"—Perry raised one shoulder—"I'm not saying you have to forgive him right now. I get it if you can't. But at least go easier on him. Understand what he's done. Maybe even appreciate it. He's stuck here with us, now—his old life is gone and he's trying to find a new place for himself. For some reason he's chosen here with you."

Here with you. That made it sound much more serious than it was. Like he...

Hells, Perry made it sound like he had a choice. It was here or death—at the hands of other pirates or the Navy. Those were his only options.

Vice gave Perry a sidelong glance, lips pursed. "That wasn't an answer, you know. Did he ask you to talk to me?"

With a snort, Perry shook her head. "No, he didn't. I doubt it even crossed his mind. He's just miserable. And so are you— I've never seen you so tetchy before."

Vice rolled her eyes. "Try a week in an iron cage and you'd be *tetchy*, too."

"Hmm, you see, I don't think it's just because of what he did. I think it's because of what you're doing to him now. Being like this isn't in your nature, and I think it's eating you up inside. I think you want—"

"Don't." Vice's fingers twitched. She wasn't sure what Perry had been about to say, but all the conversation leading up to it, the tone of her voice, *everything* set a panicked alarm bell jangling in her body.

"What you two were developing—"

"I said, *don't.*"

"—before."

"Nothing was developing between anybody." Vice shoved her hands to her sides, fisting them so tightly it felt like her knuckles would crack. "It was just sex." She might've told Knigh it wasn't just bodies between them, but that didn't mean she was about to admit that to anyone else, even Perry.

Head cocking, Perry narrowed her eyes. "And have you had 'just sex' with anyone since him?"

Vice huffed. "I've been a bit busy being imprisoned and searching halfway around the world for you, in case you hadn't noticed!"

Perry smiled, her look too much like Barnacle with a bowl of cream for Vice's liking. Her eyes glinted. "Thought not."

"Perry. Look." Vice shook her head. "It was nothing but bodies slotting together. But"—she raised her hands before she could disagree—"*but* maybe I can try to be a little kinder to him now he's got me back to you."

Perry's eyebrows rose in expectation. She wanted more.

Vice sighed, rolling her eyes. "Fine. I promise I'll try to be nice to him—or at least not horrible. Happy?"

Perry shrugged, the corner of her mouth lifting with a bitter edge that was out of place on her. "It's a start. At least it might kill this seed of discord in my crew."

My crew. Vice winced—this might not be an easy conversation, but it was a necessary one. At least it would change the subject from her and Knigh. "About that." She drew a long breath and turned to face Perry fully—she owed her that. "As you're my friend—family, even—I will warn you."

Perry's eyes narrowed in a question.

"It's time." Vice lifted her chin. "I'm going to call a vote for captaincy."

"Oh." Perry paused there, mouth in a little *O* of surprise. "Right. I see." She nodded, the motion slow as if forced. "Do... um... Do you think you're ready?"

Vice tilted her head. Perry had never been interested in captaining her own ship. Why the sudden change of heart? "Don't tell me—now you've had a taste of power, you want more?"

"Lords, no—it's more trouble than it's worth, to tell you the truth. Though I know that won't stop you wanting it. I just mean after your ordeal, perhaps you should wait a little longer. You're still regaining your—"

"Thank you, Perry." Chuckling, Vice pulled her in for a hug. Her friend was worried for her. Maybe it was because she'd missed Perry over these months of separation, but it wasn't as annoying as usual. She smiled and squeezed before releasing her. "I appreciate your concern, but my strength's improving every day. I'll be challenging a new recruit to a press-up competition in no time."

Scoffing, Perry rubbed her forehead.

That had to be her agreement. A thrill of anticipation shivered through Vice. "I'll call a vote tomorrow." Movement past Perry caught her eye—a gathering knot of sailors on the main deck. "What's—"

The air carried back the sound of raised voices just as Vice craned and spotted it. At the centre of that knot of people, two heads rose above the others, one blond, one mid-brown streaked white.

Aedan and Knigh.

A SAILOR'S WORK

Head down, Knigh found ways to work the *Respair's* deck. It wasn't easy. Much of ship life involved small teams working to one purpose. And, of course, no one wanted to work with the man who'd orchestrated Vee's arrest.

Striding fore, he braced his hand against the coil of hemp rope over his shoulder. He frowned against the sun's glare as well as the mutters rising in his wake.

The smell of salt and sweat. The sea's constant call. The wind, brisk and refreshing. It was all so familiar, and that made the one difference even more stark.

The Royal Navy had rules, hierarchy, strict discipline, and protocol. It was a framework he'd flourished in. Even after his father's death, when he'd discovered his own monumentally flawed judgment, it had been a safety net. In his uniform, he had something else to rely on.

An insubordinate junior officer? The severity determined the punishment, all in the Articles of War. For a first offence, reading the Articles to the whole crew. After that, bilge duty or some other dull, shunned task. That was usually enough to cure a headstrong boy of such foolish behaviour.

A storm approaching? Change to storm canvas, strike or reef the sails, and out-sail it, riding the winds to calmer seas.

New orders from the Admiralty? Carry them out.

Simplest of all was the matter of war.

Cannon, sail, rudder, and rifle—each of these things had its set process. Other than that, it was kill and don't die. Apply his crew's skill appropriately and do what he could to ensure as many as possible survived while achieving their objective.

Here, though, on the *Respair*, in a nest of pirates? None of that applied. Well, except for the part about not dying. They'd taken prizes since leaving Nassau, so he'd had the chance to apply his skill in battle, but it was fleeting, the fight over too quickly.

Coming this way was Clovis, a burly giant of a man with cropped coils of black hair and warm brown skin who often manned the helm. He shouldered Knigh as he passed.

He met Knigh's eye. Instead of an apology, he gave a grim smile.

Deliberate, then.

Jaw tight, Knigh lowered his head and continued on his way.

Here, he had no recourse for such behaviour. And there was plenty of it.

Vee's speech back in Nassau had saved his life, but...

He's no friend of mine, just a necessary evil.

They were only temporary allies. And although things had softened between them after he'd spoken to Billy, she'd barely said five words to him since they'd re-joined Perry. This wasn't such a large ship that she could avoid him for a week purely by chance.

He grimaced. It was deliberate, just like all the knocks from her crewmates.

"You're lucky I don't give you something to wince at, traitor." It was a voice he knew.

Aedan.

Teeth gritted, Knigh continued striding past.

"I'm talking to you."

The rope on his shoulder jerked backwards, but Knigh's fingers tightened on it and he stood his ground. In a controlled turn, he faced Aedan, finding him close, hand knotted in the coiled rope.

Knigh let a few seconds of quiet tick by, commanding that. It was a trick he'd learned in the Navy. Reply too quickly, and you gave the other person power. Make them *wait* for a response and they'd grow uneasy, realising they couldn't force a reaction.

"My apologies. Did you ask a question?" Knigh gave a smile that was anything but sorry.

"No, I didn't." Aedan's knuckles grew white beneath his tattoos. The hemp rope creaked. "But since you mention questions... Why the hells did you do it?" His chest heaved, thick with muscle.

So this wasn't avoidable. Fine.

Back straightening, Knigh lifted his chin. He met Aedan's gaze, unflinching. With fae strength on his side, he might win a fight against Aedan. But then again, he might not.

It certainly looked like they were about to find out.

The sounds of work faded around them, barefooted steps shuffling closer. Seemed the rest of the crew wanted to know, too.

No matter what Knigh said, Aedan would still be angry. Plus, he hadn't even told Vee about that—not properly.

Coward. Yes, she'd cut him off, but he could've made her listen. On board the *Swallow*, she'd been a captive audience.

His throat burned, but he forced the words out: "There's only one person I owe that explanation to, and it isn't you."

Jaw flexing, Aedan strained closer. "And have you given it to her?"

Knigh fought against the urge to swallow. It would've been a sign of weakness, a sign he was uncomfortable with that question. "Also not your business."

"No, you know what?" Aedan stepped into Knigh's space, not quite touching chest-to-chest. His eyes blazed. "I don't buy that crap. You joined *The Morrigan*. You ate with us, worked with us, chatted and joked with us." He dipped forward a fraction of an inch with each item as if he longed to poke Knigh in the chest.

Perhaps he didn't want to be the first to make physical contact. Perhaps he wanted to goad Knigh into starting the fight, to avoid Vee's wrath.

Probably a good idea.

"You celebrated with us," Aedan went on. "I called you

178

'friend'. And then…" Breaths harsh, he shook his head as though finishing the sentence was impossible.

Knigh's throat tightened. He and Aedan had chatted and laughed—it was true. They'd even sparred together a few times. Was a pirate's friendship so easily won? Maybe it was when that pirate wasn't Vee, tight and guarded underneath it all. They were easygoing folk. Perhaps their friendship was that simple.

Saying it was just a job didn't feel like an adequate response.

"Suddenly shy?" Aedan's eyebrows jerked upwards. He laughed softly, the sound without mirth. "You're a bloody piece of work, you are. Shagging a woman you're going to get hanged —that's low, even for a pirate hunter."

Heat surged through Knigh's veins, flaring through his muscles in readiness. The rope bit into his calluses; the other hand clenched, hard, tight.

Aedan needed to shut the hells up. Immediately.

Knigh bit the inside of his cheek, and the pain cut through his anger.

Was it just at Aedan? Or himself?

He exhaled, the breath rasping with a low rumble.

It was both.

Damnation, it was *both*.

Realising it didn't cool the fire in his blood, though.

Aedan was far too close, needling him with his own stupid, monumental mistake. The sharp smell of sweat and work was too much like the stink of battle. Despite the wind, the sun was hot on his back and head.

Knigh had the advantage. Aedan was already squinting into the light. It could be enough to slow him, just a touch, stop him reacting as Knigh pulled back his fist and—

"Lords and Ladies, it's a miracle!" The voice cut through the thick air, full of mock astonishment.

Vee.

"You've all finished your work," she went on. "Or at least, I assume that's what's happening, because you sure as hells aren't doing any." A growl edged those last words.

Knigh didn't take his eyes off Aedan, who also didn't move, but mutters and shuffling around them suggested most of the crew were backing away and at least trying to look busy.

"Aye," Perry said, voice a calm contrast with Vee's sarcasm, "every one of you knows better than that. A sailor's work is never done. Get back to it."

Aedan's teeth ground, so hard and close that Knigh could hear it.

"*All* of you." Perry's tone came out lower, pointed.

With a slow exhalation, Aedan backed off a few steps. He tugged on the rope, and Knigh let it go. He re-coiled it, never dropping his gaze from Knigh.

Now he had space, Knigh's breaths came more easily, but threat still laced the air like a scent.

"Blackwood," Vee said.

He flinched. That was the first time she'd said his name since they'd boarded the *Respair*. He turned to her.

She gave him a tight smile. "I need to borrow you. I have a question about the clue you might be able to help with." She said it with all the formality of a lady enquiring after a gentleman's family.

He's no friend of mine.

Breath held against a sigh, he nodded. The clue, of course. Hadn't she told everyone that was the only reason she suffered him?

Perry leant over as he passed. "I want you off deck for an hour, at least," she muttered, her tone saying it was an order, not just a request.

He inclined his head, then gestured for Vee to lead the way. Striding aft, he was sure he could feel Aedan's gaze burning into his back.

He glanced at Vee's profile. With the tan creeping back across her skin and more flesh on her bones, she was looking even healthier than when they'd left Nassau. It eased the tension across his shoulders. She almost looked her old self.

"I thought you were avoiding me." He raised his eyebrows, as if it were a question.

"What a strange idea." But she said it in a flat tone, not even trying to sell the comment.

He held back a sigh. So he hadn't imagined it.

They walked to her cabin in silence.

Although she'd lost most of her books back on *The Morrigan*, this room was still full of *her*. The clothes strewn over the floor and the back of the chair. Beneath the stern window, the desk covered in a disarray of papers, books, an inkwell with the lid half off, and abandoned writing implements. Muddled in with the papers, an assortment of threads coiled like miniature ropes and a tiny pair of scissors in the shape of a stork.

The scent of vanilla and storms.

Knigh clenched his fists as the shiver washed over him. It felt like an age since he'd smelled it, though it was only a week since they'd shared a room in Nassau.

He tore his attention away from the stern end of the cabin where Vee had taken up a position by the desk. Anything to distract himself from her—just for a moment while he grew accustomed to that smell again.

What appeared to be a dome of grey fur lay nestled on the bunk. Barnacle lifted her head and chirruped at the sight of him. Vee must've made her a new cushion—this one was black, embroidered with white thread. Around Barnacle's curled up form, he could make out the edges of letters, but not enough to read what they said.

"Hello, little lady," he said, crouching and rubbing the top of her head, right between her ears. Her eyes half-closed as a purr rumbled through her.

Vee said nothing.

He didn't dare look up to see what she was doing. Not yet. Instead, he occupied himself with the cat, letting her rub her face against his hands.

With a couple of deep breaths, he'd acclimatised to being in here.

As if sensing he was almost finished fussing her, Barnacle flopped onto her back and demanded rubs of her round belly. Her very *round* belly. "Who's been eating too many rats, hmm?"

Vee snorted. "I think she's pregnant."

"Huh." He smiled down at the grey cat, imagining a whole litter of demanding little Barnacles romping around the deck.

Chaos. Utter chaos. "I'm not sure the world's ready for that." He ran his fingertips over the soft white fluff of her belly.

Fine, he was ready to face Vee now. Nodding, he rose. "What can I help you with?"

She still stood at that desk, back to him, apparently just staring out the window.

He frowned, cocking his head. He'd expected her to pull out notes or show him a page from the mysterious book.

Neck craned, he approached and tried to follow her gaze.

Outside, the sun flashed and glistened off their wake, shifting between light and shadow. It was a bright counterpart to the sea he'd faced the night he'd dived and pulled Llyr from the depths.

"I didn't actually need you," Vee said. "I just wanted to defuse the situation with the crew." She sighed, folding her arms.

His brows shot up. She didn't need him. Of course not. She was only rescuing him from a fight, and now she'd grown as cold and distant as she'd been since they'd reunited with Perry and the crew.

"Oh."

"Perry pointed out that you're not having the best time."

He could hear the wince in her voice and knew her well enough to picture it.

Her shoulders bobbed. "I promised Perry I wouldn't add to it. Unfortunately, Aedan hasn't made the same promise. So, you can stay in here for a while, let him cool off. I'll get on with this work"—she gestured to the desk and its mess of papers—"and you can just, I don't know, read a book? Stroke Barnacle or something?" She turned, but when she saw him so close, she sucked in a sharp breath.

They were almost toe-to-toe. Looking out the window had brought him closer than he'd realised. Closer than he should be.

Her windswept hair gleamed in the light from the window, waves snaking out from the braid over her shoulder, wisps falling across her forehead and framing her face. His fingers itched to push it all back so he could get a good look at her—at the fine line of her jaw, the angles of cheekbone and brow, the mole above her left temple that rose whenever she arched her eyebrows, which was often.

It was an effort to swallow. An even greater one to keep his hands in place at his side.

As part of his naval training, he'd stood at attention on a sun-beaten deck in the Arawakéan summer for hours at a time, resisting the desire to scratch his nose or wipe sweat from his brow.

That was a breeze compared to standing here now and not touching her.

She stared up at him, eyes a deep, unfathomable green-blue today. Her arms tightened across her chest as it rose and fell deeply. A ripple passed across her jaw before she dropped her arms and gripped the back of the chair she leant on.

He blinked and shook his head. What the hells was he thinking? He didn't get to enjoy this anymore—looking at her, being around her. Not after what he'd done. Not after he hadn't even explained why.

There's only one person I owe that explanation to.

Jaw working, he backed off.

Blast. That was exactly why Aedan had got to him—he'd hit on that sore spot of truth. The fact he hadn't explained it all to Vee.

The fact he'd let her stop him each time.

The fact he'd been a damn coward.

He swallowed, frowning at the floor.

It was time.

FORTIFICATION

One hand on the bulkhead between Vice's cabin and Perry's, Knigh drew a deep breath. "Well, while I've got you as a captive audience..." He tried to keep his voice light, but his stomach twisted into a knot. Her promise to Perry might mean she'd let him finish this time. "I want to explain."

Her brows knitted together in confusion.

"About what happened. I owe it to you. And you've shut me off every other time, but you also asked me—back on the *Swallow*, the day I told you about Billy."

She went very still, the only movement her breathing.

"Look, Vee, I—"

"No." She remained so still, he wondered if he'd imagined her saying it, but then she shook her head, the movement small but fast. "You were a pirate hunter. I am a pirate. You wanted to capture me. You did. And I fell for your trick. That's it." The corner of her mouth twitched in a mockery of a smile. "You won. Well done." Her arms clamped over her body, folded so tightly it was a wonder her joints didn't crack.

Knigh pressed his fingers into the wood panelling. She might've promised Perry she wouldn't add to his hard time on the *Respair*, but clearly that didn't extend to this. "Bloody hells, Vee, it's not that simple."

Her mouth flattened. "No, I suppose a plan that involved shagging me must've been quite complicated."

The words lanced through him, sharper than any blade. He bit his tongue. He couldn't react, despite the hurt. Perhaps she was just trying to push him away again, as she'd admitted to on the *Swallow*.

Once he was sure he had himself mastered, he shook his head and met her gaze. "That was never part of the plan."

Another flicker of an expression crossed her face, too quick for him to decipher. "Ah, so it was just the icing on the cake? A little something extra while you waited for your bounty?" She shook her head again, eyes hard.

The look chilled him, colder than the sea the night he'd saved Llyr, the icy cousin to her cool hands that were normally so refreshing and welcome in the Arawakéan heat.

She scoffed, but every inch of her angled with tension. "That's *such* a great comfort. I'm *so* sodding relieved that screwing me was a nice bonus for you."

That wasn't fair. She *knew* it wasn't—

"Did you promise the rest of the Navy a go before they hanged me, tell them how great I was at—"

"You told me you'd murdered an innocent eighteen-year-old girl!" It burst out of him, almost a shout. "What was I supposed to think?"

Her expression cooled another degree. "She wasn't that innocent, trust me."

He huffed, throwing his hands in the air. "She *is* you, Vee. Wild Hunt, what's so wrong with Avice Ferrers that you have to talk about her as if she's someone else?"

Her frown changed—something about the angle of her eyebrows rendered it more desperate than bitter as it had been. "She was foolish, and she was weak. She broke when *he* died. I am not that pathetic creature." Her nostrils flared and her gaze skittered away, landing on Barnacle. "I don't need him or you or *anyone*, and I refuse to ever again be that powerless."

There it was.

Vee... Vice... Avice... Whoever she was—all of them, maybe —she'd loved her husband. And when he died, she'd broken.

If she didn't need anyone, she couldn't break again.

Perry said it had changed her, but in all the quiet, secret conversations in the time *before*, Vee had never spoken of it. She'd barely mentioned the man she'd eloped with. Even now, she didn't say his name.

Maybe it was because he'd heard the story second-hand, but he hadn't understood before how much of a turning point it had been for her. That was when she'd built her walls, and now she'd hidden behind them for over three years.

They were impressive defences, like the Tower of Lunden's fortifications, crenelated and hard as limestone.

But they'd ultimately come from a soft, vulnerable place.

He raked his hand through his hair. What had eighteen-year-old Avice been like? He'd known her a little when they were children, but who was the young woman she'd become? The still-forming personality before she'd carved walls of flippant humour and bravado to keep the world out.

Had he only reinforced them?

His chest ached.

She thought what had happened between them had been his way of penetrating those defences, and his betrayal proof of her need for them. No wonder she'd reacted as she had after they'd slept together on the *Swallow*.

This was unacceptable.

He swallowed down a leaden weight and forced the words from his throat: *"Anything to get the job done."*

She flinched, gaze flicking back to him.

"You said that before," he went on, "back on the *Swallow*—threw my own words back at me."

Gods, it had hurt, probably more than anything else she'd said. He should have told her at the time. Whether she wanted to hear it or not, she needed to.

"But it wasn't that," he continued. "What happened between us was never, *never* part of the plan."

He willed the truth of it into his eyes.

Maybe if he started at the beginning.

"I planned to capture you, believing I was ridding the world of an evil villain." He sighed, shaking his head. "But when I joined *The Morrigan*—the more I got to know you... Well, you weren't what I expected." He rubbed the drapes above her bunk between his fingers and thumb—glad of the distraction. "I knew what I'd do and how I'd do it. I made all the arrangements, contacted FitzRoy and Bricus. I had back-up plans and safety nets. I planned for every eventuality. Except you."

Now he'd broken eye contact, he didn't dare glance back to see her reaction. She remained silent—that could be a good thing. Or bad.

He frowned at the deep teal cotton, folding it between his fingers. "I was so sure you weren't the monster the Navy claimed, I'd decided I was going to submit a report to the Admiralty outlining the truth." He swallowed and bit his lip. He'd never said this part out loud before, only thought it. "I was going to recommend they give you a ship of your own—something fast and sleek, copper-hulled, like the *Venatrix*. I was going to ask them to make you a privateer."

"Oh." It wasn't much more than a breath.

"By the time *we* developed, I had no intention of arresting you. But"—there was always going to be a *but*—"then you told me you'd killed—*murdered* Avice Ferrers and... and..." He shook his head, pushing hair from his face. But he couldn't delay it. "It destroyed everything... my judgement. *Of course* I was wrong. I'd been wrong before, hadn't I? About my own father, no less. I told myself that I'd been fooled again." He closed his eyes, pressing fingertips hard into them. "It was only then I decided to go through with my original plan."

She was still quiet, but he finally dared to look at her. Her arms were crossed again, and she stared at the floor near his feet, shaking her head. "That's not—"

"What happened between us was real, Vee. Please believe me." He took a step towards her and pulled the shell from his pocket. "See?" He held it out, and the sunlight through the stern window caught in the shimmering, shifting iridescent colours of its curved interior.

She hissed in a breath, starting forward, her wide-eyed gaze on the shell. "You saved it." Her fingertips landed on the back of his hand, gently angling it and the shell so they were out of her shadow, catching the sun.

"Of course I did," he murmured. "Because it was never just the job. Wanting you and"—a shiver lifted the hairs on his forearms—"and letting myself have you—Vee, it wasn't *whatever it takes to get the job done.*"

She looked up at him, eyebrows raised, that little mole above her temple raised, too. She opened and closed her mouth, then shook her head. "I don't know what to say."

"You don't need to say anything. I—I just needed to tell you this. And it's long overdue."

She cocked her head. "I might have had something to do with that."

"I could've found a way—insisted, written it down, signal flags, *something.*"

She scoffed and lowered her gaze to his hand, still in the space between them. She dipped her fingertip into the cup of the little shell as he had done a thousand times. The surface was smooth and curved just so, perfect for the pad of a finger or thumb. The other side, the one against his palm, was rough and craggy, flecked grey and brown, giving no hint of the glorious colours inside.

He watched her run her fingertip around the shell's edge, her movements slow, almost hypnotic. Her other hand was still under his, her touch cool and soft.

This moment. His chest ached with how gentle it was. Its quietness.

This was what they could have had. Lords, this was what he *wanted*. Many, many moments with her. Some with laughter and music and, hells, even dancing.

Others with quiet, like this, where it was only them and their privacy.

"Vee," he murmured, and her finger lifted from the shell, hovering in the air above it, "I—I know I warned you that I was untrustworthy. And I've clearly proven that I am." His voice came out thick with wanting, with longing, with the heavy weight of guilt sitting on his chest. "But I want to be worthy of trust—I want to be worthy of *your* trust."

His heart throbbed, heavy and hollow. Because it was a damn foolish wish—the stuff of children's words in mirrors late at night, playing games to ask a favour of the Lords and Ladies. Not something a grown man should reasonably expect.

Certainly not something *he* of all people should ask for.

Eyes closed, he shook his head. "But I don't even trust myself—how can I expect anyone else to trust me?"

Her hand closed over his, capturing the shell between their palms.

He inhaled, eyes flying open.

This close, even in shadow, he could see that unfathomable dark teal wasn't the only shade in her eyes today. A sunburst of lighter, brighter turquoise radiated from her pupils—the same colour the sun made when it shone through a wave. Her frown had gone, replaced with a gentle crease that might have been regret or sorrow or pity.

This was the woman who'd made him believe she wasn't a monster.

She was so many other things. Compassionate, like when she'd saved him from the Grays' ball and Mercia. Noble, in her own way, like when she turned their course towards slaver ships and made sure the proceeds went to the people who'd been captured. Passionate. Funny. *Fun*. Hard-working and determined. Ferocious in her loyalty to her friends. Clever and cunning enough to challenge him, even when they'd been all-out enemies.

How had he ever believed the Navy?

"Knigh," she breathed.

And then there was no air between them.

He wasn't sure if he'd bent to her or if she'd tiptoed to him or if they'd both moved in one moment; all he knew was that her mouth was against his.

This wasn't the desperate, clinging kiss they'd started with on the *Swallow*. It also wasn't the chaste, frustrating one beneath the mistletoe.

This was a different creature entirely.

Slow, gentle, first against his mouth, but then she moved to his cheek, his jawline, his throat, grazing his stubble with a quiet rasp. His skin didn't burn at her touch, instead warmth bloomed, making his heart throb hard, fuller with every moment.

He dropped the shell back in his pocket and gathered her against him, their bodies slotting together with aching perfection. She was, once more, that delicious blend of soft flesh over the solidity of muscle. He bent his head and inhaled, her sweet-salty scent so overpowering that for a moment it was the only thing in the world.

Hands planing over her back, he kissed the curve of her ear and sighed as she ran the bridge of her nose along his jaw, something about the gesture more intimate than anything else they'd ever done together.

"Vee." But he didn't know what more to say—maybe he just needed to taste her name again.

Perhaps he didn't need to say anything more, because then her lips were on his again, slow and firm as her fingers tangled in his hair.

Despite the sweetness, his body responded to her touch, throbbing low in his belly, hardening against her.

Lords, he shouldn't be doing this. Succumbing to their attraction on the *Swallow* hadn't helped—it had only made things worse.

As if she'd realised the same thing, they stumbled apart at the same instant, breaths heaving.

Vee landed heavily on the desk, touching her lips, as if unable to believe what she'd just been doing with them.

Knigh clenched his jaw.

Self-control.

No matter how good it felt in the moment, it would only lead to more hurt after. She hadn't forgiven him. He hadn't forgiven himself. And he'd told himself he wouldn't take pleasure in her company, never mind *her.*

"I—I'm sorry." He shook his head, blinking rapidly, as if that might erase the ghost of her touch still on his scalp and lips. As if it might warm his chest, left cold from her absence. "We can't do that again. I know."

With a shaky exhale, she nodded, hand dropping to press into the papers littering the desk. "For a moment, I forgot." She tossed her hair, as though he was still touching her and she could shake him off.

Eyes closed, she gave a soft snort. "Gods, I was stupid. For a second, I actually forgot. I got wrapped up in all those moments—in *you*. Walking through Nassau together. Diving that bloody reef..." Emotion crackled through her voice. "Every time I see you, I think of it all—the good and the bad.

"And the very worst. That night in Portsmouth, in the cage. I thought I was going to die."

He rocked back on his heels, her words like a shove.

She—the Pirate Queen, the mistress of bravado, the permanent joker—she'd believed she was facing her own death. He knew she'd been scared that night—she'd been so vulnerable. But he never dreamed she'd lost hope.

It didn't seem possible.

She swallowed. "I planned it. Once I was on the beach, facing the gallows, I was going to use whatever strength I had left to bring in a storm. Maybe I could have washed it and them all away. I figured at least then my body would go back to the sea."

She hadn't believed he would go back for her.

His throat closed, and all warmth vanished from his body, leaving only an aching coldness. He clamped his teeth together and stared at a point over her shoulder, willing away the stinging in his eyes.

She thought he'd abandoned her to that hopeless cage, even after he'd known the truth about her not killing Avice.

He huffed out a breath when his voice box felt like it might work. "I said I'd get you out."

She gave a bitter smile. "A lot of people say a lot of things."

He stared at her a long while, but she gave nothing more. She didn't soften it with a joke or a grin.

Was it any surprise? He hadn't just betrayed her, he'd let her down. Badly. And others had, too. FitzRoy. Her father.

Disappointing fathers. That was a wound they shared.

"And that stupid shell," she said, shaking her head as if coming back to herself from some distant memory. "I wish you hadn't shown me. I wish you hadn't kept it."

He gripped his pocket, checking the small, round shape was still inside. It wouldn't have been a surprise if she'd lifted it during all that dangerous kissing.

She glared at his hand. "You should have thrown it overboard. But you can't let go of the stupid thing. And I can't let go of what you did." She fell silent and the aftermath of her words rang around the room, lending the silence a heaviness that weighed on his lungs.

I can't let go of what you did.

Her words chimed again and again.

I can't let go of what you did.

Of course she couldn't. He needed to—

I can't let go of what you did.

He shook his head. Gods knew what he needed to do, but it involved letting her go. His stomach turned.

"Even if I could forgive you," she said, voice firmer, "we're back with the crew now." She nodded as if that explained it all.

He cocked his head, unable to keep the confusion from his face. "What's that—"

"They know what you did, and I'm calling a vote on the captaincy tomorrow."

No wonder she'd made that speech about FitzRoy and Drake's treasure—it wasn't only to get them to agree to pursue it.

It was to show her as a leader.

"I can't afford to be weak in front of them," she continued. She pushed herself up from the desk, shoulders squaring, chin lifting. "I'll do my best to be civil to you and keep my promise to Perry. I'll even keep you safe from my crew when I'm captain. But that's all I can do. I can't be your lover or even your friend. I just can't." Even with the confident stance, her voice cracked on the last word.

She strode to the door, angling away so she didn't even brush against him as she passed, despite the narrowness of the cabin.

Then she was gone, the door closing softly in her wake, leaving him in this space that was still too full of her.

His hands shook, his breaths, too. Gods damn it, he'd just about kept hold of his self-control in the face of Aedan, but Vee could always get a response from him.

At least he'd told her all of it, finally.

But here, still surrounded by her smell, her belongings, all those little signs of *her,* it didn't make him feel any lighter. And he couldn't even escape yet—from the look of the sun outside, he still had at least half of Perry's hour before he could emerge.

Groaning, he sank to the floor by the bunk and leant over it, stroking Barnacle beneath the chin.

She purred away, eyes half-closed. At least she could bear to have him around.

As if agreeing, she rolled onto her back, revealing the letters curving around the bottom edge of the cushion.

"Non obsequiorum," he muttered.

We do not yield. Or perhaps, *We do not serve* was a better translation.

He frowned. A motto? Not the Ferrers one, that was to do with being worn, but still shining. What was it? *Splendio tritus* or something like that.

But *non obsequiorum?* That was new. Perhaps she'd chosen it for herself.

At Barnacle's miaow, he absently stroked her belly, running his other hand over the words.

Or was it *We do not submit?* Maybe that was why Vee wanted to be captain. Then she wouldn't have to submit to anyone.

Another wall of protection.

Another mile of distance between her and everyone else.

CAPTAIN

None of the crew looked surprised.

Vice smiled, looking at them each in turn, like she'd done at Nassau as she'd given her speech about Knigh. She gritted her teeth against the wince at the thought of that damned name. That damned man.

Not now.

She took a long breath, swallowed, then nodded to herself.

Right now, she had a vote to win.

Her crewmates stood in huddles beneath the mid-morning sun, muttering. It made sense to call the vote before the hottest part of the day when tempers risked growing shorter.

She'd said her piece, setting out her qualifications to become captain.

It was all quite simple. She was clever. She'd orchestrated plenty of cunning plans aboard *The Morrigan*, and much as FitzRoy often took the credit for her successes (and sometimes made a point of blaming her for his failures), everyone here knew the truth.

She could work with weather and sea to not only keep them safe but to get plenty of loot. She'd risked her life for those here on more than one occasion. She was brave and strong, and she already had a reputation—hells, even a song written about her. She'd represent the *Respair* and her crew well.

Vice had said all that to much nodding and chatter amongst the crew, and now it was Perry's turn to make her case for why she should remain captain.

Did she really want it? She'd never aspired to it before, but maybe the taste of captaincy had built her appetite.

Hands on hips, Vice took a step back and let Perry have the deck.

Blonde hair in her customary crown-braid, Perry turned, nodding to the crew—*her* crew. Perhaps the nods were meant to remind them of the fact.

"You all know Vice. That's why you're here." She met Vice's gaze and smiled. But there was something guarded to it.

Blast, she did want it for herself. Well, that was fair enough. Vice would make her quartermaster and they'd run the ship together. They made a good team, and Perry was about the only person in the world she trusted.

Vice swallowed, then smiled back.

"In fact, you're all here," Perry went on, expression turning serious, "because that bastard FitzRoy sullied the title captain with his treachery."

Don't look at Knigh. Don't look at Knigh. Don't...

There hadn't been any more incidents since yesterday's

with Aedan, but if Vice glanced his way, it would only remind them all.

Grumbles and dark words rippled through the crew.

"He didn't care if you all got caught." Perry frowned and pursed her lips. "He didn't care if you were imprisoned or gibbetted or hanged. She"—Perry pointed at Vice—"*she* cares."

Vice's eyebrows shot up as she blinked. This didn't feel like a counterargument. She cocked her head at her friend in an unspoken question.

But Perry just carried on, "You were separated from her as much because she is loyal to you as because you are loyal to her. You know Vice—many of you have sailed with her for over three years, the same as me."

From his great height, Clovis caught Vice's eye. His black beard parted to reveal bright teeth in a grin. He elbowed his partner, Erec, and murmured something—maybe about how he'd lifted Vice on his shoulder the day her gift had awoken.

Erec was wiry and short, his coppery skin a beautiful complement to Clovis. He nodded back, slipping his arm around Clovis's waist as he flashed a bright smile.

That looked like two votes for Vice.

Her heart skipped. Elsewhere there were nods and smiles.

Lords, was Perry adding her argument to Vice's? She had to stand as captain to give the crew a choice. If Vice had called the vote and Perry just stepped aside, with no one else putting their hat in the ring, Vice would've got the captaincy by default.

Those who became captain by default rarely kept the title long.

They hadn't earned it. Their crews hadn't chosen it. They won no respect.

One thing a captain needed was respect.

But arguing Vice's case—that was the closest Perry could come to handing it over.

Vice's chest warmed, full and bright, and for a moment her eyes stung with fierce gratitude and even fiercer love for Perry.

"You know Vice," Perry repeated, voice rising over the mutters rippling across the deck. "You know her skill, her bravery, her intelligence. And you know I bloody love the woman." She chuckled, and the laughter radiated through the crew. "But that's enough of me and what I think. It's time for you to vote."

VICE'S FINGERS tapped against her thighs as she paced the poop deck.

Bloody hells, how long did it take to count shells and stones?

She huffed and glanced over the rail. Three heads bent together over the crate serving as a makeshift table—Aedan, Erec, and Luned, a woman several years older than Vice who Perry had recruited a year ago. Choosing those three to be scrutineers had taken almost as long as the actual vote, but eventually they'd emerged as the trio who'd even out each other's obvious loyalties—Aedan's to Vice and Luned's to Perry. Erec's loyalty was to Clovis alone.

After Vice and Perry had made their speeches, they'd retired to the poop deck to allow the crew a chance to discuss the options in private and choose their scrutineers. Vice hadn't watched the conversation, but even she'd spotted Knigh separate from it. He'd waited on the forecastle, leaning on the rail. It wasn't as if he'd be able to sway anyone to his point of view—they'd probably pick the opposite of anything he suggested.

Then each person had dropped either a shell or a stone into a box, and the adjudicators gathered to count the vote. Shells for Vice, stones for Perry.

With a groan, Aedan straightened and rolled his shoulders, expression as unreadable as one of Knigh's. Luned backed away, face pinched.

Erec nodded to Clovis, who wore the same determined look as when he clung to the ship's wheel in heavy seas. He called for Vice and Perry.

Vice shivered as she hurried down the steps, Perry in her wake. This solemnity thickened the air. Pirates laughed and joked most of the time—probably because death was only ever a storm or a sabre away—but there were times, usually brief, when they were serious.

Choosing a captain was one of those times.

Seeing so many grave faces on board a pirate ship when there weren't bodies to commit to the sea felt wrong, curdling in her marrow.

"It's decided," Clovis bellowed, calling all attention to the trio gathered to deliver their verdict.

Vice's stomach flipped. That's why it felt wrong—too much like her trial. But this wasn't fixed against her like that charade had been. She pushed her shoulders back and lifted her chin.

At last.

She was going to be a captain.

At long bloody last.

"The votes are cast," Luned said, her voice ringing clear across the deck's silence.

"The votes are counted," Erec followed.

Aedan cleared his throat. "Our captain will be Berit Peregrina."

The smile on Vice's mouth tightened, then fell. "Perry," she breathed.

Perry?

She hadn't even made a case.

Frowning, Vice blinked, once, twice, three times. No, she'd heard wrong.

But everyone was looking at Perry, who shuffled with obvious discomfort.

Clovis appeared beside her, avoiding Vice's gaze, and raised Perry's hand. "Our captain," he called over the sound of waves and whispers.

Perry was captain. Still. And Vice was not.

"Our captain," Vice muttered as the rest of the crew shouted it back at Clovis.

Her shoulders sank. How had this happened?

The cheers were warm and genuine, if not wild like they'd been the day Vice's gift had awoken and FitzRoy had declared her the saviour of *The Morrigan*.

But they were cheering Perry's name, not hers. Vice shook her head, rubbing her brow.

"It was a close vote," Aedan said as the deck quietened. He raised his eyebrows, meeting her gaze.

Urgh, this was meant to soften the blow. She gritted her teeth, stomach turning. She didn't need his pity.

"I voted for you," he went on, oblivious. "And we all lo—we're all loyal to you. But..." His eyes lowered.

Gods, was it really that bad? Why hadn't they voted for her? Had it even been as close as he'd said? But she couldn't ask—it would seem desperate to demand answers to why she'd lost.

Luned clicked her tongue and huffed. "But you can't be trusted." She arched her brows and held Vice's eye contact with no trace of pity. Somehow that was easier.

You can't be trusted.

Vice's frown tightened. But she'd risked her life for them so many times—in battle and in clever schemes where she snuck around places she shouldn't. Like when she'd crept on board the *Venatrix* and sabotaged it to allow their escape.

She glanced to fore. Knigh stood off to one side, arms folded, alone. His brows were lowered, and he watched her, brooding.

Perhaps he thought this was payback for how she'd treated him.

"Not with our lives, anyway," Luned continued, maybe dissatisfied that her statement hadn't elicited a response from Vice. "Because you're so damn reckless with your own. You're a danger to us as well as yourself."

The words forced Vice back a step. A danger to them? "No, I—I never." Her stomach twisted and her heart thudded, creating some grotesque swirling reel of a dance inside. "I'd never—"

"Maybe you don't mean to, but your decisions endanger others. Of course we don't trust you—not with this."

Apart from Luned, everyone had gone quiet. No one argued with her.

Even Aedan looked away, cheeks red.

They really thought that. Or more than half of them did, anyway.

No one will follow you because you'll only lead them to death. That's what Fitz had said months and months ago. *You are not fit to lead. You will never be captain.* She'd thought he was just angry and lashing out in a way he knew would hurt her, but perhaps...

Vice crossed her arms to hide the trembling. It took three swallows before she could speak. "I see," she said, voice hoarse. She nodded to Luned in acknowledgement. "Congratulations, Perry." She managed a quick glance at her friend.

At least she'd lost the vote to Perry and not to FitzRoy. That would have been unbearable. *He* would have been unbearable.

"Yes—uh—congratulations." Vice nodded again, movements stiff and repetitive, as though she were an automaton. "If you'll excuse me."

She turned on her heel and swept to her cabin.

You can't be trusted.

If they didn't trust her, then she'd never be captain.

FLAWED

"**B**ollocks," Vice muttered, pacing her cabin.

We don't trust you—not with this.

"Bollocks!" If they didn't trust her with their lives, then they didn't trust her. End of story.

I'll never be captain.

It just wasn't possible. Everything led to becoming captain. Everything.

The past three years, all she'd learned about ships and crews and battle. It all led here.

Except 'here' wasn't being captain, apparently.

Maybe it was the time apart. Maybe they were concerned about her weakness and—as Knigh insisted on calling it—*her ordeal.* Perry had ensured she was only on half watch, so the crew knew she still wasn't at full health. Perhaps, if she called another vote in a few months, it would go differently. They'd have faith in her again.

Arms folded, she frowned out the stern window. No, this wasn't permanent. This was just for now. She had to prove herself to them, just like she'd been working at proving herself to FitzRoy.

"What an idiot." She slapped her forehead. "Absolute bloody idiot."

How had she not realised before? All this time she'd been trying to prove herself to the wrong person.

It wasn't FitzRoy she needed—it never had been. It was the crew.

Although maybe the same thing she'd tried with FitzRoy would actually work with them. If she found Drake's treasure, they'd have to make her captain.

She chewed her lip, watching the flickering water as the sun inched towards its zenith. If she could just—

A smart rap at the door.

Knigh?

"Vice?" Perry's voice.

Of course it was Perry. Unable to keep the sigh from her tone, she called her in.

The sun caught in Perry's hair as she paused in the doorway, expression shadowed. She closed the door behind her but waited by it as if unsure about entering.

"Well." Vice lifted a shoulder.

What was she meant to say? She'd given her congratulations on deck. And although she didn't begrudge Perry being captain—she was wise, she knew her business—it still wasn't what she wanted. "They made their decision."

Stating the obvious, but it was better than silence. And

better than voicing the stupid thought that still needled the back of her mind.

I'll never be captain.

It wasn't true. She had a plan. This was only a temporary setback.

Perry blasted a sigh. "I'm sorry." She winced and now the sun wasn't behind her, Vice could see the lines around her eyes, the downturned grimace of her mouth.

"Not your fault." Vice shrugged and angled to glance out the window. "Hells"—she scoffed—"you argued *for* me."

"Can I sit down?"

You're captain, aren't you?

Vice twitched. No. That wasn't how she spoke to Perry. That wasn't...

Perhaps she'd have said it out loud to Knigh. She'd definitely have said it to FitzRoy. But not to Perry.

She shook her head. "You've never had to ask me that. Don't start now."

"Fair point." The bed creaked as Perry sat beside Barnacle, who was curled up on her cushion. "Are you going to sit, too? And actually—I don't know—look at me, perhaps?"

Vice snorted and turned, giving Perry an over the top roll of the eyes. "If I must."

I'll never be captain.

She managed a half-hearted grin before sinking into the chair at the desk. If Perry wanted her to sit, that meant this was a serious conversation.

"Look," Perry said, leaning forward, fingers steepled, "I—I

didn't expect that outcome. Not at all." She looked away, wincing. "But I think I might understand it."

Vice's stomach plummeted. "So you agree?" If Perry thought she wasn't fit to be captain, did that make it true?

"Understanding something isn't the same as agreeing with it."

Perry stopped as if she expected Vice to reply.

She just frowned back.

It wasn't that Perry was wrong. Vice understood that Mama was afraid to leave Papa, that she didn't really have a choice, but it didn't mean she agreed with it.

It was that Perry had come here. Now she'd dropped the news that she found it understandable that someone wouldn't want Vice to be captain.

Well, she was piloting this conversation, let her lead it wherever the hells she wanted.

"What does a captain do?"

Vice blinked. What kind of question was that? "They're in charge. They get to decide where the ship goes, what prizes the crew pursues, tactics." She waved her hand. It was obvious. Even ten-year-old Avice Ferrers knew that from her adventure stories.

Maybe that was the problem and why Perry remained silent. She was looking for more. Vice should *know* more from three years at sea.

"And"—Vice screwed up her face—"and they take responsibility for those decisions." That's what Perry was looking for. She loved the R-word. "If things go south, they need to take decisive action to solve the problem."

She smiled and gave Perry a firm nod. That was better. A perfect answer.

With a slow sigh, Perry shook her head. "Well, yes, that's part of it. But it's not the most important thing."

Vice frowned, cocking her head. "Knowing what cargo's most valuable? Setting an example of bravery and ferocity for her crew? No, I know! Ensuring everyone's trained—"

Perry shook her head again.

What the hells was she looking for? What was Vice missing?

"Being a captain," Perry said, voice gentle, "is about relying on others."

Vice sat back. Relying on others? "Well, yes, you can't sail a ship alone."

"No, but I think you'd try to."

"It would be a useful skill."

"Luned was wrong about you."

Vice twitched at the neck-snapping change of direction, but at least it was a more positive one. "Glad someone thinks so."

"And for the longest time, *I've* been wrong about you." The lines between Perry's brow and her low, soft tone suggested this was anything but positive. "I always thought your greatest flaw was your recklessness."

Vice laughed in disbelief. "My greatest flaw? I'm so glad to have your faith."

"Against your many positive traits, of course." The corner of Perry's mouth rose. "I wouldn't be your friend if it was all bad, would I? And I only think about your flaws because I want to see you overcome them."

"Flaws—*plural?* Is this meant to be a motivational speech, Perry? Because you really need to work on your technique."

"Wild Hunt, Vice, would you just shut up and listen, *please?*"

Vice's brows shot up. "Sorry," she muttered and gestured for her to continue.

"Thank you. This might be hard to hear, but trust that I'm saying it for your benefit." Perry eyed her, still leaning forward, gaze intense. "I thought if you could learn to be less reckless, then you'd be able to achieve all the things you want. But I was wrong. The thing holding you back is your refusal to rely on anyone else other than when it's absolutely unavoidable."

Vice ground her teeth against responding.

"And everyone has flaws, but the problem is, this one isn't compatible with being a captain."

The air burst out of Vice as if she'd been punched in the belly.

Buggeration. Perry didn't think she'd ever be captain, either.

And if Perry thought it...

Vice's throat closed and pressure built at the back of her eyes. How could Perry not believe in her?

"The most important task for a captain is relying on others," Perry went on. "It's about placing people in positions where they can use their skill. Where they can excel. It's about trusting them to do their jobs and, in turn, making them confident of their own strengths and competency.

"You have to direct them. Your job is to choreograph all

those different people and their abilities and positions—like a conductor in an orchestra."

Vice frowned, trying to picture it. But Papa had never let her travel to Lunden for concerts or the opera.

"Or"—Perry raised a finger, a faint smile at the corner of her mouth—"like you bringing together current, winds, sails, and rudder to help us sail. That was some impressive manoeuvring to keep us from the Duke's cannons back on *The Morrigan*."

Each of those things had played their part. Vice nodded, exhaling. Knigh had even helped her, taking the wheel and coordinating it with her work on wind and sea, but only because she couldn't do that while delving deeply into her gift.

Perry cocked her head and arched her eyebrows. "Why do you think FitzRoy had you lead a boarding party? You're bold, resourceful, clever, determined. You'd do anything for your teammates—anything to keep them alive." Perry's brows fell, knotting together. "But that's just it—you try to do everything yourself."

Vice pursed her lips, leaning forward to mirror Perry. "If I don't, who will?"

"Your crew."

"Touché."

Perry huffed. "This isn't about winning an argument. It's true. The crew won't elect you captain or trust you when you won't rely on or trust them. They love you. They'd do almost anything for you. But you don't make them feel valued and skilled, which is what a captain must do."

Vice winced, sitting back. Did she make others feel so

worthless? She picked at a snag on her fingernail. As a girl, she'd been made to feel useless. It was what ladies were meant to be—or so aristocratic society would have them believe.

Pretty. Perfect. Pointless.

Or rather, with no more use than a pack-horse broodmare —to pop out babies. The husbands got to venture out and be useful while wives waited at home.

Her stomach turned. She'd decided at a young age—that wasn't for her.

"They need to feel trusted to do their jobs," Perry murmured. "You need to—"

Pounding rattled the door. "Sails, captain," boomed Clovis's voice.

Vice was already on her feet, Perry a second after. They exchanged glances and Vice grinned as energy flooded through her.

Action—that's what she needed. Far better than the twisting in her gut or the thoughts about how she wasn't trusted, how she'd never be captain.

A prize.

"Royal Navy. Blackwood says it's the *Sovereign.*"

Vice stopped midway to the door, heart flipping.

Not a prize.

She shared a wide-eyed look with Perry. "Have they come for Knigh?"

Perry swallowed. "Or for you?"

WHAT LURKS IN THE DEEP

"Why has he only brought one ship?" Vee asked, squinting at the approaching vessel. "Surely he wouldn't come after us alone?"

The cold pit that had opened up in Knigh's belly at the sight of the *Sovereign* widened, deepened. There was only one reason the Duke of Mercia would approach without even a few ships to support him.

Perry touched his shoulder. "What is it?"

"Hmm," Clovis grumbled, scanning the sea with his spyglass. "There's a strange wake pattern, captain, but no ship."

There it was.

Clovis offered Perry the glass, pointing out the V-shaped ripples ploughing through the water.

They stood on the *Respair's* quarterdeck, watching the *Sovereign* approach from astern. They'd piled on more canvas, but even with Vee's gift, it had steadily gained on them over the past half hour.

At first, Knigh had hoped Mercia's other ships were behind his or still over the horizon. But no, it was only the *Sovereign*.

That meant two things. This was personal, not naval business. And...

He swallowed past the dread blocking his throat. "He isn't alone."

Tentacles. Terrible, huge tentacles. The stuff of legends.

And nightmares.

Vee's eyes had gone distant, as they did when she dipped into her gift. "There's something in the water." She blinked, then stared at him, wide-eyed. "Something big. What the hells is it?"

"Mercia's creature," he murmured.

Rust-red crinkled skin. Impossibly huge suckers carving into solid oak. So many muscular arms, crushing ships in their grasp.

He shuddered. "The kraken."

The pulse in Vee's throat jumped. Wind whipped at Clovis's neckerchief and pulled strands of Perry's hair loose. They all watched him, unblinking. Beyond their little bubble on the poop deck, the crew worked, oblivious to the true danger.

"He woke the kraken?" Vee's eyes widened. "And you didn't think to tell us?"

"I couldn't say anything before. It's a naval secret. And after I left, I thought Mercia and *that thing* were out of my life." He shook his head, raking his hand through his hair. "We need to outrun it. It can—"

"We've heard the stories," Perry said, voice low and grim. "We don't need it spelling out."

Not when it could panic her whole crew. Knigh clamped his mouth shut.

Perry nodded, lips thin. "Everything you've got, please, Vice."

If Knigh had any fears that Vee might rail against Perry's captaincy now it had defeated her own attempt to claim it, they were erased by the determined set of Vee's jaw and how quickly she closed her eyes to work her gift.

The wind lifted, raising white tips on the waves.

"Clovis, Blackwood," Perry went on, "you two on the helm." She gave Clovis a pointed look, as if to ask whether that would be a problem.

Despite Perry's slight size, Clovis bowed his head. "Aye, captain."

Knigh hurried to obey the order. Apparently Clovis really was professional enough to not let his feelings get in the way of his work, because he took one side of the wheel and let Knigh take the other with no hint of yesterday's antagonism.

The heavy weather, summoned by Vee, made it stiff-going, but between the two of them it wasn't too much work to hold her steady and make course adjustments. Meanwhile, men and women worked aloft, unfurling every possible inch of canvas.

It wasn't enough.

The *Sovereign* grew, and so did the kraken's wake.

"Blackwood," Perry called from the quarterdeck.

He left Clovis at the helm and hurried up the steps.

Perry stood at the taffrail, Vee at her side, both watching

the approaching vessel. There was no sign of the kraken. "What do they mean?" She pointed, and Vee thrust a spyglass into his hand.

Sweat beaded Vee's brow, but she wasn't swaying on her feet as she had been when she'd used her gift on the *Swallow*. Her strength was returning. In any other circumstances, that would've made him smile.

Instead, he took the spyglass and turned towards the most dangerous man on the seas.

Signal flags rose on the *Sovereign*. Two solid white. Yellow banded red. *Truce*.

White crossed blue. White again, then another yellow banded red. Blue crossed yellow. *Talk*.

"Parley." He cleared his throat. "They're asking for parley." But they hadn't moved to force the *Respair* to halt. In fact, the *Sovereign* had stopped gaining since he'd last looked astern. Perhaps the *Respair* could even outrun them. They hadn't fired a warning shot or...

A shiver flashed down his spine. "Wait, where's the kraken?"

Lips pursed, Vee shook her head. "It disappeared to port a while ago, I can try—"

"You need to find it." Knigh sucked in a deep breath as he raised the spyglass again and scanned the waves on the port quarter.

Nothing there, just the little whitecaps Vee had lifted.

To the port bow?

Vee gave a sharp gasp. "It's—"

Dead ahead, the sea crashed in a mighty gout of water. It

splashed the deck, leaving three red tentacles in their path, each thicker than the main mast, as broad as the ancient yews of Albion's oldest groves. They slithered through the air, blocking the *Respair's* course.

That was how Mercia was going to force their parley. The spyglass almost fell from Knigh's numb fingers.

Lords, it had been such a long time, he'd almost forgotten the full horror of the thing.

Water dripped from the tentacles. He couldn't see its glassy, empty eyes or massive body that could mould from bulbous to sleek, boneless. But they were still there, hidden beneath the waves.

"Heave to," Perry bellowed as cries echoed across the ship.

Vee had already stilled the wind and must've pulled on the currents, too, because they were drawing to an unnaturally swift stop.

Her breaths rasped as she gaped at the thing. Even Perry— level-headed, calm Perry, stared, hands knotted together.

Knigh winced. Maybe he should've told them sooner, but he'd thought—*hoped* Mercia was out of his life now.

Idiot.

More signal flags from the *Sovereign* as it drew closer. Knigh frowned, watching them. *V–I–L–L–I–*

"He wants me," he muttered, a chill settling into his bones, despite the lack of wind.

He stared, stomach leaden as the warship drew alongside, four-hundred yards away.

A voice drifted across the water, helped by a speaking trumpet. "—ton Villiers will meet George Villiers in boats at the midpoint between our vessels to discuss terms."

"George," he sighed. So his foolish brother was still with Mercia and had been manipulated into doing his dirty work.

"Neither party will bring weapons. Neither ship will fire guns or make any show of aggression. Any such action will result in an end of the truce and a battle you cannot win. Lower your boat."

Silence reigned on the *Respair*, broken only by the constant sea.

Knigh's pulse pounded in his ears, in time with the headache blooming behind his frown.

Mercia still had George. And he wanted to talk. What the hells did he want? To arrest him? Vee? *Both?*

He rubbed his brow, but it did nothing to ease the tension or the pain.

Vee leant on the rail, eyes narrowed at the *Sovereign*, jaw solid. "What now?"

Perry sighed and gave Knigh an apologetic look. "You're going to have to parley."

PARLEY

Knigh rowed the jolly boat, but the small vessel moved quicker than it should've for the effort he was putting in. Gritting his teeth and heaving again, he frowned up at Vee, who stood at the *Respair's* rail. She needed to conserve her energy, not waste it on this.

But there was nothing he could do about that except row.

He glanced over his shoulder. George approached on a similar boat, except he wasn't even on the oars—Mercia pushed him through the water unaided.

The sun glared off the water, but the harsh shadows on George's face were enough to suggest he wore a pinched expression.

They reached the midpoint at the same time and Knigh stowed his oars, then hauled the two boats alongside each other while George shifted to the closest spot on the thwarts.

Flickering light flashed off the sea's surface, throwing shifting shadows across George's tanned skin.

They both sat that way for a few moments, just looking at each other. George's nose wrinkled as he surveyed his brother.

Knigh gripped the gunwale against the urge to run his hand through his hair. It had grown too long, and his jaw and cheeks were rough with stubble. His clothes, too—they weren't those of a gentleman and certainly not fit for a naval officer. Not that he was one anymore.

George glanced past Knigh to the *Respair, squinting against the sun.*

"Was it all worth it, then?" Lips pursed, he cocked his head. "Abandoning your family to go after your paramour? Mother's been beside herself, you know."

The air in Knigh's lungs stilled. He'd spent the brief trip across the water wondering what George might say. This was a topic he'd expected, but that wasn't enough to blunt the words.

Gods willing, Mother would understand when she read the letter he'd sent back with Billy. And his sister, Is, knew part of the truth—she'd help explain. But was that enough? Was a letter ever going to be enough to explain or excuse what he'd done? He'd abandoned them—abandoned everything.

But it wasn't for nothing.

Swallowing was hard, but he somehow managed it. "I had to right a wrong."

"By committing one against your own family?" Shaking his head, George huffed. The breeze mussed his hair as he looked at the water lapping against their little boats. From his frown, Knigh would've wagered he was wondering how he found himself speaking to his brother in the middle of the ocean.

He wasn't the only one.

Knigh peered past George to the dark shape of the *Sovereign* a couple of hundred yards away. George was meant to be back home, or at least on dry land. He was no sailor. And now Knigh was a fugitive, responsibility for the family fell to George. He had to take care of Mother, help Is find a husband, manage the modest pot of money Knigh had put aside.

But here he was, and there was only one reason.

Mercia.

Go on, Villiers—show them some Albionic spirit. We'll feed them to my beast.

Stomach twitching, Knigh swallowed down the bitter bile. "George, you need to understand..." He shook his head.

Why was it whenever he tried to speak about Mercia it came out wrong?

With a deep breath, he fixed his gaze on his brother and willed every ounce of disgust at the Duke into that one look. "You don't know what he's like. Being here—you're in danger."

George just rolled his eyes, huffing again. "Look, Knigh, just give Mercy the damn book. All he needs is your clue to go with his." He folded his arms. "Give it to him and no one has to die—including your pirate woman. You have an hour." The sun gleamed on his hair as he turned and gestured to the *Sovereign*.

Was that all? He couldn't go yet. He didn't understand. He didn't—

"No, George!" Knigh rose, rocking the jolly boat. "You can't stay with him—it's not safe. *You're* not safe," he said, voice cracking on the last. His fingers locked around George's arm, forcing him to turn.

He was being so flippant. He needed to take this seriously. Is and Mama had already lost Knigh and Father, they couldn't lose George as well.

His fingers bit into soft flesh.

George stared back at him, eyes wide. He was smaller, weaker, not fae-touched. Knigh would pick him up and haul him onto this boat if necessary. And he wasn't listening, so perhaps it *was* necessary.

Anything to get him away from that man.

A flutter of panic beat against his ribs. If George stayed with Mercia...

Beyond him, there was movement on the *Sovereign's* deck.

"I'm taking you home." Chest heaving, Knigh leant close and tightened his grip, ready to pull him across the gunwale.

George's lips bleached of colour. "Knighton, unhand me."

Steel and polished wood gleamed in Knigh's peripheral vision. He blinked, was that—

George held a pistol. It shook in his hand, but he had it aimed at Knigh.

Heart clenching, Knigh froze. His own brother had a gun pointed at his chest.

Shouts rose from both ships.

No weapons. No show of aggression. So much for that.

George shook his head, yanking his arm against Knigh's iron grip. "You're taking me nowhere. I'm where I want to be, just like you are—with *her*." Eyes gleaming, he jerked his chin at the *Respair*. "Lords, Mercy warned me you'd become a vicious animal. I didn't want to believe him, but"—his lip curled and his voice grew thick—"I'm glad he gave me this." He lifted the gun, nostrils flaring. "I don't want to have to use it, Knigh. Just let go."

Knigh scoffed, the sound bitter as he tugged George closer. They were both tight against the gunwales of their respective boats, the sun beating down, sweat on their brows. The boats rocked and pitched with their uneven loads.

He shook his head, eyes stinging, blood boiling. "He gave you a weapon to bring to a parley and yet he calls *me* the animal."

"Look at you!" A soft laugh of disbelief laced George's words. "You're sailing under black sails. You've turned your back on your family just so you can bed some pirate whore. And now you're trying to kidnap me. You're a mess."

The *click* as George cocked the pistol might as well have been a shot through Knigh's heart.

George's chin wobbled, but his jaw tightened. "Let go of me."

He meant it. He meant all of this.

Knigh dragged in a shuddering breath and unlocked his fingers.

George thudded to the bottom of his boat, staring up at Knigh. Horror, disbelief, relief all warred across his face. Then an instant later, both boats lurched into movement, taking George out of sight.

A gun *boomed*. Knigh's ears rang so much he couldn't be sure which ship had fired, but he heard Vee's cry of dismay a moment later.

He stumbled to his seat, hands shaking too much to take up the oars. His stomach churned. George had chosen Mercia over him—*believed* Mercia over him.

Mercy warned me you had become a vicious animal.

A splash sounded nearby.

"Not the boats," went up a shout from the *Sovereign*. Was that Mercia?

Knigh shook his pounding head. The pressure at the back of his eyes was unbearable. Bitterness flooded his mouth, only cut through by salt.

Maybe he *was* more beast than man. Wasn't that what he became when he lost control, a rabid animal? And right now his self-control was as slippery and writhing as an eel in a barrel.

Yesterday, Aedan and the overpowering desire to fight him. Giving in to that aching kiss with Vee. Today, grabbing George, breaking the terms of parley.

He cracked his knuckles. He'd held tight enough to leave bruises. His own brother.

He doubled over, face in his hands. "What have I become?"

BUYING TIME

The wind whipping past him said the jolly boat scudded over the waves, thanks to Vee.

Vee.

Rifle fire cracked overhead.

He swallowed, nodded. This was no time for wallowing.

This was a battle. Thanks to him. He gritted his teeth and dashed the back of his hand against his damp eyes. Yes, Mercia had given George a weapon, breaking the terms, but no one would've known if he hadn't drawn it. And he'd never have done that if not for Knigh's foolish error. Even if he was trying to protect his brother, he should never have grabbed him.

Now, Vee and the others needed him.

He blinked and surveyed their positions. The sea had blown up around him—Vee was pumping her energy into both current and a whirling wind localised around his boat. But he had no sail, so why? He narrowed his eyes at the *Sovereign* as another report of rifles sounded.

To throw any shots off target.

His heart clenched.

Bloody woman, wasting her energy on him.

But, again, there was nothing he could do about it.

"Focus," he muttered.

George was almost back at the *Sovereign*. Knigh still had fifty yards to go. Did that mean Mercia's gift was stronger than Vee's?

The *Respair's* guns had to be ready by now—their gunner teams were experienced and could load in a minute and a half, just like any Navy crew. They hadn't fired yet—Vee's earlier cry suggested the *Sovereign* had made that first shot. So they were waiting until he was clear. The speed he was going, rowing would only create drag with the oars, so he had to sit and wait.

There was one other factor in this battle. The kraken.

No sign of it currently, but that didn't mean it had gone. Mercia would keep the thing close. Maybe he wanted to make them surrender, rather than risk sinking their ship with his creature. The kraken wasn't a weapon known for subtlety.

Just give Mercy the damn book. All he needs is your clue to go with his.

He wanted the Copper Drake. So, FitzRoy wasn't the only one after it.

And Mercia already had a clue of his own. Revealing that must've been a slip on George's part. No way would the Duke have given him instructions to mention it.

Moments later and he was being hauled up the davits, the

jolly boat swaying as it left the water. As soon as he was clear, a riot of fire thundered from the *Respair* and wind filled her sails. When he set foot on the bustling deck, Vee was waiting, face hard, a twisted echo of the night he'd returned from saving Llyr.

She grabbed his arm, fingers knotting in his shirt as she dragged him towards the helm. She blasted out a breath and released him with a shove as if she couldn't decide whether to have him close enough to wring his neck or far, far away. "What the hells were you playing at? No aggression, they said!"

Knigh shook his head, following her aft. "I couldn't—I can't leave him there, not with him." His heart pounded against this ribcage, hard and aching. "Vee, I can't. It's not safe. It's—"

She scoffed, but her eyes smouldered as another round of gunfire reverberated through the deck. "He's safer with the Duke on a man-o'-war than he'd be with us. You know better than that." She shook her head, breaths heavy, the lines of her shoulders tense. "Have you lost your bloody—"

"He laughed." Knigh's throat closed. The back of his eyes burned. He'd never told anyone that before.

It had haunted his dreams and even his waking hours. It had pushed him from mainstream naval duties and onto the path of pirate hunting. But he'd never said the words out loud before.

She had to understand.

Her eyebrows knotted together as she stopped several feet from Clovis at the helm. "What?"

Knigh swallowed past the blockage. He'd started now. It was further than he'd ever got before. He had to say it all.

"Mercia laughed," he murmured. "When—when I cut Billy's hand off." Another shiver wracked through him and that cruel laughter echoed in his mind. "He was egging me on. When I came back to myself, he was disappointed I hadn't killed anyone—crew or surrendered prisoner. And he wouldn't let the ship's healer see Billy. He didn't—still *doesn't* know I'm a healer. I had to close the wound in secret. If I hadn't, he'd have died."

Knigh leant in until they were only inches apart and held her gaze, unblinking. "He doesn't care about the people under his command. He doesn't care if someone kills or tortures a prisoner. He's a monster. And—and I didn't realise." He closed his eyes, unable to bear looking at her as he admitted it: "I believed in him."

And if he, a man with much more experience of the world than his brother, had believed in Mercia, was it any wonder George had been tricked into following him?

"Oh." It was more exhalation than word. "Gods. Knigh." She touched his shoulder, her hand cool through his shirt.

He sighed and pressed against that touch, the coolness so welcome against the shame burning through him. "Vee, I—"

So close it made him jump and open his eyes, Perry shouted an order. "What do they want?" she asked at normal volume. She glanced at Vee, as if she feared that was their price. It would've explained his reaction out on the water.

Wild Hunt, pull yourself together.

A long breath. And another. He raked his hand through his hair. There would be time to wallow in his multitudinous mistakes later. Right now, they had a battle to survive.

Swallowing, he nodded and met Perry's gaze. He forced in place an expression more confident than he felt. "The book."

Vee took a step back—her hand had fallen away from him when Perry had appeared. "The Copper Drake? Why would he want that? Hells, how does he *know* about it?"

As they took up positions beside Clovis, Knigh explained George's slip up. Vee's gaze kept going distant, and she reached to adjust their course as they took one sharp turn after another, rifles and guns blasting all the while. They'd avoided taking a hit so far, but it was only a matter of time.

At mention of the Duke's clue, her eyes shot to the *Sovereign*. She gripped her sabre's hilt. "Of course," she muttered, shifting weight from foot to foot.

Her need for movement was infectious, but they wouldn't board the *Sovereign*. That wasn't a fight the *Respair* could win.

"There's a rumour the royal family has a clue," she said. "He must have it." She strained towards the warship, as if she'd jump straight in the jolly boat and row over there herself.

Perry's jaw clenched, and she called an order for port guns to ready. "So what do we do?"

Knigh bowed his head. "We need to flee." Even if it meant leaving George at *his* mercy.

Perry's face pinched, and she gave Vee an apologetic look. "We can't outrun them, can we?"

Vee's glower spelled out the answer: *no.* "Maybe if it was just them, but what's the speed like on that—that *thing?*"

Knigh grimaced. "Even with your gift..." He shook his head. "Kraken!"

The cry came from starboard, turning Knigh's stomach and

making everyone on the *Respair* flinch.

"Buggeration." Vee bared her teeth, hand on her sabre again.

The tip of a red tentacle lashed out over the deck. A dull smack sounded. Knigh couldn't see what it hit, but a scream pierced the air—not what it hit, but *who*.

His throat closed as the figure arced into sight, flying overboard and landing with a splash.

"Rope and barrel," Vee shouted, voice sharp, "throw it in after him. Get him back!"

"I've seen that thing in battle." He grabbed Vee's shoulder and made her face him. "It follows Mercia's commands. That was just a warning shot—a bit of idle play. It'll wrap those tentacles around the ship, destroying masts, rigging, sails, *people*. Then it will crush the hull."

"Blasted hells," Perry muttered. "It'll sink us."

Vee's eyes narrowed for a second and her back straightened. The corner of her mouth lifted. "Not if it'll sink them, too."

"What?" Perry glanced back from issuing another order.

Knigh cocked his head as Vee's twitch grew to a grin. Was she thinking... "Grapple them?" He hissed in a breath. They could never have done it with *The Morrigan,* but the *Respair* was larger. Not as huge as the *Sovereign*, but a closer match. "Risky, but it just might work. Utterly mad, but..."

Vee lifted a shoulder.

He raised his eyebrows at her. "It'll only buy us time."

"Enough time to come up with a better plan." She frowned in the direction the man had gone overboard. No sign of the tentacles. "A plan to get away from that thing." Her gaze grew distant as she sank into her gift, the ship groaning into a too-sharp turn.

They braced, and he caught her arm, keeping her upright while she concentrated on sea and sky.

One hand on the door to her cabin, Perry raised her eyebrows in question.

"Bring us alongside," Knigh said, "grapple the Sovereign as if we're going to board. If we'll drag them down with us, they can't blow us apart with shot or set the kraken on us."

She sucked in a sharp breath. "Bloody hells. I see what you mean by mad." Grimacing, she bowed her head. "But right now it's the best we've got."

Her orders shot across the deck, almost as quick as the rifle-fire whistling through the air. Set cover. Raise nets. All steps to protect the *Respair* and keep them from being boarded.

The ship shuddered as it took a hit. More shouts—check damage, patch it up, take care of the wounded.

Vee pushed Knigh's hands to the wheel, relieving Clovis. Together they executed a clever turn that brought them up on the *Sovereign's* far side—a manoeuvre Mercia wouldn't have predicted.

Grappling hooks sailed through the air and landed on the *Sovereign. Thunk. Thunk. Thunk.*

As the crew tightened the lines, Vee watched the enemy ship with that serious look she got in battle. A tense line creased between her eyebrows. Jaw knotted, she squeezed her sword's hilt. *"All he needs is your clue to go with his."* She glanced at him. "That's what your brother said, yes?"

"Mmm-hmm." He blinked, releasing the wheel now they were stationary. "Wait, what? *Why?*"

She exhaled through her nose and nodded once before striding away fore, hand slipping in her pocket, no doubt for the almonds or cashews she always kept ready.

"Vice," Perry called, starting after her. She blasted a frustrated breath, then had to stop and bark an order.

"I'll go," he muttered and followed.

He caught up with her at the gun racks—her fae-worked rifle remained. Or at least it did, until she pulled it from the rack and checked it over, nodding absently, still chewing a mouthful of nuts.

"What're you doing?" He took the only other remaining rifle and poured a measure of powder down the barrel, then continued the loading procedure without looking.

She touched each of her pistols in turn, nodding again as if reassuring herself they were there and ready to fire. "Well, if we're grappled, I may as well board."

He spluttered, almost dropping the ramrod. *"May as well..."* She'd actually said that. So flippant. He pinched the bridge of his nose. "Vee, that's a naval vessel, full of trained—"

"I'll be quick." She flipped open the leather bag that contained further shots for the breech-loading rifle, ran her fingers over the contents, then buckled it in place at her waist.

"That wasn't my concern." The fact this was madness— that was much more pressing. He stared at her as if his look alone could make her realise it.

"Noted." Flat-lipped, she inclined her head. "But I'm going after that clue."

EXPECTING

Vice dropped through the *Sovereign's* gunport and ducked behind a cannon, sweat trickling down her neck. To one side stood a companionway with steps up and down, and beside it a capstan spanned from deck to ceiling, wound with thick cable. Fore of her position, a bulkhead cut through the deck about fifty feet away, but it was hard to tell in the dim light. The distant sounds of gunfire still sounded, echoing her heartbeat hammering in her ears.

Maybe this hadn't been her best idea ever.

She gritted her teeth. No, it was quiet—no one down here; they were all occupied by the fight. And she needed that clue. Mercia had been kind enough to drop himself in her lap. It was too good an opportunity to pass up.

She'd tried to come alone, but Knigh and her usual boarding party had appeared as she'd made preparations. Of course, they'd insisted on coming along. Only Wynn and Effie had stayed behind at her instruction, and only because she'd given them a better offer to put their knowledge of fireworks to good use.

See, Perry was wrong, she knew her team's strengths and how to best use them. Wynn and Effie were Ælfwynn and Æthelflaed Brock, daughters of the famous John and Nadia Brock. When their father had journeyed to Aryavarta, he'd gone for knowledge of gunpowder. He hadn't expected to bring back a wife and business partner who'd help him found a great fireworks empire. Or at least that's what it had been before he and Nadia died and a villainous cousin swept in. But even so, Wynn and Effie knew their gunpowder and had their parents' sense of innovation.

Lords and Ladies knew she had no idea how to stop the kraken from attacking them, but maybe they would.

They'd hurried to Perry with a promise to 'cook something up.'

"Good work getting this open," Knigh muttered as he climbed through the port, his landing as light as a sabrecat's. He inclined his head as he handed over her rifle and scanned the area. "We're two decks below Mercia's quarters and"—he narrowed his eyes at the companionway—"just above sickbay. We need to move—they'll be bringing the wounded through here."

Vice blinked, raising one eyebrow at him as she slung her rifle's strap across her body. His comment was awfully specific. He didn't just know Navy ships, he knew *this* ship.

Wild Hunt, was this where he'd served with Billy?

She gave him a wide-eyed look, wanting to ask, but perhaps it was better not to know.

His jaw ticked.

Bollocks, had she led Knigh onto the very ship where he'd had to endure all that? Had he carried Billy down that very companionway to sickbay?

She tore her gaze away, biting her lip.

He'd be fine. He'd spent years training for the military. He'd been in worse situations than this.

"Gods know how we're going to do this," he muttered.

Her skin prickled. "You didn't have to come."

"I did."

Vice frowned and cocked her head. What the hells did that mean?

But instead of explaining the comment, he turned and helped Saba through the gunport.

"This way," he muttered once Lizzy and Aedan were aboard and made for the companionway. They paused at the sound of groans and voices from below.

The iron tang of blood mingled with the earth smell of sawdust and the stink of piss and excrement. Injured men. Dying men.

They pressed on.

"How many people sail this thing?" Saba asked, staring at the capstan as they passed.

"857 when I served," Knigh said, voice as stiff as his movements.

Vice's stomach tightened. She'd guessed right. He'd worked *this* ship.

Now she paid attention, tension poured off him, obvious in every line, even in this dim light—the solidity of his jaw, the set of his shoulders, the white-knuckled grip on his pistol.

This was where he'd cut off Billy's hand.

Shoulders set, she crept on. She needed to get up to the next deck, then make for the stern where Mercia's day cabin was. There she'd find his desk and papers and, surely, his clue. She didn't need long. She could sneak through, barricade herself inside, and search.

In fact, she didn't need Knigh or the others. She could spare him going any further.

"Kn—Blackwood, you should go back. You *all* should. I can—"

A thud from above, light, and the sounds of gunfire and shouts came suddenly louder. Someone had opened a hatch.

They hid behind the cannons lining port and starboard.

Vice kept her breath slow, even, quiet, but excitement crackled through her veins, prickled the hair on the back of her neck. Every step was a step closer to Mercia's clue, and every clue brought her closer to working out where Drake's treasure was. Perhaps Mercia had the cipher for the Copper Drake.

A pair of uniformed men came down the companionway, carrying an injured comrade to sickbay.

Even though they were out of sight, Knigh signalled for the pirates to wait. Sure enough, the men reappeared a few minutes later, continued up the companionway and back out the hatch.

Soon after the hatch sounded, the pirates broke cover and went up the companionway. Vice crept up first, sabre in hand.

But there was no one to use it against and when she glanced aft, she found panelled doors, more like something from a mansion than a ship. Her heart leapt. That had to be the way to Mercia's quarters. Knigh confirmed it with a nod.

In silence, she and Knigh led the way towards those doors, pulse rushing louder with each step.

Nearly there.

Maybe they would make it without any fighting.

It had been one thing sneaking onto the *Venatrix* and going through Knigh's quarters, but creeping through a first-rate warship, a giant on the ocean—this was a different matter entirely.

She gave Knigh a quick smile, but his flaring nostrils and solid jaw froze the look on her face. He had none of the same pleasure. No excitement sang through his veins at being close to a clue to Drake's treasure.

They paused at the doors, her hand on one handle, his on the other. He'd listened at it a good while, but was apparently satisfied as he inclined his head.

Her pulse thudded so hard, she could feel it in her grip on her sabre, at her throat and temples.

Almost there.

Perhaps Marines waited on the other side of these doors. She'd fight her way through, get to that damn clue if it was the last thing she did. With any luck, they were distracted by the fight above.

She nodded to Knigh, swallowing. As one, they swung open the doors, weapons ready, allies at their heels.

Inside was stillness.

The panelled bulkheads were painted a calm duck egg blue, again more suited to a grand house than a sailing ship. Her boots padded over black-and-white chequered tiles. Ahead, another set of double doors stood ajar. The day cabin had to be that way.

A frown flickered across Knigh's brow as he glanced around. "They didn't even clear for action."

Saba shrugged. "Maybe they weren't expecting—"

"Oh, we were expecting." A stranger's voice.

Vice had her sword up in a second. One of her pistols was somehow already drawn.

The doors leading aft swung open.

Half a dozen marines blocked the way, steel bared.

That prickling at the back of her neck—not excitement, but *danger.*

She gritted her teeth as more red jackets appeared. There had to be at least ten of them, maybe more out of view.

Bollocks. They would have to fight their way through.

At her side, Knigh held his sword across his body as if barring their way. His knuckles were white.

Well, if there was going to be a fight, this was the team she wanted at her back.

She smiled sweetly at the blond marine whose fancier epaulettes suggested he was in charge. "Terribly sorry, gents, I'm a bit lost. You wouldn't help a lady out, would you?"

"You're lost all right." His sun-bleached eyebrows rose as he advanced.

"You see, I was looking for the Admiral's quarters." She gave him another bright smile. In a moment he'd realise who he was dealing with—the dread pirate from the stories. She'd gladly play the part—brash and bold and everything they expected from someone without fear. "I assume the way you're blocking the path means I'm heading in the right direction. Kindly stand aside and I won't have to kill the lot of you."

"Vice." Saba's voice wavered.

Flashing a frown at the marine lieutenant, Vice backed off a step. She kept her sword raised, ready to catch an attack, and glanced over her shoulder.

At the doors they'd entered through was now a sea of crimson. Another half dozen red jackets.

Surrounded.

FRIEND & FOE

Steel rang through the cabin, too large a sound for such a small space. Too many bodies clamoured for room.

Teeth gritted, Vice caught blow after blow, each one clanging through her.

She was close to that clue.

She *would* have it.

She'd given them a chance to retreat or surrender, to let her pass. They'd declined and attacked first.

Fine.

Her shot cracked the air.

A marine fell.

The lieutenant's face tensed into an irritated frown and he lunged.

With a twist of her forearm, Vice parried his attack as she returned that pistol and drew the next. The years of practice had been worth it—she could holster and draw without so much as a glance.

At her side, Knigh was silent, brutal efficiency, his blade bloody, his strength too much for any individual to withstand.

She had that familiar dim awareness of Aedan, Saba, and Lizzy at her back, steel drawn.

If they could hold off the marines coming from the fore doors, she and Knigh would press aft and get to the Duke's day cabin. A grim smile tensed her lips. The clue was still within reach. How much would that piss off FitzRoy?

Grinning now, she feinted left. The lieutenant obediently angled to block, but her blade wasn't there anymore. She slashed up and right, catching his upper arm. He hissed in a breath, face screwed up.

Maybe with enough pain, he'd order his men to stand down.

But no order came, just more and more fighting.

Vice gritted her teeth. Shoot. Draw dagger. Parry. Slice. Lunge. Feint. Then again in a different order with a new twist, keeping these carefully drilled men on their toes.

Lizzy and Saba grunted from over her shoulder. More marines kept appearing. Behind her, even Knigh had broken his silence, a low growl in his throat. But the pirates were all still standing, and the same couldn't be said for the marines.

There could only be so many men in Mercia's quarters. If her team took down enough of them, continued aft, barricaded the doors behind them—

"What"—Aedan's voice, strained—"Blackwood?!"

A rapid report of steel on steel crashed through the cabin.

The marines took a collective breath, blades raised in defence as they paused, staring past Vice, mouths open.

Her insides twisted. Something was wrong.

"No," Saba gasped.

So very wrong.

Vice didn't have to see Saba's face to know her desperation.

The horror in the marines' wide eyes confirmed it. Some backed away. Others seemed frozen in terrible fascination.

The blood in her veins chilled.

She turned. Glacial ages passed as she kept the sabre between her and the marines and placed one foot, then the other, every movement achingly slow.

The harsh rasp of her breath was deafening. A trickle of sweat beaded down her back. The hairs on the nape of her neck strained at attention.

Steel clashed and clashed and clashed.

Her knees went weak before she consciously registered what she saw.

Blond hair matted with blood. Aedan, axe raised, braced in both hands, already down on one knee. He didn't attack, only fought to catch strike after strike after strike. He blinked away blood and sweat, teeth bared, eyes not fully focused. Crimson dripped from his chin.

Over him, brown hair streaked with white and spattered red, Knigh, his face contorted in a snarling mask, sabre crashing down with bone-shattering ferocity. Spit frothed on his lips. Every inch of his body tensed and angled and burned with violence. The air near-throbbed with it.

Four marines lay at his feet, faces pale, eyes blank.

A wordless sound heaved from Vice's lungs.

Knigh had lost control. This was no sparring match or petty squabble between crewmates. This was a matter of death. Murder was written in every line on his face, in the unseeing glaze of his eyes.

Saba started forward as if to stop him, but strong as she was, no way could she stand in the face of his fae-lent strength, never mind the force of his rage. She seemed to realise, stopping short with a soft breath, face crumpling. "Blackwood—Knigh, stop."

Even as her stomach turned and sent bile to the back of her tongue, Vice lunged, placing her blade between Knigh and Aedan.

But thanks to his fae gift, Knigh was fast—too fast. He diverted his blow, sword arcing away and finding its mark in Aedan's arm.

There was no blood. Aedan's mouth opened, but no sound came.

Maybe Knigh had pulled his strike. Maybe this was some plan they'd concocted and—

Then the blood started—a great gout of red so rich and dark it was almost black.

Aedan's eyes rolled.

BERSERK

Aedan might've made a sound, but Vice couldn't hear anything over the roaring in her own ears. It could've been her pulse, her breathing, or maybe even her own voice. It could've been anything.

As Aedan slumped to the floor, Knigh's blade rose again, covered in that terrible blood, and he added his other hand to the hilt, ready to cut down in a decimating blow.

"No." She tried to say it, but who knew if it came out, because her throat felt like sandpaper. Limbs heavy with dread, she dropped the dagger and darted into the space between Aedan and Knigh, ready to block Knigh's strike with both hands on her sabre.

It arced. A drop of blood landed on the bridge of her nose, warm and slick. She yearned to wipe it away as it rolled down onto her cheek, but she had to catch this blow.

And then she had to wake Knigh up.

Because if she didn't...

Her heart shrivelled.

The stories were clear—there was only one way to stop a berserker who wouldn't return to himself.

His blade gleamed red, bearing down on her.

She'd brought him here. If she had to kill him...

The shock of the strike rang through her, jolting through every bone, joint and muscle, driving the breath from her, forcing her to one knee.

But she kept her blade high, holding his mere inches from her face.

Teeth bared, gritted, he pushed down, down, down, trying to force his way through her defences. His grey eyes were colder than a winter sky full of snow.

Gods, he didn't even see her, did he?

She had no breath left to make a sound, but if she had, it might've been a whimper.

Forcing her burning arms to hold their line, she dragged air into her lungs.

"Knigh, please?"

What had she done before, back on the *Covadonga* to get through to him? His name. Remind him of himself.

"Knighton Villiers."

Steel ground on steel, the sound setting her teeth on edge.

No recognition sparked in his eyes. Nothing.

The leather grip of her sabre creaked in her hold. Damn it, her entire body creaked. This would've been a challenge even at full strength—Knigh's muscles were beautiful, yes, but also deadly. He would've been strong even without his fae-gift. With it, he was overpowering—impossible to resist.

Her muscles shrieked. Tears stung at the corners of her eyes —or maybe it was sweat.

Options. Another dagger in her boot. She could probably draw it and use it before he killed her. But then he'd be...

Was Aedan—?

She shook her head.

"Knigh." She gritted her teeth against the choking sob that wanted to come out with his name.

Her arms trembled with strain, with creeping weakness. She could just give in to it. But then the others would die too— to him or the marines.

One more try to awaken him. One more. She owed him that.

Right arm burning, she released the sword with her left. *Only a few seconds,* she told her muscles. He just needed to snap out of this.

Gods, please let this work.

"Knighton," she cried, left arm arcing until her hand landed on his cheek in a ringing slap.

Then she was on her feet, dragged there by his hand fastened around her wrist, swords still crossed between them.

A snarl curled his lips. His breaths heaved through flared nostrils as he dragged her closer to their blades—hers horizontal, an inch from her throat, his closing in on her cheek.

It hadn't worked. If anything he looked even more enraged. And now, instead of Aedan, he meant to kill her.

But not Knigh... he wouldn't...

Her wrist burned in his vice-like grip. Every muscle in her right arm, shoulder, chest, and neck strained to keep blade from flesh, but still weakened. It was only a matter of time.

She stared up at him and a sound that was half-breath, half-sob fell from her lips.

"Knigh, please?" The roaring in her ears had gone, though she didn't know when that had happened. All she knew is that she could hear how broken her voice sounded. "This isn't you."

She managed to bend her wrist towards him, though it made the bones shriek and his grip tighten. Her fingertips grazed his cheekbone. "Knigh, come back."

He blinked. A sharp, deep inhale sucked out the air from between them. The snarling lines of his face faded, leaving wide eyes, raised eyebrows, parted lips. "Vee?"

Harsh breaths heaved through his chest as if he strived to control them. The grip on her wrist loosened and the pressure against her blade disappeared.

She tried to give a reassuring smile, but her face was too tight and there was too much blood underfoot.

Gods, please let Aedan be alive. She held her breath to stop another sob.

Knigh took a step back, shaking his head, staring at his blade. "Vee, I—I'm sorry. Did I—"

His gaze fell past her. She knew the moment he saw Aedan, because it twitched through him, a convulsion of horror. "Oh, gods"—he shook his head again and again—"no. *No.*" He sank to the floor, reaching for Aedan.

Vice's heart crumpled as she blinked and turned to the rest of the room. They'd been in the middle of a fight, hadn't they?

That felt like hours ago. She shook her head, a wave of dizziness tilting through her.

Both groups of marines stared, shifted, exchanged glances. In the aft group, the lieutenant's grip tightened on his sabre as if the spell of this terrible spectacle was breaking. With a little luck, they feared facing a berserker. Or maybe seeing Knigh return to himself so distraught had doused that fear.

Blade raised, weighing a ton, Vice glanced over her shoulder.

Lizzy was bent over Aedan, staunching the wound. She'd tied a strip from her shirt over it, but it was already stained red, and Aedan's eyes were shut. At Lizzy's side, Saba stared up at Vice, cheeks tear-stained.

Vice's heart lurched to her throat. "Is he...?"

Lizzy pursed her lips, wiping her bloodied hands on her breeches. She nodded once. "Alive for now. We need to—"

"I know." Vice bit it out. They needed to get him back to the *Respair* where he could be treated. Maybe Knigh could heal him. If he'd saved Waters, he could save Aedan, couldn't he? But they couldn't do that on the deck of an enemy ship surrounded by Royal Navy Marines.

Something salty and stinging pressed on her eyes.

They were only on this bloody ship because of that clue.

No, because of *her*.

And now she had to get them out. She had to be strong.

Jaw clenched, she lifted her chin and raked the marines with a first-rate glare. "Blackwood, take Aedan." He was the only one strong enough to carry Aedan's bulk on his own.

And she couldn't ask him to fight again.

Her throat closed.

Wild Hunt take her. She'd known the *Sovereign* was his former ship—or at least she'd worked it out before they'd walked into this trap. She knew the ghosts this place held for him. Her skin rose in goosebumps.

Hc should never have been here. *She* should never have allowed it. She should've sent him back the moment she'd realised.

If Aedan died, it would be her fault. She'd led him here, just like she'd led Evered halfway across the world. He'd died, Aedan couldn't as well.

No more thinking—that might break her—now was the time for action.

"Lizzy, Saba," she said, and damn her voice, but it wavered. "To me."

One of them pressed the worn hilt of the dropped dagger into her left hand. She nodded a thank you. That was better: both fists full, weapons for parrying and attack. If they were going to cut their way out of here, at least she'd do it fully armed.

They were five feet from the doors they'd entered. Only four marines stood in their way.

"Gentlemen," she said in a low tone, "we're taking our injured and we're leaving." *Please Lords and Ladies, let my fae charm do something useful for once—something important.* "Step aside."

The sound of her own voice prickled the back of her neck. The quality of it was almost as if many spoke at once. It thickened the air, making it leaden and difficult to breathe.

Three of the men between her and the doors sidled away. Even the aft group, with the lieutenant, backed away a step. They all still held their weapons ready.

It might end up being a fighting retreat, but at least the way was clearer.

"Let's go." She nodded at Lizzy and Saba. "You two first, then Blackwood. I'll bring up the rear."

With a brief clash of steel, Lizzy and Saba had the last marine in the doorway disarmed, his nose bloody, and they led the way fore, back towards the companionway.

Vice couldn't bring herself to look. She might glimpse Aedan's lolling head or the blood that had to still be dripping from his arm, because perfect droplets marked their route across the chequered floor.

Besides, the lieutenant was advancing now, his eyes hard, sword ready.

As soon as she was through the doors, she slammed them shut. Shoulder braced, she held them closed against a shove from the other side.

"Rope," she called. Heels dug in, she closed her eyes and pushed as hard as she could, despite her muscles' complaints.

A ring of steel and a *thunk*, then Saba was there with a freshly cut length of rope. Between the two of them, they held the doors. In no time, Saba's clever maker's hands got the rope lashed around the door handles in a figure of eight.

"That'll slow them," she huffed.

Vice nodded, jaw tight. "Let's go."

CUT LOOSE

They ran—no point in stealth anymore. At first, all was quiet, but then a hatch above opened with a flash of daylight and red uniforms.

The next few minutes were a blur of fists and steel and evasion as one handful of marines appeared after another. Vice ducked behind the capstan head and rolled over cannons. She tipped round shot from its racks, sending it wheeling across the deck, treacherous underfoot.

She held the top of the last companionway as her team got the gunport open, but glancing blows sliced her shoulders and knee, sending sharp pain through her battle-abandon.

"Cut the cannons loose," she called down to the others, punctuated with a grunt as she fumbled a parry and only just caught the marine's blade on her knuckle-bow.

"Gunport ready," Saba called from below.

Now Vice needed an opening to get down the companionway.

Her arms were jelly and that slice on her knee throbbed every time she flexed or lunged.

In a long fight, these were the injuries that got you killed.

Not a slice across the throat or being run through with a rapier—they only finished off the inevitable. It was the little energy-sapping cuts that leeched blood, that made you pull a strike because of the pain, that tired you out and distracted you until you missed one block too many and someone cut through your shoulder, leaving you on deck drowning in your own blood.

Not today.

She gritted her teeth, kicked at one man's knee, and grimaced when it bent the wrong way with a crunch of bone. His shriek made the others flinch.

Her chance.

With a huff, she slashed wildly, forcing them back a step, then leapt into the companionway opening, dropping her dagger to grab the edge and swing through. She staggered the landing, breath huffing from her lungs.

She glanced around, sheathing her sword. Cannons trundled back and forth with the ship's sway, their gun carriages creaking. Any more movement from the ship and they'd turn deadly. A little luck and the Navy lot would insist on securing the cannons rather than chasing them back to the *Respair*.

She checked the floor. No sign of her dagger, and she didn't have time to search. Knigh was already out the gunport, pulling Aedan after him, with Saba and Lizzy guiding his legs through.

Good. Almost there.

She swung her rifle from her shoulder and cocked it. The first flash of red at the companionway opening and she fired.

Crack.

Her ears rang with the sound contained between decks.

No time to watch the marines' reactions or check whether she'd hit. She flipped the breech block open, flicked the cartridge case out, grabbed a new one, then slid it in place. With a snap, the block was shut again.

A head peeked over the companionway.

Crack.

Gods only knew if she hit, if she killed him. She needed to keep them back long enough for the others to escape.

Another cartridge. That's all that mattered.

"Vice," Saba called.

Crack.

Reloading, Vice ducked behind a cannon.

Saba peered in through the gunport. "Come on."

Vice huffed a breath and nodded. Everyone was out. Thank the gods.

Arms shaking, she threw the rifle strap over her shoulder and staggered for the gunport. In seconds, fresh air and spray washed over her and the sun shone on her head.

Her shoulders and knee stabbed with renewed pain as she crossed the gap and clambered through the *Respair's* gunport, fresh blood oozing from the wounds.

She crouched and caught her breath as Saba closed the gunport and the others crowded around Aedan's prone form.

Vice grimaced. Her little slices were nothing compared with the gash Knigh had dealt him.

If Aedan died...

His life, and Saba's, Lizzy's, even Knigh's—they were far more important than any clue to Drake's treasure. Hadn't she cursed FitzRoy for not thinking the same—for treating the crew as worth less than riches? He'd sacrifice anything for the treasure. Had she truly become the same?

A PLACE FOR BLAME

K nigh bent over Aedan, shaking. Shallow breaths. Face a ghastly shade of grey. Blood still oozed from the gash in his arm.

Before Lizzy had tied her makeshift bandage in place, he'd spotted that telltale white of bone.

He'd done it again. His madness. His loss of control. And once more, someone else was paying the price.

Pull yourself together, Knighton. He forced his breaths slower and swallowed back another wave of nausea. He'd been fighting it all the way from Mercia's dining cabin.

Aedan was alive, his limb still attached. He wouldn't pay the price if Knigh could master himself enough to heal him.

From Aedan's sluggish pulse, they didn't have long.

Nearby, the ship's pump sucked and sloshed. A couple of shots sounded from above.

"Come on," Lizzy said, lifting Aedan's uninjured arm as if

demonstrating what she wanted Knigh to do. "We've got to get him to sickbay."

No time to hide his gift. They'd all see. But Aedan's life and not having it on his hands was more important.

He shook his head, gently removing Aedan's arm from her hold. "No. Leave him here." Hands clenching and unclenching, he took a deep breath.

"But he needs—"

"Lizzy," Vee said, voice soft but full of command, "do as he says."

Knigh gritted his teeth until his jaw ached. *Breathe. Just breathe.*

Because looking at Vee right now was impossible. When he'd blinked back to himself, her wide eyes had been afraid, desperate, dark as a ship-killing storm. She had to have bruises on her wrist—his knuckles ached where he'd held her so tight. Gods, he'd marked her, hadn't he? He'd hurt her just like he'd hurt George.

Wild Hunt, take me. At least if they did, he couldn't hurt anyone else.

He bit the inside of his cheek until the salty-metallic taste of blood crept across his tongue.

Focus.

Eyes shut, he placed his hands over Aedan's wound. He sank into the place where his core of power blazed with golden light.

How ironic that as Aedan lay in front of him, life force so dim, his own gift shone brighter than ever. Bitter, bitter irony.

He dived deep, as far as he dared, until it was achingly

difficult to resist the song calling, promising. He could surrender, follow it, then none of this would matter anymore, would it?

No. It would matter. Aedan would be dead and whether or not he was there to endure the guilt, it would still be his fault. It would still be wrong.

Despite the trembling in his muscles, he drew and drew from that bright energy. He needed to knit bone as well as muscle and flesh. He needed to restore lost blood. So much lost blood. His fault. His—

This is not a place for blame.

It wasn't his own voice, but it sounded in his head as clear as any thought. Maybe a woman, but who?

There was nothing more, only that eternal song that always lived in this place.

He exhaled and pushed the power into his hands, then beyond that, beyond his own skin and into the too-hot flesh under his fingertips.

Bone was slow to heal. His power creaked through it, slow as an ancient wood growing. Shard by shard, it filled the notch he'd gouged out.

This is not a place for blame.

A memory of the voice, or perhaps it was still here.

Aedan was far too still under his touch—this had to be hurting by now. But there was no time to slow down or to check. There was too much to do if he was going to save the man's life, never mind his arm.

Voices—the boarding team, not the strange ones that sang with his gift—registered dimly. They weren't raised, so there couldn't be any immediate threat. And Vee would keep him safe if there was. Despite all he'd done.

... not a place for blame.

He nodded and gathered more from the golden glow, pressing it into the careful weaving of muscle strands, their fibres so like rope. Veins and arteries threaded through, the blood bright in his awareness as ends reconnected, their flow restored.

Aedan jolted under his hands with a low, wordless cry. On reflex, Knigh gripped him in place. More voices, gentle, comforting. Perhaps the others were helping to hold him down.

Two more deep breaths and raw flesh met raw flesh, closed, and smoothed.

When he opened his eyes, Saba and Lizzy were staring at him. Vee watched Aedan, combing hair from his bloodied brow as he blinked up at her.

There was no wound on his head anymore, either.

She let out a soft breath, shoulders sinking.

"You two *do* have a lot in common, huh?" Lizzy said eventually, narrowing her eyes and glancing between Knigh and Vee, attention remaining on the latter. "But you already knew that, didn't you?"

Vee lifted one shoulder and stood, making a noncommittal sound before offering Aedan her hand. "Come on. We're still in a battle"—she grunted as she helped Aedan to his feet, catching his arm as he swayed slightly—"one involving a bloody kraken."

They hurried up on deck, except for Aedan who was sent to sickbay but could walk without help. Before he left them, he gave Knigh an awkward look, mouth lifting in what was almost a smile.

If that was an expression of thanks, he didn't deserve it, not when he was the cause of the injury in the first place. Knigh bowed his head.

Both crews still exchanged shots through the netting, but much of the melee had dried up. A brief skirmish clashed and dissipated as they ran from cover to cover towards Perry's cabin. It seemed more a matter of marines testing the pirates than a concerted effort to break through their defences.

For now.

Knigh chewed the inside of his cheek. It certainly looked like a test of their strengths and weaknesses ahead of a full-scale attack. With their superior numbers, the *Sovereign* had to be planning it. They'd be foolish not to.

Mercia was a lot of things, but a fool wasn't one.

This stalemate was only temporary. If the *Respair* didn't escape, the *Sovereign* would eventually win.

For now, the two ships were bound together. The *Respair's* best shots had holed up at strategic points, ready to dispatch anyone on the *Sovereign* who attempted to get close to the grappling hooks and dislodge them.

The air was thick with sulphurous smoke. The sun still blazed overhead as if none of that on the *Sovereign* had just happened.

And somewhere in the ocean, the kraken waited.

BLACK POWDER

They found Wynn and Effie in Perry's cabin. Perry stood with arms folded, one eyebrow raised. It was a look Knigh recognised—one she normally wore when Vee explained a wild plan.

Perry glanced up when he entered in Vee's wake, shoulders sagging with relief as she eyed them each in turn.

"You're alive. Good." Her lips pursed as her gaze landed on Vice. "That means I can kill you for filling these two's heads with... with..." She rolled her eyes, huffing. "I have no words strong enough for this particular insanity."

Knigh folded his arms, raising one eyebrow. They'd concocted a scheme, then. Well, that was what the *Respair* needed, even if it was as foolhardy as one of Vee's.

And he needed the distraction. A set of commands to follow. An objective. A plan. He could throw himself into that, mad or not.

Vee grinned, but it didn't flash in her eyes and something about it was brittle. "Let me guess—it involves gunpowder?"

"So it *is* your fault." Perry's jaw flexed.

Outside, shots still cracked and boomed.

Vee lifted one shoulder.

Knigh approached the table littered with boxes and inkwells in an oddly familiar arrangement. The field of battle. He cocked his head. "So what *is* this plan?"

Vice and Perry both flinched, attention tearing from each other to him as if surprised by his interest or interruption.

He placed his fingertips on a low rectangular box, the type that held spare pen nibs and housed an inkwell at each end.

Blood crusted under his nails and around their edges. For a moment, all he could do was stare at it.

Aedan's blood. The marines', too. People he'd killed. An ally he'd almost murdered.

Focus. His attention needed to be on this battle, not what he'd done to Aedan. He had to suck in a sharp breath before he could speak. "This is the *Respair*, is it not?" And beside it, touching, a wooden stand for a decanter and two glasses, larger and empty of the glassware. "And the *Sovereign.*"

"Exactly," Wynn said, smiling as she joined him at the table. She swept a lock of reddish-brown hair from her face. "Idea is, we break off—preferably with Vice's help"—she looked up at Vee who inclined her head—"and chuck some special presents in our wake."

"Presents that you've already gone and bloody prepared," Perry said, voice raised above her usual calm, "before you even put the plan to me."

Effie's hand cut through the air. The way she lifted her chin emphasised her upturned nose and for a second Knigh had the impression of a young woman who'd once walked through balls the way she now strode across decks. "Time is of the essence."

"Besides," Wynn stepped in, "we suspected you'd respond better to a demonstration than an explanation."

With a flourish that wouldn't have looked out of place coming from Vee, she gestured aft. Vee must have been in here sewing because her threads and needle book littered Perry's desk. In its midst sat a small barrel with a hole cut in its lid and a bottle's neck poking out.

"Gunpowder around a bottle of strong rum," Effie said as the room's attention fell on their creation.

"Oh, you *have* been busy," Vice murmured, running her finger over the bottle's cork. "Let me guess—a rag in the top to act like a fuse?"

Effie nodded, grinning. "And that's why we like you."

A massive bloody explosion, that's what they had planned.

Knigh huffed a soft breath. "Well, the kraken dislikes loud noises and bright light. This ticks both boxes."

"I thought that might be the case," Wynn said. "We have a dozen of these. That's"—she winced and avoided Perry's gaze —"*a lot* of our gunpowder. But that thing... I haven't even seen it all, but I've seen enough to know it's huge."

"Accurate." Vee nodded. "I felt it cut through the water— it's easily the size of a ship. So, how do these little presents work?"

Eyes narrowing, Wynn cocked her head. "Saba, you have your hunting bow, don't you?"

Saba inclined her head, a confused frown on her brow. "Of course."

"Do you think you could hit a rag fuse from, say, fifty feet?"

She scoffed. "I'm insulted you're even asking."

Another grin dawned on Effie's face. "See, I told you!" She bumped her hip into her sister's. Bent over the table, she slid the box representing the *Respair* away from the *Sovereign*. "Vice gets us away nice and quickly. The barrels go in." She tapped the space left by the *Respair's* retreat. "Saba shoots them with flaming arrows."

Vee flicked a cashew nut into her mouth and munched, nodding along with the explanation.

Lizzy leant over the table, hands pressed into the surface. "Bang, bang, boom. And the kraken beastie's gone."

Wynn and Effie pointed at her, matching smiles of triumph on their faces. "Exactly."

The room fell silent, all eyes on the table.

Knigh cocked his head.

It wasn't a bad plan. Noise. Bright flashes of light. It probably wouldn't be enough to damage the *Sovereign*, unless she tried to pursue and ended up with one of the barrels against her hull as Saba set it alight.

He narrowed his eyes at the decanter stand representing the *Sovereign*. No, Mercia wouldn't chase them, not when he could have his creature do it for him.

A shudder crept over his skin.

To tackle that thing, it wasn't a bad plan, no. But it could be better.

"If I may make a suggestion?"

All eyes turned to him. Perry exhaled with a smile, nodding encouragement. The others lifted their eyebrows.

"Heated oil in a bag—the same as you'd use to calm rough waters, but warmed first." He traced his finger over the stretch of desk left between the two boxes. "Let it coat the surface, follow up with your exploding barrels, and we'll leave a strip of flaming sea in our wake."

Vee exhaled so hard it was almost a laugh. "Knigh Black-wood"—she shook her head, eyes glinting at him in something like admiration—"closet pyromaniac. Well, I never!" She chuckled. "Fire and oil, that's almost as good a match as rhubarb and custard."

Despite himself, Knigh scoffed. Trust her to come up with such a comparison.

Perry clicked her tongue, scowling at him. "And here I was hoping you'd help me put an end to this madness, not encourage it."

Knigh screwed up his face in apology. "Ordinarily, perhaps. But the kraken requires more than *ordinary*. The fire will help scare the beast away a little longer—it's our best chance for an escape."

"I hate to say it, Perry," Vee said, though she didn't sound like she hated it in the slightest, "but I don't see that we have any other option."

Lips pursed, Perry eyed them each in turn as if there was

the slightest chance one of them would put forward an alternative.

There was none.

Sighing, she pinched the bridge of her nose. "Fine. Fine!" She waved a hand at the barrel, then the door. "Make it happen. Heat the oil. Saba, set your arrows alight or whatever it is you need to do. Just do it quickly."

"Aye, captain," Vee said, touching her temple in a mockery of a salute before leading to the door.

"Oh, and"—Perry raised her eyebrows as they all turned back—"I know we're talking about explosions, but please *try* to do it safely, for all our sakes."

THE GETAWAY

V ice took deep breaths, awareness half on the deck, half with the sea, rolling steadily around them. She tightened her grip on the wheel.

They'd taken damage, but the carpenter's crew had patched the holes for now and the pumps had flushed away the water they'd taken on. They were seaworthy enough to escape.

Each grappling line had been untied on the *Respair's* side, with the loose end hidden so the Navy lot wouldn't realise they were about to break away.

Aloft, a handful of men and women had crept up behind the masts' cover, ready to start unfurling sails. The others would have to follow once they were in motion or else the *Sovereign* would catch on. Or, worse, begin shooting them down.

The dozen rum-and-gunpowder concoctions sat at the stern, ready for Clovis and a few others to launch over the rail.

They also had three big old barrels, so rickety they'd fall apart when they hit the water. Inside were the sacks of heated oil, as per Knigh's suggestion.

There was no sign of the man himself.

After she'd made it clear she didn't need his help to steer the ship, she'd gone to her cabin to grab the Copper Drake and tuck it in her waistcoat pocket. Now she knew Mercia wanted the book, she would keep it with her at all times. Fetching it in that precise moment, though? That had been an excuse to get away from Knigh.

She tightened her jaw. She couldn't be around him right now. Hells, she couldn't even *think* about him right now. Not the frothing spittle on his lips as he'd gone berserk. Not the way he'd cut into Aedan so mercilessly.

And certainly not that it was her fault.

Her stomach clenched, threatening to bring up the fruit and nuts she'd been nibbling on for energy.

Not now. Not now.

Eyes closed, she took another long breath.

Once she'd exhaled, she surveyed the final preparations as her crewmates slipped from cover to cover and down the hatches, ready to fire cannons as they broke away from the *Sovereign*.

Right now, there was the fight. That's all she needed to think about.

A flaming torch waved from the poop deck. That meant Saba had her arrows ready and Lizzy was on hand to help light them.

The weight of dozens of gazes fell on her. Next, it was her

signal to say they were breaking away.

With current, wind, and wheel, she began turning the *Respair* and raised her fist.

The shout went up. A sudden report of shots peppered the air from the *Respair's* rifle-folk as they kept attention from the real action. The men and women who'd crept aloft hurried along the yards.

The *Respair* crept away from the *Sovereign*, her grappling lines running loose as she gained speed. Moments later came the unmistakable flap and furl of sails filling with wind.

Cries rose from the *Sovereign*.

Good—they weren't expecting this.

Vice turned the wheel, pushing harder now they had sails. As she angled the current, she cast her awareness through the water. There was a vague sense of something large on the far side of the *Sovereign*. It might've been a few hundred yards away, but it was hard to get a scale.

One thing for sure—it was coming this way.

The Duke must've already told the thing they were disengaging. How did he control it? Was it even possible to communicate with something like that?

Another shout said the team at the stern was hauling the barrels and oil over the rail.

Her heart pounded. Almost time to light it all up.

Lords, Ladies, gods, please let this work.

The shape in the water was just a hundred yards away now, passing beneath the *Sovereign*. Lords, that thing was quick.

Her muscles ached as she pushed the *Respair* away, faster now. They couldn't outpace the kraken, that was clear, but it was best to get some distance between them and that floating oil, which was about to turn deadly. She sent wind over the sea's surface, blowing the oil and barrels towards the *Sovereign*.

Cannons boomed across the water. Some shots splashed into the waves, others crashed into the *Sovereign's* hull, winning cheers from her crewmates.

A strike.

No fire from the Sovereign yet—maybe they still had loose cannons they were trying to make safe.

Vice completed the turn, sending them astern from the naval ship. It put the *Respair* on course to join a natural current that would help them speed away, and it gave her gunning crews more chance to keep firing on the enemy.

Plus, she'd be able to see the fire-show.

She only needed one hand on the wheel now, keeping it steady, so she leant to starboard and peered back. Squat shapes bobbed in the water. The barrels were ready.

A form parted the water beneath the surface, massive, fast. Hungry. It was easily as big as the warship, probably bigger, and in a few breaths, it would close on the *Respair*.

Goosebumps on her arms, Vice's hand tightened on the wheel. She had to hold them steady to help Saba fire.

Flashes raked across the *Sovereign's* broadside and an instant later the air split.

Boom.

The *Respair* shuddered, once, twice, three times.

Crashing, cries, shouts for help.

Vice's stomach dropped. "Blast it all to *all* the bloody hells," she muttered. She clung to the wheel even as every muscle in her body twitched, telling her to run and help. But she had to do this. She was the only one who could.

It wouldn't take the *Sovereign* long to reload. Her stomach tensed, tight as a rope twisted too many times. She couldn't even manoeuvre to avoid the shots. "Come on, Saba," she muttered. The sooner she sent this lot ablaze, the better.

Red shapes slithered through the water, mere feet from the hull. They danced into clarity beneath the glinting waves, rising. A sucker bigger than a dinner plate broke the surface.

A breath fell from Vice's lips as cold engulfed her.

That thing. It was huge. Vast. And—she shuddered—old. Unutterably old.

She couldn't have said how she knew, but she did. And there was something—a presence at the back of her mind, like a fingertip placed on the nape of her neck.

Her eyes pricked with tears.

It could rip her apart as easily as a child blew seeds from a dandelion's head. And it could do the same to every single person on this ship.

Fire arced through the sky.

Heart in her throat, Vice watched the burning arrow reach its zenith. In a graceful crescent, it began to fall. She couldn't breathe, not until—

BOOM.

Orange, yellow, smoke, and splinters.

A blast of air crossed the deck, throwing loose hair from her face.

It was nothing like a cannon firing. That must've been what

she'd expected, because all she could do was stare at the debris falling through the air and landing in the—

Fire whooshed across the sea's surface, billowing from that first explosion.

Vice swallowed and shook her head, waking from the shock. That was just the first barrel. With the sea on fire, the rest would follow quickly.

Fist tightening on the wheel, she urged the wind and current on, pushing them faster, harder, further from the flames.

They were hundreds of yards away when more thunderous explosions sounded, one after the other, so close together they were impossible to count.

There was no sign of the kraken, even when she reached out with her gift.

It had worked.

They'd burned through a chunk of their gunpowder, but it had worked.

Even better, the *Sovereign* couldn't follow through the flame —not without risking damage.

She huffed a relieved laugh, shoulders sagging. Now to sail and put as much distance as possible between them and the Duke.

Thank the gods. Thank the Lords and Ladies for Effie and Wynn and for her gift.

She rubbed her face, and that's when she saw it.

A crimson stain on her sleeve.

Not her own blood.

Despite the afternoon sun, a shudder swept through her.

Aedan's blood. She flexed her fingers. It was still caked in the creases of her palms and edges of her nails.

Her breath shook as she scrubbed her hands over her breeches.

Aedan's blood on her hands and Knigh's berserking on her shoulders. Both her fault.

Knigh had spent years beating himself up over Billy. This time, only sheer luck had stopped him from taking Aedan's arm.

Eyes screwed shut, she shook her head. But she hadn't done it, she hadn't...

A harsh breath blasting out, she bent over, hands on her knees. Her stomach spasmed.

No, she hadn't held the blade, but she was the one who'd led them both into battle. She'd taken Knigh on board a ship that held such terrible memories. She'd pushed him too close to Mercia, to the man who'd laughed as Knigh had almost killed unarmed men.

Wild Hunt damn her, but maybe the crew had been right not to vote her captain.

She was going to throw up.

Lords, she was going to puke over the side like a raw recruit with their first taste of a storm.

Deep breaths. Deep breaths.

Teeth gritted, she breathed through her nose.

"Vee, are you—"

She bolted upright. Knigh, far too close, looked far too worried.

Swallowing down the bile, she swatted away his hand and backed off.

"Are you all right?" He grabbed the wheel that she'd left unattended.

Yet another reason she shouldn't be captain. *You can't be trusted.* As if she needed the reminder.

"I'm fine," she snapped, limbs trembling. Lords knew she didn't need his concern—she certainly didn't deserve it. What she needed was for him to go away before she cracked. "Absolutely bloody fine. I don't need your help or *you*, thanks. Now piss off."

He flinched and a small, hurt frown flashed in place for an instant before he smoothed it away as if it had never been there.

She clutched her stomach as it plunged. It wasn't true. She didn't mean it. But that hadn't stopped it hurting him or him shutting her out.

If she could swallow the words back up, she would. Eyes shut, she shook her head. "I—"

"Come on, Blackwood."

Vice flinched and found Lizzy close-by, shirt bloody, expression pinched.

"You're a healer, no?" Lizzy looked up at him, though his eyes were still on Vice.

He nodded slowly, mouth set in a grim line. Jaw flexing, he tore his gaze away and raised his eyebrows at Lizzy.

She jerked her chin towards the main hatch. "There are men and women who need you or they won't see tomorrow."

Vice shivered. Lizzy must've been down in sickbay. "Aedan, is he—"

"He's fine. He's giving me a hand with the wounded." Lizzy dismissed Vice with a wave, already starting for the hatchway. "None of us will be as much help as you, though, Blackwood. Come on."

Without even a glance at Vice, Knigh followed, leaving her alone on the bustling deck.

She clung to the wheel, pressing her forehead to a smooth-varnished handle. She'd apologise to him later. It wasn't something she was good at and it left a bitter taste in her mouth, but she'd do it.

It had been a silly momentary snap. He'd understand that, wouldn't he? If she caught him alone and said sorry, that she hadn't meant it, he'd understand and it would smooth away his hurt.

Besides, right now, the crew needed him more than she did.

She straightened, stared ahead, and steered the *Respair* into the swift current.

THE LONGEST DAY

Weary right down to his bones, Knigh emerged from belowdecks. He paused for a moment, closing his eyes and letting the sinking sun warm his face.

This had to be the longest day ever. Had the vote for captaincy only been this morning? Then George, the *Sovereign*, Aedan, and those blank moments in his memory where he'd tried to kill him.

He scrubbed his face, hands still cool and damp from having washed them down in sickbay.

And Vee's face, inches from his blade, bloodied.

Too much.

He shook his head. It was all too damn much.

A deep cold ache settled in his muscles and spread to his bones, as if the weariness had prised open cracks and now a chill could seep in.

The deck was calm now, just the usual work of sailing, punctuated with the sawing and hammering of repairs. Above, sails had already been patched. Belowdecks, he'd heard the pump's steady flush and whoosh stop some time ago. The *Respair* still sailed, but she was in dire need of repairs—*proper* repairs at a dockyard, not quick fixes carried out on the move.

Seemed Perry had the same idea, because unless he was mistaken, that was Nassau ahead.

Maybe a bit of time ashore was what he needed. Time and space to process the day – losing control, hurting George, almost killing Aedan...

Most of all, time and space away from Vee. Especially after earlier. She'd looked in such a bad way, pale, doubled over. He'd thought she was going to be sick, or that perhaps she'd hidden a more serious wound. But, no, all she'd thrown up had been snapping, snarling words.

He'd only tried to help—he had to after coming so close to hurting her today.

He flexed his hands, joints sore. No, he *had* hurt her, hadn't he? That grip on her wrist...

Still, that didn't give her licence to treat him like scum washed up on shore.

And it didn't mean he would just lie back and let her stamp on him again and again.

He'd thought they were past that. After all, hadn't she made a promise to Perry? It seemed Vee's promises were easily forgotten.

"Blackwood." Perry's face appeared at the door to her cabin. "Can I borrow you?"

He blinked, inclined his head, and followed her inside as the crew prepared to dock.

With a sigh, she perched on the edge of her desk. "I heard what Vice said to you earlier." The skin around her eyes creased as she sucked in her lips, shaking her head. "I—I'm sorry. I know she didn't mean it. I'm sure you know that, too." Her gaze fell away. "I think she was just frightened, guilty after"—she swallowed, waving towards the door—"after the boarding didn't go as planned."

Knigh clenched his jaw. On one level, Perry was right—Vee probably didn't mean what she'd snapped. Perhaps it was the relief of battle being over and all her tension needing another outlet.

But on another level, Perry was very wrong—*she* wasn't the one who should be apologising.

"It's my fault," she went on. "I shouldn't have let her board a naval ship. Certainly not after that vote." Sighing, she swept a hand through her hair, which was spilling loose from its braid. "Of course she'd feel like she had something to prove."

The look on Perry's face, like she was the one who'd caused all this, made his skin prickle. Perhaps she should have a firmer hand with Vee, but she was not to blame in this. *She* hadn't hurt him. He bit his tongue.

"Vice does care about you." She winced as she met his gaze. "I think that's why she can be so harsh towards you. She... she just struggles to deal with those emotions. Like with FitzRoy on *The Morrigan,* you know?" Sighing, her shoulders sank. "All I'm saying is, please, try not to hold it against her. She is trying. She does care. I'm sure she'll come around." She sat back, raising her eyebrows.

What a defence. She hadn't even made a case for her own captaincy with this much vigour. He folded his arms, mouth twisting. "Anything for an easy life, eh Perry?"

"An easy life?" Her brows knotted, and she straightened with a quick breath. "You think I'm apologising because it's easy? That's not fair."

His eyes narrowed. "No, it isn't. Perhaps not an *easy* life, but a peaceful one."

Parts slotted together as he spoke, the words coming far too easily. "You're content as long as the world glides past you on its little rails, everything in step as it should be. You'll do anything to keep the peace so your boat isn't rocked too hard. But Vee bloody well needs her boat rocked. She"—he scoffed—"she's done some ridiculous things."

Perry's face screwed up. "But it's not her fault, she's just—"

"Stop defending her!"

His outburst left a ringing silence in its wake.

They stared at each other, Perry's mouth open at his raised voice.

It had been a long day – longer than midsummer. Maybe he shouldn't have shouted, but maybe it needed saying.

Licking his lips, he took a steadying breath. "Stop taking responsibility for her. She's an adult, she can deal with her own feelings." He huffed out through his nose. "Or at least she should be able to."

Perry bit her lip as her gaze slid away. She knew he was right.

He plucked an inkwell from the box that had represented the *Respair* in their earlier planning. Held up to the stern windows, it gleamed in the late afternoon sun.

"We all make mistakes. Gods know, I have—every single day I think about how I handed her over to the Navy." His skin rose in goosebumps and he couldn't help but notice the way his voice thickened as he said it. *Hurting Billy and Aedan.*

He flicked the inkwell's lid shut, pressing it down until he felt a little firmer. *"Every day.* And I did that because I couldn't trust myself. I didn't believe in my own assessment of who she was. I let those stories of the notorious Lady Vice fester even once she'd shown me that wasn't who she was. So when she told me one stupid, flippant thing that aligned with that rotten story, I was only too ready and willing to believe it."

He shook the inkwell until the blackness coated the glass, blocking any light from shining through. "But *I* chose to act upon it. *I* made that mistake. And I have tried to make up for it ever since."

Perry nodded slowly. "I know," she murmured. "And Vice knows, too. She just—"

"She just needs to deal with her feelings." He squeezed the inkwell, gritting his teeth. "Accepting she has them would be a start. And"—he sighed away the stiffness, limbs suddenly heavy—"and you need to let her take responsibility for the things she's done because of those feelings. Just because you're the only one she lets through the door, doesn't mean you're responsible for what's behind it."

She exhaled, shoulders sinking as she nodded again, eyes shut as if defeated.

"I'll say it again: she isn't your responsibility." He cocked his head, heart sore for Perry. She loved Vee—she'd said as much this morning. Perhaps she was a stand-in for the daughter she'd never had. Perhaps she was the bright spark that kept her world exciting, even as she fought to keep things on the same course.

They stayed that way a long while, just the sound of work outside and the sea's constant song at the stern windows.

"I'm not without blame," he said at last. "I acted. I accept that and I'm seeking forgiveness—although sometimes it feels like I'm asking the sea itself to forgive me for all the good it does." He scoffed, the sound of it bitter even in his own ears.

"But"—he raised a finger—"she played a part in it too. She's so terrified of her own feelings, of being vulnerable, that she pushed me away. She made the decision to tell me she'd killed Avice Ferrers because she wanted to get rid of me. And it worked."

That was it. All those times she'd been deliberately cruel to him, she'd been trying to push him away. She'd admitted it on the *Swallow,* but she hadn't once accepted even the possibility that she'd played a part in the whole sorry business.

Perry had crossed her arms over her belly, as if hugging or protecting herself. She frowned at the table, lips tight. "Not a word you've said is wrong," she murmured.

Gods, if even Perry agreed with him, maybe his judgement was right for once.

The ink in the well trembled as he ran his thumb over the smooth glass. He returned it to the holder as the familiar bump of a ship coming into its berth shook through the deck.

"She needs to take responsibility for her actions and, Perry"
—he gripped her shoulder, making her look at him—"I respect
you, but you need to stop shielding her."

A soft sound somewhere between a harsh breath and *huh*
came from the far end of the cabin.

Vee stood in the doorway, mouth open, staring at him and
Perry.

How long had she been there?

Her eyebrows met in a peak, creases heavy at the meeting
point above over-bright eyes.

Long enough to be hurt.

A second later, she sucked in air and that peak inverted to a
frown. It was as if someone had shouted the order to batten
down the hatches. Even her eyes had gone dull and dark,
closed off.

"I see," she said, voice cold and crisp as an icy morning in
Albion. She lifted her chin, a bitter smile thinning her lips. "So
nice to hear what you really think. Good to know all your apologies are nothing more than hot air."

Shaking his head, he started towards her. He wasn't going
to apologise for what he'd said, but he could explain. As he'd
said to Perry, it was past time that she took responsibility. "Vee,
it isn't—"

"It isn't like that?" She scoffed, tossing her head. "I see
exactly what it's like. It really is so wonderful to hear my
closest friend and my"—she pressed her lips together as if she
bit back a word—"to hear the pair of you in such a cosy
conversation."

Surely she didn't think he and Perry? But, no, the way she

stood there angled with tension, simmering—there was no jealousy there. She was just hurt and angry at what they'd said.

He squared his shoulders. "Well it's true. I'm sorry you had to hear it like this, but I'm not sorry I said it. And I'm not going to apologise *yet again*. I've done enough of that. You've had your pound of flesh from me. You've pushed. You've prodded. You've clawed and scratched and bitten me. But enough's enough." His voice shook with the force of how much he meant it all.

She stared back at him for a long while. "Well, of course you're not going to apologise—after all, it was my fault *you* arrested me."

Her gaze snapped to Perry. "And you think it, too." She scoffed, not sparing either of them from her sneer. "Do you two really have nothing better to do with your time than talk about me? How sad. How pathetic. How—"

"What do you want from me, Vee?" His heart thundered in his chest. He hadn't meant to say it, but... "I've apologised. I've broken you out of a cage. I've brought you halfway across the world and got you back to Perry and your friends. I've done everything in my power, but it still isn't enough, is it?" He clenched his hands against the trembling. "What do you want? What more can I possibly do?"

The cruelty faded from Vee's face. Her lip trembled for the barest second. She swallowed, then drew a long, slow breath. "I wish you'd never done it."

There it was. That was the thing standing between them, the barb she couldn't pull out of her flesh, its match buried in his own.

Sighing, he rubbed his face. "I can't... It happened. I did it. I admit it and, gods, I wish things were different. But I can't change the past. I can't undo it."

She stared back at him. Her nostrils flared, but she said nothing.

"He's right, you know," Perry murmured. "What's done is done."

Vee stiffened, that softness vanishing behind hard lines and tight lips.

Her head jerked away and her gaze landed on the sideboard. Silver glinted, together with the sheen of iridescent feathers. Her earrings.

"Save your words of wisdom for him," she spat. "I won't keep you from your little chat any longer—I only came to get these. You two need plenty of time to blame me for a few more things, eh?" She grabbed the earrings and jammed one in before yanking the door open.

"Vice, please." Perry started forward, brow creased in anguish.

Vee whirled, lip trembling like a loose stone in a wall. "'Not a word you've said is wrong'—that's what you said. And don't insult me by denying it. I heard you." She shook her head. "*I heard you*, Perry." She sucked in a breath and her back straightened, that moment of vulnerability gone. Her gaze flashed to him again, eyes narrowing a fraction. "I heard you both."

Accusation. Hurt. Anger. She was a seething mass of feeling, no matter what she said about being immune to *soft* emotions.

She shoved the other earring in. "You don't have to say anything else to me. *Ever*. I've heard plenty." With a nod, she spun on her heel and strode out, slamming the door in her wake.

Perry started forward, a low sound in her throat.

"No." Knigh put his hand in her path. "Let her go."

He stared at the door. Just the other side, she'd be storming across the deck. Well, Nassau held plenty of distractions. "She'll blow off some steam, then we can talk properly tomorrow." His stomach knotted and his feet itched to follow, but he had to stand firm. "Give her a bit of time to think about it. She'll come around."

"You sound like you're trying to persuade yourself."

Lips pursed, he gave Perry a sidelong look.

She cocked her head, eyebrows raised. "Well, you do."

He sighed. Perhaps he was.

"But"—Perry raised her hands—"maybe you're right. A bit of space, a bit of time to rage, then we can discuss this." She snorted softly, shaking her head. "Hells, maybe she'll be too hungover to be angry come morning."

He nodded, but a hangover had never been known to improve Vee's mood.

Wild Hunt, it wasn't a conversation he relished having, but it was a necessary one.

It was going to be a long night waiting.

CATCHING UP

Vice stomped through Nassau, jaw ticking, teeth grinding. Even fearsome pirates scattered at her approach, backing away against walls to let her pass.

Good. If only everyone would piss off in the same way.

When she'd found the door to Perry's cabin slightly ajar, she'd gone to push it open. But then she'd heard Knigh likening seeking her forgiveness with apologising to the sea and had paused with it half-open, a slight smile in place. Neither of them had noticed her.

Maybe if they had, they wouldn't have gone on.

She played a part in it, too.

Was he right?

Oh yes, because she asked him to arrest her. She'd practically begged him to have the Navy lock her in an iron cage.

How dare he?

And Perry! That was the kicker. *Not a word you've said is wrong.*

She shook her head, veins searing with rage.

Knigh had already betrayed her once, so his words shouldn't have been a surprise. But Perry? Of all the people in the world, Perry had her back.

Or at least that's what she'd thought.

Idiot. You can't trust anyone.

Not even those two.

Talking about her like she was a child who needed managing. Like they were the wise parents, and she needed to learn a lesson at the knee of their astonishing wisdom.

Talking about her feelings as if they could know what she thought or how she felt. As if they could understand a bit of it.

She huffed a tight breath, chest aching and heaving, knuckles and palms sore from her bunched fists.

It wasn't as if she understood her feelings half the time herself.

Her head dipped.

Much easier not to bother.

A familiar form ahead—all compact muscles, face creasing with a smile that flashed against his terracotta skin. Waskar—a friend and sometimes more.

The way he peered past the man he was speaking to, eyebrows rising, was an invitation. Ordinarily, yes, he would've been an ideal candidate to drag into a tavern and drink away the evening with, before wheeling back to his rooms to screw away the night.

Not today.

She winced and ducked into an alley, angling away. No particular destination in mind, she twisted and turned through the streets and lanes, always putting noise at her back.

Quiet. Her feet understood—she needed quiet. And this clear, cooling air as the sun set. Already her boiling blood had eased.

A long walk, then she'd loop back and hit a tavern. Rum would soon make her forget Knigh and Perry.

And what she'd said.

When she'd realised what they were discussing, she'd been frozen in place. The world around her had cracked, like it was made of thin ice and someone walked across it. Her heart had stuttered in its beat.

The pair of them locked in such a deep conversation, so united in her terrible flaws.

When was the last time something had hurt that much?

The spell had only broken when they'd looked at her. Had they seen how she'd felt? The raw flesh beneath the tough shell their words had cracked apart?

Her first instinct had been to run away. But that would've been admitting weakness, letting them win.

Far better to lash out.

And, Wild Hunt take her, she really had lashed out, hadn't she?

She bit her lip, the back of her neck tickling.

You don't have to say anything else to me. Ever.

Maybe she had sounded like a petulant child.

Just a little bit.

And she'd been cruel—then and at the helm when Knigh

had tried to help her, and a million times before. All that after —How had Perry put it?—*his life as it was is over* and he'd given it up to save her.

She squeezed her eyes shut, taking a familiar left turn.

No wonder he'd said *enough's enough.* She shivered, the hairs on the back of her neck straining to attention. Did that mean he was done with her? Completely?

"Well, well, well."

Her step landed heavily, jolting to a stop. That voice, male, low, laced with violence, it threaded through her as cold and dark as her nights in the gibbet. Her hand was already on her sabre as she looked up and actually took in her surroundings.

At the end of the alley stood a man around her height, but far broader. His thick arms were bare except for the tattoos, which gleamed. His pale eyes caught the light, too, glittering and cold.

Vane.

Four men flanked him. A creak of shoe on sand suggested at least one other crept behind her.

"Vane," she said with a bright smile. "What a pleasant surprise."

She turned, keeping him to her right, and angled her head only enough to catch a glimpse back the way she'd come.

Two behind her. One big and burly, the other short and lean. That they'd paired up meant the little one had to be vicious with the two long knives glinting in his hands.

Vane smirked, cocking his head. "I must admit, I'm disappointed. Hadn't expected you to be so easy to sneak up on." He sauntered closer, his men closing in, too. "Not when I've been trying to catch up with you for nigh-on a year now. You're a slippery little fish, Vice."

It would've been easier to respond if she knew exactly what she'd done to piss him off so much. There were rumours, yes, but she had only the haziest of memories of the night in question.

Singing—*loud* singing. An overflowing tankard of rum, the smell sweet and powerfully alcoholic. Standing on a table—dancing. Laughing. Lots and lots of laughing.

Problem was, asking Vane what she'd done to insult him was only likely to wind up his over-tight cable even more. He'd take it as her sticking the boot in by making him recite her terrible crime.

Instead, she raised an eyebrow at him. "One against seven?" She scoffed, shaking her head. "That's hardly 'easy'. Looks to me like you're scared of facing me on your own."

So maybe trying to piss him off further wasn't the best idea. But he was clearly intent on a fight, and perhaps she could make him approach on his own.

The skin around his eyes twitched and his jaw hardened. His face darkened a shade.

Bollocks. Maybe she'd misjudged.

After all, this wasn't some newcomer, green around the gills, who'd bought a ship and fancied himself a pirate.

This was Garlon Vane.

She touched the back of her neck. That's what her body had been trying to warn her about. Her instincts had been paying attention, even if she had not.

Another fight, perhaps.

Her limbs were heavy and sore from facing the *Sovereign's* men and using her gift, but it didn't seem likely Vane would give her a reprieve so she could get food and a nap.

Not when he'd been waiting so long for this.

Fine. So she'd probably end up with a bruised eye, maybe a broken nose. Maybe even a wicked scar. But it wasn't as though he'd kill her. Especially if he didn't know she was no longer with FitzRoy.

She clung to that thin line of hope.

"Fitz is expecting me back, you know."

Vane's eyes widened, and he glanced right—the direction of the docks. "FitzRoy is?" He huffed. "Really? Damn." His eyes narrowed, glinting as he cocked his head at her.

Every inch of her went cold.

"Because," Vane went on, "you'll have a long, wet walk to Inagua to catch up with him. That's where we saw his flash new ship, wasn't it, Fleet?"

The skinny man behind Vice snorted. "That's right. Said he was done with this wench."

Bugger, so that was Fleet? She knew Vane's first mate by reputation only.

The reputation was more than enough.

Not only vicious with his knives, but cruel. If the stories were true, he took great delight in violence.

Well-matched with Vane, by all accounts.

She swallowed, clenching her jaw in an attempt to hide the action. They couldn't know she was afraid.

Because Wild Hunt take her, she was.

Because Vane had her alone in an alley with six of his crew, and he knew she wasn't with FitzRoy.

She pushed a smile on her face and lifted one shoulder. "Can't blame me for trying."

"No, I can't blame you for *that.*" Vane's eyes narrowed, hands straying near his cutlass.

A fight it was, then.

She drew her sabre, and the alley exploded in movement.

Metal sang, boots scraped across sand and cobbles, and Vice grunted, catching one strike, then another.

Light on her feet, she kept the wall at her back and darted for the burly man with Fleet. He was as slow as she'd hoped, and her blade met resistance at once as she slashed his upper arm before reversing her strike and catching his thigh.

Nothing deep, nothing deadly, but it sent him staggering away, clutching his wounds. Out of the fight.

No time even for a sigh of relief, as a cutlass swept in from her right.

Vane.

Muscles sluggish, she barely blocked him. The bandaged cuts to her shoulders and knee pulled with the movement, stinging.

Fresh pain flashed across the back of her calf. That had to be Fleet.

"Bastard," she hissed.

He leered, dodging her half-hearted swipe. "Not according to my mam."

Teeth gritted, still lashing out with her sabre, she sank to one knee, pretending she'd been forced down by the wound.

The sand was cool and dry on her skin as she scooped up a handful.

She parried another strike from Fleet. Their blades rang. Spinning on the balls of her feet, she stood and flung sand in the faces of Vane and the men at his side.

They backed off and scrubbed their eyes, spluttering. Their blades swung wildly.

She ducked away and shoved Fleet. He was wiry but smaller than her and weaker. Without his partner, he was vulnerable to her height and strength.

Good.

He thudded against the wall with a grunt. Blinking and shaking his head, he tried to catch her next blow, but she was too quick for his dazed state.

Red bloomed across his chest. Again, not too deep, but it'd need stitches. As long as he kept it clean, he'd live.

Yellow teeth bared in a wince, he stumbled back.

The way was clear.

She could run.

Running away would be admitting defeat to Vane.

Running back to Knigh and Perry would mean admitting she needed them.

But—

Pain burst. Blackness flashed in her vision. She staggered forward, knee jarring on the floor.

One hand went to the back of her head. It came away warm, wet.

She blinked. She was in a fight. She needed to—

Spinning, she lifted her sabre, but the thing was so heavy,

same as her eyelids.

Come on, Vice.

She pulled in a long breath and shook her head.

The strike jangled through her blade and arm, but she'd caught it—that was the important thing.

She smiled, huffing.

Vane did not.

Movement to her right. Then her face exploded.

White. Black. Sparks and shadow.

She coughed and spat blood. Gods, her cheek had to be on fire. She ran her tongue over the inside where it was already throbbing and tight. Jagged, metallic, raw. It was a mess, she could tell that much.

Was her sabre still in her hand?

She blinked, and the darkness faded. That was the floor, tilting. And her hands were on it, too. No sword.

Everything was a few seconds delayed as she swung her head left and right. It had to be here somewhere. She'd just—

Warm flesh closed around her neck—too tight. Hair tickled her chin, then she was on her knees, someone at her back. She grabbed at—at *an arm*, that's what it was.

Sweat and rum and salt—she could taste it, smell it.

"Don't you worry your pretty little head," Vane murmured in her ear, the hold on her throat tightening. "You're worth more to me alive than dead, much as I'd rather string you up."

The barest whisper of air wheezed into her lungs. Her burning, burning lungs.

Buggeration.

Bollocks.

Bastard.

She clawed, blood hot under her fingernails. She thrashed, but more hands closed on her aching legs and pinned her.

Still. Compliant. Powerless.

Their faces swam into view, grinning and grotesque.

No. She tried to shake her head, pulling at his arm, his flesh.

Nassau was home. Nassau was safe. This couldn't be...

She flailed over her shoulder. If she could get his eyes—

Fingers closed around her wrists. She couldn't move, couldn't breathe.

Her ribcage spasmed, desperately trying to pull in air, but...

Grey crept in at the edges of her vision.

Her head hurt. Her face hurt. Her chest and throat...

Sparks of white light flickered.

"Bloody hells, woman," Vane said in her ear, breath tickling, "you don't give up, do you?"

Never. She wanted to say it, but even her jaw wouldn't work. And her eyelids were drooping. And...

And then, nothing.

THE MORNING AFTER

Light seeped through the stern windows of Knigh's cabin. Even with just a sheet, it was too hot. He grumbled. His eyes burned, and he hadn't even opened them yet. Inhaling long and slow, he reached across the bunk.

Except Vee wasn't there. And never had been.

He sighed. Of course, it had been weeks since they'd shared a bed.

Was she in someone else's right now?

He buried his face in the pillow and groaned.

To keep him from having to share with any crewmates who might want him dead, Perry had given him a small private berth just below Vee's. There was no sound of footsteps above. Or a creaking bunk—at least that was something.

Grimacing, he swallowed back the sharp jealousy that needled him at that thought.

He had no claim over her.

They weren't anything to each other anymore—she'd said herself, they weren't even friends. But it was almost six months since he'd first joined *The Morrigan*, and they'd seen each other almost every day. For a good portion of that time, they'd shared a room.

Her absence was a gaping hole in this little cabin.

He shoved his face harder into the pillow until the air he inhaled was hot and stuffy. Thanks to over a decade in the Royal Navy he was normally an early riser, but right now it was sorely tempting to stay like this.

Last night, sleep had not come easily. He'd played that conversation over in his head a thousand times. Could he have phrased things better? He should've said this, replied with that. He should've made her understand.

He should've gone after her.

No, he'd given her time. That was the right decision. She'd had the evening to stew and the night to come out the other side clearer. This morning she'd be in a better frame of mind to actually speak rather than just lash out.

Which left only one thing to do. Go and face her.

With a huff, he pulled his face from the pillow and rolled out of bed. He splashed last night's water on himself and dressed quickly.

He needed to tell her what he'd told Perry, just in a slightly kinder way. It sounded more like she was angry about the fact they'd been speaking about her than the content of that conversation.

Or was he just trying to convince himself? Hands running through his too-thick hair, he winced in the cracked mirror.

There was no more putting it off. Or trying to comfort himself.

This wasn't going to be a fun conversation, but it had to be done.

He had to find Vee and have it out, once and for all.

THERE WAS no sign of her up on deck. No surprise, if she'd been out carousing until late. With her lingering weakness and propensity to overwork herself, Perry still had her on a strict half-watch. And being in port, they only had a handful of crew on duty at a time. Vee wouldn't be needed for some hours yet.

But there was no answer at her cabin door, either. Still asleep, perhaps? It wasn't locked.

Just a glance. But when he opened the door, her bunk was empty. It hadn't been made, exactly, certainly not by any naval measure, but the fact the blanket had been pulled up and Barnacle's cushion placed in the middle was Vee's version of making her bunk. That was usually done some time around midday when she almost tripped over said blanket discarded on the floor.

So the bed hadn't been slept in.

His stomach clenched.

No claim on her. She can do what she wants.

But he ground his teeth all the way up to the quarterdeck, where Perry was speaking to the ship's carpenter about repairs. She acknowledged him with a quick nod, finished her conversation, then wandered over wearing a look that was equal parts wince and smile.

Her green eyes skimmed over him. The look became more wince than smile. "Have you spoken to her, then?"

"I was coming to ask you the same thing—I haven't seen her yet." He stood at the fore rail and scanned the rest of the ship in case, by some miracle, she was already up and working.

Perry scoffed. "I did wonder if she might come to you late last night for a drunken argument." She lifted a shoulder, cocking her head. "I wouldn't worry too much. I'm sure she was out drinking. She usually finds her way home, eventually, sleeps a few hours in her bunk, and emerges just in time for her watch."

The sun was already warm enough to seep through his shirt and bring sweat on the brows of men and women on the docks, sawing timbers for their repairs, but goosebumps rose on his skin. She must've spent the night with someone else. His stomach wrung as tight as sheets in a washerwoman's hands.

She can do what she wants.

He cleared his throat. "She—uh—she's not in her bunk. I've already checked."

"Oh?" Perry glanced up at him, eyebrows raised. *"Oh."* She turned away, but not before he spotted the grimace wrinkling around her eyes.

He shuddered. Even Perry thought it, and she knew Vee better than he did. At least Aedan was on deck helping the carpenters, so she hadn't found her way to him last night.

Was that really any comfort?

He raked his hair, sighing. He should've gone after her. No

matter how much she snapped back at him, he could've explained it then and there, got it all over and done with.

"Come on," Perry sighed. "Let's go and find her, since I'm clearly not going to get any work out of you before we do."

They checked the deck and the sleeping quarters below. No one had seen Vice, and she hadn't ended up in some empty hammock by accident.

Perhaps she was still drinking.

But most of the taverns were shut. The owners Perry knew well enough to rouse at this time in the morning opened up their doors and let them have a look around, just in case she'd crawled under a table and passed out. No Vee under any tables, benches, or even in cupboards under stairs.

Perry kept up a steady stream of cheerful chatter as they checked the handful of taverns that were open, ready to serve pirates ale and rum at whatever time they saw fit. But no, Vee wasn't in a corner, stewing.

By the time they entered the first of the shops Vee included in her errand circuit, Perry had stopped bothering to fill the gaps in conversation when Knigh didn't reply. When they were halfway through the town, her conversation stopped altogether. And by the time they went to Waters, who had fully recovered from his attack, her face had grown pinched.

Knigh's stomach had dropped so far over the course of the day, it was somewhere below ground. As they left Waters' shop, he shook his head. "What if she got so drunk, she fell off the jetty on the way back to the ship and drowned?"

Perry raised an eyebrow. "You really think Vice could drown?"

He screwed up his face and sighed. "Do you have any better ideas?"

Any amusement evaporated from her face and she pursed her lips, looking ahead, towards the docks. "I bet she's back at the *Respair*. Nassau's a big place. We just missed her." She chuckled. "Yes, I bet she's just starting her watch now on no sleep with a raging hangover, whilst cursing you and me and the sail she's repairing. Let's go."

But Vee wasn't at the *Respair* and hadn't been all day.

Where the hells could she be? Was one of her friends hiding her? Waters would—she'd mentioned how they'd spent evenings chatting and drinking in the rooms above his shop, so they were good enough friends for that.

"Don't worry," Perry said, but her smile was tight. "Wherever she stayed last night, she'll want her own bed tonight. She'll come crawling along the dock as the sun sets, give you and me a good glare, gather up Barnacle in her arms, and slink away to her cabin. Just you wait and see."

His jaw clenched. Waiting sat wrong in his bones, a heavy, creaking feeling, but there was nothing more he could do right now. Constantly glancing at the wharves, Knigh found himself some busy work on deck—replacing lines, hauling fresh and repaired canvas, lifting new planks and joists wherever the carpenters ordered.

Aedan nodded and stayed silent as they worked together to move the timbers, but that didn't matter. All that mattered was Vee coming back soon.

As the sky lit up with jewel tones of pink and orange, Aedan finally cracked. "Nearly sunset and she's still not back?" He chuckled, but his brows were drawn together into a frown. "She'll be bloody knackered."

Knigh opened his mouth to reply, but no words would come out. Instead, he nodded and continued working and watching the jetty.

Sunset faded and stars came out, twinkling in the deepening sky.

With the dying light, the work had stopped, but Knigh still stood on deck, leaning on the rail, eyes burning as he stared at the approach to the *Respair*. Most of the crew had gone drinking, but Saba, Lizzy, Aedan, Wynn, and Effie had swapped with others so they could stay on watch. They loitered on deck, jumping every time someone walked past.

Saba's knife scraped against the piece of driftwood she was whittling into another animal. This one, long and thin, looked like it would become a lizard. She barely looked at it, but apparently her slender fingers knew what to do, because the shape still emerged, sinuous and sleek.

Knigh couldn't decide if the constant scrape, scrape, scrape was comforting or irritating.

Perry appeared at Knigh's side, hands resting on the rail. "Still nothing?"

The back of his neck prickled and goosebumps flooded his skin. Hearing someone refer to her absence out loud somehow made it much worse.

You don't have to say anything else to me. Ever.

He swallowed twice before he could speak past the blockage in his throat. "She's gone."

IN THE HOLD

Rocking, creaking, salt, and... burning? Her wrists were too hot. And, gods, the back of her head throbbed. Her face, too, as she screwed her eyes shut tighter. It was definitely swollen and her mouth felt like something had died in it.

Vice ran her tongue over the inside of her cheek.

Hmm, yes... She'd had a fight with Vane and his gang, hadn't she?

Maybe the blow to the head had been worse than she realised, because her stomach churned. Couldn't be seasickness—she'd never had that, even on her first voyage, even in the worst seas.

At least the others must've found her and brought her back to the *Respair*. Amongst the briny scent of a ship lingered honey and something herbal—Lizzy had checked her injuries and applied a salve, then.

Every inch of her body ached. Getting up was too much effort. Why hadn't they put her on the bed?

She gave a wheezing sigh, throat tender from Vane's crushing hold. She tried to rub her face, but weight dragged at her wrists and there was a *clink* as she moved.

The back of her neck prickled.

That feeling in her stomach. The too-hot, almost burning feeling at her wrists.

Iron.

Gasping, she opened her eyes and tried to spring upright. The world tilted, stopping her in a sitting position.

Shackles bound her, only the linen of her shirt between iron and skin. She'd been secured to a seeping hull by a length of chain.

This was not her cabin.

In the dim light, black spots bloomed at the edges of her vision.

Past the honey and salt, a dank stink hung in the air—dirt and stale water and dead rats. She wrinkled her nose. The bilges.

Buggeration, this wasn't even the *Respair*. Its hull didn't leak like this. No part of it was this dirty. They were pirates, but Perry kept a clean ship and Barnacle was a fine ratter.

She swallowed back nausea.

Where the hells was she?

Lights flashed in her vision, shocking against the black splodges as she turned her head. She managed to pick out bars and a corridor beyond that ran left to right. Dull lamplight came from one end.

The dizziness—she closed her eyes as it rose higher and higher, threatening to close over her like a rising tide.

Bile in her mouth. Her head knocked against something. Was she lying down now?

Voices. Distant, echoing along the corridor.

She forced her eyes open, groaning. The bars swam in and out of focus beyond the shifting bright and dark spots invading from the edges of her vision.

Louder. They were coming closer.

Who was it? She had to stay awake. They couldn't—

The dizziness rose and consumed her like a great wave. The blackness blotted out the bars, the light, the voices.

Everything.

When she woke again, her head didn't hurt so much, but her stomach still turned and her body was stiff like she'd been in the same position a long while. There was someone in the cell. Just a faint scrape of boots on the deck, but it was enough to give them away with her eyes still shut.

Light pressed through her eyelids. Someone with a lamp.

Scowling, despite the way it made her cheek throb, she opened her eyes and pushed herself to sitting.

The lamp was only a few feet away, too bright, too harsh against the darkness. Once she'd blinked away the shock of it, the face beyond started to resolve into something more than yellow light—into Garlon bloody Vane.

Her stomach clenched. So he hadn't just beaten her up and

left her in the alley, he'd taken her. *Kidnapped* felt too ridiculous a word. She was Lady Vice, the terrifying bane of the Royal Navy, the Pirate Queen; she didn't get *kidnapped*.

Until now.

"Oh, look," Vane said, breaking into a grin, "Sleeping Beauty's woken up." His eyes narrowed. "Although the way your cheek's all puffed up, you're more beast than beauty."

"Different stories, dickhead," she muttered, checking the back of her head. A bump the size of half a lime. Her hair was thick with blood and that salve she'd smelled before. She'd had worse. That he'd had it treated suggested he wasn't about to murder her.

Now there was a lamp in here, she could see her cell better. Iron rings and bands studded the deck and bulkheads. A former slave ship. Her stomach turned.

It had brought men and women captured in war from Noreg, the seas around Albion, the Inland Sea, and further south in Alkebulan and transported them here as the cheapest possible labour for those who'd bought parcels of land from the Arawakéan Union.

So Vane had taken such a ship for his own. What had he done with the enslaved people on board? Some pirates gave them back their freedom, others made them join the crew. Many offered the choice. There were others who sold those people, just as the slavers originally planned. A few, though, men like Ned Low, tossed them overboard. *Too much trouble*, they said.

She grimaced at Vane. Those words wouldn't sound out of place coming from him.

"Ah"—he waved a hand—"same difference. And stories are all lies, anyway, so what does it matter?"

Lies, maybe, but they told the truth all the same. That conversation was destined to go nowhere, though.

"You've messed up, Vane," she said loud enough that any crew in the corridor would hear.

"How'd you figure that? You're the one in my brig."

"Do you really think you or your crew will be able to buy a single thing in Nassau ever again when this gets out? You know they all love me there." Shaking her head, she clicked her tongue. "And that's not to mention what my friends will do when they come for me. You do know we've got a berserker in the crew now? And I think he might well be in love with me."

Her throat closed as soon as she said it. It was rubbish, of course. Just crap to scare Vane, but...

She coughed away the discomfort and went on, "When he finds out what you've done, he'll murder you with his bare hands."

"A berserker?" he asked, head cocking. "Is that who you were having a go at right before you stormed out?"

She froze. Even her lungs paused, mid-inhale. How did he know?

"What was it Fleet heard you say?" He narrowed his eyes as if racking his brain. "Oh yes! 'You don't have to say anything else to me. Ever.'" His teeth bared in a slow grin.

Bollocks.

Fleet must've been on the docks and overheard—she hadn't exactly been quiet. No doubt, Vane's crew knew to always keep an eye out for her.

"Yeeeeesss"—he dragged out the word in a way that made her want to punch him in the face—"I don't think I'm going to be too worried about your friends coming for you. Not after that bust-up. They'll just think you've walked out."

Her eyes burned as she stared up at him. No, they wouldn't think that. Maybe she spat and hissed, but she was loyal. That ship was her home. That crew...

No, they knew she wouldn't leave without a word over something like this. Without her things, without the clues, without Barnacle, especially now she was expecting kittens.

Never.

But if he was wrong, why were her eyes stinging so much?

JETSAM

The day after her chat with Vane, the ship's movement changed.

Head cocked, Vice frowned. Her first instinct was to reach out with her gift, but thanks to the damn shackles, that was impossible. Also thanks to the shackles, queasiness was her constant companion, but at least it wasn't that same bone-deep weariness and horrible wasting that she'd faced in the iron cage.

She rubbed her stomach, focusing on the deck beneath her. The sea outside was quieter. The ship moved less. They must've set anchor.

From above came shouts. Orders. Greetings. Not surprise or fear or the start of battle.

There was no bump of arriving at a jetty, so they'd pulled up by another ship. One sailed by allies of Vane's and thus enemies of hers.

Within ten minutes, Fleet appeared at the bars, knife in one hand, key in the other, and a burly woman at his side.

"Time to chuck the jetsam," he said as he unchained her shackles from the wall.

She ground her teeth against the desire to wring his throat with her bound hands. She wouldn't get far on a ship full of enemies. Instead, she let him lead her up on deck.

The sunlight burned, blinding as she stumbled from the companionway. Quick as her eyes were to adjust to the dark, thanks to her fae blood, they were slow to recover after days belowdecks, and the journey across the ship was nothing more than shapes, some still, some moving.

Men and women's voices rose in work, others only muttered. Fleet's fingers bit into her arm, guiding her.

"Here's your stop, Vice," Vane said. Gods, the bastard sounded smug.

There was a step up, then a wobble—a gangplank? They were moving her to another ship. Whose?

Her heart pounded as she squinted ahead. Shadows, dark blue, white sails above, a quieter crew. Those few voices she caught were all male, all with Albionic accents, rather than the riot of different speech patterns and lilts heard on a pirate ship.

The hairs on the back of her neck tickled.

No. He wouldn't...

Teeth gritted, she blinked again, hard, and angled her face from the sun.

Dark blue uniforms on every man. All of them staring at her. And this ship—it was huge.

A warship.

He bloody well had.

Vane had sold her to the Royal Navy.

She glared at the back of his head as he led the way to the stern, down a companionway and through a set of double doors.

Like a creature waking from winter hibernation, her stomach turned slowly.

Some part of her knew before she saw the familiar white and black chequered tiles, but at the sight of those, there could be no doubt.

This was the *Sovereign* and Vane had sold her off to—

"Your Royal Highness," Vane said, voice smooth as oil. Beyond him was a table, surrounded by empty seats. She couldn't see past him to the person sitting at its head, but there was only one man it could be. "I've brought a gift."

He bowed, arms flourishing ridiculously, then stepped aside, revealing a gilded chair, more suited to a throne room than a dining table. And on it—the Duke of Mercia.

His darkest brown eyes locked with hers. A smirk twitched at the corner of his mouth as his thumb stroked his chin, but the glint in his eyes was far from amused.

It was triumphant.

"Bow for the prince, then," Fleet hissed in her ear.

A jab at the back of her knees sent her to the floor. She sucked in a breath, ready to turn and growl a threat, but the iron links between her shackles brushed the back of her hand, searing her skin and making her cry out instead.

Pain streaked through her and sparked along her nerves. She yanked her hands as far apart as she could, holding the shackles taut until there was no danger of the links slipping against bare skin. Head bowed, she focused on her breath.

Slow. Deep. Think about that, not the pain, not the pain.

The Duke made a thoughtful sound, drawing her attention. "A gift, is it, Mr Vane?" His gaze slid to the pirate, the smirk fading. "I prefer my gifts to be better treated."

Had he guessed the iron had burned her? Or was he just commenting on her bruised face? She clenched her fists against the urge to touch her cheek and see how swollen it was. At least it didn't throb anymore—the burn across the back of her hand eclipsed that.

"And," the Duke went on, "gifts tend not to be presented with the expectation of reward."

Vane raised his open hands as if helpless. "She didn't give me much choice."

"No, I suppose she wouldn't." Eyes narrowing, the Duke turned back to her.

Not amusement in his eyes, maybe not even triumph. *Evaluation.*

A chill threaded down her back. Evaluation *for what?*

"Well, I have her now. That's the important thing. Good work, Mr Vane." He nodded to one of the men nearby—this one wore a black suit rather than uniform. A personal servant, not a naval man. "I will always reward loyalty." He dismissed Vane with a flick of his fingers.

With another theatrical bow at Mercia and a sneer at her, Vane followed Fleet and the servant out. Was she better off with him or the Duke?

Once the door closed, Mercia nodded at one of the two

remaining men—these both in Navy uniform. "Get those *things* off her." He wrinkled his nose, shaking his head as if Vane had left a bucket of excrement behind.

The younger of the two, blond, perhaps a couple of years younger than she was, unlocked the shackles, while the other gripped her arm tight enough to bruise. Despite that dull pain, she huffed with relief as the iron's heat left her wrists and the queasiness subsided.

"And out of my sight, in fact, Evans." He waved off the blond man holding the shackles. He didn't stop to watch Evans open the door and hand them to someone outside, just narrowed his eyes at her, head cocking. "Come here." He sat back and indicated the chair to his right.

He didn't say it unkindly, just with the manner of someone who'd always been obeyed. Like Papa.

That thought was enough to make her grit her teeth and stay put.

He sighed and rolled his eyes. "Bring her."

The next thing she knew, the man who'd been holding her dragged her to her feet. He grunted, maybe surprised to find a woman so heavy, but she was tall and not built like a damsel. Evans made an uncertain sound at her side, his grip light on her other arm, encouraging her along, rather than forcing.

She gave a grim smile, even as they deposited her on the chair. They returned to their posts by the double doors and she tried not to look like she was watching them. They were maybe twelve feet away, armed. The Duke had no visible weapons, but that didn't mean—

"Madam," he said, voice laced with another sigh, "even if

you did overpower me *and* my men, where would you go? I have an entire ship full of the Royal Navy's best, including riflemen in the tops. And you"—he narrowed his eyes, leaning closer—"are clearly weakened." He held out his hands. "Give me your wrists."

She blinked at the request, stared at his pale palms. If she refused, he'd just grab her or have his men do it.

Huffing, she offered her wrists for inspection, but she kept her hands fisted and didn't place herself in his grasp. It was a small rebellion, but that was all she had, for now.

With a heavy exhale, he took her wrists, surprisingly gentle, and pushed up her shirt cuffs. A few times, her sleeves had slipped, mostly in her sleep, leaving several little brown burns. The fresh one on the back of her hand was raw and red, already blistering.

He clicked his tongue and shook his head. "Iron. Vile stuff." A shudder shook through him.

Was that *empathy?* From the Duke of Mercia? Frowning, she watched him run his thumb over one of the burns.

"Interesting, though." He released his grip and eyed her for a long while. "Such little marks, and yet they reveal so much. It appears I owe you an apology." His crimson eyebrows rose. "I offered a reward for your capture, but I made it clear that you were not to be harmed. Had I known, I'd have included an instruction not to let iron touch your fair skin."

Damnation. He knew what she was. Fae-blooded, descended from the fair folk, rather than only blessed by them like fae-*touched* magic-users. More powerful and with more than one gift. Did that make her more valuable to him? Or more of a threat? Did it mean he wouldn't take her back to Albion for execution? She clenched her jaw.

"Don't look at me like that, as if I couldn't possibly apologise. I'm not a monster." He chuckled, then leant closer still, a conspiratorial edge to his tone. "I detest iron—unsurprising for someone fae-blooded, perhaps—but even its use on an enemy fills me with distaste. I know well its terrible burn." He smiled bitterly. "At the Grays' ball, you praised my mother for her wisdom, but kindness is a different matter entirely. I owe my knowledge of iron's caress to her. She made my sister and me both touch it as children." He scoffed and sank back in his chair, gaze drifting away from her to somewhere far away and long ago. A diamond stud glittered in his ear as he tugged the lobe. "A warning, she called it." He opened his hand, revealing a silvery burn across his palm.

A chill cloaked Vice. The queen had forced her own children to touch iron?

No, the woman she'd known wouldn't...

But she couldn't keep her eyes off the thin, raised line marring his pale skin. It was the exact same colour as the silvery padlock burned into her own palm. That had been iron, used against her by her own father.

How well had she really known the old queen?

She shook her head, exhaling. Gods, no, what was she thinking? Was she so weak-willed to let him get into her head this easily?

Remember what Knigh said. He laughed. He egged Knigh on to kill men who'd surrendered.

But when she looked back at the Duke, he was staring at

the burn, expression drawn into a frown, something sad in the set of his mouth.

Good, he was distracted. And now she was rid of that iron...

She reached for the sea, letting out a shaky breath when it greeted her, as cool and comforting as fresh bed sheets after a fever. Maybe she could turn the ship off course or find clouds to raise into a storm and force them to a safe harbour. Once on land, she could make a run for it. Or, perhaps—

"My word," he breathed.

She flinched—she'd drifted away with the sea and hadn't realised his attention was back on her. An innocent smile flashing in place, she blinked.

He watched her like a sabrecat assessing prey. "Such power. It's rolling off you. I'd assumed you were a fae-touched sea witch. But you're not just fae-blooded, it's..." He shook his head, eyes narrowed in thought. "*Recent* blood. You have more power than my own sister, you know." He scoffed. "And what do you do with it? Throw it away on piracy. You could have the world at your feet, but instead you drum up silly songs amongst your adoring fans."

"I didn't ask for any songs," she said, but his words echoed in her mind.

You have more power than my own sister.

Her magic was stronger than the new Queen's?

"And yet they sing them all the same." He watched her, calculation in the tilt of his head. "It's a shame you won't hear them do so again."

She smiled at him through gritted teeth. "My friends will come before you execute me."

He chuckled, shaking his head. "I'm sure they will." He sat back, half slumping against the arm of his almost-throne, casual in that way only someone born to power could be. With a smile, he sent the hairs on the back of her neck to attention. "But if they try to rescue you, I'll have my creature kill them all."

She shuddered, goosebumps chasing across her flesh. Those tentacles.

He nodded to his men. "Do not mistake my mercy for weakness, madam. I'll not hesitate to crush your friends should they become an inconvenience. And much as I loathe the stuff, I'll return you to irons if you attempt to use your gift without my express permission."

The two guards appeared at her sides, taking her by the elbows as if to pull her upright.

A low sound in her throat, she shook them off and rose, glaring at the Duke. He knew the pain of iron to someone fae-blooded, yet he still threatened her with it. What a piece of work.

She followed the guards to the doors, glowering.

Then it dawned on her—he spoke of iron, not execution. If he was planning to execute her here or take her back to Albion to face the hanging she'd avoided, surely he'd have threatened to bring such a punishment forward or do it more painfully?

He wasn't the sort of man who'd shy away from reminding her exactly what trouble she was in.

If you attempt to use your gift without my express permission.

Did that mean he was going to give her permission to use her gift at some point?

At the doorway, she turned and frowned at him. He still lounged in his almost-throne. "You said you didn't want me harmed. Normally with pirates it's 'dead or alive'. And if you were planning to have me executed, what does it matter if I'm hurt?"

He arched one eyebrow, the corner of his mouth rising. He said nothing.

The guards grew impatient, hands wrapping around her arms, dragging her out the door.

She twisted in their grasp, still staring back at the Duke, cold dread tickling down her back. "What do you want with me?"

He only smiled.

SEARCH PARTY

Knigh poked his head through a tavern doorway. He'd already checked this one at lunchtime, but perhaps...

The barkeep glanced up from cuffing a wayward customer around the ear and met Knigh's questioning gaze. Her rouged lips thinned with an apologetic smile and she shook her head.

Still nothing.

It was two nights since Vee had stomped away from the *Respair*, angry and hurt. No one had seen her. No one had heard from her.

Or at least no one who'd say anything.

He clenched his useless fists, backing out the door.

Above, the sky was bright with orange and red splashes chasing the setting sun. It had no business being so cheerful when she was gone.

With a glower at the offensive sunset, he made for the

waterfront tavern where he'd arranged to meet the others. Perhaps they had news.

When he walked in, the drawn looks on Perry and Aedan's faces said they had no answers, either.

He bit back a sigh and waved for the barkeep's attention before joining them. At least he and Aedan had found their own brand of camaraderie while looking for Vee. It was about the only thread of hope he could find in all this.

"Nothing then?" he asked, slumping into his seat.

"Not even the proverbial sausage," Perry said, staring into the dregs of her drink swirling around the bottom of her tankard. "Wynn and Effie have already reported in—nothing from them, either."

Aedan's jaw ticked, and he shook his head. "It's like she's disappeared."

"Or doesn't want to be found," Knigh muttered, nodding thanks to the barkeep as he deposited a brimming tankard on the table.

Perry's brows contracted, and she also shook her head as a smile creaked into place. "Maybe Saba's heard something." Her gaze slipped past him to the door and her brows rose expectantly. "Or Lizzy—here she is." She waved her over, calling for another drink.

Lizzy's freckled cheeks were pink and her breaths laboured as she dropped into her seat.

Knigh leant forward, lowering his tankard from his lips. "News?"

"Tracked down Waskar"—her eyes slid from him to Perry—"her fella around here."

Knigh's fingers twitched around the cup. A lover, then.

Lizzy caught her breath. "He saw her that night."

Knigh stilled, chest tight and aching as his stomach plummeted. Did that mean...? He swallowed, windpipe suddenly too narrow. Did he really want to know?

Lizzy quaffed her drink as soon as the barkeep set it down and wiped her mouth with the back of her hand. "On the road near the Straw Mare. Didn't get to speak to her—she met his eye but ducked away before he could catch up to her. Not seen her since."

In different circumstances, he might've sighed with relief. But if she wasn't staying with this Waskar, where the hells was she?

He shook his head. "So, she's left. That's the only remaining answer. Someone must have helped her get away or saw her on another ship. Surely?"

Perry's eyes widened. "No, she wouldn't—"

"Wouldn't she, Perry?" He stared back at her. He didn't want to believe it, but... "We've both seen her do some impressively stupid things when..." *When emotionally spooked* was what he wanted to say, but it didn't feel right to discuss Vee's feelings when she refused to even talk about them herself. Not after last time.

"No," Aedan huffed, shaking his head too hard too many times. "She wouldn't just walk out without saying anything."

The man was in love with her. It was written all over his face, in those deep lines between his brows, in the anguish dulling his blue eyes.

Most of all, in the way he steadfastly refused to believe she'd leave.

"I hate to say it," Lizzy murmured, watching him with an awkward twist of her mouth, "but I think Blackwood's right. She's gone."

Teeth grinding, Knigh picked at some fluff on his cuff. Grey fur mixed with a loose thread.

Barnacle's fur. The same fur Vee had buried her face in and sobbed against the night he'd taken her from the gibbet.

Vee might be pissed off enough with him and Perry to disappear like this, but she'd never leave Barnacle. Not through choice. And not when she was expecting kittens.

Or maybe she figured Barnacle was safe with them for the moment and she'd come back for her later? Was he being as much of an overoptimistic fool as Aedan?

He cocked his head at Lizzy, who was watching him over the brim of her tankard.

Wild Hunt, did he look as love-struck as Aedan?

He raked his hands through his hair. *Get a grip, Knigh. Vee is off-limits.*

Lizzy cleared her throat. "You could—"

"Saba!" Perry was on her feet, eyebrows raised, mouth open and turned up at the corner—the picture of hope. "Have you...?"

Saba sauntered over, silent, but her jaw was tighter than a brawler's fist—that must've been what had cut Perry off. Her chest heaved as she shook her head. She opened her mouth as if to speak, but just let out a heavy breath, lower lip wobbling.

Every one of Knigh's veins ran cold. Saba had been cheerful

when they'd set out this morning, smiling and joking about how they'd find her asleep in a bush somewhere or tucked up in someone's jolly boat, still stewing.

She dropped something on the table, metallic and bright. Knigh darted forward, scooping it up before Aedan or Perry reached it. A hoop of cool metal, bright feathers.

Vee's earring. One of the pair she'd snatched from Perry's room that night and rammed into her ears.

"I made those for her," Saba said, voice raw. "She'd never leave them. Not through choice." She gave each person at the table a wide-eyed look, still standing even though Lizzy had pulled out a chair.

Knigh blinked slowly, glanced down at the earring, then back up at Saba. "Where"—he stopped, voice too loud in his ears—"where did you—?"

"In an alley on the other side of town." She took Aedan's tankard from his hand and drained it before slamming it on the table, eyes closed, deep lines between her eyebrows. "There was"—she shook her head, eyes still shut—"the sand had been scuffed up and—and..."

Knigh's stomach roiled and a dull roaring began in his ears. The earring left behind... sand disturbed...

Saba dragged in a shuddering breath and fixed her eyes on her captain. "Perry," she said, voice cracking, "the place was covered in blood."

Knigh blinked, the motion slow. He'd misheard. This blasted roaring had made him think she'd said... "Blood?" He swallowed, making his ears pop. That was better. He could hear properly now.

He held his breath, ears straining, muscles thrumming with how tightly he held still.

Saba sank into the chair, hands over her face.

He tried to push a comforting smile in place. She was going to tell them the alley was covered in—in... something else. Not—

She nodded. "Blood."

GIFTS

Abath? Vice narrowed her eyes.

It was a few hours since she'd arrived and she was in the small quarters she'd been given, watching cabin boys fill a copper bath with steaming water.

Being Mercia's captive became stranger and stranger. First, her wounds had been healed—the *Sovereign* had a fae-touched healer on board, just as Knigh had said. That she warranted healing where Billy hadn't suggested she was worth more to Mercia than his own men.

Then there was the comfortably furnished cabin with its cosy bunk, brocade-upholstered armchair, and even a washstand.

And now they'd brought the bath and all these buckets of gloriously warm water.

But a bath in itself wasn't dangerous, so she took advantage of the opportunity to wash away the dirt from the fight and Vane's ship.

Besides, it wasn't the bath that had her wary—it was *why* she was being bathed.

And the fact the bath came with a beautiful gown of deep purple silk. The fabric was still crisp, not softened with wear, so it was new. The skirts were long enough to cover her ankles, despite her height, so perhaps it had been made for her or at least another tall woman.

That was cause enough for suspicion.

Still, they were clean clothes, unlike her bloodstained waistcoat, shirt, and breeches.

But there was only one reason she'd be dressed up so prettily.

She waved off help from the grey-haired man who'd brought the gown and dismissed him, insisting she'd get herself ready. Although she'd grown up with a maid, she was used to dressing herself. Plus, it would be difficult to hide the Copper Drake in her pocket if he helped with her clothes.

Eyes narrowed in the mirror, she pinned up her hair in what was almost an elegant style, except that the twists were loose and a few too many tendrils fell around her face and down her neck. She smiled at the effect.

Artfully messy.

She might be wearing the gown he'd sent, but she'd still stamp her own identity on her appearance. Other than the Copper Drake, the only things here that belonged to *her* were the jewelled drake pin, Evered's opal ring, and one earring of the pair Saba had made her. When she'd woken on Vane's ship, the other had been missing. She took it from the sideboard, feathers tickling her palm, and poked it through her earlobe. A large hoop with dangling feathers and just the one, not a matching pair—decidedly un-ladylike. Maybe it would annoy Mercia. At the very least, it would remind him who she was.

A short while later, four guards appeared at the door and her efforts were rewarded with their lingering looks. The one who'd removed the shackles was amongst them—Mercia had called him Evans. He too stared a moment too long before looking away, cheeks pink.

That was an angle she might be able to take advantage of— after all, she was on a ship full of men. Wasn't that why so many captains had denied her a place on their ships when she'd first tried to run away with Evered all those years ago? What had they called her? *A distraction.* Good. Let her looks be a distraction she could use this time. Perhaps if she flirted and played the helpless lady, she'd find a way to escape.

The uniformed men escorted her through the ship, Evans' hand a light guidance on her elbow. Up a companionway, turn right, right again. She followed the route, committing it to memory. There was no Knigh to help her find her way around the *Sovereign* now.

Her stomach seethed, part-anger, part something else.

Urgh, the *something else* was horribly close to regret. If he were here, or Perry, it would be a comfort. She wrinkled her nose at the admission, even if it was only to herself.

Eventually, they reached the now-familiar checkerboard tiled cabin, which had been transformed into a luxurious dining room with three places set and two already occupied.

Mercia and George, in smart silk suits that gleamed in the candlelight.

Both watched her enter, offering formal greetings before the Duke dismissed his guards.

So confident? There were knives on the table. She could probably overpower the pair of them and maybe the two midshipmen at the doors, even if Mercia was also fae-blooded. The grey-haired valet who'd brought her clothes and bath was here, arranging dishes on the sideboard. She'd spotted him straining to shift the bath after it was part-filled—he wasn't especially strong.

With a sweet smile, she inclined her head to the two gentlemen, trying not to look like she was checking for other weapons or working out whether the windows were locked.

Grab a knife, threaten one to force the other to back away and keep them silent. Get the window open, then jump out and trust herself to the sea.

Her heart sped as she took the seat the valet pulled out. The gown would drag in the water, yes, but with her gift she'd be able to stay afloat long enough to shuck off a few layers.

The question was, how far would she need to go?

"It's good of you to join us, madam," Mercia said, gesturing to the valet without looking at him.

She arched an eyebrow. "I was powerless to resist such a charming invitation."

He chuckled and quaffed wine, gaze lingering on her single earring.

George frowned, looking away from her to his finger tapping on the tabletop.

"I'd quite forgotten about your pert wit." Mercia scoffed, raising his glass to be refilled, then gesturing for the servant to attend to hers.

He approached, offering a decanter of white and another of red. Mercia was drinking red, so she chose the same—at least that meant it was unlikely to be poisoned.

But he didn't seem to want her dead, so maybe that wasn't something she needed to worry about. As a flurry of boys brought in more platters of food, she ground her teeth. She'd already asked what he wanted with her and the look he'd worn said that not only wasn't he going to tell, but that he'd enjoyed seeing her powerless, uncertain, desperate for information.

She'd be damned if she'd give him that satisfaction again.

And for now, the roasted meats, stewed vegetables, and thick gravy wafted a rich savoury scent through the air that had her mouth watering. They had brought lunch to her cabin. Other than the locked door, she couldn't accuse Mercia of being a poor host. But that had been hours ago, and her body was still repairing itself.

Mercia raised an eyebrow as she selected the correct knife and fork from the half dozen at her place setting, but didn't ask about it. Still, it had to be a hint to him that she knew etiquette and all the other stupid aristocratic rules, even if she didn't always choose to obey them.

He and George made small talk as they ate. George even asked about her accent and where she was from. She didn't answer.

"Well, we know she's Albionic," Mercia said, eyeing her as

she sliced through a plump chicken breast. "After all, she's fae-blooded."

George's eyebrows rose, and he turned to her, head cocked.

I can't change the past.

Vice's stomach lurched. It was the exact same angle Knigh's head tilted to when he was curious or teasing. She gritted her teeth and sawed into the chicken until her knife shrieked against the plate.

"The royal library includes records of all families with a fae bloodline, you know." Mercia's eyes bored into her as if he wished the records were before him and he could find her name amongst them.

Well, he wouldn't find the Ferrers family even if he had every record that had ever been made of fae-blooded families. Hers was not official.

George still watched her, hazel eyes ablaze with curiosity, mouth slightly pursed.

Lords, it was unbearable—his expressions reminded her too much of Knigh. George's were the unguarded versions of those little tells she so often glimpsed in his brother.

She kept her head down after that, focusing on the food until they stopped trying to engage her.

Then she let her attention drift out to sea. With any luck, Mercia wouldn't realise she was using her gift and follow through on his threat of iron. Besides, just *feeling* the sea surely didn't count as using her gift. She wasn't making anything happen. She kept her eyes lowered to be on the safe side.

Wide, deep ocean.

She bit back a sigh of relief at the welcome sensation of

water, currents, tides, waves. This ship was strange, too large, but the sea? That was familiar.

But—she frowned—it was also wide. Too wide. They were far from land. Even if she could get a window open and jump out, she had nowhere to go.

The roasted chicken might as well have been leather.

Mechanically, she chewed and chewed, but swallowing was suddenly impossible. She took a long draught of wine and choked it down.

Nowhere to go. No escape. At least for now.

There would be a chance. They'd have to put in at a port at some point or even a little island. And she'd be ready. Maybe she could sneak a knife away from the table.

Once the dessert plates had been cleared, Mercia dismissed the valet and the midshipmen who'd helped serve them. If they'd been close to land, this would've been an even better chance to escape.

"Come now, madam," he said, smiling as he tapped a claw on the table, "you can't expect us to call you *Lady Vice*. We're not asking your true name, just your real one—the one people must have called you at feast day balls. There's no power in giving us that."

Admit nothing. She smiled back, baring her teeth a little too much for politeness. "My name is Vice."

He exhaled, lips tightening.

George shifted in his seat. His expression was all relaxed friendliness—the one aristocrats learned to wear even when seated opposite their bitterest rival at a dinner party. But tension rang in the press of his fingertips against his glass and the angle of his shoulders.

"You know," Mercia said, sitting back casually, although his gaze on her was anything but, "I could just order you to tell me."

She lifted a shoulder. "You could. I wouldn't have to obey, though."

His nostrils flared as his eyes narrowed.

Good. Let him remember that whatever rank he had in the Navy, whatever power he held in Albion, this was not Albion. And she was not Navy.

Eyes closed, he gave a slow exhale. "Madam, my apologies." He opened his eyes, agreeable once again.

Although she was immune to fae charm, she could feel it radiating off him. Perhaps he could consciously control his. It was certainly potent.

George's shoulders sagged, and he drained his glass.

Mercia sighed, shaking his head. "It's only that—"

The door opened and one of the young men who'd escorted her here paused, bowed stiffly and cleared his throat. "I apologise, Your Highness. May I—"

"Approach," Mercia said, tone bored as he beckoned with a twitch of his finger.

The officer did so, pausing and whispering in Mercia's ear, too softly for her to pick up.

Mercia's jaw knotted and huffed out a breath through his nose. "Wild Hunt take the lot of them." He rose and touched George's shoulder, a regretful smile on his mouth for such a brief instant, Vice almost doubted she'd seen it. "You'll have to excuse me a moment—duty calls." With a nod to each of them, he left with the officer.

The double doors clicked shut and Vice swallowed. Just her and George: this would've been an even greater opportunity to escape if they weren't so far from land.

"How did you do it?"

Vice blinked, tearing her gaze from the doors to find George glaring across the table at her. She shook her head. "You're going to have to be more specific."

"Ruined my brother. Made him abandon his family. He's lost—"

"Everything because of me." She rolled her eyes even though her stomach dropped at the reminder. All the things he'd given up that she couldn't give back. "Yes, yes, so everyone keeps telling me. I did nothing to your brother. He merely realised the error of his ways."

George watched her, brows knotted as his gaze swept over her face. Maybe he was looking for a sign of regret or apology. Maybe he was just wondering how his brother had been drawn in.

I can't change the past.

Her throat closed. Whatever George was looking for, it felt horribly close to that expression Knigh had worn so many times looking at her—the one that made it seem as though he was trying to work out how to untie a complex knot.

She couldn't help Knigh with the law or the Navy or his family back in Albion, but maybe she could do something about George.

She gulped the last of her wine to clear her throat and leant across the table. "Knigh hasn't abandoned you," she hissed. "In fact, he's desperate to get you out of here."

"As he made abundantly clear when he tried to drag me from that boat." Sitting back, he raised an eyebrow, the picture of an unimpressed lordling.

It was an odd glimpse of who Knigh could've become. In his rich suit, a diamond glinting at his earlobe, George looked like a version of Knigh who'd never joined the Navy, whose father hadn't gambled and drunk away their fortune and instead had left it to his eldest son.

It hollowed out her chest.

George lifted his chin. "He normally shows a greater degree of self-control."

She scoffed. "On that, we're agreed. But doesn't that tell you how desperate he is?" She straightened her expression and held his gaze. "He's afraid for you."

The cool façade ebbed away as George exhaled. He mirrored her, leaning closer, lines etched between his brows in confusion, rather than irritation. *"Why?"*

The way he said it—so forceful with a tiny shake of his head, suddenly vulnerable in the midst of all the posturing he'd done until now—almost made her blurt out what Mercia had done.

But she bit her tongue, because to tell George that, she had to tell him what Knigh had done.

And in that talk on the *Swallow*, Knigh had made it clear in a way that had gutted her: he'd never told anyone what had happened that day. Only her.

George already thought Knigh had abandoned their family. She couldn't shatter his image of his brother further.

And Knigh already burned with shame from what he'd done. It wasn't for her to spread word of it.

"I—I don't know exactly what happened," she said, stumbling over her words as she tried to choose them so carefully, "but the Duke did something that—"

"Just like Knigh." George huffed, rolling his eyes. "Why can no one give me a straight answer?"

Damn it, he had to understand. If Mercia didn't care about the lives of the men he'd been trusted to command or of those who'd surrendered, surely George's didn't mean a great deal, either.

She surged to her feet, bending over the table, over him. "If lots of people are warning you off him," she hissed, "maybe you should take the bloody hint!"

The door opened.

She froze.

Silence for a second too long.

This had to look bad, like she was threatening George.

Bollocks.

"Thank you, Miss Vice," he said with a bright smile, "the white I think, yes." His gaze flicked to the decanter of golden wine near her left hand.

He was saving her arse.

She nodded, swallowing. "You are quite welcome, Mr Villiers." She dared a glance at Mercia as she filled George's glass.

He watched them, an odd look on his face as he crossed the

369

room. He wasn't convinced by their charade, but he resumed his seat and let Vice pour him a glass of the red.

It gnawed on her to serve him like this, but it was better than him thinking she'd threatened his lover. Whether he cared for George's life or not, he considered the young man *his*.

For tense minutes, they sat and drank in silence.

IRRESISTIBLE

"Leave us," Mercia said at last, watching Vice over the rim of his glass.

Thank the gods for that. With a sigh of relief, she rose.

"Not you." He nodded at her chair before turning a warm smile on George. "She and I have some things to discuss."

George shot her a look, the skin around his eyes tense. But he inclined his head and stood. "Of course."

Mercia caught his hand, stopping him from turning away quite yet. He looked up at George with eyebrows raised as their fingers tangled together. "You understand, don't you?"

There was something about the angle of his brows, the tone of voice—hopeful? Apologetic?

From the enmity between Knigh and Mercia, she'd assumed his relationship with George was a way of getting back at him—but this?

George scoffed and nodded. "Of course," he repeated, but this time the tone was gentle and warm where before it had been much cooler.

Mercia gave a bright smile and kissed George's knuckles.

Vice looked away. This was a private moment, and either Mercia was a terrifyingly good actor or it was genuine. She didn't know him well enough to tell which and that made her shift in her seat.

Maybe even wicked dukes could love.

Then George was gone, and it was only her and Mercia.

Knigh hated this man. Wanted nothing more than to be many miles from him. Was maybe even scared of him—for a man who'd taken down Bonny Steed that said a lot.

She shuddered and drained her glass, feeling Mercia's eyes upon her.

"I cannot work you out."

She snorted and reached for the decanter. Her cheeks were already warm. Maybe if she got drunk enough, he'd get too frustrated for whatever chat he wanted to have with her.

"Those burns confirm you're fae-blooded, not merely - touched. The power I can feel"—he shook his head—"it rolls off you. And yet..." He exhaled heavily through his nose and held out his glass now hers was full again. "You should be much more powerful than when I saw you in that battle. Unless you were holding back, but I don't understand why you'd do that."

Jaw clenched, she poured the wine. "Yes, you returned George's boat before I got Knigh's. Thanks for the reminder." The now-empty decanter thudded on the table.

"Being locked in an iron cage for a week will do that to you."

With a wince, he lifted the glass to acknowledge her point. "Perhaps it's just that." He took a sip, eyes boring into her. "But you should still have been able to reach past your own power to the wellspring."

She couldn't help the confused frown or cocked head. What the hells was 'the wellspring'? She looked away and gulped her drink. Maybe it was—

"You don't know what it is, do you?"

She gritted her teeth and raised an eyebrow back at him. Knigh was far better at schooling his expressions than she was. But was there any harm in admitting her lack of education on this front? It wouldn't give away who she was or anything he hadn't already worked out.

As a prince, he must've been trained in the use of magic—of course he'd know a few tricks she didn't, however much that irked her.

"I'm self-taught." She shrugged. "No magic tutors for me."

"So, your gift awoke in secret." He watched her, eyes narrowed. "Or perhaps after you'd already become a pirate." His gaze drifted to the table. "Certainly, your parents didn't know what you were, otherwise they'd have seen to your education in that area, just as they saw to your manners. The plot thickens." With a smug smirk, he sipped his wine.

"And they'd have sold me to the Navy." Rather than trying to sell her to the Villiers family and Uncle Rufus.

"Now, now"—he frowned—"we don't *own* our sea witches. They merely work for us."

"For life. With no choice in the matter. Sounds a lot like ownership to me."

"They're paid generously for their service to the realm. But come, I don't want to argue with you—not on this, at least." His teeth flashed in a grin.

She snorted into her glass, despite herself.

"I am loath to see such potential go to waste," he went on, all amusement evaporating. "I have a modest library on board" —he gestured aft—"you must avail yourself of it. The books on magic are off limits to my men, but I'd be only too glad to unlock the shelf for you and make recommendations."

She held her glass an inch from her lips, the sip she was about to take forgotten. It all seemed so reasonable—*he* seemed so reasonable. Not exactly the monster Knigh had painted.

Maybe that made him all the more dangerous.

She drank to delay responding.

Why would he want to help her? It had to be some sort of trap. Had to be. But how?

After all, she was already his prisoner. A well-treated one, perhaps, with a glass of wine in her hand and silk gown on her back, but still not here through choice. And she was a fugitive —he'd be well within his rights to have her executed in Port Royal, or even on the deck of this very ship.

She'd already fallen into his trap. Could reading a book really make it any worse?

Could this 'wellspring' prevent her ever feeling as power-less as she'd been on the *Swallow?*

Maybe he offered this in the hope she'd feel obligated to do something for him in return. Well, more fool him—they'd made no bargain, and even if they had, she didn't have to keep her side. He was too used to dealing with honourable types.

And just because she accepted his offer, didn't mean she couldn't escape. Not tonight, but she'd stay alert to a chance, and in the meantime, she'd take advantage of his library.

She swallowed the rich wine and returned the glass to the table a little harder than intended. Her limbs were heavier than when she'd arrived.

Exhaling, she nodded. "Thank you."

She never had been able to resist a good book.

AN UNWELCOME GUEST

Knigh gripped his tankard, knuckles white. He hadn't been able to stomach any more drink or even the food the others were eating since Saba had confirmed it.

Vee's earring found in a blood-stained alleyway.

He stared ahead, chest tight, stomach churning.

She had to be alive. The alternative...

It just wasn't possible.

"Berit Peregrina! Just the person I was looking for." A familiar male voice rose over the tavern's general hubbub.

It was as if someone had rammed dozens of pins into Knigh's flesh.

Breaths harsh, movements mechanical, he turned to the door.

In a green coat covered in an excessive amount of gold

braid, black hair freshly trimmed, arms raised in an expansive gesture, he was unmistakable.

FitzRoy.

With a rakish smile flashing, he swaggered over.

It's the first time I'll watch a woman I've bedded die... I'm curious what that will feel like.

Yes, they'd both betrayed Vee, but FitzRoy hadn't even had the good grace to see the error of his ways. He could've helped rescue her, but he'd been happy to while away the evening in luxury, so he'd be well-rested to watch her hang in the morning.

Knigh's blood simmered. His muscles quivered, stuck between adrenaline roaring for action and his will telling them to remain still.

"You've got a cheek, FitzRoy." Perry's voice was level but carried into every corner of the tavern. "What the hells do you want?"

At first, Knigh thought it was that the pulse in his ears had drowned out all the sound, but, no, the place had gone quiet. Every pair of eyes watched their table or the man approaching it.

Knigh couldn't even occupy himself with the dregs of his drink. If he moved the barest inch, he'd explode.

"Come on, you can't still be upset at me over that unpleasantness back in Albion." FitzRoy gave Perry a charming smile, apparently ignorant of Knigh's barely contained rage. "It was only business."

Only business.

That's what the man was like. He'd taken Vee—he must

have. He was after the Copper Drake, and he hadn't thought twice about hurting Waters to get it. He wouldn't give a solitary damn about hurting Vee for it, either.

"Besides, thanks to our friend here"—he turned that smile on Knigh, though his skin paled a shade when their eyes met—"our dearest Vice is absolutely fine. Or, *was*. I hear you've lost her. *Tsk*. How careless."

Chairs shrieked across the stone floor, Knigh's included.

He was on his feet. He didn't remember telling his body to rise, but it had. His knuckles cracked, fingers aching.

"Now, now, Blackwood"—FitzRoy raised his open hands, scoffing—"nothing for you to worry about. I've just come to parley with your captain."

Bugger control. Let the adrenaline win.

He surrendered to the rage, and his muscles roared into action. Unleashed, he closed the gap between them.

FitzRoy's eyes widened as if he hadn't actually expected Knigh to follow through on the threats his body had made.

But Knigh's fist arced, the full weight of his charging body behind it. And it wasn't quite right, because Vee wasn't here, but this was the closest thing to right he'd felt since she'd disappeared and like a starving man offered a skewered rat, he'd take it.

The sound of his fist connecting with FitzRoy's nose was blunt and wet and glorious. The grunt after, even sweeter.

FitzRoy staggered back, clutching his face as crimson blood spilled over his hand and pretty coat, all the brighter against the green. "What the bloody hells was that for?" he spluttered.

Aedan circled the table, coming up behind him.

Breaths heaving, Knigh gave a grim smile and shook out his hand. He and Aedan might've had their disagreements, but on this they were united. "Where is she, FitzRoy?" Somehow his voice came out soft and smooth, like the approach of a hunting sabrecat. "Gods help me, if you've hurt her—"

"What?" Eyes wide, FitzRoy adjusted course towards the door, glancing from Knigh to Aedan and back again. He threw a chair to the floor between him and them. "You think I've got her? Are you bloody mad?"

Knigh laughed, raising his eyebrows. Didn't feel too far from it right now. "Maybe I am."

"Perry, come on"—FitzRoy grabbed another chair, swinging its legs through the air to try and ward them off— "are you really going to let these two... Look, I came to talk. I don't have her. Do you think I'd come here like this if I did?"

Knigh's muscles thrummed, ready for more violence.

FitzRoy could break that chair over his back for all he cared. He should've done this back in Portsmouth.

"Knigh," Perry barked, every inch the captain. "Enough."

He clenched his jaw.

"He's come alone," she went on, "and openly. If he was after a ransom, he'd have sent a message, don't you think?"

Think.

He had to think. Engage his brain, not just his fists.

Losing control was not something he could afford to do. He could've killed Aedan on the *Sovereign*. The man only stood here now because Knigh was a healer as well as berserker.

He *would not* give in to the rage, no matter how good it felt.

He tore his gaze from Aedan and backed away a step,

though his hands remained clenched at his side and his muscles ached at being idle.

"*I* don't have her," FitzRoy said at last, lowering the chair with a solid thud. "But I know who does."

The breath stilled in Knigh's chest.

A bluff? Or truth? It could explain why he'd come here—perhaps he wanted to sell the information.

FitzRoy's throat bobbed, and he squared his shoulders. "And I'm going to help you get her back."

THE FITZROY QUESTION

"My cabin, *now,*" Perry muttered when they arrived back at the *Respair*.

Knigh nodded. He knew that tone. He was in for a talking-to. Well, he'd had his share of those in the Navy and he'd take it like an officer.

Maybe it was for hitting FitzRoy or for refusing to accept his help. Whatever reason he was in trouble, they had far more important things to worry about.

Mercia had Vee.

His stomach lurched again at the thought.

It was something that should've been impossible. Unimaginable.

And yet FitzRoy heard it from Vane himself. He said the smug bastard hadn't been able to keep his mouth shut, not after a couple of drinks, anyway. Figured he was doing FitzRoy a favour, while also lining his own pockets with the Duke's generous reward.

Knigh trudged across the gangway, teeth gritted as his throat tightened. Hadn't he pursued Vee for his own 'generous reward' not so long ago?

And, in a roundabout way, isn't that what had put Vee into Mercia's path? If Knigh hadn't come to Arawaké hunting her, she'd only be a song to Mercia. She'd still be on *The Morrigan*, safe and carefree, not the bitter, irritable woman he'd betrayed.

He scrubbed his face.

Hells and damnation.

They had to get her away from Mercia. Either the Duke wanted to hurt her or he planned to use her in some way. He was a master manipulator, after all. Promises. Lies. Whatever it took to get what he wanted. And if that failed, he wasn't above threats or even torture.

Stomach churning, he followed Perry into her cabin and squared his shoulders, ready for the inevitable dressing down.

She turned and folded her arms. Eyebrows raised, she perched on the edge of her desk. "You mind telling me what that was about?"

"We don't need his help," he said, shaking his head. "I already worked with FitzRoy once and I regret it every day. I'll use my contacts from..." He worked his tongue around his mouth.

FitzRoy had said one of Vane's men had overheard their argument with Vee—best not to talk about pirate-hunting or the Navy here in Nassau, even aboard the *Respair*.

He cleared his throat. "From *before*. I can get false information to Mercia."

He'd been turning it over and over in his head on the walk back from the tavern. He still had contacts—he could plant misleading information somewhere it would be sure to get back to the Navy and then to the Duke. "We can lure him somewhere of our choosing or divide his forces." He scoffed. "The man's arrogant enough to sail with a minimal escort. He believes the kraken will keep him safe from everything."

"Reducing his escort would be useful." Perry nodded thoughtfully. "But that doesn't mean we don't need FitzRoy as well." She held up her hands before he could object. "I don't like the man either, but he's always been good at getting information. He found out where Vice was before any of us had the slightest idea, didn't he?" She exhaled, jaw tensing as if the thought of Vee in Mercia's hands hit her every time she thought of it, too. "And he's got a frigate—*seventy-four* guns. We'll need more than just the *Respair's* thirty-six if we're going to face the *Sovereign*."

Knigh bit the inside of his cheek. She wasn't wrong.

FitzRoy, though? "You know what he did to Waters."

"You heard him: he didn't order his men to do it and he punished those who did."

"Oh yes," he scoffed. "Because FitzRoy is known for his honesty, isn't he?"

"No, he's as big a liar as any of us. This isn't a job for honest folk. But I was his quartermaster for years. I know him. Attacking an old man isn't his style, and neither is ordering his men to do it for him. Vane? He wouldn't hesitate. But not Fitz-Roy." Her lips lay flat, certainty in the set of her jaw.

He made a low, frustrated sound in his throat. "But we can't trust him. What if this is a trap to draw us in?"

She snorted. "As soon as we discovered where Vice was, we'd've gone after her, no matter who had her, no matter where they had her, no matter the danger. If it's a trap, so be it."

Knigh crossed his arms. Again, she wasn't wrong.

"But"—Perry cocked her head—"I think FitzRoy, in his own way, has some degree of regret for what he did. It might be hard for you to understand—you weren't there when they met, but... He was fascinated with her from the start. Even before her gift manifested, when she was just an aristocratic girl wanting a place on his ship. You heard him at the tavern."

"'Absence makes the heart grow fonder,'" Knigh muttered. It rose his hackles afresh.

"Exactly." She opened her mouth as if to say more, but instead just exhaled, gaze slipping away to the silver violin ornament on the cabinet. Lips pursed, she stared at it for a long while.

Something else was troubling her. He narrowed his eyes. "What is it?"

She huffed and met his gaze. "FitzRoy helping us or not isn't what I wanted to talk to you about." She waved at the chairs around her small central table where they'd planned the escape from Mercia. "Sit."

"It's that bad?" He raised an eyebrow but obeyed.

She sat opposite, wincing. "Your behaviour with FitzRoy was excessive. I'm a five-foot tall woman who's worked with the roughest of pirates for longer than I care to admit. I've faced down Clovis in a mood and ordered him to do some crappy jobs. I've never let a single one of them scare me. But today"— she exhaled—"Knigh, you looked frightening, like you were about to lose control."

His mouth dried. His blood had been screaming for it—he couldn't deny that.

"I've seen you in battle," she went on, green eyes intent. "You're explosive. With gunpowder, we take precautions. What do I need to do with you? How can I stop *you* exploding?"

You can't. I can't be trusted.

It ached, but it was true. He just needed to keep a tighter rein on himself. Once they had Vee away from Mercia, it would be easier.

Although she'd avoided him for most of their time on the *Respair*, he could usually catch a glimpse of her each day and her laugh had a way of ringing through the air. The past couple of days, her lack had been a palpable thing, hollower than the empty feeling in his chest.

He worked his jaw until he could swallow. "I—I'm sorry, Perry." He shook his head, heart squeezing tight. "I'm normally better at maintaining my self-control, but all this with Vee... What does Mercia want with her? What if he's hurt her? What if—"

"With all respect, Knigh, the way you boil over so easily, I don't think your self-control was really working, was it?" She raised her eyebrows, but the lift at the corner of her mouth was soft—apologetic or pitying, perhaps. "It's just oil poured over churning waters—under the surface they still roil. You need to look deeper. What's the source of this anger?"

His fingers knotted, knuckles white. That wasn't somewhere he could go. Too raw, too shameful, too...

He shook his head.

Too much.

In silence, Perry rose and went to the cabinet with the silver violin on it. She produced a bottle of amber liquid and two dented tankards and sloshed a generous glug into each cup before placing one in front of him. It sweetened the air, strong and spiced.

She swirled hers, leaning against the cabinet and running a finger over the ornament's strings. "You were right about me and Vice, by the way."

Knigh's brows shot up at the whiplash change of direction. "Pardon?"

"When we were talking that night." She sighed and took a long gulp of rum. She didn't even wince. "Maybe I'm too much like an indulgent mother when it comes to her." She smiled softly, gaze turning distant. "I am too calm, too content. Vice, though? She has a fire in her—a curiosity, striving, this... drive and ambition and the optimism to think she can actually achieve all the things she imagines. They're attractive qualities." She lifted a shoulder. "Maybe part of me wishes I had that spark. Perhaps I'm calm water rather than bright flame. But"—frowning, she met his gaze at last and there was disappointment, perhaps even shame in her eyes—"I'm not helping her, I'm just enabling her worst behaviours. Thank you for helping me realise it."

It felt like he was meant to say or do something in response. Everything she'd said made sense. Vee was a force of nature—literally, when it came to her gift. Perry clearly adored her and only meant well in all the things she did for her, whatever the outcome.

"I'm sorry I said it so harshly." He inclined his head.

"No, I think *harsh* might've been what I needed. I don't want to keep enabling those behaviours." The skin around her eyes tightened, lines forming. "And... I don't want to enable yours, either."

Ah, there it was—the relevance of this to their conversation.

His worst behaviours. His berserking, his rage. His all-too-frequent loss of control. He usually managed to hold it together, only cracking twice in the years since Father's death. Since meeting Vee, though...

"Don't bottle it all up." The corner of Perry's mouth quirked, apologetic, kind. "That just lets the tension build and build until eventually you explode."

He lowered his gaze, unable to take that kindness in her eyes. He didn't deserve it. He didn't deserve this—the space in this cabin she'd carved out for him to...

Just the *thought* of speaking about it set his heart racing. He'd told Vee bits and pieces, her hand on his arm or draped around his waist had been a calming influence.

He sighed. "You have to understand, I haven't—it's not the done thing to speak of such things in the Royal Navy." He frowned, running his thumb over the dented rim of his tankard. "Especially not for a captain—we're meant to maintain our authority and, thus, distance. And—and…"

Speaking to Mother, George, or Is about Father or his own anger had been out of the question. He was the head of the family—he had to protect them, even if that was from himself and his destructive emotions.

Perry nodded with a gentle smile. "I get it. Men aren't exactly encouraged to speak about their feelings at the best of times."

He exhaled his relief. She understood, then. He nodded and took a mouthful of rum. Sweet and spiced and bloody strong— it cut through the sour taste that had haunted his tongue since FitzRoy had appeared.

If he'd given in entirely, he could have smashed the man's face to smithereens. Killed him with his bare hands.

Was that who he wanted to be?

The man who'd looked frightening to Perry, this tough woman who could captain a ship full of men twice her size?

The man who'd hacked into Aedan's arm?

The man who'd cut off Billy's hand?

The man who'd come back to himself with Vee staring up at him, desperation on her face?

Something inside him cracked.

He bent over the table and buried his face in his hands.

He wanted that man gone.

Maybe Perry was offering a solution.

It couldn't hurt to try.

CERTAINTY

Knigh scrubbed his eyes and took a shuddering breath.

"I always thought my father was this great hero, discharged from the Navy because of an injury." He shook his head, smile bitter. More rum to sweeten it. "Let's just say I was so wrong in so many ways."

The gambling, the *professionals*, the mistress and bastard child. A litany of father's failings and his own inability to spot them.

"Then there was Mercia." He scoffed, but his face burned with the shame of it. "I thought he was someone I could follow —a great leader. Wrong. Again." He squeezed the cup. What he wouldn't give to go back and tell his younger self the truth.

He stared at the late afternoon sun glinting on the pewter tankard. Looking at Perry while he said this next part was impossible. "Then there's me."

He'd already told Vee about this—that should make it easier. Nodding, he shut his eyes. "I lost control when the *Sovereign* faced a Hesperian warship. The men surrendered—I was told partially because of the number of them I killed in battle and how 'fearsome' I looked. But because I'd lost myself, I couldn't stop." He sucked in a sharp breath. "It would've been a massacre, but my friend—my *brave* friend stepped in to stop me." His voice cracked on the last part.

Billy had forgiven him. He had to remember that.

"By way of thanks, I cut off his hand. And that was when I came back to myself." He couldn't look at Perry, but she was still here, still listening. She hadn't run away. "So, you see, I'm capable of anything." He snorted. "Except for knowing what's right or who to trust. I mean, look at what I did to Vee." He raked his fingers through his hair.

His hand trembled.

The hand that had killed. The hand that had taken Billy's. And here it was quaking, too cowardly to face the truth.

"All these years," he went on because it was too late to stop, "I've been relying on the Navy to tell me what's right and wrong, and yet I somehow still failed in this judgement."

He exhaled, no more words coming.

Maybe this was a start. Maybe Perry had an answer.

He drained his cup, the rum-fire snaking down to his belly. Then he dared to look at her.

She still wore that same expression from earlier—gentle, open, calm.

"Please don't look at me like that, Knigh. I don't have the answers." She said it kindly, but it still deflated him. "There isn't one of Lizzy's herbal tinctures that will 'cure' you. It's not as simple as stitching together a sail. But I have something for you to think about."

She cocked her head. "The Navy was wrong about Vice. But what did your instincts tell you about her? Because even if your conscious mind isn't sure, *I* could see it. You trusted her—believed in her. I saw you fighting side-by-side, steering the ship together, protecting each other. Your instincts were right about that, weren't they?"

He frowned and stared into the empty cup.

All those times—evading the *Sovereign,* diving the coral reef, the fight on the *Covadonga...* He'd placed his life in Vee's hands willingly.

Despite being her enemy, he had found himself trusting her. Far too easily, in fact.

He sighed. "I hadn't thought of it like that."

Perry smiled gently. "I thought not. Let's talk about this some more—when you're ready. But in the meantime, think about what I've said."

With a deep breath, he sat up straight. "I will. Thank you." With a tight smile, he stood and headed for the door. His throat was still raw from talking about Father, Mercia, and Billy, but his shoulders were a little lighter.

"There's still the matter of FitzRoy helping us."

Knigh turned on the balls of his feet, grimacing.

"It would be a necessary, *temporary* alliance," she said, "nothing more." It sounded like an explanation, but her eyebrows arched like it was a question.

He narrowed his eyes. "Are you asking if I agree?"

"I am."

He scoffed and shrugged. "You're captain, it's your decision."

"And in Vice's absence, you're my first mate."

His lips parted. Perry was wise. He respected her and her judgement. She generally made sound decisions. *This*, though?

He shook his head. "You can't be serious."

"Why not?" She lifted her hands. "I trust you, Knigh. And—"

"Please tell me you're joking. You heard all that, didn't you? Wild Hunt, I don't even trust myself."

She cleared her throat. "As I was saying—*I* trust you. You freed Vice despite it costing you so much. You got her here, despite the huge risk to yourself. And you are uniquely qualified—your training and experience—"

"No, no, no. You have a whole crew of experienced sailors. I'm—"

"Let me bloody finish, will you!" She huffed, almost laughing. "Yes, others may match those criteria, but"—she leant closer, elbows on the table as she pointed at him—"*you* have the courage to admit when you've made a mistake. Many don't. Even fewer also have the grit to then right that wrong, no matter the cost to themselves."

He frowned at her, shaking his head. "How can you be so sure? About me, about this"—he lifted his hands, helpless— "about any of it. I wish I could be as confident in my decisions as you are. I wish I had this strong voice in my mind saying 'this is right'." His eyes stung. Was that what she had that he lacked?

She chuckled. "Wouldn't that be nice?"

He gritted his teeth—this was no joke. "How do you always know what's right?"

With an exhale, her amusement faded. "I don't."

"But—"

"I listen." She lifted her eyebrows. "To others, to the situation, to my instincts, too, yes, but not those alone. I look at the information I have. I try to examine different facets of the problem, consider different outcomes, how it might affect others. But ultimately, I can only make a best guess. I *think* this decision will be for the best, but no one really knows until it plays out."

He'd never heard anyone explain their decision-making process like that before. In the Navy it was always down to protocol and procedure or, even simpler, orders from higher in the chain. And before that—well, the Navy had been his life since the age of twelve, and who explained decisions to a boy?

"So," he said, a half-smile tugging on his lips, "you *guess* your way through life?"

She grinned and shrugged. "An educated guess, sometimes. An informed guess, most of the time. But I can't know everything, I can't have every piece of information or predict every possibility." Her expression grew gentler. "You have to do the best with what you've got. That's all anyone can do."

He cocked his head. She was making a frightening amount of sense, and it sounded so simple, but—

"So do you accept?" She raised her eyebrows. "You'll be my first mate and accept FitzRoy working with us for a while, anyway?"

Perry had never steered him wrong, even early on when she'd advised him on what to wear for that first visit to Nassau.

Dizziness hit him for a second as he tried to reconcile the fact that had been only months ago and not years.

Back then, he'd respected Perry's judgement. Who was he to argue now?

He exhaled. "Fine. Just until we get Vee back."

Which would be soon.

ESCAPE

The cabin door was unlocked.

Vice stared at it, holding perfectly still. Evans and one of the others had brought her back three minutes ago, according to the clock on the wall, and she'd stood here all that time, watching... waiting.

No one had come back and locked it.

Had they forgotten? Had she played the part of the willing guest well enough over the past week that Mercia thought she didn't need locking in anymore? Evans had been gentler than his colleagues—he never tried to drag her around like the others. Could it be that he didn't like her being held captive and had done this deliberately?

Maybe it was just that he and his companion had been distracted by the prospect of shore leave. During her daily walk around the deck with Mercia and George, the *Sovereign* had entered a harbour, and she'd been hurried out of the way so they could drop anchor. No one had told her *which* harbour this was, and if she'd asked, she'd have seemed too interested.

But they were near land. Even in this gown, she could swim to shore. Then she could disappear, stow away on another ship. Or make it *look* like she had, when actually she was hiding somewhere in town.

She didn't need much of a plan; she just needed to get off this ship. Once she was away from Mercia, she could work out the next step. But if she didn't get off the *Sovereign,* there would be no next step.

She had to get back to her friends. Barnacle would need her when she had the kittens. And she had to...

She licked her lips, glanced at the clock. Five minutes.

They weren't coming back to lock the door.

It took no time to gather her belongings—the Copper Drake was already in her pocket, as always, and she'd taken to wearing her drake pin on her stays, hidden beneath her gown. She removed her earring—best not to get it caught on anything while she snuck around.

"I'll get back to you soon, Saba," she whispered and kissed it before slipping it into her pocket.

No sword or dagger. That made her fidget. No weight at her side, nothing to hold.

Not even a makeshift weapon. For all that she'd been treated like a guest on the surface, the cutlery had been checked at the end of every meal, so there'd been no chance to steal so much as a butter knife.

She sighed. She *was* a pirate, after all—she probably wouldn't trust herself with the silverware, either.

Gods only knew where her sabre was. She hadn't seen it since Vane had knocked her out in that alley. She clenched her jaw and ran her thumb over her opal ring.

That had been Evered's sabre. Maybe he hadn't been the best husband, but the foolish girl she'd been had loved him. She'd trusted herself to him, and maybe things would have been different if she hadn't dragged him halfway across the world.

Now this ring was all she had left.

She squared her shoulders. "Here and now, Vice," she whispered. "Here and now."

Bundled up clothes made a convincing shape under the blankets of her bunk, especially once she snuffed out the lamp.

Two deep breaths, then she crept to the door. Quiet outside.

If anyone saw her in the corridor, she could always claim to be feeling unwell and looking for water. As long as it wasn't Mercia or the fae-touched healer, she'd be able to charm them into believing her.

She eased open the door and peered into the corridor.

No one out there.

Glancing left and right, she crept out. She could move silently, thanks to her fae blood, but silk gowns were not made for silence. A rustle accompanied every movement.

She made her way fore, wincing at the sound.

She'd asked for different clothes, for breeches and shirt,

rather than a lady's fine dresses, but Mercia had only smiled and denied her. Maybe he thought it gave him control over her. Maybe he just liked to be surrounded by pretty things, like the embroidered silk suits he gave George.

Despite the impractical clothes, she'd paid attention during her time on the *Sovereign*. Her little cabin, an interior one with no windows or gunports, was one deck above where they'd boarded during the battle with the *Respair*.

To fore, the squat mass of the capstan head glinted in the dim lamplight. Once she reached that, there were cannons on either side—she could get out through a gunport.

Voices drifted through the gloom and footsteps sounded from above. Muffled, perhaps a couple of bulkheads away, men sang and laughed. Probably a mess room.

Her neck prickled. It had been quiet belowdecks when she'd snuck on board with Knigh and her boarding party, but now the ship was alive.

Still, she was almost there.

Footsteps, growing louder. Someone coming this way.

She hurried around the corner and ducked between a cannon and the hull. She forced her breathing slow and soft as a pair of men strode past, grumbling about dinner.

Buggeration. Now she was tucked against it, she could see the cannon was too close to the gunport—it would block the flap from opening. She'd have to wheel it about four inches away from the hull.

Even with her fae blood, it would be a challenge—these were far larger than any on *The Morrigan* or the *Respair*.

Once the men had gone, she counted to thirty before bracing herself against the cannon.

She could say a lot about naval discipline but they maintained their equipment well—it was as heavy as she'd expected, making her muscles groan and her hands ache. But its carriage wheeled smoothly away from the hull with only a soft squeak.

Even better, its breeching rope stretched just far enough.

Perfect.

She grinned and flexed her fingers, loosening the knuckles.

Now, she only had to pull on the—

"—spending it all in town. Who knows when we'll get the next chance. You know what he's like."

Close. Coming down a nearby companionway.

She dived behind the cannon.

Riiiiiiip!

Her gown. A loud, unmistakable sound.

"What was that?"

She hunkered down, as small as she could, and pulled her skirts close so they wouldn't be visible to anyone walking past.

"Sounded like... tearing fabric?" Louder. Lamplight spilled through the companionway. "Coming from below."

"That's what I thought."

Bollocks.

"Don't tell me a cat's got into the hammocks again."

Three sets of footsteps came down the companionway, grew louder. Light pooled and shifted as if they held up a lamp.

If she moved, she'd make more sound, and they'd notice

that damn rustling now they were alert. There was nothing she could do. Either they'd spot her or they wouldn't.

Stillness, silence. She held her breath and closed her eyes.

Go away. Go away.

But of course, they didn't, and the footsteps came unerringly closer.

When she opened her eyes, an officer stood over her.

PRACTICALITY

"How disappointing." A sigh ran through Mercia's voice as he sat back in his ridiculous gilt chair.

Vice stood before him, jaw clenched. The way she'd been bundled in, it was like she was a traitor being presented to the king.

This bloody dress. If she'd been wearing normal clothes, she would've made it.

Or if she'd had a weapon. She could've taken one of the officers at knifepoint and forced the others to keep quiet and open the gunport.

She'd tried flirting and bribery.

She was here, so neither had worked.

"You can't expect me to just roll over and accept being your prisoner, however pretty the cage." She gave Mercia a bitter smile.

"I suppose not." He raised his eyebrows, gaze trailing over

her as if taking her measure. "Not the notorious Lady Vice. Perhaps I forgot who I was dealing with."

The corners of his mouth rose. There was nothing warm about it. "But perhaps you don't realise who *you're* dealing with. Let me be clear." His voice came out clipped, cold, sharp, each word cutting through the air like a blade. "I told you not to mistake my mercy for weakness. You'll find none of that here."

Something about his look made her shift, aching for a dagger or sword to hold between them in defence.

"Your cabin," he went on, "your food, your clothing, access to my library—these things are not signs of weakness, merely practicality. Perhaps it's my fault for not explaining sooner. Allow me to rectify that."

He lifted his chin. "You and I need a working relationship."

Her brows contracted. *Working relationship?* Did he mean to make her join the Navy? She was a sea witch—if she'd stayed in Albion, she'd have been forced into service, even as a woman. But he hadn't put her into uniform. She glanced at the two guards, still standing beside her, but they only stared ahead at perfect attention.

When they'd dragged her in, Evans had been stationed at the door. He didn't have Knigh's control—shock and concern had been written clearly in his wide, blue eyes. If he'd been the one to find her trying to escape, would he have turned a blind eye?

Mercia leant forward, brown eyes intense below his frown. "I need you powerful."

Gods, he did mean to enlist her. Bollocks. She wouldn't last five minutes under naval discipline.

"Such a waste. You are capable of so much more than petty piracy." He sighed, shaking his head as he rose. He took a step forward, then paused, glancing at the officer to her right. "Did you check her for weapons?"

He hung his head. "No, Your Highness. We—we thought it best to bring her to you immediately."

"Despite the fact she might have a knife in her pocket?" Mercia raised an eyebrow, acid in his look. "Good Lords and Ladies, check her now, you imbeciles."

They did as they were told, and Vice gritted her teeth. At least they were looking for weapons, and with any luck, they'd ignore the Copper Drake—it was only a book, after all.

"What's that?" Mercia squinted over as the younger one pulled it from her pocket.

Despite her pounding heart, Vice forced herself not to react, aiming for that blank expression Knigh assumed so easily.

"Just a book, Your Highness."

Mercia held out his hand, finger motioning for the young man to approach. "Here."

No way could she keep up Knigh's mask. Head bowing so he wouldn't see, she muttered, "It's just my diary."

"Really?" he drawled. *The Secret Diary of Lady Vice, Piratess Extraordinaire.* I do hope you've portrayed me sympathetically." He flashed a smirk and snatched the book from the young officer.

"Well, then," Mercia murmured, looking at his prize, "I do believe you've been holding out on me, madam." Fingertips stroking the cover, his gaze roved over it. With a soft exhale, smile building, he opened the book and turned its pages, drinking it all in.

Vice watched, teeth grinding. He *knew*. He bloody well knew what it was. The very thing he'd attacked the *Respair* for and she'd delivered it to him.

Now he had it, maybe he'd let her go. He must've been holding her in the hopes of luring in Perry and Knigh and taking the book from them. Or he meant to hold her ransom in exchange for it.

A silver lining—she'd get her freedom, then she'd find a way to get her book back.

"To think," he murmured, finally looking up at her, "all this time and I hadn't realised Mr Vane had delivered me *two* gifts in one neat package."

Two gifts. Did that mean she was the other gift? That didn't sound like she was merely a tool towards getting what he wanted.

"Now"—he clapped the book shut, all amusement vanishing—"consequences." Lips thinning, he rose and stalked closer, leaving the book on the table. "You disobeyed me. There must be an appropriate punishment."

A flogging, no doubt. The Navy was so fond of that. She'd seen deserters who'd turned pirate—the scars on their backs told harsh tales. Knigh had no such scars, though—of course not. He was too much of a good boy to ever earn a punishment. Or at least had been until very recently.

Her chest tightened at the thought of him off somewhere, thinking she'd walked away without so much as a goodbye.

"This time your punishment will be mild and temporary," he went on. "But if you disobey me again, if you try to escape or use your gift without my sanction, the effects will be much more long-lasting." He stood a foot away now, close enough that she had to lift her chin to meet his gaze.

No way was she going to look away, be cowed by his attempt to intimidate her. His men didn't hold his gaze—let him remember she wasn't one of them.

"You do any of those things," he said as softly as a lover, "and I will have Knighton Villiers flogged before you. Then"— he leant even closer, the corner of his mouth rising—"I'll feed him to my beast."

Her stomach turned. Those tentacles—blotchy red with huge suckers, the great muscles writhing. That hard, blunt sound as it had slapped a man off the *Respair's* deck.

Show no fear.

She swallowed it down.

Shaking her head, she dragged out a laugh from some- where deep inside. "You couldn't get to him. He's not stupid enough to come running after me, and he certainly doesn't care enough to, either." After the laugh had faded, she forced the grin to stay in place, even though her hollow chest echoed with the words.

Knigh didn't care enough to come, not after what she'd said and all she'd done.

Mercia scoffed. "I managed to get to *you*, didn't I? And you're far more beloved than Captain Knighton Villiers, former pirate hunter. Hated by pirates, hunted by the Royal Navy. Do you think anywhere's truly safe for him now?" A smug, sneering smirk on his face, he shook his head. "I could have him brought to me in a matter of days."

Her grin turned rictus. He was right. Gods damn it.

Gods damn *him.*

"Besides," he went on, "even easier would be to lure him in with you. You said when you first arrived that your friends would come for you. And you're forgetting—I saw the way he looked at you at the Grays' ball. He's quite taken with you. Bewitched, I'd say. If I made it known where you were and that you were in danger, he'd come running."

She snorted, bitterness at the back of her tongue. "Didn't Vane tell you about our argument?"

His smirk faltered. His brows twitched.

Vane hadn't. Good.

"I turned my back on them," she went on, "and they on me. They won't come. They're probably glad you've taken me off their hands." She said it all with a cavalier toss of her head, but the words stuck in her throat.

They probably were glad. It would be easier, wouldn't it?

Easier for Perry—no one to apologise for all the time.

Definitely less painful for Knigh—no one sniping at him, reminding him of what he'd done. Hadn't he found it hard living on Billy's ship because of the guilt? It wasn't as if she'd made it easy for him to be around her.

Enough's enough, that's what he'd said.

"Interesting." Mercia chuckled softly before flicking his fingers. "No matter. Even if what you say is true, I have George here and, as they say, blood is thicker than water. If Villiers thought his brother was in peril, he'd come."

Vice gritted her teeth. He had her there. *Of course* Knigh would come for George—he'd tried to pull him off a boat in the middle of parley, even though it had smashed the terms of their ceasefire.

"There, you see I'm right." Smug smile returning, Mercia backed away. "Now, your punishment for this transgression." He nodded to the guard on her right again, who went to one of the cabinets. "Since you clearly believe my threats are idle, I see I must make it crystal clear that I mean what I say." That clipped tone had returned to his voice, and his smile faded to something grim.

Back stiffening, Vice swallowed. She'd never been flogged —for all his bad points, FitzRoy didn't believe in it.

They'd probably strip her to the waist and do it up on deck for everyone to see.

Fine. They could see all they wanted; it wouldn't bother her. She'd meet their gazes. Let them be shocked that she was no shrinking violet, no delicate lady. She clenched her fists, palms slick.

"Despite my distaste for it," he went on, "I fear this is the only punishment you'll take seriously."

She blinked. *Distaste?*

The guard to her left went for her wrists.

Distaste. Oh no. Not that. There was only one time she'd heard him use that word.

She twisted out of the guard's grasp. "Don't you—"

"Madam," Mercia said like a parent losing patience with a child, "these shackles are lined with wool. If you resist, I will have my men remove the lining. Do you understand?"

Her stomach twisted, pushing bile up her throat as she watched the other guard turn from the cabinet and come closer, the black, bleak sheen of iron in his hands.

He *knew*. Mercia knew how it felt. The burn. The cold emptiness where it blanked out his gift. The bitter sickness, the sapping weakness.

He knew, and yet he was still doing this. And if she disobeyed, tried to escape, did anything to displease him, he would do whatever it took to get what he wanted—her obedience.

Head cocked, he raised his eyebrows as if to say she'd brought this on herself. "Tomorrow they'll be removed and we'll continue our developing friendship and say nothing more about it. Understood?"

She stared at him, not able to trust her voice. Pleading would be useless. Begging was beneath her. And even a scream of rage would only feed him.

He was every bit the monster Knigh said.

DEPENDABLE

The *Venatrix* arrived a week after Vice's ill-fated escape attempt.

Sat at Mercia's dining table, Vice fiddled with the feathers of her earring and waited for the ship's commander to arrive. She bit her lip, trying not to let her interest show.

The *Venatrix* was a small ship. Too big for Vice to sail on her own, true, but maybe some of the sailors could be bribed. Hells, she didn't need to *sail* it—she could sneak it out, sails struck, purely under the power of her gift on the currents. It would be slow going, but...

She forced her breaths slow, even.

Perry would tell her to be patient, bide her time and all that.

With a little luck, the *Venatrix* would stay with Mercia's small fleet. She would keep eyes and ears open and watch for her opportunity. This could be her route back to the *Respair*.

To her left, Mercia and George shared a quiet conversation. The warmth between them felt too genuine for her to bring herself to try and listen in.

As for her punishment, Mercia had been true to his word and left her in irons the whole night. But afterwards, he'd ordered his healer to tend the burns and had sent an entire pineapple to her cabin. They were expensive in Albion— perhaps it was meant to be some sort of peace offering. He hadn't said a thing about her escape attempt since.

She eyed him sidelong. He was an odd man. The iron—no denying it, that was cruel. But it was as if the punishment shut the door on the crime. Maybe he was just trying to fool himself that she wasn't a prisoner and was one of his crew, needing discipline when she strayed.

But *why?* He had the Copper Drake, why keep her?

They went on daily walks around the poop deck, discussing his books, with him giving advice on using her gift. They made small talk over dinner, when Mercia would sometimes prod for more information about who she was, where she came from.

But he still hadn't given away why he kept her here, other than this 'working relationship' he'd mentioned before.

"I'm afraid, madam," George said, pulling back from his tête-à-tête with Mercia, "you won't find the *Venatrix's* commander nearly as dashing as her previous captain." He flashed a teasing grin that had too much of his brother in it.

Her heart skipped a beat, sending a sharp pang through her.

Wild bloody Hunt, she missed Knigh Blackwood.

Who'd've thought it possible?

She was supposed to hate him, not be pining for him.

Mercia watched her, eyes narrow, sharp. "Indeed, Munroe's rather less dynamic than Villiers. He's... *dependable.*"

George scoffed. "That's kinder than what you said earlier. 'No chance of becoming a real captain' were your exact words."

She was saved from responding by the double doors opening.

Lips pursed, she stared at Evans as he entered, avoided looking at her, and announced Munroe, though she barely heard his words because the ones in her head chimed louder.

Truth was, she'd stopped hating Knigh a long time ago. Even if she couldn't forgive him for what he'd done, she couldn't hate him for it either.

But after what she'd said as they'd docked at Nassau, maybe he hated her. Maybe Perry did, too.

Especially if they believed she'd left through choice. Her throat closed. Surely they'd realise she wouldn't leave them, Barnacle, *and* all her belongings. Unless the fact the Copper Drake was gone was enough—she'd been so single-minded with the clues, she couldn't blame them for believing it.

When he entered, Munroe with his mousy hair and kind brown eyes looked every bit as dependable as Mercia had said.

Once he'd handed over the sealed missive, Mercia introduced them before sitting back, ankle resting on his knee, to read the message.

At her name, Munroe turned, eyebrows rising. "I must apologise, madam," he said, soft borders accent lilting in a way that made her miss Lizzy. "We almost met once before, on the

Veritas, but I only saw you from a distance. I didn't recognise you when I walked in."

"No, I was in a *slightly* different outfit on the *Veritas.*" She gave him a lopsided smile. Gods knew he had no reason to expect to see her on the *Sovereign* of all places.

"Hells and damnation!" Mercia's foot stomped on the deck as he sat upright, glowering at the paper. He jerked his chin at Munroe. "Did you know the contents of this?"

"No, Your High—"

"Out"—Mercia sprung to his feet, brows knotted fiercely— "the pair of you." He threw the key to her cabin at Munroe.

Face tensing, George leapt up and bent close to Mercia, voice low and soothing.

Mercia leant over the dining table and waved the message towards the doors. "Wild Hunt damn the bloody lot of them, George! Look!"

Vice exchanged a look with Munroe. He winced, opened the door, and escorted her out.

Evans and the other guard looked askance as there was a clatter from inside the Duke's rooms and more swearing. Munroe closed the door. "I'd maybe leave His Royal Highness for a while."

Evans offered to take Vice to her cabin, but Munroe declined, "It's no bother."

She gave Evans a smile and inclined her head in a way that said she'd be fine with Munroe.

"Does madam"—Evans grimaced, blond eyebrows crinkling—"*need* anything?"

She bit back a laugh. Bless the boy, but no wonder he was

pulling that face. The day after her escape attempt, he'd winced at her burns as he'd taken her to the healer. Softly, he'd asked if there was anything she needed—he was the only one of her guards who ever spoke to her. Seemed to be the only one who saw her as a *person* rather than just a prisoner.

Without the preventative, her bleeding had started, and she'd explained that she needed cloth or sea sponge and the healer had been no help on that front. Evans had paled when he'd understood why, but when she'd returned from sickbay, a parcel of sponges had appeared in her cabin.

Her chest had tightened at the sight. That little act of kindness had cut her more deeply than Mercia's iron cruelty.

"No, but thank you, Evans," she said, holding his gaze so he'd understand she meant for the sponges as well as for this offer. Perhaps Mercia had got wind of the fact he'd helped her, because this was the first time she'd seen him since.

"Very good, madam."

Munroe watched the exchange with a soft frown before escorting her away.

When they were out of sight of the guards, his pace slowed and he glanced up and down the corridor.

Vice tensed. Could he possibly still be in touch with Knigh? Could this be a rescue attempt? She'd thought Knigh and Perry weren't coming, but on this she wouldn't mind being wrong. Her heart pounded as she cocked her head at him in question.

"I shouldn't ask," he murmured as they inched along, "he's a traitor after all. But I hear he helped you, and I can't help but wonder... Is Blackwood well?"

No rescue, then. A stupid hope. She'd been right before—she was on her own.

"He was the last time I saw him." With a snort, she raised a shoulder. "He's not exactly popular with my—uh—*colleagues*, but he's safe enough." Perry would see to that. "If he's a traitor, though, why do you care?"

Mouth twisting, he looked ahead. "I shouldn't, but..."

I shouldn't, but...

Did Knigh leave everyone feeling that way about him? *I shouldn't care, but...*

She shouldn't have cared when he was so distressed about Billy, but...

She shouldn't have cared when Aedan wanted to kill him, but...

Munroe sighed. "I don't know what madness came over him—maybe you bewitched him for all I know—but I owe Blackwood my life. *And* my position. He sent a recommendation to the Admiralty that I should command the *Venatrix* after he joined *The Morrigan*."

As they reached her cabin door, she laughed softly. "Of course, it's *my* fault." She rolled her eyes and entered.

Munroe paused in the open doorway. "It must be." He watched her, brow creased. "Blackwood and I weren't as close as some, but around our duties, we talked. And I know the Navy was the making of him. He could've ended up like his father—"

He drew a sharp breath and clamped his mouth shut, no doubt realising Knigh perhaps didn't want his family's secrets shared.

She folded her arms. "I know what his father did."

"Then you know the great contrast between him and the man the Navy forged his son into. Could you imagine Blackwood ever turning his back on duty like his father did?"

His father had drunk and gambled away the family fortune. He'd fathered at least one bastard—Knigh had told her as they'd talked, entwined in the dark.

She could call him a horrible name right now. She could say that he was just like his father. That wasn't true though, was it? She shouldn't care, *but...*

Eyes closed, she shook her head.

"And yet," Munroe said, "in breaking you out of that gibbet, he turned his back on all of it."

Her heart shrivelled. The way Munroe spoke, he clearly disapproved.

It mattered what he thought of Knigh. Gods knew why, but it needled at her. She didn't give a damn if someone thought ill of her, but Knigh? Not when he'd finally done the right thing, and that was what he was being judged for.

What about what you think of him?

Urgh. She grimaced and looked away from Munroe, unable to bear his gaze. Not when these thoughts seethed to the surface, all writhing and complicated and uncomfortable.

Yes, Knigh had betrayed her. And yes, that had damn well hurt.

But... did she want to cling to that and let it rot in her gut forever? Did she want to let it destroy her and eclipse all the good that she found with him?

Because much as she'd never admitted it out loud, there

was good between them—or had been. Teamwork with him felt effortless—in battle, at the helm. It had warmed her to see him grow more comfortable and relaxed back on *The Morrigan* compared to the stiff man she'd first met.

And damn it, but she enjoyed his company. As simple as that. He made her laugh, and on the rare occasions when she made him laugh, it felt like an achievement.

Above all, she wanted good things for him—she wanted to see that laugh more often.

And for some stupid, weak reason she couldn't work out, she wanted him to think well of her.

But if she clung to her hurt and anger, all those things would forever be tainted. He'd worked hard to make things right. He'd paid the price.

Wild Hunt damn her. It was too late to tell him.

Her insides twisted, turned, tightened.

She could defend him, though.

"You're wrong," she said, squeezing her arms as she finally met Munroe's gaze. "He wasn't shirking his duty, he was *embracing* it. He realised he'd made a mistake, that I'm not the monster the Navy makes out. There"—she winced—"there are facts you don't know. He discovered one. Maybe it was wrong to leave his family, but he knew if he didn't break me from that cage, I'd die. He had to weigh up those two duties—one to provide for his family and the other to—to..." She shook her head, hands in the air.

"To justice," Munroe murmured.

She blasted out a breath, shrugging. "Maybe."

He opened his mouth as if to respond, but instead just

closed it and rubbed his forehead. He paused there. Maybe he was trying to reconcile this new information with what he already knew—what he already *believed*.

At last, he sighed, arms dropping until he stood nearly at attention. "I should return to the *Venatrix*."

Maybe they'd bonded over Knigh. "Can you get me out of here?"

He cocked his head at her, frowning. "No," he scoffed. "Why would I help you, anyway?"

"For Knigh?"

His lips tightened, and he gave her an odd look. "I'm not sure why you think..." He sighed. "Anyway, I'm not going anywhere. My orders are to stay here with the *Sovereign* while the rest of the flotilla is redeployed."

That must've been the message that had irritated Mercia so much.

It had crossed her mind before—if he wasn't returning to Albion to take her to justice, maybe he was using the Royal Navy's resources for his own ends. They certainly hadn't done anything naval since she'd been aboard—no assisting Arawakéan interests, escorting merchant ships, or attacking pirates.

She lifted a shoulder. "Can't blame me for trying."

He tilted his head in acknowledgement. "It... it's been interesting meeting you, madam. You aren't what I expected—I wonder if that's why Blackwood did what he did."

With that, he closed the door. The lock clunked a moment later.

Vice sighed and slumped onto the bed.

"Bloody Blackwood."

The Navy was the making of him.

Hadn't Perry said something like that, too? Back when she'd persuaded Vice to promise to stop being so cruel to him. *A man who was made by his uniform.*

She couldn't picture Knigh ending up like his father, but maybe Munroe was right—maybe he'd have been another wastrel of an aristocrat if he hadn't joined the Navy and found purpose. Knowledge. The true confidence that came from skill and expertise, rather than the arrogance he'd had when they were children. That had all been overconfidence without justification.

And he'd walked away from all of it to save her life.

It twisted her stomach. Such a high cost.

She flopped back on the bed, grimacing. From the way she'd acted ever since, he had to think it a poor exchange.

THE WELLSPRING

"That light in the centre," Mercia said, voice little more than a murmur, "you see it, yes?"

With her eyes closed, Vice nodded and her earring's feathers tickled her bare neck. That and the sounds of a working ship were the only things that registered from outside.

Inside was endless, stretching away beyond sight, all dark, except for here. Here a violet light crackled, an orb of lightning and smoke.

On the edge of hearing, a song sounded in a language that stirred something in her bones. Something like home.

Occasionally when she used her gift, she was vaguely aware of it, but she tended to focus more on the sea or sky than the song.

One of Mercia's books she'd borrowed said it was the 'well-spring', that word he'd mentioned before.

Bright. Powerful. Like a too-close lightning strike.

"I see it," she whispered, voice merging with the crew's work-shanties drifting back from the quarterdeck and fore.

She and Mercia stood at the ship's stern, hands on the taffrail. During today's walk, he'd tried to explain the idea of the wellspring to her and how to use it, but words alone hadn't been enough.

Still, *why* was he helping with her gift?

Maybe it was part of his charm-offensive.

When she'd asked, he'd looked genuine as he'd explained how because of his gift for the sea, he'd never had a fellow sea witch assigned to his ship, even though his magic didn't affect the weather. Some could work the oceans, while others could work the skies, but not many had the gift for both. "We don't need to be at odds," he'd said. "We're both Albionic, both fae-blooded, both sea witches. Perhaps I'm merely trying to help someone for whom I feel kinship."

It had been a few days since the *Venatrix* had arrived, but she hadn't seen Munroe again. Just as he'd said, all but the little frigate and three other ships had split from the flotilla, leaving on a mission from the Admiralty.

It left the *Sovereign* vulnerable, which left Vice on edge, all the more alert for a chance to escape. But there had been none. Her door had been locked without fail and guards ghosted her wherever she went.

Even now, four waited on the other side of the poop deck, standing at attention in the afternoon sun while Mercia taught her about her gift.

"What you normally do," he went on, "is the equivalent of

scooping up a bucket of the stuff from the edge of the spring and carrying it where you need it. Hard work, if you ask me."

She could hear the half-smile in his voice.

"*Physically* hard work," he said. "It strips your body, strains your muscle, just like hauling water up a well and lugging it about would—like some common farmer."

She snorted. "Because you'd know all about that."

"Concentrate," he snapped.

Grinding her teeth was the only way to keep her mouth shut. She wasn't one of his men to order around, but he had agreed to show her how to make better use of her gift. *Make more of your potential,* he'd said.

"Now"—his voice was soft again—"hauling those buckets is what our common cousins the fae-touched must do. They have no choice in the matter. And we *can* do that—a crude method, less powerful, but it's often quicker and requires less focus. However, we *do* have a choice."

She edged closer to the wellspring. The air around it hummed. If it counted as air, since it was in her mind or—or some other place, not *here*. "What's the other option?"

"It is the true strength of the fae-blooded. Yes, those who are touched have just one gift and we can have two, sometimes three. But that's not the key. *They* cannot enter the very centre of the wellspring—it would destroy them. Utterly."

Utterly. The way he said it rang with excitement, as if he'd like to see it or had and enjoyed it. She shuddered.

She'd never been taught to use her gift formally, but even children knew the stories of gifted folk burned away by their magic.

"But you and I have nothing to fear," he continued, "we may go right to that source and divert it, like the clever farmer who digs an irrigation channel. Your body must become a channel for the power to travel through, bridging this place where we stand and the one inside. It's still a strain, but not in the same way that carrying each individual bucket is."

She paused short of touching that shifting, swirling mass of cloud and lightning. Was this a trap? Did he want to see *her* destroy herself in it?

She exhaled and opened her eyes, squinting at the sudden brightness of the day. "Is it still dangerous?"

"Our fae blood protects us. We're safe to follow the song to the source of the wellspring and draw directly from it." He chuckled softly. "How do you think I brought George back to the *Sovereign* so much more quickly than you pulled in his brother?" He looked out over their wake, the edge of a smile on his lips. "I'd say it's a fair trade for the burn of iron."

Arms crossed, she frowned. He had beaten her in that little race, true. And when she'd first encountered him, he'd blocked her gift entirely, stopping her from even feeling the sea across the area he controlled.

All that, despite the fact she had more fae blood than he did. Her father, whoever he was, had been one of the fair folk, whereas Mercia's fae-blood had been diluted by humans for generations. It stood to reason that she should be stronger.

But if he went to the source, while she worked with one arm behind her back, using only the most basic magic skill...

She huffed. It seemed logical, but he was her enemy—it could be a lie, a trap.

"You're unsure of whether to believe me." He turned to face her, lounging against the rail. "I suppose I can't blame you. But consider this: if your body and mind are honed enough to channel it, to take that energy, then your power could become limitless. It merely requires control." The skin around his eyes tensed as he said that last word and his gaze bored into her, eyes even darker in the harsh afternoon shadows.

Control. As if he wanted to control her. She clenched her jaw. What did he want with her? It couldn't be the Copper Drake—he would've got rid of her already if that's all he wanted. And he'd called *her* a gift.

If she could work out what he was after, she might be able to use it to trick him into letting her go or putting her in a position where she could escape.

She rubbed her wrists. His healer had got rid of her burns, but the memory of dull, aching iron still lingered.

Right now, it felt like he was the one tricking her. But into *what?*

He squinted up and gestured. "Channelling the wellspring, you could summon a storm from this clear sky."

She scoffed. Maybe he was just mad. That was an angle she hadn't considered. "I can't do that. I have to use the weather that's already there and manipulate it to do what I want. Clouds become a storm, wind turns to my course or gets stronger. I can't conjure a storm from nothing."

"Can't you?" He raised an eyebrow at her. He looked so sure. "Try it." He nodded astern. "I know you can. You just need to prove it to yourself."

The book that mentioned the wellspring *had* suggested it

could be used. That was the only volume written by someone who was fae-blooded. The others were all by fae-touched magic users, as if those with the blood of the fair folk running through their veins were loath to trust their secrets to paper and ink.

Another book, this one written by a sea witch, had mentioned another interesting idea. Something Mercia hadn't yet mentioned during their chats. A sea witch could battle another for control. It was possible, with enough will, enough physical strength, enough focus, enough hold on pure magical power to splinter someone else's hold on the water.

Mercia had blocked her before. Maybe she could break that if she learned enough about her gift. There had to be some silver lining to this captivity.

Hells, maybe she could even use it to stop him from communicating with the kraken. It might not rely on his message getting through the water in any way she could affect, but it was worth a try. Stopping him from ordering it after her as she escaped—that could be the difference between freedom and another night in irons.

Or death.

She brushed the sea with her thoughts. It was so much like smoothing the top of Barnacle's head, it made her heart clench.

Something—*a ship* moved through the water, just around the other side of the island they were passing. Two, in fact, their draughts shallower than the *Sovereign's*, hulls sleeker, faster.

Her heart sped, and she eyed Mercia sidelong. He hadn't reacted. The action disguised with a wipe of her brow, she glanced aloft and fore. None of the men on watch looked on alert or expectant, like they were due to liaise with other ships.

Could it be…?

No, they weren't coming. After all the things she'd said, she was on her own.

Some idiotic pirates thought it was a good idea to attack a warship. That was all. More fool them—this one came with a sea witch and his kraken. The creature regularly went off hunting and sometimes Mercia sent it away to do his bidding, but today it stalked the ship a short distance to starboard.

"Hmm." Mercia's head snapped up, and he scanned the island, gaze in the exact direction of the ships.

She forced her breaths even. He couldn't know she was hoping for rescue. It was silly and weak. Not to mention, it would blow a hole in her argument that Knigh and Perry wouldn't come for her if he tried to lure them in.

"Sails," went up the shout as the ships rounded the island's steep hills. "Flying the black!"

Heart in her throat, Vice gripped the rail, straining over it to catch a glimpse.

Three-masted, all square-rigged. She knew that sail plan—she'd scaled every inch of that ship.

The *Respair*.

And the other vessel had to be their ally.

She grinned, a stupid, wild hope flaring in her chest. They *had* come for her.

Mercia's hand closed on her arm, the grip bruisingly tight as he yanked her away from the rail.

She whirled, off balance.

All hint of his earlier friendliness had disappeared behind a rigid smile.

"Here's your chance," he said, nostrils flaring. His gaze flicked to her earring and his lips thinned for a second, bloodless. "Summon a storm, drive them away."

She scoffed. "Why the hells would I do that? And even if I wanted to, I can't."

She tried to pull away, but his grip tightened, points of pressure sharpening to spots of pain as his claws pierced first her gown and then her skin.

Teeth gritted, she glared. He thought a few scratches would scare her into obeying him?

Idiot—she'd faced far worse.

She bared her teeth in what was more a snarl than a grin. It didn't waver as he pulled closer, body heat reaching her, breaths on her face.

"You can," he hissed, "you just need the proper inducement. Try this: if you don't get rid of them, I'll have my creature crush their ships. Your choice."

FROM THE DEEP

Could the kraken really crush a ship? The stories said so, but Vice had only seen Mercia use the creature to menace vessels with its tentacles and sweep one person off the *Respair's* deck. The crew had managed to pick the poor man up and Knigh had healed him. No harm done.

It didn't seem as dangerous as the stories made out. Hells, Mercia was more of a monster than the kraken.

"You're full of crap," she scoffed. "You wouldn't let George see you murder his own brother. What would he think of you then, even *with* your fae charm?"

His eyebrow twitched. "Really? Am I?" His gaze shifted, and she got the sense of him drifting away, focused on his gift in the sea. "There!" His face lit in triumph and she glanced at the *Respair*, expecting to see the kraken's tentacles surface beside it.

But when she cast out into the water with her gift, the huge shape wasn't heading in that direction.

Mercia dragged her to port. "Still you doubt me," he muttered, fingers biting into her arm. "Very well."

He shoved her against the rail and it took her every instinct of self-preservation to just hold the smooth timber, rather than turn and punch him in his cruel face. He had a ship full of armed men and she had nothing. Attacking him would only get her injured or killed.

Beneath the waves, the kraken jetted away, swift and sleek and unseen.

"Look." He pointed to port, along the kraken's course.

Amongst the glistening waves, triangles of white canvas and the froth of a wake marked the passage of a fishing boat. A two-masted vessel, it was smaller than the *Venatrix* or *The Morrigan*.

Was that what he meant or was there something else she was missing? She frowned from it to him.

"Look," he hissed, eyes fixed on the boat.

A chill shook through her before the suspicion fully formed in her mind. No, he wasn't going to...

The kraken's wake closed in on the little boat.

Wild Hunt, he *was*.

"No, you can't attack them." She stared up at him. "They're just a fishing boat. They're civilians—"

"I said, *look*." His claws sank back into her flesh, jolting pain through her.

Chest heaving, she stared at the little boat cutting through the waves. He couldn't mean this. He was bluffing.

Please, gods, say he's bluffing.

The rippling shape of red tentacles broke the surface, and she felt the ghost of the spray, like she had on the *Respair*. From here, she couldn't see the fishing boat's crew, but in her mind, they cried out in terror, just like her friends had.

One rust-red tentacle snaked around the hull, and it was as if it tightened around her own heart.

"Stop," she whispered, "please. You don't need to do this. I'll do as you ask."

"No." His voice was cold and distant. "You haven't learned your lesson."

Another tentacle unfurled from the deep and writhed through the air before closing on the fishing boat.

"Please." It was begging, but she didn't care. He had to stop. Her hands shook at her sides, despite the pain in her arm where he'd pierced the muscles with his claws. *"Please."*

A third tentacle and a fourth. Just above the waves rose a huge yellow eye with a narrow slash of a pupil and behind it, the top of that massive, bulbous body she'd felt in the water.

Stomach turning, she looked away. Her knuckles were white where she gripped the rail.

"No, no, no," he said, voice chiding like he was teaching a lesson to a naughty child. "You're going to see it all." His hand closed on her cheeks, claws threatening to break the skin. Fingers crushing into her jaw, he forced her gaze back to the struggle between the kraken and the little boat.

Except it wasn't a struggle. Every tentacle was wrapped around the pathetically small vessel now. It wasn't even as long as the kraken's round body.

When she closed her eyes, he scraped a claw along her cheekbone to brush her lashes.

"Watch, or I'll take your pretty little eye."

She huffed out a little breath, almost a whimper, and forced her eyes open.

The boat tilted, tentacles tight around it. The arms thickened as if the creature tensed.

It was squeezing.

Her stomach turned and sour bile coated her tongue.

Maybe she heard it from this distance, maybe it was just in her mind, but there was a groan of timber.

Mercia's fingers flexed against her as a mast snapped and fell. The other followed a moment later.

Then splinters and water burst beneath those red tentacles.

Vice's belly heaved just as Mercia released her.

She puked over the side again and again, a cold sweat dripping off her.

That creature. Those people. Had they—

"I'd rather not upset George," Mercia said, as if they were in the middle of a friendly chat, "but I will if you force my hand— like you forced me to do that."

When nothing more came, she shuddered straight. Mercia was...

She had no words for what he was.

"Those lives are on your conscience—do you want your friends' to be, too?" One red eyebrow raised, he looked to the stern.

She'd been wrong.

The kraken could do it. Easily.

Wiping her face, she heaved in fresh air and followed his gaze.

The *Respair* and its partner were turning, making directly for the *Sovereign*, black sails full. They'd chosen their approach well—the wind was with them and the sun behind them.

They'd come for her. They knew about the kraken.

That meant they had a plan.

Maybe they had some more of those clever barrels Wynn and Effie had made to scare the creature off.

But that whole scheme had been expensive, as had the repairs to their ship—no way could they afford to restock her powder stores after, not with enough gunpowder to do it all again. Besides, it had only worked thanks to her gift helping them speed away before the kraken returned.

And even if they did have a plan—a *better* plan—it would be at a cost.

A human cost.

It was too big a risk. If the kraken got to them—well, she'd seen exactly what it was capable of.

Her stomach tightened like a knot soaked and left to dry in the sun, but there was nothing left to vomit up.

No one needed to die for her. Whatever they'd said after the vote for captaincy, she wouldn't risk them.

She'd almost cost Aedan his life boarding this very ship.

And Knigh... She'd already cost him so much. Family, career, *sanity* if his berserking was anything to go by. He didn't owe her anything more.

The thought hit her, painful in its truth.

He'd paid enough.

What she'd been pushing for—it simply wasn't possible. *I can't change the past.*

Breaths sharp, she tore her gaze away from the approaching ships and turned to Mercia.

With his charm all dried up, there was no doubt. This was his true face. Hard. Cruel. If he couldn't win with charm, he'd win with force.

But he *would* win.

Except there was one problem. She swallowed. "I—I can't—"

"Storm," he spat, *"now."*

Lightning from a clear sky. A storm from nothing. The impossible. If she didn't—*couldn't* do it, Knigh, Perry, Saba, Aedan, Barnacle, *everyone* would die.

Better her than the kraken.

Eyes stinging, she opened up her awareness to the sky.

THE SEA WITCH

T he *Sovereign*.

That meant the kraken was probably nearby.

Knigh had ordered watches at the fore top and mizzen top to call out at the first sign of that telltale wake pattern.

Nothing so far.

His jaw was still tight, though.

Despite the kraken's threat, here they were, closing in on Vee.

He gripped the rail, leaning over, letting the spray wash over him. Almost there, just a matter of a few hundred feet.

Only the *Venatrix* and three other ships remained with the *Sovereign*. His false information had worked, then. He allowed himself a small, tense smile.

Stage one of the plan, complete.

Next, the *Sea Witch* would attack. While the *Sovereign* was distracted by that, the *Respair* would cut across close to their stern, rake it with a broadside, followed by a boarding party he'd lead. They'd swing across ropes from the yardarms, making a swift entrance in the gun smoke. Once they were aboard, they'd need to move quickly and find Vee, while the *Respair* joined the distraction efforts.

If they could spot Vee before boarding, that would help, but he'd drawn a layout of the ship in case anyone got split from the team. In particular, he'd pinpointed the cells where she was probably being kept. Aedan could pick locks, so chains wouldn't be an issue.

It was perhaps a lunatic plan, but it was a plan.

Perry appeared at his side. "I see her," she said, voice taut. "Look." She pressed her spyglass into his hands.

At the stern in a lapis-blue gown, hair streaming around her face, stood Vee. His heart leapt to his throat. She looked... *well.*

No sign of injury. No chains. She seemed more guest than prisoner.

"I thought she'd be in a cell or chains," he murmured, unable to lower the spyglass.

Someone had hold of her arm. He blinked and followed— oh, of *course.*

Mercia, red hair impossibly bright in the sun.

They faced each other, deep in conversation. Close.

Jaw even tighter, he scanned the deck. No sign of George. They were putting on more sail but didn't seem to be making any preparation for battle.

He returned the spyglass, exhaling. What could they be talking about with such intensity?

"We'll have her back soon." Perry squeezed his shoulder.

"Are the barrels ready?" They only had spare powder for two, and the *Sea Witch's* crew had a few more, but it was better than nothing.

"Aye, and Saba's arrows." She nodded, smile turning stiff. "The boarding party are ready, too."

"But I need to—"

"You're not going." Her voice was firm, and she raised her hand to stop his protests, every inch the captain. "I know you say our chats have made you feel better, less angry, but"—she shook her head, sighing—"I can't let you go. Not after last time, and not with so much at stake. We need to get across as quickly as possible, get her back, and get away. I cannot have any complications slowing this down."

He gritted his teeth. The worst thing—she wasn't wrong. There was no good counter argument other than that his muscles itched to get over there and his hands ached to take Vee's and bring her back.

"We might have reinforcements"—Perry's gaze slid past him to the *Sea Witch*, its great bulk keeping abreast with the *Respair*—"but there are still only two of us. We cannot win a battle, we can only get what we came for."

He nodded and swallowed back the ache. "Get Vee. Nothing else matters." *Even my wounded pride.*

The quality of light changed. Subtle, but *off* somehow.

"What's—"

The sky had darkened. Clouds loomed where moments ago there'd been none.

More now, even just a second later, coalescing, churning, deepening from fluffy white to grey to black in the matter of heartbeats.

"Blackwood," Perry said, voice wavering, hair whipping in the wind, "is this the Duke?"

Shouts rose from the crew as they too spotted the changing conditions.

"No." He stared at the still-gathering clouds, a chill pressing its way through his shirt and down his spine. "He can shape water, but he has no gift for weather." The hairs of his arms rose as tingling static charged the air.

It wasn't Mercia, it had to be some freak occurrence. But his chest was too tight to take a deep breath and say it.

Because there was another possibility...

But—no, he'd never seen weather like this—a storm from a clear sky in a matter of moments? Impossible, even for a sea witch.

A blinding arc of violet lightning flashed from sky to sea, striking directly in their path, forcing Knigh to shield his eyes.

Almost instantaneously, a crack rent the air, loud as any cannon.

A sharp smell, metallic and clean, filled his nostrils.

Perry barked orders to reef sails. No time to change to storm canvas.

The cloud wasn't done—electricity still crackled in the air even though the storm remained localised to the stretch of water between the pirates and the *Sovereign's* reduced fleet.

Breaths ragged, Knigh stared at the spot lightning had struck—exactly where he would've placed a warning shot to stop someone coming closer.

It was no accident. And this storm was no force of nature, either.

"Could he have another sea witch?" Perry looked up at him, eyes wide.

Stomach clenching, he shook his head. They were so few, no ship would be allowed more than one, duke or otherwise. However manipulative that duke was.

Another two strikes lit up the air in quick succession, their booming thunder shaking the *Respair's* timbers.

"We have to turn back," he said at last. That was a safe thing to say—something he could push past his tight throat. The other words...

Face screwing up, Perry huffed. "You're right."

Across the water, FitzRoy's *Sea Witch* was already turning. Someone on its quarterdeck waved to the *Respair*.

Knigh hurried across the deck to give the orders to change course. Those words he could shout out. "Brace the yards. Helm, hard to port."

The other words, a proper answer to Perry's question, stuck in his throat.

Mercia already has another sea witch.

A STORM FROM A CLEAR SKY

P ower.

Pure, unbridled power.

Crackling through her veins. Sparking through her muscles. Tingling against her skin.

As bright as flashes of lightning in the storm she'd created. As searing as Avalon's forge. As overwhelming as a tidal wave.

She was nothing. It was all.

What was her name? Did she even have one?

Somewhere, a body shook, every fibre tensed as it tried to hold together and direct the power surging through it.

That was her.

Yes.

She was Vice. A person. Not this snapping, cracking energy. A person.

Focus. Breathe. In. Out.

The power throbbed now, intense, consuming like a lover's skilful touch, but no longer obliterating.

She was Vice, and she was channelling this. She was in control.

The storm—*her* storm still churned the sky, shaking the air with thunder and lightning. She couldn't leave that there.

Inhale. Exhale.

Electrical potential still crackled in her hair. It needed discharging.

With a push, one last bolt of lightning ripped the sky, kicking up the burning stink of ozone.

She wrung out the cloud—a sheet of rain gushed into the sea, so heavy it roared.

And then the air was clear.

She huffed out another breath and opened her eyes.

The sky spun, the deck tilted, and her body trembled.

"Well," Mercia said, catching her elbow, eyebrows raised, a flicker of a smile on his lips.

She blinked hard, scrubbing her face. Her fingertips still tingled and she wouldn't have been surprised if tiny sparks of lightning had danced across her skin. She drew a deep breath, and the world spun a little less.

Had she just...?

"That was..." He exhaled, shaking his head as he looked off the stern where the only evidence of her storm was a damp freshness in the air.

She'd made a storm. She'd done that before, of course. Back in Portsmouth she'd raised one as she'd left court, before they'd thrown her in that iron cage. But there had already been clouds in the sky, potential she could use and build upon.

This? The sky had been that bright blue that made her eyes ache without a cloud in sight.

Swallowing, she nodded. His lessons had been right.

"I'm impressed," he said, returning his gaze to her, an edge of calculation in his narrowed eyes. "Some—even the fae-blooded—have been burnt away dipping into the wellspring."

The breath burst from her as she stared at him. "Thanks for the warning!" But even his carelessness couldn't tarnish her triumph. A storm from a clear sky!

He scoffed, but stopped abruptly, head cocking. "What's that?" He grabbed her chin, angling her face.

Teeth gritted, she yanked away. It was bad enough she was his captive, she wasn't going to let him paw her like a posses-sion. "I'm not your—"

"Look at me." He bit out the words, so serious it made her pause.

She glared back.

"My word, I've never seen *that* before." With a forefinger he tilted her head back, the tip of his claw grazing her skin. "Your eyes..." He exhaled, and it tickled her face. "There's a violet-blue glow in them, like flashes of distant lightning."

"What?" She touched her lower lids as if she might somehow feel it with her tingling fingertips. Ever since her gift had awoken, her eyes had changed colour with the sea, but this? This was new.

And that wasn't all. Using the wellspring had affected her body, but the trembling had already stopped and she wasn't as hungry as she usually got after using her gift heavily. There had been that initial disorientation when she'd opened her eyes, but she hadn't collapsed and her muscles didn't burn like she'd climbed the shrouds twenty times in a gale.

If anything, she felt refreshed, like she'd had a good sparring session followed by a long, cool drink. She was *energised*.

Although, she'd been much more vulnerable while she'd used her gift. Normally she still had some awareness of her physical surroundings, even when her thoughts dived into the sea, but this time she'd barely remembered she *had* a body.

Still, she'd never tasted power like this. What could she do with it?

A half-smile caught her mouth. So much potential.

Limitless.

"What an intriguing fae mark." Mercia's mouth curved slowly as he dropped her chin, expression turning thoughtful. "You've done well today, Vice. Even better than I'd hoped." He raised his eyebrows and scanned the sea. "You thoroughly frightened your friends away. I'm sure I can come up with some fitting reward."

The smile withered on her lips.

That's what she'd been doing—scaring off Knigh and Perry and the others. The kraken. That little fishing boat. The puff of wood and water exploding as it had been crushed, those lives wiped out in an instant.

The wellspring had obliterated all thought until she'd known nothing but the storm. She'd completely forgotten the *why*.

Those lives are on your conscience.

The tingling fled her skin, chased by a chill even though the sun was bright overhead.

All that power. The greatest magic she'd ever worked. A storm from a clear sky—it was the stuff of legends.

But it was no triumph.

Eyes burning, she tore her gaze from Mercia and scanned the seas. No sign of that poor fishing boat, not even flotsam on the waves.

Close to a small chain of islands, black sails retreated, already smaller than her thumbnail. Perry, Knigh, Barnacle— they'd been so near, but now...

Her chest tightened until she could barely breathe.

In Nassau, she'd joked to Knigh that she couldn't strike him down with lightning from a clear sky. Maybe now she could.

Her throat ached to laugh and tell him that. He'd chuckle and make one of his rare jokes—something about how he preferred it when she couldn't do that. But he'd know he was safe, that she'd never do it, that it was all bluster, that they weren't enemies. That she didn't want to hurt him.

Except she couldn't tell him and would never hear his stupid joke.

And after that storm, he'd think she *did* want to hurt him.

Who could blame him after all the sniping, the spite?

Mercia had no power over weather—Knigh knew that, and he'd know she was the one who'd made it. Maybe he'd be glad of it.

Enough's enough.

Inside, something—*everything* crumbled. There was nothing left, just a hollow ache.

A clawed grip fastened on her wrist and with a yank, Mercia had her facing him. His smile was anything but friendly. "Don't you look after that ship so longingly. You won't be returning to it. We have treasure to find."

She stared at him, blinked, ran through the words again before they would go in.

That was why he'd captured her, to help with Drake's treasure? Lords, riches were such a distant concern right now. She shook her head, trying to make sense of it all. "Why do you need me?"

"I have a map. I know where it is." His eyes glittered, smile turning smug. He must've seen the surprise on her face. "You will dispel the storm around it for me."

That was all he wanted from her. A bit of weather magic?

She huffed out a laugh of disbelief, despite the tightness in her chest, despite the threat of his claws still at her wrist. She could get rid of the storm, help him reach the treasure, then he'd let her go. That wasn't so bad. Of course, he wasn't counting on the fact she'd then find a way to steal the treasure from him and get back to the others. Somehow.

"Is that it? All this just to ask me to still a storm? I didn't need to—to do that. You didn't need to..." Her voice came dangerously close to cracking as she gestured first to port, then to the now-clear sky. "If you'd let me tell them this was only temporary, that'd I'd meet them in a couple of weeks in—"

"You misunderstand." His chin rose and that cool, imperious, princely look slid into place. "I only wanted you to help me get Drake's treasure," he went on, "but with your power, you will be useful to me for so much more. When I return to Albion with the treasure and Excalibur to claim my throne, *you* will be at my side."

Her head pounded. Useful to him. Excalibur. Claiming the throne. There were rumours the ancient sword, the mark of a true ruler of Albion was with Drake's treasure. But that was nonsense—why in the world would Ser Francis Drake have it? And why would it be in Arawaké?

Mercia went on, "Why do you think I've been teaching you how to use your gift?"

For his benefit. Of course. She'd known it was some trick. Well, more fool him. "Why the hells do you think I'll stay with you?"

He chuckled, the sound low as distant thunder. "Why the hells do you think you have a choice?" His eyes glittered, hard as his diamond earring winking in the sun. "I won't give you up. You are mine."

You are mine.

"I'm no one's." Teeth bared, she twisted out of his grip.

Threads of pain marked the course of his claws, but it was nothing against the ache still in her chest. She could do nothing for those people on the fishing boat. Despite her power, she'd been powerless to save them.

And if she never reached the *Respair*, she wouldn't be able to explain to Knigh and Perry that she'd only raised that storm to keep them safe.

If she never went back, she wouldn't be able to apologise to him for being so awful.

If she never went back, they'd always think the worst of her.

Muscles flaring to life, her hands clenched into fists. Her blood boiled. If she—

Steel rang from every direction.

She blinked and tore her gaze away from Mercia. Her chest heaved as the rest of the world rushed in.

Sails overhead with naval pennants—a red kraken on white highest of all. Uniforms to every side. Men armed with sabres, pistols, rifles. One held iron manacles.

All she had were fists and a gift that iron would nullify at a touch.

Shoulders sinking, she unclenched her hands.

"Good," Mercia said, closing in and lifting her chin with a claw, forcing her to meet his gaze. He glanced at her earring, flicking it with disdain. "I will quash every inch of rebellion in you. Even if I have to lock you in irons until you comply. Even if I have to capture a friend of yours or some relative from Albion and hold them against your obedience."

Was that why he'd been trying to puzzle out who she was? Disguised as simple curiosity. And more iron? Did he really hate it so much, or had that all been a lie to soften her?

He searched her gaze, eyes narrow. "You may be the notorious Lady Vice, ruthless pirate, but there's someone in the world you care about. That new captain-woman of yours, or maybe one of the people you led onto my ship. Villiers, certainly—that's an easy one. Even darling George, at a pinch —I don't think you'd like to see him hurt, if only for his brother's sake." He smiled and the cold light in his eyes, so hard, so sharp, made her believe him. Just like he'd had his creature crush that ship, he would do it all. "I will find someone you care for and have no hesitation in using them to break you."

He leant close until their noses almost touched. "You are mine, and you will obey."

She stared back, goosebumps over every inch of flesh.

Earlier, everything inside her had crumbled and, gods, it had hurt. But now even the dust left behind blew away in the sea breeze.

Her power was a curse.

Her triumph was ashes.

She was nothing.

He must've seen he'd won, because he smiled and released her, stepping away.

By that chain of islands, only sea remained. The black sails were gone.

OVER THE HORIZON

Knigh gripped the ship's wheel like a drowning man. Gaze dead ahead, he kept the *Respair* on her new course, skirting an island chain. Away from the *Sovereign*.

The flaming arrows had been cleared away. Wynn and Effie were in the powder room dismantling the explosive barrels. The would-be boarding party had all been reassigned to other duties.

And the storm thundered in their wake like distant gunfire.

It must've been Vee. But *why?*

In the half-hour since that first strike of lightning, he'd asked himself the question until his chest ached. And he still had no good answer.

"Do you think it was her?" Perry's voice came softly just beside him.

He hadn't been able to say it. Didn't mean it wasn't true, though. Eyes closed, he nodded.

"A storm from a clear sky," she said. "I didn't think she could do that."

"Me either. But there's no other explanation."

Perry hunched in on herself, folding her arms, frowning ahead. "But... *why?*"

He almost laughed to hear the question said out loud, but his face was too stiff.

The wheel pulled to starboard as the *Respair* rode a wave trying to push them off course. He gripped harder, arms bracing. It wasn't the action his muscles had craved today—he'd wanted a battle. But it was something, and it gave him an excuse to stay silent a moment longer.

Eventually, the wheel was stable, and he dragged in a long breath. He knew the answer. Hells, he'd known the moment he'd heard who had Vee. He knew the man well enough, knew what he was capable of.

"Mercia has turned her. Maybe he's offered her..." He shook his head.

What could tempt Vee into working with him? *For* the Navy? She hated strict discipline, unbending rules and order. What in the world could make her put up with that?

Unless she thought she had no other option.

Unless he and Perry had hurt her so badly that she really was ready to push them away for good. Then even Mercia might seem like a better option.

He bit his lip against the shudder that pulled on his muscles.

"I don't know," he said at last. "A ship? Treasure? *Drake's* treasure. Mercia already has a clue of his own." He rubbed his face, shoving the hair from it.

A ship. The *Venatrix* was with the *Sovereign*, wasn't it? His throat closed. She wanted it. Badly. And she'd just been rejected by the *Respair's* crew the morning of the argument. Mercia could promise it to her and make her a privateer. As an admiral, duke, and prince, he had that power.

And the weight of that promise, together with losing the vote *and* what he and Perry had said...

"No." Perry shook her head, the movement tossing her hair. "No, I don't believe that. Maybe—Yes, of course!—she was keeping us out of danger." A smile crept across her mouth, but her brows were still drawn together. "Maybe she was keeping us safe. Maybe..." She licked her lips, the smile fading.

She was trying to persuade herself.

Knigh's insides shrivelled, leaving him empty. If even Perry thought Vee could choose Mercia...

He squeezed his eyes shut. "We hurt her too much." He exhaled, shoulders caving in. "Even if everything we said was true, that—that was *not* the way to deliver it."

He leant against the wheel, exhaustion overwhelming. He hadn't only been geared up for a fight—he'd been ready to see Vee. To speak to her, to explain, to even have that hard, horrible conversation.

And instead, he had this. Sailing further away with no prospect of speaking to her, perhaps *ever*.

"Mercia didn't turn her," he murmured, voice thick, "*I* did. And I've put her in danger because of it."

I pushed her to him. It gnawed at him. *I pushed her to him. I pushed her...*

"If he's as bad as you say, we can't leave her at his mercy." Perry's lips tightened, paled, and she blasted a breath out through her nostrils. "Even *if* she's chosen him for now."

For now. He searched Perry's gaze. She believed it. She thought there was still hope.

For someone who was generally wise, Perry could be so blind when it came to Vee.

"Pull into this cove," she said, chin jutting to port, "I've signalled we'll meet FitzRoy and talk about next steps." She kept nodding as if that would make the situation better. "We'll follow at a distance—use the horizon and any land to stay hidden. I'll put a watch as high as possible—they'll keep eyes on the tips of the *Sovereign's* masts. That's all we need to see to know which way they're going." She exhaled and dropped her arms from where they'd been so tightly folded. "Wait and see what happens."

Delay making a decision, that's what she meant. But she was captain, and it wasn't endangering anyone. He'd object as soon as it did.

Perhaps it would be comforting knowing he was just over the horizon from Vee.

Perhaps it would be torture.

"Your hope is admirable." He gave Perry a stiff smile. "But I'm sure of it—Mercia has offered her the *Venatrix* and another clue. With the Copper Drake *and* his clue and all his other resources—if that treasure exists, she'll find it." He shook his head, throat too tight to speak for a second. "He's offered her everything she's ever wanted."

How can I compete with that?

RESPAIR

Knigh scribbled out another row of nonsense letters. Sighing, he threw the pen back in the inkwell.

This blasted clue would be the death of him.

He'd tried the first letter of each sentence, of each word, the last letter, all the capital letters. None of them had spelled out a secret message, a clue, a riddle, or a location.

No wonder it had irritated Vee so much.

Vee.

Eyes screwed shut, he grimaced. "Not thinking about her, remember?"

That was the whole point of trying to work out this damn clue. He'd spent days stewing about her and Mercia and that damn storm. Any time he wasn't working on the clue, his thoughts drifted back in that devastating direction.

Even when he'd sat up with Barnacle last night as she'd had

her kittens, all he'd been able to think about was that Vee was missing it. The four little things were healthy and wriggling, suckling from their mother in a blanket nest at the foot of his bunk. He'd slept on the floor out of fear of squashing them.

Wild Hunt, how Vee would've laughed at him.

"Clue," he muttered. "Distraction."

He scowled at the page. What the hells did Drake's poetry have to do with his treasure?

Smoothing his hand over the sheet of paper he'd used for notes, he shook his head at the gibberish scrawled all over it.

Hells, he'd even resorted to tallying the number of times each letter had been used. It hadn't added up to an intriguing set of coordinates or anything else he could work out a use for.

At least it kept his mind occupied.

The last thing he needed was to be left to think about—

Two raps at the door.

Perhaps it was Perry wanting another chat. Despite all this business with the woman he wasn't thinking about, his talks with Perry had helped him feel a little better about his father and his anger. It was the tiniest glimmer of the faintest silver lining to Vice's storm.

"Yes?" he called, turning his chair.

When the door opened, it wasn't Perry, though—a far larger form blocked the evening light. Even with his face shadowed, the gold glinting on his ostentatious coat was unmistakable.

"FitzRoy." Every muscle tensed. "What are you doing here?"

"Blackwood," he drawled, stalking in and surveying the room with a quick glance. "So good to see you, too." He narrowed his eyes at Barnacle's cushion still on the bed. "So this was Vice's cabin, eh?" Eyebrows rising, he nodded. "I'm sure she won't mind you leaping into her grave *at all.*"

Perry had asked him to take the room, just temporarily, while he was first mate, so he'd be close by if she needed him.

A long breath. And another. Knigh pulled his teeth apart from where they'd clamped together far too tightly. "It isn't like that and you know it. What do you want?"

FitzRoy closed his eyes, exhaling through his nose. "This isn't going how I intended." He shook his head and gave what might've been an apologetic smile. On him it was hard to tell. "Look, I... I know how you feel. I suspect I'm the only one around here who does. Say what you like about Vice, but she has a way of getting under your skin, doesn't she?"

Knigh raised an eyebrow. FitzRoy had come here to have a heart-to-heart about Vee? If the man wasn't so irritating, he'd have laughed. Hard.

"I do care about her." A softer look flickered over FitzRoy's face, obliterating his usual smugness for a moment. "But it's complicated. We've been through a great deal together—I met her three years before you appeared, you know." He lifted his chin as if that made him important.

Knigh forced his breaths even, but his fingers itched to form fists and pulverise the man. Not because of what had happened between him and Vee, or how long they'd known each other— his mere presence was enough.

"Good for you," he managed to push out from between gritted teeth.

He bit his tongue against the desire to say that he'd been

engaged to her and had known her since before she could fire a pistol.

But keeping that from FitzRoy was something he could cling to—a little piece of control that he could balance all the rest upon.

His shoulders lowered, and he managed to ease a faintly mocking smile in place—a look he often wore when dealing with this man.

FitzRoy pursed his lips, stalking closer. "I can see you don't believe me." He stopped by Knigh's chair, folding his arms. "After I saw you in Portsmouth, I drank myself into a stupor because I couldn't get it out of my head that she was about to die. Lucky for me, you saved her. Don't get me wrong, I want to wring her neck as often as I want to take her over a desk—"

Knigh bit the inside of his cheek. He would not react.

"—but... damn that woman if she doesn't drive me utterly insane." He raised an eyebrow. "I'm sure you understand."

Long breaths. Several of them. Knigh smile brightened as his muscles eased. "What is this, FitzRoy, the inaugural meeting of Lady Vice's Former Lovers Society?" There, he'd even managed a joke. He was in control.

"Oh, Lords no, we'd have to invite *a lot* more people for that. Aedan, for starters." The corner of FitzRoy's mouth twitched as if he expected a reaction. When none came, he huffed a little breath of surprise. "She told you, then?"

"I'm busy. Get on with something meaningful or get out. And I'm only humouring you on the 'something meaningful' because Perry practically begged me not to murder you on sight."

FitzRoy shrugged and scooped up a handful of papers from the desk. "I'm just trying to offer some friendly advice. After all, you seem so damn tense all the time. Look, we have her in common, but I understand her in a way you couldn't possibly. I saw the girl she was before she was Lady Vice and I saw her become the woman you know now." He sighed, gaze dropping to the nonsense notes. "What I'm saying is—you need to forget about her. It was inevitable."

Knigh stiffened.

"She turned coat," FitzRoy continued, "but can you blame her after what we did? She's disloyal, but we played a part."

There is no 'we'.

You're wrong.

She isn't disloyal.

It all fought to come out of his mouth at once.

Wild Hunt, if FitzRoy told him the sky was blue, he'd have argued.

The self-importance. The assumption that Knigh would want to speak to him of all people about Vee. And the bald-faced hypocrisy of *him* calling *her* disloyal.

"She was lusting after that ship of yours the moment she saw it. If your Duke offered it to her, she'd sell her own mother for a pop at it. *Of course* she abandoned us and changed sides."

"She hasn't changed sides," Knigh snapped. "She's many things, and she has plenty of failings, but being disloyal isn't one of them."

Breaths heavy, he fell silent.

Damnation.

It was true.

That hadn't just spewed out of his mouth because he was driven to disagree with anything FitzRoy said—it was bloody true.

The way she followed Perry's leadership, despite it standing between her and her own captaincy. Loyal.

Even back in Portsmouth, she'd insisted on helping his family. Loyal—to a man who'd betrayed her, no less.

What was I thinking? Of course she'd never turn coat to Mercia of all people.

Perry had to be right—Vee had used that storm to turn them away for their own good. It was the only thing that made sense, and he'd been a fool not to see it.

Only his fears around Mercia had made him think anything different.

FitzRoy was a fool, too.

Vee hadn't abandoned them.

And Knigh couldn't damn well abandon her.

Chair squeaking across the floor, he stood. Muscles thrumming with energy, movement was suddenly very necessary. He clenched his hands, trying to hold it in.

FitzRoy chuckled softly. "Your optimism is admirable, albeit unexpected for—"

"Shut up, FitzRoy. And, while you're at it, get out."

He had to go out to the main top, check what the watch had seen.

They—the whole crew had to be ready. There *would* be an opportunity they could exploit to get Vee—perhaps the *Sovereign* would anchor in a quiet bay and they could swim from shore under cover of darkness. If she was being treated like a guest, she'd be much easier to reach than if she was locked down in the hold. They only needed to get in and out quickly.

Wynn and Effie could re-make their explosive barrels to scare away the kraken and buy time for their escape. FitzRoy could distract them with his seventy-four guns.

FitzRoy's brows lifted slowly, and he dropped the papers back on the desk. "Hmm"—he reached down, apparently unconcerned that he was crowding Knigh's space—"my clue." He turned the page towards himself, frowning.

"It's not *your* clue. Vee and I dived for it, not you. You were swanning around 'supervising' *The Morrigan's* careening, as I recall."

Eyebrow raised, FitzRoy straightened. "I think you'll find I was biding my time until we could intercept the *Covadonga*. And—oh yes, of course! This *is* the *Covadonga*, so I'd say I timed it pretty damn perfectly. Wouldn't you?"

Smug bastard.

"It still isn't your clue," Knigh bit out, pinning the page to the desk beneath his fingertips.

FitzRoy shrugged and pulled his hand away before sauntering to the door. "Fine. Fat lot of good it'll do you, anyway. Doesn't look like you've managed to solve it, either." He flashed a sharp smile, then left.

Knigh turned from the door with a sigh. "Prick."

And he'd messed up his desk.

He gathered the notes, re-stacking them with a satisfying

rustle of paper. Good, the clue was still there. He wouldn't have put it past FitzRoy to try and pocket it.

The fact he'd left it wonky was enough to set Knigh's teeth on edge. He rolled his eyes, catching a glimpse of the mountainous islands outside, their lush green edged with gold by the setting sun.

He'd go to Perry, tell her she was right, and apologise for letting his fear rule him.

Nodding, he smiled and went to straighten the clue.

Mountains.

The white space left by the edges of the poetry looked like a pair of mountains side-by-side, one taller and steeper than the other.

His breath caught as he lifted the page, leaving it on its side.

Perhaps the words themselves weren't the clue; perhaps the clue lay in their shape.

It didn't match the islands out the stern window, but it was faintly familiar.

With the paper against the setting sun, the random lines on the other side ghosted through.

Only they weren't random.

His heart skipped a beat.

"Rivers."

Tributaries feeding into larger rivers running down the sides of the twin mountains.

"Damnation."

They'd been looking at the clue wrong all this time—literally. They'd focused on the words and letters. Even keeping the page upright had been wrong. But *sideways*...

He gave a cautious laugh. He knew this island.

Just wait until I tell Vee.

His insides dropped. The laugh deflated.

She wasn't here, and if they didn't get her back from Mercia, he'd never get to tell her.

LIMITLESS

Almost two weeks after summoning the storm, Vice sat in Mercia's study, curled up with a book. This one was about the work and adventures of sea witches since the days of Elizabeth I, when the fae had returned to Albion and, with them, magic.

She scrubbed her eyes, which were gritty from lack of sleep. The kraken's red tentacles had slithered through her dreams every night. Sometimes it crushed the little fishing boat again, but she was *there*—she could see the crew's faces, hear their screams, see their blood. Other times it destroyed the *Respair*, and it was the cries of her friends and desperate mews of Barnacle's kittens that woke her.

Last night, its tentacles had wrapped around her.

She shuddered, squeezing the book. Had Barnacle had her litter yet? Her eyes stung at the thought of the cat—*her* cat labouring alone.

"Here and now," she whispered.

Today they were due to reach the island where Drake's treasure was hidden, according to Mercia's map.

Vice flipped the page, unable to summon an ounce of excitement. What did finding the treasure matter if she didn't have her freedom? That was more important than gold or jewels or even Excalibur.

Munroe had come aboard yesterday for a meeting about roles and duties for the approach to the island. As Mercia's 'pet'—that's what the men had started calling her out of his earshot—she'd attended, but hadn't roused herself to speak. Even catching a glimpse of Mercia's map, which he guarded jealously, hadn't piqued her interest.

Afterwards, she'd managed to corner Munroe alone and asked him to try and get a message to Knigh. If she couldn't escape, at least she could explain she'd raised the storm to keep them safe, so they'd know she hadn't betrayed them. But Munroe couldn't—even if he had a way of reaching Knigh, the risk was too great.

"I *am* sorry," he said and looked at her strangely. "You were quiet in that meeting. Hardly what I'd expect from the great Pirate Queen."

"The great Pirate Queen wouldn't get herself captured by a monster."

He flinched, glancing towards Mercia's quarters. He huffed a sigh, shoulders loosening when he saw the Duke wasn't nearby. She walked him the rest of the way to the ship's boat before wishing him goodbye and turning away.

"You've given up, haven't you?"

She stopped mid-step and looked over her shoulder, missing the tickle of her earring. It sat in her pocket, unworn since the day she'd sent the *Respair* away. She tried to scoff but couldn't summon even a hint of laughter. Did he really expect an answer?

He was giving her another odd look, a troubled frown between his brows. "Blackwood didn't give up on you. He wouldn't expect you to give up on yourself."

She wanted to say she didn't have a choice or ask him what the hells he knew about being captured by someone like Mercia. But her jaw was too stiff, and he was already climbing into the boat waiting to take him back to the *Venatrix*.

Her shoulders and jaw had been knotted with tension ever since.

It wasn't that she'd given up. There just wasn't any way out.

She was under constant supervision—guards waited outside the doors right now, iron manacles at their belts. The stern windows were all locked. And even if she somehow managed to get out, the men in the mizzen top were always on watch for anyone in the water, rifles loaded with iron shot.

Then there was the kraken.

She turned the page, huffing. All the stories were the same: reading between the lines, the sea witches pressed into naval service were little more than property. They only left when they were too ill or injured to use their gifts or once they were dead.

Anyone whose gifts worked sea or weather ended up as the Royal Navy's working prisoners. Maybe this had always been inevitable.

A sharp rap came from the door. One of the guards—not Evans—entered and nodded. "Madam, we approach the island."

She left the book out—maybe it would annoy Mercia—and followed him to the poop deck, gown rustling with each movement.

Mercia and George waited, both staring intently ahead. The skin around Mercia's eyes was tight, his jaw too. She followed their gazes.

Close to the water's surface, a ball of dark cloud churned. No storm would normally sit that low or stay in one place. She frowned, watching as they approached.

Lightning flashed within the seething mass, soon followed by a boom of thunder.

The hairs on her arms and the back of her neck stood on end. Mercia was right—this was no natural storm.

"How have they made it last so long?"

"Hmm?" Mercia finally tore his gaze from the storm and raised an eyebrow at her. "What do you mean?"

"When I work on the weather, it lasts while I focus on it and pour energy into it, but once I stop, it dissipates over time. This must've been put in place when Drake hid his treasure. How is it still here?"

Was there some trick to it—yet another technique she didn't know? Mercia's books hadn't so much as hinted at any way of using gifts to leave a permanent mark on the world like this.

"Perhaps the answer lies with the treasure." His eyes narrowed at her, calculating. No doubt he wondered if this was a way to make his 'pet' stronger. "Come ashore with me."

She plucked at her skirts. "Not the best idea in these."

He blinked, then scanned her from head to toe as if he hadn't really seen her before. "Of course." When he clicked his fingers, his valet hurried over. A few words, then the servant was off putting together a 'more practical outfit' to leave in her cabin.

Asking for different clothes had got her nowhere. Now her gown was no longer convenient to him—*Poof!*—breeches, shirt, and waistcoat could just appear.

"Now," he drawled, "about that storm."

From this distance, she could see the water below the clouds. More white than blue, it twisted and foamed. Thirty-foot waves peaked, their steep sides more mountain than sea.

She reached out with her gift.

It was even worse.

The waves whipped high and powerful, just like she'd seen, but that wasn't all. Seething, sucking, spinning. It swept together, turning over and over, before dragging froth and water to the sea bed.

Wild Hunt, this wasn't only a storm, but a maelstrom too.

"There's a whirlpool," she murmured.

"I know. Focus on the storm—I can take care of the water."

But she shook her head and pulled on sky and sea at once.

The storm writhed against her grip, electricity crackling, thunder shaking. Jaw clenched, she willed it still and quiet. *Seep between my fingers. Dissipate.*

Clouds thinned, grew lighter, but lightning went on striking, bright and fierce.

The sea, too, bucked and twisted from her grasp.

Bugger it.

Her limbs ached—she was only using her own strength, not the wellspring. She couldn't focus on the wellspring *and* both her gifts.

She huffed, shaking her head. "Fine, you sort out the whirlpool."

With long breaths, she closed her eyes again and gathered her focus. Somewhere in the distance she clasped her hands—maybe that sensation would be a reminder if she came close to losing herself again.

When she dived into the power, she was blind.

It was everything.

And she was nothing.

But...

Pinpricks of pain. Nails against the backs of hands—*her* hands.

She was not nothing. She was Vice. And she was here to call sea and storm to her command.

The energy condensed, no longer everywhere and everything, now fizzing and snapping through her veins. It sparked across her skin, leaving her tingling in its wake.

This, she could direct.

The immense power of that lightning striking over and over was nothing to this. She pushed her power into the storm. Instead of the static in those clouds bursting outwards in more flashes of lightning, it streaked inwards, converging on the crackling core of her gift.

It was like being hit. Sudden and hard, shocking a gasp from her.

An instant later, it shifted, more like power and lust and fierce joy buzzing through her.

The clouds were gone and somehow she'd sucked energy from the lightning itself.

Her body trembled—no, shuddered. She was a wine glass quaking at a note that, held too long, would eventually break it.

This power—the lightning and the wellspring together—it was too much. Glorious as it felt, it would rip her apart if she didn't discharge it. Maybe that was what a storm cloud was—power that couldn't be held too long, that needed release.

If her body could act like a channel and bring power from the wellspring to the world, maybe it could carry it in the other direction, too. She held her hands in the glowing core of the wellspring, but instead of pulling, she pushed.

As if that thought was all it needed, the trembling energy cracked through her and into the wellspring in a blinding flash.

With a jolt, she opened her eyes.

The deck spun as if they'd sailed into the maelstrom, but she was ready for it this time and braced her feet in a wide stance. After a few long breaths, it stilled.

She'd done it. And done something with that lightning. Maybe something she shouldn't have.

She winced, rubbing her aching arms with stiff hands. Hunger gnawed at her stomach. Her muscles felt like they'd been pummelled in a fight—not tired, but sore. Creating the storm hadn't hurt like this.

Maybe mortals weren't meant to draw power from nature.

Still, she'd done it. She scoffed and shook out her arms.

"Well done," Mercia said, an odd tone in his voice making her look up at last. *"Very* well done." But he frowned as much as he smiled, as though even he wasn't sure whether he meant it.

Perhaps he didn't want a pet more powerful than he was.

He'd underestimated her. He thought she was all raw power. True, she might not have had any training in her gift, but she'd used it almost every day for the past three years. She'd calmed storms, saved lives, steered ships out of cannon fire. It wasn't a formal education, but she hadn't been idle.

And now he'd taught her to use the wellspring.

Maybe that meant she was limitless, like he'd said. Maybe he'd just exaggerated to win her over. Either way, she was definitely stronger than she had been—perhaps even stronger than he was.

Perhaps that was what he saw as he frowned at her.

She smothered her smirk and turned away.

The island rose from calm waters, a lush emerald green. A cove of pale sand lay ahead, the perfect place to make landfall, while a forested headland climbed to the left before dropping into the sea in a sheer cliff face.

At the very top of the highest part of that cliff, the regularity of the rocks caught her eye, and she squinted. Were they walls? A pillar? Not natural rock formations, but ruins.

"There it is," Mercia breathed. He chuckled as if he hadn't expected there to really be an island beyond the storm and maelstrom. "Well, madam, you'd best get changed while they ready the launch. Drake's treasure awaits."

MOSS & CANOPY

The storm was gone, but rainwater still dripped from one leaf to the next and eventually to the forest floor. One droplet splashed down the back of Vice's neck as she hiked up the headland.

It didn't make much difference—her shirt and breeches were already soaked through with sweat and humidity.

More sweat beaded the brows of six of Mercia's men who huffed their way uphill, Evans amongst them. They blocked any path she might've taken if she wanted to run. But she was close to Drake's treasure—now was not the time to try and escape.

Besides, the *Sovereign's* boat was the only way off the island, and that was guarded by another half-dozen men.

Sighing, she trudged on.

After an hour, shadows rose in the green gloom. Vice

493

blinked, looking up from the root-strewn trail. Evans' pale hair gleamed in the scant light as he stopped and peered up.

The shadows resolved into low stone buildings, one and two storeys with open doorways that were little more than yawning blackness. Vines snaked their way across hewn rock and saplings grew from rooftops, their roots veiling the dark doorways.

The building style was local, none of it Albionic. These had to be remnants of an old civilisation, ancestors to one of the cultures that still ruled Arawaké and traded with Europa. Drake must've appropriated these ruins to hide his treasure. It made sense—he probably hadn't stayed in one place long enough to build something of his own.

Ahead, more green, but this was moss blanketing stone steps that led up and up, eventually piercing the forest canopy. Bright daylight flooded a structure at the top of the terraced pyramid.

Vice cocked her head, staring up with narrowed eyes. The tree growing in the middle of the steps, with another fallen at its side. The square faces carved either side of the path, mouths open as if they'd speak. The stylised carvings around them, still slick and glossy from the earlier rain. It was all familiar.

She'd seen it in the Copper Drake.

And she knew where to go.

She directed them not to the top, but to a narrow door hidden behind one of the stone heads. She couldn't read the Copper Drake, but she'd studied the drawings until her eyes had burned.

Lighting lanterns, they slipped inside a stone passage

barely wider than her shoulders and low enough that she had to stoop.

No footprints marked the mud outside, and it was so overgrown this ruin must've been abandoned long ago. They were the only ones here—she had no reason to be stealthy.

But there was something about this place—the quiet, perhaps, or the age—that made her creep along. Maybe it was the sense that this was somewhere she shouldn't be.

If this was a temple, it was to gods she didn't know the names of, never mind follow. If it was a tomb, it was for someone she'd never heard of. Whatever the purpose of this place, it wasn't for her or Mercia.

Or Drake. The building wasn't his, but he'd still used it for his own purposes. Had he also felt unwelcome? Or had he been blind to it? Had he been more like Evered—looking at the world like it was all his to own and do with as he wished?

Saba would love and hate to see this. She'd know what the buildings were for, which local culture they were by the style of lintels. She could perhaps even work out their age. But she'd also rage against Drake for having taken this place that was not his. Had he desecrated a sacred location to hide his treasure?

Still, Vice wished Saba were here. And Perry, Knigh, and the others. Her chest tightened.

After a few minutes, the passage turned then opened into a chamber that stretched roughly twenty-five feet left, twenty-five right, but only a dozen feet ahead. Braziers filled with blackened charcoal stood at regular intervals. Every inch of wall and ceiling was decorated in bas-relief sculpture, so detailed, all she could do was stare.

The criss-crossing, spiralling textures, the paint—ochre, orange, red, black, blue-green—and the gleaming jade in the shape of...

She blinked—ah, that was a necklace at someone's throat. On the ceiling, jade and obsidian adorned a throne.

Evans appeared at her side and lifted his lantern to help her make sense of it all. As the rest of the party filtered into the room, exclaiming at the sculpture, the shapes had resolved into recognisable figures and features.

A feathered, winged serpent. A man with a lizard tail and face. A woman with claws, fangs, and white skulls bright against her red clothes. And many more.

Were they just carvings, though? Thicker shadowed lines stood out on the wall ahead. Eyes narrow, Vice crept closer and gestured for Evans to lift his lantern.

A groove ran around the edge of a hanged woman as if the whole thing was separate, not just carved into the wall. A door?

Her pulse sped. This was the way forward.

But—she cocked her head, taking a pace to the right—the lizard-man was also outlined. And the lady of skulls, too.

Vice stepped back, taking Evans' lantern and shifting it so the light and shadows danced and deepened.

Each carved figure was a door.

Thirteen doors.

She chewed her lip. Which was the right way? And did she really want to alert Mercia to her discovery? If he couldn't find a way forward and had to abandon this, she could escape later, to return and claim Drake's treasure for herself.

"What's this?"

She flinched at his voice right beside her. So much for keeping quiet about the doors.

"Hmm." Mercia raised his eyebrows, gaze tracing the lines she'd been examining. "A door. Good find, madam." His eyes glinted, dark like the obsidian chips in the walls.

Evans stepped forward, taking in a jaguar-featured woman with a soft exhale, his blond hair bright in the lamplight.

"Look." He chuckled and pressed a spot on the jaguar-woman's shoulder. A click, then the door opened, and he grinned at her, then one of his colleagues. "I'd say you owe me a drink for that, Flanders." Still grinning, he nodded to Flanders and started inside.

Stone scraped upon stone. Something rumbled beneath their feet.

A trickle of fine sand hissed from the ceiling, then stopped. With a clack, a pebble fell loose and hit the floor.

The hairs on the back of Vice's neck prickled.

A distant clink echoed like a shard of pottery landing on a floor below.

She tensed, hand going to her belt. No hilt to grab, though.

An uncertain sound rose from Evans' throat. He glanced back, face pale. "What—?"

Then he was gone.

DUST

Staring at the puff of dust, it took Vice a moment to register the crash of rock, the scream, the thud.

Where Evans had stood, the ground had fallen away, leaving a maw of darkness.

The other men hurried to the edge, bending over. "Evans?"

Agonised cries came from the hole. So he was alive, but whether he could hear or understand them over the weight of his own pain was anyone's guess.

Vice's stomach turned. She'd heard cries like that before from a man who'd been trapped beneath a cannon that had burst from its breeching ropes. It had crushed his legs and chest. He hadn't been able to make that sound for long.

"Rope," she said, "I need rope." She'd spotted coils on the men's shoulders as they'd hiked up here. "I can climb down and—"

"Out of the way." Mercia pushed her aside. He waved the

men from the hole and strode towards it, boots clicking across the stone floor.

Mercia was going to do it? She blinked. Maybe he did care about his men.

When the officers backed away, their faces had a green cast.

Small wonder. The sound of Evans' whimpers made her insides shrivel. Once Mercia brought him up, she would soothe him and help carry him back to the boat.

One hand braced on the stone edges of the doorway, Mercia bent over the hole, peering down. Tongue clicking, he shook his head. "Spikes. A trap—not an accident."

"Mother," Evans whimpered. "Mama. Help me."

Eyes stinging, Vice gritted her teeth. They had to get him to a healer *quickly*. Maybe one of these bags of equipment had willow bark or laudanum—something to help the poor lad's pain.

She shook her head to dispel the horror that held her frozen in place and glanced at the equipment Mercia's men had brought with them. One of those who'd backed off had a coil of rope over his shoulder.

"Give him your rope," she hissed at him, jerking her chin at Mercia. "What do you think he's—"

The crack of a pistol shot rang out.

Vice ducked before she even registered consciously what it was.

There were no more cries.

Mercia turned with a sigh and slipped his pistol back in its holster.

She stared at him, chest so tight she could barely breathe.

Her ears rang.

He'd killed Evans.

They had a healer back at the *Sovereign*—the man trapped under a cannon on *The Morrigan* hadn't been so lucky. Evans had been young and fit. Even with severe injuries, he'd stood a chance with a fae-touched healer.

That boy—because he wasn't much more than a child. He'd been kind, gentle, thoughtful. He'd treated her like a human being. He'd... he'd had a whole life ahead of him.

"Hmm." Mercia raised his eyebrows again, no change in the sound or expression from earlier, like he hadn't just killed someone or lost a man under his command. "One door down, twelve to go."

A shudder shook right through to her bones. That was all he saw.

Evans had been his to command, yes, but that also meant Mercia had responsibility for his safety, his *life*. And although Mercia had made his kraken kill those fisherfolk, he hadn't been able to see their eyes, *see* them die. But he'd killed Evans just as easily, even as he'd begged for help.

Then she was only a foot away from Mercia, breaths shaking. "You're a monster. How could—?"

"He was already dead. I just ended his suffering." Lips pursed, he turned a cool look upon her, apparently unconcerned by her closeness.

Footsteps and the ring of steel. Mercia's men closed in, ready to stop her attacking him. Still loyal, even after that?

No wonder he didn't think her a threat. No weapon, outnumbered six-to-one—she stood no chance.

Mercia raised a hand, keeping his men at bay as his hooded eyes stayed on her. "My assumption is all but one of these doors is a trap. If you care so much, you'll work out which is safe so we all make it to the next room."

Cold settled over her. He didn't give a damn whether his men survived. It was down to her.

She would've gladly fought any of them in a battle and cut them down to save her own skin. But this wasn't a battle—it wasn't a choice of her life or theirs. This was a needless waste.

Muscles tight, she paced the room.

Jaguar-woman. Winged serpent. Lizard-man. They had to be gods of the people who'd built this place. Gods always had their own domains and meanings. The Morrigan were the sisters of war and fate in Albion. She knew all their stories and associations—crow, warrior-queen, hag.

While these figures on the walls looked familiar, she didn't know their names, their stories, their *anything*.

She huffed. One of them could be the god of treasure, for all she knew!

But, then again, had Drake known anything about them, either? The age of this place—it must've been old and deserted even before he found it. He could have simply made up his own associations.

She stopped before the winged serpent—that was like a dragon or a drake, wasn't it? Maybe this was the way.

No, he hadn't built this place and set its traps. She had to stop thinking about *his* viewpoint.

For a long time, she paced. Mercia still examined the carved forms, eyes blazing with curiosity. His men hung back, watching her, hands on their weapons. She could've laughed—they were afraid of the wrong person.

Mercia blasted a frustrated sigh. "They're so damn familiar, I feel like the answer is right there and I'm just not seeing it." His face screwed up, so unlike his usual genteel elegance it made her pause, even though she hadn't acknowledged him since he'd told her to find the right door.

She tugged on her bottom lip. The man was a monster—worse than the notorious Lady Vice, every bit as bad as Knigh said. But she was stuck with him, and they were close to Drake's treasure.

He was a necessary evil.

She had to speak to him, to work with him. Even if it was only to delay him pointing the pistol at her once he decided she was of no further use.

Swallowing, she folded her arms. "Stands to reason—they must still worship these gods or variations of them now. You've probably seen similar statues in nearby towns and cities."

Lips pursed, he shook his head. "That can't be where I've seen them—I never visit Arawakéan settlements. I leave diplomacy to my sister and her errand-boys."

"No, I suppose that wouldn't be your strong point."

So, if not in nearby towns, where could they *both* have seen these figures?

She stared at the winged serpent.

Actually, it wasn't just that the idea of a winged serpent was familiar, it was...

Her fingertips traced over the stylised feathers, the lightning-bolt crown—even these little details were familiar. She couldn't have seen this carving before because she'd never been here, but a drawing of it...

"The book," she breathed. Her heart sped, the beat light and fast against her ribs. "The Copper Drake—do you have it with you?"

His eyes narrowed at her—no doubt he thought this a ploy to get her hands on the book again. "Why?"

"That's where I've seen these figures before. You must've seen them too. It's the only place we'd both recognise them from."

He gasped, eyebrows shooting up. "Well I'll be damned. You're right." He pulled the book from his waistcoat breast pocket. Frowning, he flicked through it.

"Give it to me," she said, peering at the pages as he spent far too long pausing at every image.

He gave her a look that said he wasn't mad so he wouldn't be doing that.

"Even if I did snatch it off you, where would I go? You've got them blocking the way out. The *Sovereign's* the only ship around. I can't exactly escape. I've spent weeks obsessing over that thing—I know exactly what page we need."

Face still angled at the book, he looked up at her from beneath lowered brows and held her gaze a long while. His jaw ticked. "Fine."

Within a second, she'd flicked to the right page.

The drawings leapt out, fresh after she'd spent a few weeks away. She looked from them to the carved doors before her. All perfect matches.

Beneath each one, a word—thankfully written in Albionic,

rather than the ciphered Ancient Hellenic. *Onion. Beet. Parsnip. Lettice. Radish.*

She huffed. What the hells did leek and cabbage have to do with the right course?

"Wait," she breathed. *Lettice*, not *lettuce*. Lettice Archer was the sea witch who'd served with Drake for years. Old books sometimes spelled words strangely, but the fact this one was also a name... It certainly fitted with humour of the time—Joan Shakespeare's plays were full of silly wordplay.

"What is it?" Mercia craned over the book.

"Maybe nothing."

Lettice had been written under the winged serpent drawing. She stalked to the carving. Its sinuous lines caught the light, making the feathers seem to move as her lantern shifted.

Leek. Onion. Beet. Parsnip. Lettice. Radish. Cabbage.

This had to be the answer. Lettice Archer had set Drake's ships on the right course—he could have used her to signify the right path.

Frankly, no other option made sense. Besides, it would explain why these had been written in Albionic—the wordplay wouldn't work in Ancient Hellenic, even ciphered.

"This one." She nodded. "And I think..."

The serpent's eye clicked under her fingertip and the door scraped open on tracks.

"There." She exhaled and raised her eyebrows at Mercia.

He smiled, and it conjured Evans' cries in her mind. Sour bile burned her throat.

Eyebrows raised, Mercia peered into the corridor beyond. "After you."

THE KEY

Heart pounding, Vice crept through the door. Her leg muscles wound tight, ready to leap the instant the floor so much as creaked.

But it didn't.

Her ears strained as an ugly thought registered—each door could have a different trap behind it.

But there was no whirr of cogs or rumble of rock falling from above. No tripwire crossed the path.

Three steps in and nothing.

Another three steps and she was still alive.

She hadn't realised how tightly she'd been holding her shoulders until they dropped.

"It's fine," she called back and stalked down the corridor.

For five minutes, they made their way through a narrow, winding passage. The way the passage dog-legged, they might've only travelled a few dozen yards from the room with the doors. With the encroaching jungle shrouding the building, it had been hard to get an idea of its full scale.

For the sections where the corridor ran straight, it stretched beyond their lamplight into darkness. Vice smoothed her fingers over the hair at the nape of her neck. It lay flat and had done since she'd started along this route, in fact. Maybe there were no more traps. Each corner still sent her hand to her belt as if she might find an enemy when she turned.

The corridor finally opened out into a square room—this time the carvings weren't only painted in red and ochre and set with jade and obsidian, but flecks of gold leaf glimmered in the light. With a low gasp, Vice spun in the centre of the room. Some depicted recognisable objects and creatures—a face below a tasselled headdress, a bird with spotted feathers— others were so stylised she could pick out nothing but patterns.

And in one corner stood a chest—not of Arawakéan design, but plain and sturdy and of Albionic oak.

The others filed in. There was no gleam of Evans' pale hair, no gentle smile amongst the grim faces.

"Is this it?" Mercia approached the chest. For the first time the curve of his lips was uncertain, paired with a crease between his brows.

"I hadn't expected it to be so small, either." She shrugged. But it was Drake's treasure. His book and map had pointed them here. If it was so simple, why bother with the rest of the book though? And the cipher?

Unless this wasn't it.

She swallowed and tried to look nonchalant as Mercia

ordered his men to check the chest, the room, and its other door.

This could just be another clue, pointing them on elsewhere. Hells, maybe the chest was a red herring. The real clue could be somewhere in this room. That was the sort of thing that happened in adventure books.

Steps silent, she circled the room, fighting to keep her breath steady. Dust and fine sand covered the floor as it had in every other room, but here dried leaves and thin branches crinkled under the men's feet.

Placed here deliberately, to hide something?

The marines who'd checked the door reappeared. She kept her eyes on the wall carvings as if that's all she was interested in. They reported to Mercia—a short corridor led outside, opening to a plaza, half of which must've crumbled into the sea. This was the last room on this level.

While they helped examine the chest and work out how to open it, Vice scuffed her feet across the floor, sweeping the leaves away. Smooth stone. She didn't know what she was looking for, but if there was something here, it would stand out. Paint or the outline of a trapdoor. There could be another level below, hiding the real treasure.

The corner of her mouth twitched, and she scratched her nose to hide it. But when she glanced at Mercia, he was too absorbed in the chest to notice. *Good. Stay occupied.*

More smooth stone.

She kept going and as she reached the last corner, she kicked away a pile of leaves, revealing a scratch.

Deep. Not an accident. Angled lines, nothing like the serpentine and linear designs on the walls.

She pushed away another leaf, revealing a symbol she knew. *Sigma.*

Breath caught in her throat.

Keep calm.

She yawned, throwing another glance at Mercia. Still distracted.

Leant against the wall, she toed away the rest of the leaves.

A grid of Ancient Hellenic letters.

Her heart squeezed. This was the cipher's key.

With this, she'd be able to read every word in the Copper Drake.

She swallowed back the excitement that was trying to push its way out in a laugh. She might've found it, but there were practicalities. Most importantly, how could she copy it down? She flicked through the book—her folded sheets of notes were still tucked in the back. That was a start, now for something to write with. If she asked Mercia for a pencil, he'd want to know why.

Rolling her shoulders and neck, she circled the room again. Something sharp would give her blood. Or—

She reached a brazier. *Charcoal.* Perfect. She palmed a few pieces of burnt wood.

With another theatrical yawn, she sat beside the key, legs stretched out to block their view. As if absorbed by their swirling shapes, she stared at the carvings on the wall opposite. She unfolded a sheet of paper with one hand and placed it over the top half of the key. It took a few seconds to take a rubbing from the carved letters and fold the paper back up.

She glanced at Mercia as she unfolded the next sheet. His men had a hammer and chisel out and he was ordering them to take off the hinges. They'd be in the chest soon and she needed to look riveted by that or else he'd realise she'd found something more interesting.

With a few swipes of charcoal, she'd taken the next rubbing.

The metallic clink of hammer on chisel filled the room.

She blew away the charcoal dust and folded the paper before leaping to her feet.

As she crossed the room, she tucked the pages down her shirt and the Copper Drake into her waistcoat pocket.

When she reached Mercia, she smiled, eyebrows rising in question.

He countered with a smug smirk and gestured as a hinge clattered to the floor. "You're just in time."

Fool. She had the real prize.

A couple more minutes and Mercia's men had the other hinge off and the chest open

No yellow glow of gold under lamplight. No gems or silver.

No traps, either, by the look of it, which was something.

In fact, no sign of *anything*.

Mercia blasted out a breath and craned right over the chest. "What the devil?" A scowl creasing his face, he pulled out a folded piece of cloth. Not silk, either, but simple linen. It might've once been white, but now it was yellowed and stained with age and brown marks that looked like water damage.

Eyebrows raised, Vice peered in the box. Nothing else.

Chest rising, falling, deep and harsh, Mercia shook out the cloth. No treasures fell out, just sprigs of lavender and another rectangle of fabric. This one was also linen, but a deep, rich purple with a jagged white line in the middle. A lightning bolt. The whole piece was maybe three feet by five, while the stained one wasn't even half that size.

He looked from one to the other, mouth opening and closing as a vein pulsed at his temple.

She fought to keep her expression blank but, Lords, the urge to laugh was overwhelming.

He bundled the fabric into one shaking fist. "You," he hissed, turning to her, lips bloodless. "You!" He waved the cloth at her, sending a waft of lavender up her nose.

Why bother to keep the fabric fresh and insects away with lavender if this was only a red herring? And why bother to put anything in the chest at all? Unless the cloth was also a clue, or of some use—

"Look at me," he spat.

She jolted, blinking from the cloth to him.

His face was red, nearly purple like the fabric. Nostrils flaring, he shook his full fist again. "How did you do it? Where did you hide it?" He shot a wild-eyed look at his men. "Search this place and outside."

Pain lanced through her as he grabbed her arm, letting the claws sink into her flesh. There was a scuffle as he dragged her towards the plaza, claws deepening every time she tried to resist.

He huffed and ranted, not even pausing once they reached the ruined terrace. Thick jungle nibbled at the stelae and low buildings to left and right, while ahead, beyond the cliff, the glistening sea stretched to the horizon. Underfoot, smooth tiles hinted at glazes of green, blue, and red beneath a layer of dirt.

From Mercia's chain of spluttered questions, she pieced it together—he thought she'd somehow broken into the chest already and swapped the real treasure for the fabric scraps.

Still he marched on, the cliff edge coming closer and closer.

Bollocks, was he going to throw her off?

She swallowed. "Look, how could I have done all that? I haven't left your sight since we landed on this island."

Feet planted, he spun her to face him.

She skidded to a halt on the debris-strewn tiles, huffing with relief. They were still a few yards from the precipice. If he charged, she'd just side-step and let him fling himself over.

Breaths heaved through him. "You love how much of a fool I look. All this for a water-stained old rag." He laughed, the sound more insane than amused.

"I want Drake's treasure just as much as you do." Not a lie.

"You've tricked me. I don't know how you've done it, but— but you must have. Led me here to—"

"*You* led us here, *Your Highness,* I had nothing to do with that. I didn't even know this island existed until you told me about it."

His shoulders inched down. "But the map"—he shook his head—"this was the only symbol on it. A key. The treasure must be here."

A key. She'd only glimpsed his map from a distance, so she hadn't seen any symbols. It had to stand for the cipher's *key.*

She bit her tongue against any reaction, but Mercia was staring at the fistful of linen as if seeing it for the first time. "Treasure," he muttered. "Excalibur. The sword of the rightful king. Not this." He shook the cloth again. "*This* isn't treasure, it's rubbish!"

Teeth bared, he stomped over and shoved the cloth at her chest.

She staggered backwards, barely catching herself and the fabric.

The ground rumbled. Rock clattered. Soil and sand hissed down the cliff face.

She froze, knees bent to stay steady as the floor shook.

Then it jolted from beneath her, like a deck dropping over a storm-tossed wave. She yelped, stomach dipping.

Falling. She was falling. The ground beneath her feet was—

The air drove from her lungs and she fell to one knee in a jarring stop.

The ground—she blinked, waited—it was still.

The section of terrace she stood on had dropped only five feet, but Lords, it had felt like miles.

She laughed, half-mad with the rush of relief flooding her, hot and intoxicating, making her heart pound wild and fast.

Up on the original level, Mercia stood at the edge, staring past her. "Vice"—he took a long swallow—"stay very still."

"I mean, I wasn't planning to dance a..." But the wideness of his eyes and the fact they were fixed on a point behind her killed the joke in her throat. Slowly, slowly, she turned her head, looked down.

From her toes there was a foot of tiled ground, then nothing more than air, sheer cliff, and the sea roaring against its base.

Their gifts had stopped the whirlpool and storm

temporarily, but even now the water grew choppy and the air thickened with cloud and static.

And this platform of terrace might only be temporary, too. If she moved too quickly, it could crumble away as the rest had. She'd be dashed on the rocks.

She tore her gaze from the tiles teetering on the edge of the precipice.

Beyond, the *Venatrix* and the three other ships left in Mercia's division bobbed at anchor, oblivious to the traps they'd faced or this crumbling cliff.

And to the east, more sails peeked around the opposite headland.

Black sails.

Vice's heart missed a beat, as jolting as the terrace's sudden drop. Was that the *Respair?*

"Vice?" Mercia's voice came out strained and when she turned there was none of the bored aristocrat left in his expression. His eyes were intense, desperate, not those of the man who was used to obedience.

The ground shifted. More tiles clattered away.

He knelt, holding out his hand, chest heaving.

He was afraid for her—wanted to save her.

Wonders would never cease.

She gave an incredulous half-smile, easing away from the brink.

The corner of his mouth ticked, and he nodded in encouragement. "That's it. Closer, now. Do you still have the book?" His eyes flicked over her as if checking for its outline.

Her eyes narrowed. "I do."

"Pass it to me, then," he said, a strained laugh lacing the words. "Better keep it safe, eh? We don't want it falling in the water."

With a grinding of rock, her platform slid another few inches. She pulled deeper into her half-kneel, keeping her balance. The cloth was still balled in her grip and she hugged it tight against her chest, pressing the hard edges of the Copper Drake into her breasts.

When the ground stilled, she caught her breath.

The book. Of course. Mercia didn't give a damn about her, like he hadn't given a damn about Evans when he'd fallen into that pit or Billy when Knigh had taken his hand.

"I see," she murmured.

She glanced over her shoulder. The empty air, the sheer drop were dizzying, despite her years of climbing the shrouds. But they were nowhere near as dangerous as Mercia.

He'd use her up, suck out every ounce of use he could get, and leave her to die.

Or he'd kill her himself.

The storm and whirlpool were gone for now...

She could use her gift to blow herself away from the rocks...

If they were black sails...

This could be her chance to escape.

The ground trembled, rattling her teeth.

There was no time to decide.

Him or the drop.

She staggered to her feet and smiled at Mercia.

His expression brightened, and he strained towards her, fingers beckoning. "Come along, quickly."

"No."

She shook her head, positive now she'd said it. "I'd rather take my chances with the fall and the sea than stay with you."

His eyes widened, face dropped.

Then the ground fell.

ON WATCH

Every sail billowed with a fair wind. Every gunner stood ready. And every crewmember worked with grim determination spelled out on their faces.

From the fore top, Knigh nodded approval, body thrumming with nervous energy as he scanned the ships ahead. The *Venatrix* and three others, all fifth-rate frigates—far smaller than the *Sovereign*.

Each top had someone on watch with a spyglass. They had two tasks: watch for the kraken's approach and look for Vee. Even so, he hadn't been able to help himself and had climbed aloft to search for himself. No sign of Vee or Mercia yet.

As the *Respair* and the *Sea Witch* streamed past the headland, he turned his spyglass to the cove where the *Sovereign* had anchored, facing out to open ocean. Why had they separated?

The seas around the island were choppy with whitecaps that grew by the minute, and the wind whipped his hair. Overhead, the sky darkened, but the sun still shone on the *Venatrix* and her three companions.

Brow tight, he scanned the massive warship's decks. Still no sign of Vee or the Duke.

Ah-ha—on the pale sandy beach, a launch. That had to be the *Sovereign's*. That explained why she was in the cove while the other ships remained out in deeper water. Was Mercia on the island?

Knigh shook his head. No time for that puzzle—they were closing with the smaller vessels.

The frigates were sluggish at setting sail—clearly not expecting company. If Mercia was on the island, the *Sovereign's* crew would be loath to leave him stranded and join battle. The ship's captain, Phillips, was a poor leader—precisely why Mercia had chosen him. He was no threat to Mercia's command and allowed him to use the *Sovereign* for his own ends rather than purely for naval work. But that meant he was also no threat to the pirates. He wouldn't be decisive enough to order the *Sovereign* into battle without his admiral.

If Mercia was on the island.

So much rested on too many *if*s, and yet this was their chance. Gods knew if they'd have another. When they'd spotted the *Sovereign* at anchor separated from her escort, the crew had voted on whether to attack or wait.

The vote had been unanimous.

Drawing a deep breath, he slid the spyglass to his belt and hurried down the shrouds.

Lords, Ladies, Wild Hunt, please say the kraken is away hunting. We could use that little stroke of luck.

Wynn and Effie had re-assembled their explosive barrels, albeit after huffing at him and Perry, "Make the barrels. Un-make the barrels. Make them again. Wish you two would make your minds up!"

He'd given them an apologetic smile but hadn't been able to air the worry lurking at the back of his mind, its tentacles as insistent as the kraken's. What if the explosions didn't work this time? What if the creature had grown used to the scare tactic?

Brow aching from frowning so hard, he swung the last stretch to the bustling deck. Spray cooled his skin, kicked up from those whitecaps he'd spotted from above.

"Blackwood," Perry called from the helm as he jogged towards her, "you have the ship."

His brows shot up. All eyes turned to him and the crew fell silent.

"We're up against the Navy and you know them best. This is your command." She inclined her head.

His command? He couldn't even argue—they were seconds from battle.

With a sigh, he shook his head. Perry knew exactly what she was doing—forcing his hand. He narrowed his eyes at her, before turning and barking orders.

"Clovis—broad on the port bow. Starboard guns, load—even guns use chain, odd guns take round shot." He pointed at each of the four smaller warships in turn. "That's the *HMS Arrogant*, the *Unicorn*, the *Siren*, and the *Venatrix*. Odds rake the *Arrogant's* stern as we pass. Evens, take her mizzenmast."

Despite the crew's surprise, they leapt to follow his orders.

It would've been easier with Vee's gift to regulate their speed and give the gun crews the best angle and opportunity to strike.

But if Vee were here, they wouldn't be doing this.

His chest clenched at the thought of her, but he pushed out the next set of orders, calling on the riflemen and women stationed at the tops to fire the instant they were in range and had a target. They'd already agreed the plan with FitzRoy: officers on the poop deck were the main priority, but they'd refrain from striking the *Venatrix* until she made an aggressive move.

In the final seconds of the *Respair* turning and getting into range, Knigh chewed his lip. Was that the right decision?

Munroe was an unknown quantity. He might be torn about attacking Knigh, especially if not directly provoked. But then again, he might not give a damn about a brother in arms who'd deserted.

At the very least, he might hesitate, and that was better than nothing. With two pirate vessels against four warships, he had to take advantage of every possible weakness.

That was all assuming Munroe was still in command.

Sweeping to starboard, the *Sea Witch* closed with the *Unicorn*. Good, FitzRoy had read the unfolding battle well. Much as Knigh hated the man, he had to give him credit—*The Morrigan's* success hadn't been wholly thanks to Vee.

The *Arrogant* inched towards port, but her crew was too slow to put on canvas, and the *Respair* drew level with her stern.

Naval battles went much the same—broadside against

broadside—and ships' hulls were strongest at their sides. At the bow and stern, they were most vulnerable.

Another weakness he was only too willing to exploit.

Starboard guns boomed, the shots so close together it was all one thunderous sound, reverberating through the deck.

Jagged holes scarred the *Arrogant's* stern. With a crack and a creak, her mizzen yard swung, broken in two, useless.

Cheers rose on the *Respair*, drowning out the sound of the sea.

Knigh exhaled and allowed himself a nod. Progress, but this wasn't a victory yet.

"Starboard guns, same again," he bellowed. "Clovis, as tight as you can to starboard. We'll take her bow and foremast."

Strike quick and hard. That was the plan. If they could disable the *Arrogant,* and Munroe stayed out of the fight, the *Sea Witch* could keep the other two occupied while the *Respair* went after the *Sovereign*. Board, find Vee, then get the hells off that ship.

That simple.

And that hard.

He clenched his jaw. One step at a time.

Gunfire flashed in his periphery from the *Arrogant* before the crack split the air.

The *Respair* shuddered. Splinters burst across the deck. Men and women screamed.

The sounds pierced him. They were his responsibility.

He was a healer. And he was also a captain, even if he'd given up the official title. But he couldn't be both at once.

He raked his hand through his hair, fingertips trying to push away the headache forming.

As a commander, he needed to be here and be decisive. He was the one who had to make decisions for the greater good. With his knowledge of the Royal Navy's tactics, he was best placed to lead this battle. It wasn't callous or arrogant, just a fact. Perry had made the right call.

He gritted his teeth and let the teams take the injured below to sickbay.

"Repair crews, damage report."

Two shots had hit, the rest had fallen short or sailed over. Damage all above the waterline, thanks to their approach from windward.

He nodded, exhaled. All manageable.

The spray. The crack of rifle shots. The boom of broadsides from the *Unicorn, Siren,* and *Sea Witch* exchanging fire. This could've been a naval vessel for all that familiarity.

But he was Navy no longer. Here he was striking at Her Majesty's ships, his desertion complete.

Something inside him shrivelled, cold and tight.

Not now.

He squared his shoulders and gestured to Clovis. They angled to starboard, gunners ready to strike the *Arrogant's* vulnerable bow.

Again, the thunder of gunfire and more cheers. The *Arrogant's* fore topsail flapped, torn. Another successful strike.

Knigh gave the next set of orders—back to port, reload guns.

A distant *boom* echoed across the water, far to stern, followed by a clinking sound.

It grew louder.

Chain shot and spinning this way.

Knigh shouted, turning, but before he could finish his warning, the air burst in splinters and a sharp crack. Canvas fluttered and the *Respair's* mizzen topmast toppled, then splashed into the sea. The riflemen and women stationed in the mizzen top cried out as they fell.

Damnation.

Smoke rose from the *Sovereign's* bow chase guns. The captain must've gathered himself together enough to fire from anchor.

She hadn't set sail, so Mercia had to be on that island where they wouldn't leave him. But they had enough range that they didn't need to move.

"Get lines and floats in the water," Knigh shouted, "we'll pick them up as we manoeuvre. And cut any stray rigging—we can't have it dragging us down." *Or giving the kraken a lure.*

They were down a mast.

He winced, but Perry ran past with a reassuring smile. "Just one of those things," she called as she went aft. "I'll make sure it's cast off before it sinks us."

Losing those sails would slow them, but that would allow the *Arrogant* to catch up, placing her perfectly to take another broadside. If they took her main mast, she'd be dead in the water, allowing them to go after the *Sovereign* and find Vee.

Under his instruction, they turned again and fired, smashing more of the *Arrogant's* yards, tearing her sails.

Someone gripped his arm. "Saba's hurt."

Knigh tore his gaze from the enemy's mangled ropes and canvas to find Perry staring up at him, eyes wide.

His hands tightened. He should've been healing the injured. No matter the logic, he couldn't shake that feeling—it was his gift, his responsibility, something only he could do.

And while his decision earlier to stay and command had been for the greater good, this time...

Saba was the most accurate with a bow and arrow—the rest of the crew favoured pistols and rifles. Their plans for dealing with the kraken depended on her.

"Perry, I—"

"Your gift. I know." She nodded, eyebrows drawn together. "She's the only one who can light the barrels. Go. I've got the ship."

His muscles burst, finally releasing their pent-up energy as he ran aft to heal Saba.

On the main top, the metallic glint of the watch's spyglass caught his eye. No sign of the kraken.

Yet.

PRESENT & CORRECT

Gunfire tore the air, relentless. The *Respair* shuddered with each report she delivered. She'd lost a second mast, but she wasn't defenceless.

Amidst the shouts and clang of reloading, Knigh made his way fore, bent over to counter the tilting deck. He'd healed Saba's injuries—a huge splinter from the mizzenmast had pierced her shoulder. Thankfully, it had missed her heart and lungs, but pushing out the remaining shards of wood and closing the wound had still drained his gift and left Saba pale and breathless. All the while, the ship had taken more strikes.

Another boom, this one not accompanied by a tremble through the *Respair's* decks—one of the other ships firing. Knigh ducked on instinct, even before he registered the clinking approach of chain shot.

A crash above, then a spray of splinters on the back of his neck as he shielded his face.

Buggeration, what had they hit this time? Shaking off the debris, he squinted up.

Ropes strained, snapped, whipped away, and another yard creaked and splashed into the waves.

It had been broken in two and a chunk was missing from the mainmast—a strong wind would be enough to send it toppling after.

He gritted his teeth. They only had a few sails left. They were practically dead in the water.

Expression neutral, he sent a further team belowdecks to check on damage and another to see what could be done to make the mast safe. He stopped to crouch and quell a man's bleeding with his gift. Just closing the artery wasn't too great a strain on his energy, and without it, the man wouldn't have survived to reach sickbay.

Smoke hazed the deck, swirling around what was left of the masts. Knigh grimaced at the acrid air scratching his lungs.

But it wasn't the worst thing aboard.

That tilt—it wasn't the pitch of a ship on waves. Just a few degrees off level, sloping aft, it remained persistent, even as the vessel bobbed with the sea. The *Respair* had lost her balance.

They were taking on water.

The pumps gurgled, seawater gushing up from the hold and out through the scuppers, but they still listed. It was more than they could handle.

Damnation.

There was only one thing left to do.

Pausing to help the injured where he could, he made his

way to Perry at the waist, where she was taking a damage report from Luned, face taut.

Once Luned had gone, Perry raised her eyebrows at him in question.

"We need to abandon ship," he said, stomach leaden with the words.

Smoke and shouts crowded them and the air was thick with sulphur and copper and gunfire, but Perry's wide, green eyes were drops of stillness in the chaos. She stared up at him, creases between her brows.

"We're taking on water, and the pumps can't keep up." His voice sounded so calm and somehow the sentence felt distant, as if he wasn't the one saying it. "Those breaches are too close to the waterline."

As if the ship understood his words, the deck listed further.

Eyes closed, Perry hung her head. "I know." Her shoulders rose with a long breath before her head snapped up, that momentary despair gone. "Get anyone who can't swim to the boats."

"Perry," he murmured, "that's almost everyone."

She winced. "Then do your best. The rest will have to go in the water—grab anything that floats."

He drew a long breath. She was right—that was all they could do. "I'll put the best shots at bow and stern." He waved Aedan and Effie over. "They can protect everyone else from..." He'd seen sharks and rays in the clear seas as they'd skirted the island. But what did they matter when the kraken lurked some-where out there?

"Good thinking." She frowned, worrying her lip between

her teeth. "And Saba and the barrels—we might need them yet."

He nodded and managed a reassuring smile, squeezing her shoulder. "We only need to get everyone to the *Sea Witch*. We'll make it."

Perry exhaled, tension easing out of her stance before she turned and began issuing orders to ready the two boats and make for FitzRoy's ship.

Aedan and Effie reached his side, eyebrows rising.

"Are we really abandoning ship?" Effie looked up at him, eyes wide, suddenly child-like.

"Think of it as evacuating to the *Sea Witch*, rather than abandoning the *Respair*."

Again, that reassuring smile. It felt like a lie. If the kraken came...

He swallowed away the bitter taste of that thought. "Get the injured, the worst swimmers, and as many guns as you can to the boats."

Aedan cocked his head, brows knotted. "What about Barnacle and the kittens?"

"That's where I'm going."

"Good man." Aedan clapped Knigh on the back, then went to his duties with Effie.

The order to abandon ship spread like wildfire.

Men and women streamed past in the opposite direction as Knigh ran aft. The deck's tilt grew worse by the minute.

By the time he reached Vee's cabin door, guns strained on their breech ropes, trying to roll from their stations. Thank the gods his efforts to distract himself from Vee's absence had included checking every rope and tackle on the *Respair*. If those guns broke free, they'd throw the ship even more off balance and crush anyone who got in the way.

In the cabin, Barnacle circled the blanket nest, her kittens mewling inside. She glared at him as he entered, her back arched, tail fluffed up.

"Come on," he murmured, hands wide as he approached. "Let's get out of here."

But she hissed as he got close, and when he reached for the blanket nest, her paw shot out, streaking needles of pain across the back of his hand.

"Bloody hells, cat!" He shook his head, teeth bared. "I'm trying to help you."

She only stood between him and the kittens, hackles raised.

The deck shuddered and dropped, sending books sliding along the shelves and the inkwell clinking in its holder as they tilted further towards the stern. Out the window, the sea bobbed closer, little wavelets frothing white.

"Buggeration." He grabbed his duffel bag, shoved the papers and clue inside, and slung it over his shoulder. "Right, Barnacle. I understand that you're scared, but we haven't got time for this." Bracing, he slid his already bloodied hand under her and scooped her up.

She yowled, she scratched, she hissed and spat, but he managed to keep hold of her wriggling form and drop her in Vee's sea chest. When he closed the lid, she scrabbled against it.

"Sorry," he muttered, wiping blood from dozens of scratches, "it's only temporary."

The kittens mewled and wriggled in their little nest. So small. So helpless. His heart clenched.

He sliced a length of blanket from the nest and folded it in half, deck tilting, ship groaning all the while. With the ends tied around his neck and the middle tucked down his shirt, it formed a pocket.

"Come here, you." He scooped up the grey female first. She was a perfect copy of her mother. She pedalled in the air, little pink tongue showing as she mewled, before he dropped her into the pouch, soon followed by her brothers and sister. All four fitted inside, snug with their heads poking out the top.

Outside, the sea loomed closer to the window.

"Now for the fun part," he sighed and opened the sea chest.

Barnacle streaked out, eyes wide.

"They're here, they're safe." He braced himself for more scratches as he picked her up, but she must've spotted the kittens in his shirt because she let him place her on his shoulder. "There."

Pinpricks of pain crossed his shoulder as she settled in, head next to his as she surveyed her babies.

"All present and correct, see?" Wincing, he nodded and pulled Vee's fae-worked pistols and rifle from the chest. The pistols went in his belt, the rifle over his shoulder.

The only other thing left to take from the cabin was the sea chest itself—it would float, and someone might need that help once they were in the water. Careful not to squash the kittens, he carried it out on deck.

It was like hiking uphill now.

The boats bobbed in the water, and crew waited at the rail to board, their low hum of conversation tense.

Saba grumbled at being sent to a boat when she could swim well.

"You're the only one who can light the barrels," Wynn snapped as she hauled her sea chest over the side—evidently she'd had the same idea as Knigh.

The *Respair* gurgled and groaned, sea dragging at her.

"Come on." Knigh clapped Saba on the shoulder and nodded to the boat. "No time for complaints."

With a sigh, she clambered over the rail and down to the boat.

Opposite, Perry stood, gripping the gunwale, her jaw tight.

As others passed between them and down to the boats, he nodded to her and gave that lying smile again. "Just to the *Sea Witch.*"

She exhaled, loosening as she counted those passing, and he helped the injured down to the boats. Anything that floated went overboard—chests, barrels, doors ripped from their hinges...

The boats filled too quickly, and soon enough men and women began dragging themselves onto the jetsam. Their breaths were barely this side of panic from being in the sea when they couldn't swim.

"Er, Captain?" Clovis stood at the tiller of the jolly boat, shielding his eyes as he looked dead ahead.

Perry mouthed *forty-five*. She threw the giant a questioning glance.

Hand dropping, Clovis turned, brows drawn tight together.

"I know you said we only need to get to the *Sea Witch*, but does FitzRoy know that?"

Knigh followed his gaze, frowning.

The *Sea Witch* had to be at least 800 yards away, sails full and silhouetted against the darkening sky, stern towards them as she shrank into the distance.

THE FALL

Air whistled in Vice's ears, tugged at the cloth in her hands, pulled her hair from its braid. Rock and tiles fell, scraping her shins and knees. Her pulse roared.

The sea was coming up too fast. And the rocks, too.

Maybe this wasn't the best idea.

She'd be in the water in seconds—or dashed against the cliff. If she could focus for a moment...

Slower breaths. She reached for the breeze.

Come on.

Turn this way, turn this way.

It bent to her will, pushing on her chest and face. Lords and Ladies willing, it was enough to keep her from—

Boom.

Gasping, she opened her eyes. Grey rock, blurring past, just for an instant and then the shock of cool water smacking against her feet.

She plunged below the surface, muscles braced ready to strike rock, all noise drowned by the gurgle and murmur of sea against her ears. Had that been cannon fire? Had she pushed herself far enough from the cliff?

No rock yet. Thank the gods.

When she opened her eyes, bubbles streamed from her clothes and caught the daylight filtering from the surface. They wavered, buffeted by the currents and waves above—the maelstrom was returning.

She clutched the cloth and Copper Drake against her chest and kicked for the surface.

Bloody hells, I hope this thing is written in waterproof ink.

Drake was a sailor through and through—surely he'd have thought of that. And the clue she'd taken from FitzRoy had been underwater in that chest for at least a few months before she and Knigh had recovered it.

Then there was that cannon fire...

Those ships—if that was the *Respair*, they must've come for her, right? But they couldn't stand against the *Sovereign*, and four other warships—not for long. She had to get to them, then they could leave and the battle would be over before the *Sovereign* got involved. Right now Mercia had to be running back through the ruins and the rainforest to get back to the ship's boat. Surely his crew would wait for their admiral.

But what if they didn't?

Gods, never mind drowning in this water, she was drowning in thoughts, in worries.

Teeth gritted, she kicked harder, reaching out with her gift to still this small area of sea. The daylight above grew brighter and brighter until, at last, she broke the surface.

She trod water and caught her breath.

Cannons thundered over and over, the shots so rapid, they bled into one another, crowding the air. Even from here, she could taste sulphur and charcoal past the sea's salt.

Above, clouds already regrouped, forming a blanket of mid-grey.

Ahead, the *Sovereign* still sat at anchor. Good. They were waiting for Mercia.

Then to the right, hundreds of yards away, five ships shrouded in smoke—three with white sails, two with black.

She knew one of those sail plans well, even though it was only partially visible behind the naval vessel—the *Respair*. Her heart leapt.

They'd come. Despite the argument, despite the storm she'd made to scare them off, they'd come.

The *Venatrix* stood separate from the battle, sails balanced in a heave-to as if Munroe had ordered them to stop. None of her cannons lit up.

She tied the soggy weight of the two pieces of cloth across her body and swam towards the battle, never taking her eyes off what she could see of the *Respair*. As soon as she got close enough, she'd be able to use her gift to help.

The naval ships parted, revealing the *Respair's* full length.

Except it was wrong—all wrong. She hadn't only been able to see some of their sails because of the other ship in the way, it was because they'd lost their mizzenmast and the top of their foremast.

They wouldn't be making a swift escape any time soon.

Bollocks.

Huffing, she called on her gift and pulled the currents to help her swim faster. She had to get to them. She had to help.

Another boom joined the general tumult, but this one came with a flash from the *Sovereign*, firing from anchor. The *Respair* rocked and a dark line opened up on its hull.

Her blood was ice. Her arms and legs kept going, kicking and pulling on the water, but it was all mechanical, her muscles numb.

That was bad damage. If she could see it from here, *really* bad. Not something easily patched up. And it was close to the waterline. They'd be taking on water, maybe more than the pumps could handle.

At best, they couldn't leave on the *Respair:* she'd taken too much damage.

At worst, she could sink.

The sky opened, a cold, heavy rain pelting from the re-gathering storm clouds.

Vice's stomach clenched as if someone held it in their fist. Knigh, Perry, Saba, Aedan, *everyone,* even Barnacle—all here because of her.

If they sank...

Who knew if that other pirate ship would stop and help? That's assuming they didn't also take too much damage to escape—once the *Respair* was disabled, the *Arrogant* would be free to gang up with the *Unicorn* and the *Siren*.

Even through the rain, Vice could see the *Respair* barely limped on, course painfully slow. The pirate ship placed the

Arrogant between herself and the *Sovereign*. A shield, but one that could still fire back.

Vice grimaced, chest tight. She had to get there—she could help them manoeuvre, give them speed. But not from here.

And they might not last long enough for her to reach them.

There had to be some other way.

She blinked away the rain pouring in her eyes—it grew heavier by the second.

The *Venatrix* still sat off to one side, bobbing in the water and taking no part in the battle. Did that mean Munroe didn't want to attack Knigh? Or did he have some other reason for holding off?

Maybe that was their route away. If she could take that ship...

There was no time to puzzle over it. She changed course, aiming for the smaller vessel.

Her breaths came harder and harder and her limbs heavier with the dual ache of swimming and her gift. She didn't dare use the wellspring when she needed to focus on swimming—it consumed her attention too much.

Eyes stinging from salt and rain, she stared from *Respair* to *Venatrix* and back again, until eventually the *Respair* took another strike to her masts and fell still.

A grunt came out with her next breath. Perry, Knigh, Saba... they could already be dead for all she knew, killed by a falling yard or a rifle shot, throat pierced by a huge splinter from the hull.

She couldn't think about that—about anything.

The swim. That was all that mattered right now, and she threw every ounce of herself into it.

After an eternity, she escaped the cloud cover and reached the *Venatrix's* hull.

Now for Munroe.

During her approach, she'd spotted the crew gathered on the far side, watching the battle. The sounds of sea and cannon covered the splashing as she dragged herself up the starboard steps.

She peeked onto the deck. Angular figure unmistakable in his uniform, Munroe stood on the quarterdeck. She bit back a groan—she had to clamber round, then step up on deck. Just walking across from here was too open. Even with the distraction of the battle, one of Munroe's men might spot her and they all had pistols while she still had no weapon.

She clambered aft, panting. Sticking to the rail meant the handholds were much better than the route she'd used to take Knigh's false clue all those months ago. By the time she reached the quarterdeck, her arms shook and her face had started to tingle. Too much energy used up. But...

There was no backing down, no giving up.

Teeth gritted, she dragged herself on deck.

She landed without a sound and crept towards Munroe, gaze on the sabre at his belt. That would keep his men away, stop them attacking her on sight. She just needed time to speak to him and the sword would buy it for her.

The pounding of her heart was deafening. If this failed...

Once she was a foot away, she seized his sword. The feel of a hilt in her hand was so right she could've moaned with relief.

All at once, a shout from above, Munroe turned, she grabbed his arm.

By the time she had the blade at his neck, his men had a dozen pistols aimed at her.

"Hello, Munroe," she said in his ear, voice calmer than the blood roaring through her veins. "Back off," she called to his crew, "or I'll slice his throat."

Their guns remained levelled at her, muzzles black as oblivion.

To port, cannons still thundered.

ABANDONED

Knigh's throat clenched as a streak of anger seared through him.

Hells and damnation.

"They're leaving," Lizzy gasped.

"The bastard," Saba muttered.

The news made its way around the crew, radiating across the listing deck from the rail, reaching boats and those already on the floating debris.

FitzRoy had abandoned them.

The only silver lining was that the three frigates were in pursuit, bow chase guns still firing at the *Sea Witch*, rather than attacking the *Respair*.

Perry's face had frozen, disbelief etched in the frown between her eyebrows as she gripped the rail. She glanced ahead again, as if hoping she'd see something different.

But the *Sea Witch* only grew smaller.

Knigh gritted his teeth. The coward really had abandoned them.

The crew's mutters went quiet, leaving only the lapping water, distant gunfire, and the groaning corpse of the *Respair* slowly sinking beneath Knigh's feet. When Perry gave no orders, they glanced at each other, eyebrows rising in question, in hope... in desperation.

But no answers came.

They were afraid, and they needed direction. Knigh had seen it before in the Navy. A frightened man could cling to direction like a drowning man clung to flotsam—like men and women clung to their floating barrels and chests right now.

He swallowed and lifted his chin.

"We're not far from land," he shouted over the choppy waves and bobbing, tilted deck. "There are beaches further along the coast—past the cliffs."

Every pair of eyes turned to him. Those in the water panted as they kept their heads up, but they nodded.

"Here," he called and threw one of Vee's pistols to Lizzy in the boat. He swung the rifle by its strap to Saba. "We only need to get to shore, but let's make sure everyone makes it, yes?"

Saba's brows lowered, and she nodded. "Aye."

Lizzy scanned the waves, jaw tight. "Anything comes for us, it's dead."

He couldn't help the grin that pushed its way to his face. "That's the spirit. The plan stays the same, it's only the destination that's changed." He squared his shoulders, all confidence, as though he wasn't gripping the rail of a sinking ship.

"If you're in a boat and you have a gun, you're keeping everyone in the water safe. You watch for sharks like your life depends on it." He raked his gaze over the upturned faces. "Because it does."

With one click after another, pistols and rifles cocked. More nods. Those faces were less frightened now, more determined.

He squeezed Perry's shoulder. "Right, Captain?"

Blinking, Perry drew a long breath, seeming to wake from her shock. "Aye," she called, "work together and we'll make it. If you can swim, help those who can't. Blackwood and I will bring up the rear and make sure no one's left behind."

She met Knigh's gaze and exhaled before mouthing *thank you.*

He inclined his head. He might not work for the Navy anymore, but this was what he did, who he was. He didn't need thanks.

Glad for the excuse to break away from her gratitude, he retrieved a kitten that was trying to climb under his armpit, its furry paws tickling as much as its little needle claws hurt.

Someone cleared their throat. "What about the sea monster?"

Whispers across the waves. "The kraken."

He kept his head down as if still absorbed with adjusting his precious load. He didn't have an answer for that.

They had a handful of explosive barrels, but no oil to light up the sea's surface.

They had Saba and her bow. But the explosions were only ever a short-term measure to allow a swift escape.

With two rowing boats and scores of men and women in the water, there was no such thing as a swift escape.

If the kraken comes, we're all dead.

NO HERO

A dozen pistols. A dozen men who wanted her dead— and more of them in the tops.

Vice swallowed. "I just want to talk," she murmured to Munroe. "This was the only way I could think of to get close without your men arresting me."

"Yes," Munroe muttered, looking at her over his shoulder, "holding me at swordpoint is definitely a way to make yourself less threatening to my crew."

"I'm a pirate, there's no way they'd see me as unthreatening even without a weapon."

He huffed a soft sigh. "They don't see you as a pirate. To them, you're a lady." His eyebrows rose at her before he turned back to his men. "Lower your weapons. Give the lady some room and I'm sure she'll calm down."

So bloody patronising. Her jaw ticked, but she bit her tongue as the crew obeyed and backed off.

Munroe returned to eyeing her sidelong. "I presume you want my help?"

"Not me." She eased her grip, letting him turn to see her better. *"Knigh."*

His brows shot up.

"I know you think he betrayed you, the Navy, his duty. And gods know I'm the last person you'd expect to sing his praises, but he's a good man and he's on that ship." She jerked her head at the *Respair*, which now listed unmistakably. There was no saving the ship, but the crew...

"A good man?" Munroe arched one eyebrow. "You'll forgive me if I don't take a pirate's word for that."

She scoffed. "Fair point. How can I persuade you?"

"I'm not sure you can," he murmured, shaking his head. "Desertion's a terrible crime without assisting a criminal— never mind one quite so notorious. At least if you *had* bewitched him, he wouldn't be responsible for his actions. But you say he *chose* to help you, to leave everything, and yet you give only the vaguest explanation for why that makes him a 'good man'. Surely you can see the impasse here?"

Her insides knotted. *Notorious. Bewitched.* Munroe had swallowed the Navy's stories hook, line, and sinker, just like Knigh had.

The truth had made Knigh see. Maybe that was the only thing that would work on Munroe.

Urgh, not someone else knowing her secret. Avice Ferrers was meant to be dead. Then no one would come looking for her. Not her cruel father, not Uncle Rufus, who was even worse.

Not Mama or Kat—the last thing she wanted was them in danger on her account.

Vice glanced at the *Respair*—what remained of her masts tilted at a drunken angle, and the dark breach in her hull had disappeared beneath the waves. She'd be taking on water quickly now.

No matter how loath she was to tell the truth, if it was the only chance to save the others, she had to try.

"He believed I was the notorious Lady Vice, too." She gave a bitter smile and met Munroe's gaze. "But I swear on the gods, the Lords, the Ladies, even my gift—and the Wild Hunt can take me if this isn't true—I've never tortured anyone. I've never murdered a child. I've never killed someone who wasn't armed and trying to kill me or someone else, too. I give quarter. I chase slavers. And I'm no hero, but I'm no villain, either."

Munroe's lips sat flat, thin, his gaze unreadable.

"Knigh saw all that. He started believing it, realising the Navy's stories weren't true. He decided he'd ask them to make me a privateer in service to the Queen." She heaved a long breath, but she had to spew out the next words while she still could, before she lost momentum. "But I told him a stupid lie to push him away and keep my reputation intact. I told him I'd murdered his former fiancée, Lady Avice Ferrers."

"Ferrers? Wasn't she the girl who went missing?"

Vice inclined her head, throat closing against the words that had to come next. "And he believed it. That's why he went through with the plan in the end."

Munroe nodded like it all made sense.

Her stomach twisted at having to make the confession, but this wasn't about her. "Except I didn't kill her. I *am* her."

"Oh," he exhaled, mouth hanging open.

"That's the fact he discovered. That's why he had to help me—to undo his mistake. He knew, if he didn't, my death would be a mark on him forever."

"Damnation." He shook his head, blasting out another breath. "He wouldn't have been able to live with himself."

She nodded, all words dried up now.

Eyebrows drawn together, he looked at the *Respair*. "And their ally appears to be fleeing."

She nodded again, swallowing. Whoever the hells that was, they'd abandoned the *Respair* to her fate and the crew to naval hospitality. For pirates, that was the noose.

"I'm not asking you to fight," she said once her voice could be trusted again, "just to pick them up—stop them drowning or..."

Sharks. The kraken. The Navy wasn't the only danger at sea.

"I..." Grimacing, he shook his head. "Blasted hells, what position have you put me in?" He glared at her, a war playing out across his features—determination in the set of his jaw, but a question in the crease between his brows. "I don't want to see him die. And perhaps he *was* wrong to arrest you in the end, but I can't turn my back on the Navy like he did." Desperation laced the tightening of his lips. "If I order my men to help, that's mutiny against our commanders."

Her insides seethed. Munroe understood why Knigh had helped her, but it still wasn't enough.

Across the glittering sea, the *Respair's* stern was almost completely submerged.

Her grip on Munroe's sabre tightened until her knuckles ached. Fighting was easier—why couldn't she be doing that instead of this?

She tore her attention from the sinking ship, though her every fibre strained towards it.

What position have you put me in? Munroe was torn. There had to be a way she could persuade him. She ran through all he'd said.

Perhaps he was wrong to arrest you in the end. Arriving in Portsmouth—the stink of the docks and cry of gulls was every bit as clear as it had been that day. The Vice Admiral waiting for her, arrest warrant ready. FitzRoy stumbling from his cabin in that stupid charade, accusing her of holding him hostage to force the crew to obey her.

A hostage.

Her heart leapt as she stared at the blade close to Munroe's throat.

"What if there was a way I could make it not your fault? What if everyone thought *you* had no choice?"

He cocked his head. "I'm not sure I follow your meaning."

"You already ordered your men to back down—as far as they're concerned, it's because I have this." Allowing herself a half-smile, she tilted the sabre, still several inches from his flesh. "And, of course, I'm an *unstable woman* and a dangerous pirate. If you're my hostage, no one could blame you for giving in to my demands, just while you wait for an opportunity to disarm and recapture me."

Eyebrows rising, he opened his mouth, closed it, then nodded. "That... Actually, that could work." He drew a long breath, still nodding. "But you're going to have to hit me and take my pistol, too—that will make it more believable."

"I'm not going to hit you!"

"You must. Just bloody my nose a bit. We have to sell this. Besides"—the corner of his mouth quirked—"I'll be able to tell everyone about the time Lady Vice punched me. And it will read better in the report, especially with all these witnesses." He jerked his chin towards his men.

Their guns were lowered now, but they still watched her, a couple murmuring to each other. Maybe they were hatching some foolish plan to rescue their commander from her wicked clutches. With a gun, they'd be less inclined to try anything foolish.

"Fine, I'll hit you. Then we go and pick up the *Respair's* crew, right?"

"Right." Munroe nodded. "In ten seconds, I'm going to reach for my pistol. That's your cue to hit me and take it. Then we go and save Blackwood."

Bollocks—could she trust Munroe? Maybe he was trying to get her to slip so he could get his sabre back? And would his crew even comply?

It was an insane plan, no escaping that fact.

If even she thought it was mad, what the hells would Perry think?

But for Perry to survive to hear about all this, Vice had to go through with it.

And there was no time to think, because Munroe was going for his pistol.

It was a left-handed strike, and she softened it at the last minute, but the impact against her knuckles still made her wince.

Munroe grunted, eyes closing as he clutched his face and blood seeped between his fingers.

His men shouted.

She had to be quick.

Heart hammering, sabre still to his throat, she grabbed the pistol and turned it on the crew. "So much as *think* about attacking me and you'll see a lot more of his blood."

"Do as she says, gentlemen." Still holding his nose, Munroe made a good show of looking at her wide-eyed with fear. "Surrender your weapons and set sail for the *Respair*."

She inclined her head, holding his gaze. She had control of the *Venatrix*, now to save her friends.

Gods, please let us be in time.

WHITE SAILS

"Grab anything that floats," Knigh called. The waves below were littered with barrels, sea chests, doors, and loose timbers. One woman even clung to the figurehead, which someone had pried loose. She and others stared up at him, eyes wide. Many scanned the water, tension etched in the stiff lines of their jaws and brows. Their grips on the poles they used as makeshift oars were white-knuckled.

He held the *Respair's* rail, just about keeping his footing on the steep deck. It was close to the sea's surface now—those evacuating didn't need to climb down, they could just jump a few feet.

The injured lay or sat in the bottom of the jolly boat and the longboat, Lizzy and others seeing to them. Saba stood at the jolly boat's stern, rifle in her hand as she watched for danger. Her bow sat beside her, ready. In the longboat, Wynn and Effie sat at the last set of oars, explosive barrels by their feet. He'd tried to put Barnacle in one of the boats, but she'd sunk her claws into his shirt and flesh, refusing to be separated from her kittens. In the end, he'd relented and left her to observe the evacuation from his shoulder.

He and Perry helped the remaining crew into the water or a boat. Perry counted each one, while he pointed out what piece of jetsam they could cling to.

"Start heading north." Expression flat, he waved in that direction. "Aim for the island chain we saw on the way here."

Inwardly, he grimaced at what he left unsaid—*because we'll never reach this island.* It was far closer than the archipelago they'd seen *en route,* but the sea between them and the shore churned now and the island itself was barely visible through dark clouds and lashing rain. Another magical storm—fierce but contained in a strip around the coast. If they tried to get through that, they'd all drown, whether they were in a boat or otherwise.

Beneath his feet, the ship shuddered and bubbles gurgled to the surface, splashing his legs. "Come on," he called, slapping a man on the shoulder as he paused by the rail, "quickly, now."

He'd seen vessels wreck before—the danger wasn't only in being trapped on board, but in the sucking water as the ship sank beneath the surface and to the sea floor. Even he probably wasn't a strong enough swimmer to resist that.

"That door." He pointed it out for Luned, who balanced beside him now. "There's space—just be careful not to tip it over."

Mouth flat, she gave him a grim nod, then eased into the

water. Those already on their floats reached out and helped guide her to the door.

"Who's next?" He turned, forcing a smile in place.

"That's it." Perry sighed and ran a hand over her face. "Just you and me left. Everyone else is accounted for—alive or known dead." She sucked in her lips and glanced over what remained above the surface—the stump of the foremast, the bowsprit, and the forecastle, its steps disappearing into the water. She shook her head. "The *Respair* is lost."

She'd told him what that word meant. Regaining hope. The opposite of despair.

This wasn't only about losing the ship... Mercia still had Vee. But he couldn't think about that. If he did, he might break, and the crew needed him. Perry needed him.

He reached across the gap and squeezed her hand. "But we'll live to fight another day."

Her nostrils flared, but she inclined her head. Her green eyes were too bright, too sad.

Off the starboard bow, movement.

He sucked in a breath, some part of him saying *danger* before he'd fully registered what it was.

White sails, a sleek hull. The *Venatrix*.

Coming right this way.

Hells and damnation, the Navy wasn't leaving them alone after all. His stomach sank. "We need to hurry."

"Bollocks," Perry muttered. "We're bloody sinking, is that not enough for them?"

He'd never have pegged Munroe for a man to attack the crew of a sinking ship, but if those were his orders...

Knigh bowed his head, grimacing.

Beneath the glinting waves to starboard, a red shape slid through the water.

Sucking in a sharp breath, he strained from the rail, staring until his eyes burned. But it was gone, if it had been there at all. He might've imagined it.

Lords and Ladies, please say I imagined it.

Because that colour had been the exact rusty shade of the kraken.

ON THE QUARTERDECK

Sweat bathed Knigh's skin, sticking his shirt to his back as he sat astride Vee's sea chest and paddled it away from the *Respair's* sinking wreck. Only a few feet of forecastle, the bowsprit, and the splintered ends of the fore-mast remained above the waves.

Barnacle's claws were a collection of pinpricks across his shoulders, and she complained with every sweep of his makeshift oar through the water. The kittens kept wriggling, occasionally poking their heads out and squeaking.

Around him, every uninjured crewmember paddled or kicked, pushing the boats and floating debris further from the *Respair* as the *Venatrix* drew closer and closer.

She hadn't fired yet.

Breaths huffing, he clung to that as tightly as he clung to the plank of wood he used to paddle. He hadn't seen any more hints of red in the waves. It must've been a trick of the light—his fears playing with him.

"Crew of the *Respair*," came a shout from the *Venatrix*. "Do not fire. We've come to parley."

Knigh gritted his teeth and sought out Perry amongst the dozens of figures around him. This would be a call to surrender.

And capture for a pirate meant death.

In battle. Drowning. Sharks. The kraken. It would all be the same in the end. At least if they were taken to Mercia on the *Sovereign*, he might get to see Vee and George one last time. His heart sank as surely as the *Respair*.

Perry's face came into view as she craned past another crewmate. She met his gaze, frowning.

"Blackwood?" That was Munroe's voice.

Knigh bowed his head, paddle poised above the wavelets. Here he was surrounded by pirates—hells, he was a pirate himself now—dressed in worn shirt and breeches, hair too-long, chin covered in what was more beard than stubble. No wonder Munroe wasn't sure.

Was Knigh ashamed, though? He'd served this crew as loyally as he'd ever served the Navy. He'd tried to save their lives and the ship. He'd worked as hard on the *Respair* as he'd worked aboard any other vessel.

He might be a pirate and a deserter now, but he'd done the right thing in saving Vee from the gibbet and he'd do it again in an instant. That path could only end with him becoming a pirate—or dead.

And the heart pounding in his chest right now was very much alive.

With a deep breath, he lifted his chin and turned.

The *Venatrix* had circled the *Respair's* wreck and was now less than a hundred feet away and closing. Her longboat hung from the davits, ready to launch. Ready to gather them all up for arrest.

Munroe stood at the quarterdeck rail as the ship hove to, stopping twenty feet from the edge of the scattered pirates. "We've come to help." He gestured to his crew, and they threw a couple of dozen lines into the water.

Knigh's brows shot up and when he exchanged a look with Perry, she wore the same expression.

Munroe had said *help,* not *arrest.*

When she cocked her head in question, Knigh lifted one shoulder. They had no other option, even if the help was only a precursor to arrest—even if this was a trap.

"You heard the man," Perry called to the questioning looks from her crew as the *Venatrix's* longboat lowered. "Get yourselves aboard."

It took perhaps a quarter of an hour to get everyone aboard, and once they were on the *Venatrix's* deck, the injured were carried to sickbay. No one arrested them or took their weapons.

Knigh shared another look with Perry. Perhaps Munroe *was* simply helping. And if he was helping, maybe he'd be willing to help some more—maybe Knigh could persuade him to get Vee from the *Sovereign.*

Whatever it takes to get the job done.

Knigh deposited the kittens—all uninjured and mewling for milk—and Barnacle in an open sea chest and charged towards the quarterdeck where he'd last seen Munroe.

None of the crew tried to stop him. Although none of them were armed, either.

Perry hurried after Knigh, Aedan and Saba trailing behind. "Do you have the slightest idea what's going on?"

"Honestly? Not a clue. Either Munroe's truly helping or this is a way to capture us."

"Well," she muttered, "we haven't been arrested yet."

He frowned at the yards above, all braced to take a fair wind that channelled them directly away from the storm that circled the island. "And we seem to be leaving the *Sovereign*." *And Vee.*

He couldn't let that happen. They'd come all this way, lost the *Respair*, lost crew. They couldn't leave without her.

The crew watched them pass, mistrust clear in their glinting eyes and tense brows.

The *Venatrix's* helm stood at the front of the quarterdeck, and as Knigh approached, he spotted Munroe up there manning it himself. He had only the bare minimum of sailors with him. Strange. Maybe he wanted his men watching the pirates he'd now invited on board.

At the base of the steps, an officer stopped him and asked for his weapons, which Knigh hurried to hand over. He wasn't planning to fight anyone, he just needed to get to Munroe and persuade him quickly.

Climbing the steps, Knigh called, "Munroe, turn around! We need to get—"

His feet faltered on the top step.

Past Munroe, dark hair streaming, eyes closed, a frown of concentration between her brows. A pistol and sabre hung limp in her hands.

"Vee?"

He couldn't breathe. His heart stilled. He blinked. She was still there when he opened his eyes.

She was why Munroe had stopped to pick them up. That had to be the reason. But why wasn't she on the *Sovereign?* Had Mercia moved her? Had she escaped? Was Munroe helping her get away?

Too many questions. He shook his head and forced his feet to close the distance between him and Munroe, rather than going to Vee.

Wild Hunt, he wanted nothing more than to walk up to her and pull her against him or at least touch her shoulder—some confirmation that she was really here and safe and well. But she was away in her gift, and everything about this situation was uncertain.

He clenched his hands and bit his lip against a hundred questions, and a hundred more things he wanted to say. *What happened? I should have come to you and had that conversation sooner rather than letting you overhear it.*

And most of all, *I'm sorry.*

He tore his gaze away from her and raised his eyebrows at Munroe in question.

With a stiff smile, Munroe surveyed him. "You made it, then." He glanced over his shoulder at Vee. "She's holding me hostage."

Knigh narrowed his eyes, head cocking. Vee was armed, true, and there was blood on the front of Munroe's shirt, even though the *Venatrix* hadn't joined the battle. Still—"You don't look like much of a hostage. She's..." But he bit his tongue. She wasn't aware of her surroundings right now, too deep in her gift, but best not to make Munroe's crew aware of that fact.

At least this explained their tension and the lack of men on the quarterdeck.

"Captain!"

Knigh, Perry, and Munroe all snapped their heads towards the call as Aedan ran up the companionway onto the quarterdeck. He paused, stared at Vee, and exhaled with a laugh. "I should've known." He touched his chest before turning to them, the gesture full of tenderness.

With a quick shake of his head, Aedan's expression flattened to seriousness. "The *Arrogant* and *Unicorn* are breaking off from the *Sea Witch* and changing course to intercept us." He addressed Perry, but then gave Munroe an awkward look as if realising this wasn't the *Respair* and he was in command.

Perry sucked in her lips, frowning at Munroe. "They wouldn't attack you, though."

"Well." Munroe's nose wrinkled as he winced. "I—I suppose as far as they're concerned, they just saw us not join the fight and now we're fleeing the area. Perhaps they suspect we've been taken over by pirates."

Knigh cleared his throat. "Fancy that."

He squinted ahead at the familiar shapes of warships approaching, their white sails full and bright in the sunlight.

What wasn't familiar was their split course, aimed at passing either side of the *Venatrix* so they could both unleash the full force of their guns against her. He'd executed that manoeuvre himself many times, but he'd never been on the receiving end of a Royal Navy broadside, let alone two.

A shadow passed over those sails as they sagged, the wind no longer with them. Dark clouds threaded between the warships and the *Venatrix*, a swift and neat storm blocking them off.

A streak of lightning, and another, both directly in the warships' paths.

Power. The air buzzed with it. Every hair on his forearms and the back of his neck stood on end. He could only stare at Vee, but at his side, he was dimly aware of Perry, Aedan, and the others shifting with unease.

Just like when the *Respair* had chased the *Sovereign*, the lightning strikes did no damage, placed perfectly to warn away pursuit. She *had* been trying to scare them off without hurting them, and she was doing the same now.

His heart soared to have that hope confirmed. Perry had been right all along. Of course she was right. He scoffed—how could he have doubted her—*or* Vee?

Knigh smiled at Perry, exhaling. "I don't think we need to worry."

He turned to Vee.

Her hair lashed in a wind that only seemed to hit her, whipping as if she were the centre of a vortex. Her eyes were open now, but they stared ahead, flickers of violet light in their depths.

His breath caught as if the vortex had sucked it out. What on earth? What was happening? He'd seen Vee work her gift dozens of times, but this?

This was...

Frowning, he glanced at Perry, about to ask her if she'd seen it before, but her open mouth and wide eyes were all the answer he needed.

With a *clunk*, the sabre and pistol fell from Vee's grasp. Lines carved between her eyebrows as they drew together. Still, she stared, unseeing, unblinking.

Knigh swallowed, hands clenching and unclenching at his side against the desire to go to her, grab her shoulders, and check she was all right. But despite all that power crackling through the air, she wasn't swaying or looking the slightest bit tired. What had happened to her?

Beyond, the thread of storm she'd placed between them and the other ships traced all the way to the black clouds surrounding the island, as though she'd syphoned it from them.

The air crackled like static charges constantly sparking, and when he tore his gaze from the ribbon of cloud, he saw the lights in Vee's eyes flashing—brighter, more frequent, like an intense storm raged within her.

She looked... inhuman.

He shivered.

Was this still Vee?

Past the howling wind, a different movement caught his eye.

A flash, but of reflection, rather than an inner glow. Navy blue and gold. Steel.

Knigh blinked, feet already propelling him forward before he fully understood what he saw.

Behind Vee, one of Munroe's lieutenants approached her, sabre drawn.

"Vice," Perry cried.

Then Knigh couldn't hear anything over the roar of his pulse in his ears.

He ran.

The air was thick and slow. He sucked in harsh breaths, legs pumping, muscles burning, different from the flame of rage he felt in battle.

This was all determination.

Directing the storm, Vee's body was defenceless. And he couldn't let this man hurt her—*kill* her.

Because murder was carved in every line of his snarling face.

The blade gleamed, rising, and the lieutenant closed in—only six feet from her.

Knigh was still a dozen feet away. His heart clamoured against his ribs as if it could leap out and reach her quicker.

Wild Hunt, take me before you so much as touch her.

His throat was raw as if he shouted, but the only sound was that frantic pounding in his ears again and again and again.

Maybe the shouts would reach Vee through her concentration. But her expression didn't so much as twitch.

Damnation, he didn't even have a weapon.

The sabre reached its peak, ready to slice down on the crook between her neck and shoulder—a place he'd brushed his lips a dozen times.

There was no more running. No more time.

But Vee had dropped a sword, hadn't she?

Muscles bunching, he fixed his gaze on the hilt lying inches from her feet.

As the lieutenant began his downswing, still charging, Knigh leapt. He tucked into a dive mid-air, so near to Vee, he could've reached out and touched her. The wind surrounding her buffeted him, refreshing upon his sweat-soaked skin.

The world righted as his hand closed on the sword's hilt.

Please, gods, let me be fast enough.

Springing to his feet, he lifted the blade, braced it in both hands.

He'd barely stood when the strike rang through the sword, through him, jarring his teeth and bones.

He blinked up at the blades locked together. Their fading ring pierced the rushing pulse in his ears. Both blades were clean.

The breath burst from him. He'd blocked it.

Face still creased, the lieutenant's mouth dropped open, staring at Knigh in bewilderment. He stumbled back.

Chest heaving, Knigh advanced. He wouldn't kill him, but he wouldn't leave him armed, either—not so close to Vee while she was vulnerable.

He batted away a half-hearted strike, then flung his own sword to the deck. Jaw clenched, he closed one hand around the man's wrist and the other around the knuckle-bow. With a crushing grip, he prised the lieutenant's fingers apart and ripped the sabre from him before throwing it overboard.

His fist shook at his side, ready to punch the man in the face. Once, twice, hells, twenty times wouldn't be enough, not for threatening Vee's life—for so nearly taking it.

But he hadn't.

She was safe.

And this man only thought he was doing his job.

With a long breath, Knigh shook his hand loose and backed away.

He watched her while Munroe had the lieutenant escorted from the quarterdeck. No change—she was still away in her gift, still thrumming with strange new power. It wrung his heart to be so close and yet without her.

Teeth gritted, he made a sound low in his throat. They needed to talk, but it would have to wait until she was really here.

The Lords and Ladies only knew what her reaction would be. Just because she'd forced Munroe to pick them up didn't mean she wasn't still angry at him—it only meant she didn't want the whole crew to die. She loved Perry, Saba, Aedan, all of them.

But maybe she hated him.

Above, the sails flapped and below, the deck pitched. Their course was changing, but Munroe hadn't moved the wheel.

That was Vee's tug on the ship. Despite the question mark hanging over Vee's feelings about him, he smiled to himself at the familiarity. It had been too long since he'd felt it.

As he approached the helm, Perry grabbed his arm and Aedan slapped his back. Saba nodded, lips still tight from tension that must not have uncoiled for her yet. Perry sent them to guard Vice until she 'woke up.'

His heart still pounded quick and hard, but it eased with every moment. She was safe.

Knuckles white, Munroe wrestled with the wheel, staring from it to the sails. "What the hells? It's as if the sea itself is fighting me."

Knigh grinned and clapped him on the shoulder. "That's because you're going the wrong way." One eyebrow raised, he nodded at the wheel. "May I?"

"Well, I'm clearly not in charge anymore, so why not?" Munroe huffed and let Knigh take over.

They quickly fell back into their old pattern, Knigh as captain, Munroe as first lieutenant. Knigh gave him orders to adjust sails and brace yards to take best advantage of the wind Vee gave them, steering past the storms that blocked the other vessels, and Munroe passed those orders to the crew.

It was smooth sailing for perhaps ten minutes, then the sea ahead erupted.

Knigh gasped, gripping the wheel all the harder as shouts and spray rose. Stomach plummeting, he stared at the all-too-familiar gouts of water.

Out of the depths writhed huge red tentacles.

THE KRAKEN

As soon as she'd heard someone report to Munroe that everyone from the *Respair* was safely aboard, Vice had sunk into her gift completely. Much as she wanted to run to Perry, Knigh, Saba, and the others, she had a job to do.

She let the storm around the island re-form completely, shoved the currents together, bringing the maelstrom back to full force, and, with the *Sovereign* blocked, she pushed the *Venatrix* away.

All that took energy, though, so when the other naval vessels returned, she reached into the wellspring and let its power lance through her.

Now, the sea, the sky, the throbbing energy danced to her choreography. She pulled a strand of that unnatural storm from the island, like fraying an end of rope. It tore through the sky, shielding the *Venatrix* from the *Arrogant* and *Unicorn*. Below, a current cupped the small frigate, carrying it away on a course smooth and swift.

She gave herself to the hum of power, the shift of water and air, the teeming life that was everywhere. Surf on a beach, dragging sand with the outgoing tide. Crashing waves upon cliffs, force and fluidity against stubborn stone. Waves climbing, peaking, falling, churning into the depths.

Something cut through the water. Something massive. It shot from the direction of the island, tracing the line of the *Venatrix's* wake, and slid beneath them.

She knew only one thing that moved so quickly.

Every tendril of her awareness retracted to this ship slicing through this stretch of water, this breeze pressing on canvas.

The storm might've cut off Mercia and his ship, but not his creature. She couldn't see it, but she could feel the sea's absence in a telltale shape.

Around her, through her, the wellspring roiled, uneasy, as if it knew her fear of the kraken. It could kill with a casual tentacle swipe. It could eat a man whole. It could splinter a ship with its embrace.

Not this ship.

It burst from the sea ahead, but Vice was already drawing every drop of moisture from the air, every spark of static.

Its tentacles snaked for the hull. No doubt others above the surface reached for the deck and the vulnerable men and women there. With a shift of awareness, she diverted the *Venatrix* to port—they couldn't avoid the kraken entirely, but she could make it work to hit them.

That done, she returned to the sky.

Every scrap she'd gathered, she reeled in, balling it above the kraken.

Clouds formed, light and fluffy at first, growing heavier, thicker, livelier. If she had her eyes open, she'd see they were darker now—grey deepening to black.

Her thread of awareness left in the sea picked up the kraken's movement. One arm curled around the ship's bow. Another unfurled.

There wasn't much time. That thing could pull the ship under, crack it in two, destroy, maim, kill.

Vice pulled harder. Just a few seconds more.

Static crackled inside, but she needed to hold it as long as she could bear. It tore through her, thrilling, potent, relentless... overpowering... excruciating.

All focus on the kraken, she let go.

It burned. It blinded.

It cracked open the sky.

Streaking from cloud to kraken, lightning shook the air.

In the waves, the creature convulsed, frothing the water as each tentacle shuddered.

Pain!

The word lanced through Vice's mind. Not her own thought. Not her own pain.

Hurt!

Something brushed her awareness—something old.

No!

Another awareness—not her own, but... a being—a person, in a way.

It was alien and old and huge, and as she grasped for

understanding, it stretched on and on. Like the sea, it was too massive to sense all at once. It slipped between her fingers, leaving behind one word: *Please!*

The kraken was intelligent. And its mind—because that had to be what had touched hers—was beautiful and labyrinthine, like a vast cave system of glittering quartz.

Vice stopped the lightning, letting it run crackling along the edges of the clouds. She couldn't attack the kraken anymore.

The great mass of its body sank into the water, releasing the *Venatrix*, relief palpable in its sagging muscles.

Did Mercia *ask* it to help him, leaving the creature with power over its own destiny? Or did he dominate it with his mind, holding it in thrall? Perhaps the shock of her lightning had broken his power over it.

Thick tentacles rippled through the sea and with a jet of water, the kraken darted off to the open ocean, faster than any ship.

Vice reached after it with her mind, but she had only the sea and sky as her tools. Mercia had the gift to work with or control sea animals. Had the kraken reached out to her in desperation to communicate? But how, when she didn't have that gift? Or did the kraken have its own power?

So many questions, her head buzzed with them.

And Wild Hunt, was she tired.

She fought through a mental fog to spread her awareness. The naval ships must've given up their pursuit, because she couldn't reach far enough to sense them. There was no sign of the kraken.

She let go of the storm and eased off her hold on the

currents and winds—their natural directions and speed were enough to keep the *Venatrix* sailing away from the *Sovereign* and Mercia.

Eyes opening, she exhaled. Her body wasn't too sore, thanks to using the wellspring, but it took several blinks before she understood her surroundings.

The *Venatrix's* quarterdeck. A scattering of clouds overhead. People at the helm, staring at her. One who turned from the wheel, eyebrows drawing together in a peak.

Grey eyes she knew well.

"Knigh."

BEWITCHED

Her feet started towards him before she even realised she was moving.

What if he didn't want to speak to her? She hadn't apologised for her behaviour yet. Her last words to him had been horrible, and their last interaction before today had involved her threatening him with lightning. Gods, there was so much to explain.

But maybe it was all right, because he was coming this way, one corner of his mouth rising, tentative.

Her chest clenched so tightly it was a wonder she could breathe. Somehow she managed.

She also, somehow, managed to keep one foot moving in front of the other.

All this time apart, she'd expected he'd be glad to be rid of her, permanently, if possible. No more nasty comments from her, no more guilt for him, and no more obligation to help her because of it. Out of sight, out of mind.

But here he was, striding towards her, all tall and broad, shadows around his eyes like he hadn't slept, damp hair tousled around his gorgeous face.

She'd pushed him away again and again.

And he'd let her down, yes. Once.

But that wasn't the whole story, was it?

Because here he was.

Crossing this bloody deck was taking a million steps— maybe two million.

At last, he was within arm's reach and damn her, but instead of pushing back the hair falling in her own eyes, she did indeed reach for him. Her hand landed on his chest, maybe to reassure herself that he was real and not a lie her mind told while she was, in fact, still channelling the wellspring.

A solid heartbeat throbbed against her palm.

They stopped inches apart, and she managed to drag her eyes from that point of contact to rove across him.

Dishevelled wasn't a strong enough term—his shirt was torn. His hair was a mess—a glorious, wind-swept, sea-damp-ened mess. What had been stubble when she'd last seen him had grown into a trimmed beard, setting off his jawline and cheekbones in a way that was thoroughly unfair.

His fingertips feathered against her brow, brushing back that lock of hair as he sought her gaze. He had this little crease between his eyebrows, like he was confused, but that tentative smile still hovered at the corner of his mouth.

Gods, she wanted to kiss it.

But *words*—that's what she was meant to do.

There was too much to say, and it all piled up in her throat. Lords and Ladies knew where she should start.

When she opened her mouth, two words fought their way to the top.

"You came." The same thing she'd said when he'd taken her from the gibbet cage—another time he hadn't let her down.

His hand closed over hers, skin warm and rough from work as he pressed it against his chest. His pulse hammering harder under her palm made all this suddenly more real.

"Of course I did," he murmured, voice rumbling through her, grey eyes more intense, more vulnerable than their steely colour. "I'll always come for you."

She huffed out a breath.

I'll always come for you.

No one had ever sounded so sure of anything.

Her own heart thundered, so loud it was a wonder he couldn't hear it. She leant towards him, his heat radiating across the gap in that familiar, delicious way.

The crease between his eyebrows faded. His chest rose and fell, steady, breath brushing her face, then he bent closer, lips barely parted.

Someone coughed.

Other people. On the ship. They were on the ship and...

Blinking, they took a step apart and her hand dropped, cold now it wasn't touching him.

Perry, Saba, Aedan, Lizzy, Wynn, Effie, Clovis, and Munroe had formed a horseshoe around them, some staring with raised eyebrows, others studying their nails or the deck.

They were alive and safe. But gods damn it, did they have to come and make themselves known right this second?

She chuckled, hanging her head. It was a good problem to have.

"Hold on." Knigh reached over, fingertips gliding up her jaw in a way that sent shivers across her flesh. He angled her face to him and for a moment she thought he was going to kiss her, damn everyone watching, but instead he stared into her eyes, frowning. "I thought I..." He exhaled. "Your eyes—yes. Like storm clouds. It's fading now." A smile flickered on his lips.

"Lightning? Mercia said something about that."

He stiffened, and the smile vanished as he took a step back. "I didn't think you could call down lightning on command."

Scoffing, she shook her head. Hadn't she wanted to tell him when she'd first done it? "I've learned a few tricks from Mercia."

Biting his lip, he nodded and angled towards the others, as if bringing them into the conversation.

She sighed—all those things left to say would have to wait. She tried to catch his eye as the others approached, but he studiously avoided her.

Perry looked the same as always, just a little damp and bedraggled. When Vice squeezed her close, she smelled of the sea. "Took a quick dip, huh?"

"Fancied the exercise." Perry grinned, but tears glinted at the corners of her eyes and she stroked Vice's hair as if to reassure herself she was really there. "Barnacle's safe and well—her kittens, too."

Vice sagged with relief.

Between the hugs and the greetings, she kept trying to make eye contact with Knigh, but he'd closed up, stiff and unreadable and looking everywhere but at her.

A man who was made by his uniform. Did being on the *Venatrix,* surrounded by those uniforms, remind him of everything he'd lost?

Of everything he'd thrown away because of her?

Eyes closed, she pulled her whole boarding party to her at once. She could lose herself with them—warm bodies, familiar smells, all with breath still in their lungs. Thank the gods.

With a grin, she ruffled Aedan's cropped hair. "I bloody missed you lot." She glanced at Knigh as she finished the sentence, and *finally* he looked back. His mask was firmly in place, but she'd take the eye contact. She nodded—that would make him understand she meant him too, right?

"So how the hells did you find me?"

While Perry and Saba explained how they'd found signs of a scuffle and her lost earring, Vice tried to keep her attention on them, but her gaze kept wandering back to Knigh. Still stiff, yes, but his eyes were on her as often as they were on whoever was speaking. That felt hopeful. Her heart certainly thought so, skipping a beat every time it happened, and she found herself smiling foolishly.

Damn Knigh, he had a way of making her feel like a teenage girl.

But... perhaps she should just enjoy it. Maybe he was still furious at her and that greeting had been a lapse—relief at seeing her alive. Maybe he wasn't going to accept her apology.

Maybe he'd only stuck around long enough to find her and reassure himself she was safe, and soon he'd leave.

At the moment, everything was still unsaid, still unknown, and this yearning tension fizzed between them, and maybe it was all going to end once they talked.

But for now, she had it.

"... Then FitzRoy came and told us what had happened." Perry pursed her lips and everyone's expressions darkened. Even Knigh's jaw twitched, a slip of his mask. "Vane had been drunk in a tavern, boasting that he'd sold you to the Duke."

Knigh sucked in a breath as if to speak, but someone called from fore: "Lizzy! Blackwood!"

They all turned as Luned hurried over. "We could use some help in sickbay." She glanced at Munroe, before giving Knigh a meaningful look, eyebrows raised. "Good to see you back, Vice." Despite her words during the captaincy vote, Luned's smile was genuine before she trotted off again.

Lizzy ducked in, kissing Vice's cheek. "Duty calls. Don't tell all the exciting bits while I'm gone."

Vice laughed at her retreating form.

"Excuse me." Knigh nodded, all unnecessary formality, and turned to follow.

Vice grabbed his hand, making him look back. "We'll talk later, yes?"

His fingers flexed around hers and he gave the most puzzling look she'd ever seen—half-frown, half smile.

What the hells did that mean?

"Later." He nodded and released his grip before hurrying after Lizzy and Luned.

Saba slung her arm around Vice's shoulder and Perry appeared at her other side, holding out a soggy pouch of cashews. "Might be a bit salty, I'm afraid."

Laughing, Vice took a handful and tried not to watch Knigh disappear from view.

She failed.

RISK

Limbs heavy, Knigh emerged from belowdecks to the cooling air of an orange sunset. He huffed a long sigh, running his hand through his too-long hair.

He'd been tending to the wounded for what must've been hours, but before he left, the ship's surgeon had eyed his bloody clothes and had his assistant fetch a clean shirt and breeches. The man had a good head on his shoulders, because he'd also brought a comb, soap, and a bowl of water.

Clean, yes, but he was still woefully underprepared to face Vee.

Despite that, despite the exhaustion dragging on his arms and legs, excitement buzzed through him.

When he'd seen her blink awake, there had been no question about going to her, even if he was meant to be piloting the ship.

It had taken every fibre of self-control to stop himself from holding her crushingly close. Although, he'd been unable to resist pushing her hair back from her brow or angling her face towards him.

Any excuse to touch her.

He brushed his fingertips together, the ghost of that sensation now gone.

He'd been worried that she'd changed, that something had happened to her. Seeing that power coursing through her, who wouldn't have thought it? There were stories of changelings, of people being taken, of creatures that looked like but were *not* them being left in their beds. And who truly knew what the fae were capable of?

But when she'd spoken, that had been all Vee.

He scanned the forecastle for her—perhaps she was by the bowsprit enjoying the breeze in her hair. But no, no sign of her there. Nor at the ship's waist.

At the port rail, Wynn and Effie stood, heads together, whispering. They looked at him, one eyebrow raised each, mirror images of each other. Their teeth glinted in matching grins.

"Taffrail, if you're looking for the Pirate Queen."

His face heated, and he opened his mouth. But was there any denying it? Especially after everyone had seen that moment on the quarterdeck. He clamped his mouth shut and nodded, then flashed them a quick smile.

Hands clenching and unclenching, he started aft.

The way she'd said they'd talk later made it sound like she

wanted him alone. Good—there was so much to say. Things just between the two of them. Things that should've been said a long time ago.

Good, perhaps, but also with the potential to be terrible. After all, she'd mentioned Mercia twice in the brief conversation they'd managed to have before they were interrupted.

He chewed the inside of his cheek. What had happened on the *Sovereign?* She certainly didn't spit out Mercia's name like he was a mortal enemy, and she hadn't whispered it like she was afraid, either.

He reached the steps to the quarterdeck and squared his shoulders.

"Blackwood." Not Vee.

He bit back a sigh and turned. "Munroe." Despite the interruption, his smile was genuine. Undoubtedly, his former lieutenant didn't approve of his desertion, but he'd still been a willing accomplice to Vee's 'hostage-taking' and rescue. "I haven't had the chance to thank you."

Munroe's mouth twisted in what was half-grin, half-grimace. "The lady's done that enough times for both of you. Do you have a moment?" He inclined his head towards the door to his cabin, formerly Knigh's.

Quieter, away from prying ears, of course. But also away from Vee. Still, Knigh accepted the invitation.

"Tell you the truth," Munroe said once the door was shut behind them, "I was grateful for the excuse to help." Shoulders sinking, he exhaled.

"I understand what you've risked." Even with the hostage

ruse, this could still end up costing Munroe his position, if not his life.

"And I intend to risk a little more." His jaw flexed as his gaze fell away. "That's what I wanted to talk to you about…"

HARD-WON

L eaning on the *Venatrix's* taffrail, Vice closed her eyes to the setting sun and inhaled long and deep. The air was salty and fresh and all the sweeter now she was free.

The day was done. She'd escaped Mercia and the *Sovereign*. She'd reunited with Perry, Knigh, and the rest of her friends.

She'd even gone and seen Barnacle, who'd nested in a sea chest and showed no sign of vacating. She'd purred ecstatically at Vice, butting her hand again and again, rubbing it with her cheeks, before parading around her nest of kittens as if to show them off. With tears in her eyes, Vice had given her a good fuss and told her she'd done well.

Perry, Saba, and Aedan had grabbed her and bombarded her with questions until she'd lied and told them Munroe had given her duties. Much as she'd missed them, she needed a moment alone. She'd spent weeks only speaking to George, Mercia, and Munroe, where every word had to be guarded, where she was living with the enemy. Being around friends was, somehow, *hard*.

With a sigh, she leant out over the rail and let a light dusting of spray hit her face.

Maybe there was also an element of wanting to save words for *him*.

He was still off with the injured, helping them. Much as she was dying to catch him alone, they needed him more than she did. She needed to apologise, but that wasn't a matter of life and death, even if it did wring her stomach.

The way he'd closed off earlier—maybe he wouldn't forgive her. Or couldn't.

The fact he'd kept looking at her meant nothing—or, rather, only that he liked to look at her. They'd always found each other physically attractive, after all.

"Ahem." That was him, just behind her.

Every inch of her tensed and for a second she couldn't breathe.

"'Madam, I understand you can show me to my new cabin.'" Nearer now. "That's what I said when I joined *The Morrigan*, wasn't it? But this sunset is far more beautiful."

Here they were at the stern of the ship, at sunset, just like that evening. Damn the man, but his reference to that moment did unfair things to her insides.

She exhaled, almost laughing as she turned, but she gasped the breath back in because he was far, far closer than she'd expected.

If she hadn't gasped at that, the sight of him would've done it.

He wore fresh clothes and had combed his hair, but the thick lengths on top were already trying to flop in his face. That telltale white streak was perilously close to falling in his eyes. Knigh Blackwood might have excellent self-control, but his hair refused to obey orders.

As broad and muscular as always, he blocked out the rest of the ship, making it feel like they were utterly alone.

And that was dangerous.

The sight of him, the scent of him, the sheer intoxication of him just a matter of inches away made her heart throb so hard she could feel it in her chest, at her throat, and low in her belly.

The knowledge she had of his body and what it was capable of...

Very dangerous.

But she'd made her decision: no matter the chemistry between them, whatever temptation called to her, it had to be talking first, kissing later.

So she gripped the rail at her back. It was the only way to stop herself reaching out for him, grabbing his shirt front, pulling him against her, claiming him.

She glanced over her shoulder, half-wanting an escape, half-wanting anything *but*. Above the blood-orange sun, the sky was already deep indigo, scattered with stars. That moment of looking away gave her the chance to catch her breath. She raised her eyebrows at him. "It *is* a beautiful sunset, isn't it?"

Coward. This wasn't the conversation they were meant to be having.

"That's not"—eyes closed, she shook her head and sighed

—"that's not what I want to talk about. But I owe you so many apologies for so many things, I'm not even sure where to begin."

She didn't dare look at his face—staring at his chest felt safer. He'd gone stock-still. Well, she had kind of blurted it out, hadn't she?

"I've been an arse. Not just since we left Albion with all those little daggers designed to hurt you... but also for telling you that I'd murdered Avice." That name made her grimace, but she pressed on. "You were right, I pushed you away *so* hard." She lifted her shoulders. "I panicked. I was being an idiot. Fitz told me you were leaving, and I didn't know how to handle it. So I did the only thing that made me feel like I was the one with the power, and I shoved as hard as I damn well could."

Her heart pounded with even more force to be talking about her feelings like this. It was too much truth, gushing out all at once. But it was unstoppable.

Besides, hadn't she spent all these weeks on the *Sovereign* desperate to apologise, to explain? This was her chance. And chances were all too easily snatched away. She had to take this one while she could.

She owed him that much.

A long breath calmed the frantic beat so she could go on without her voice shaking.

"And I apologise for leading you onto the *Sovereign*. I was blinded by the promise of getting that clue." She hung her head, voice going soft. "I was no better than Fitz. I should've known what it would do to you. What happened with Aedan—

that was my fault. And I am *so* sorry. I already apologised to the others earlier."

She sighed, flopping back against the rail. Lords, having feelings was tiring work. But she'd done the hardest bit.

"And there's one more thing—maybe the most important." At last, she met his gaze—it felt necessary for this.

He watched her, eyebrows slightly raised as if surprised. He wasn't quite smiling, but there was something soft in the set of his mouth and for a second it was all she could do not to tiptoe up to cover it with her own.

No kissing. Talking, remember?

Especially now. This *was* the most important part.

She swallowed and dragged in a deep breath. "I forgive you. Arresting me... all of it"—she waved her hand—"I forgive you."

His lips parted, and he blinked several times in rapid succession. Chest rising and falling heavily, he crossed his arms, hands squeezing his own flesh as if he, too, needed something to cling to.

"I couldn't get past it before," she went on, because the silence was unbearable, "but on the *Sovereign*, I barely thought about it. I was more interested in the fact it looked like I'd never get the chance to see you again, and that my last words would be such spectacularly stupid ones." She scoffed at herself, gaze dropping to his hand against his bicep, which strained the slightly too-small shirt. "I couldn't bear the thought that you and Perry would always think I was so stubbornly tied to my mistakes that I'd walked out."

The sea shushed behind them. Overhead, a gull cried out.

She chewed her lip. Should she break the silence or leave it to him? He had to say something back to all this, didn't he?

At last, he drew a long breath and blew it out, nodding. "Thank you," he said. "I know that must have been hard. *Thank you.*" His throat bobbed in a slow swallow. "So, Mercia didn't change your mind about us—the crew, I mean, not..." He gestured between them.

"Mercia?" she scoffed, even though *us* rang through her again and again in his low voice. *Us* sounded good coming from him. "Lords, no—he's a monster."

He huffed, shoulders sinking as he looked past her. The wind tugged at his hair, making it even more dishevelled. "I'm sorry... I've been an idiot. When you mentioned him earlier, I thought"—he shook his head—"I don't know what I thought. I suppose that you didn't talk about him like he was an enemy."

A fair point. "Sometimes enemies are... complicated." Then somehow her fingers were at his hair, pushing it from his face. He went still as her fingertips paused on his cheekbone for a fraction of a second. Only a moment of soaking up his familiar warmth, but gods, it was glorious. She lowered her hand, exhaling shakily. "Rest assured, he didn't turn me against you, he didn't win me over to his side or any of that. But he did help me, despite himself. I'll tell you more about it another day— right now I'm just glad to be away from him."

He nodded slowly, letting the quiet stretch on for a moment.

"You know," he said, "I was terrified I'd never see you again, too." He gave a smile laced with bitterness. "When you didn't come back, I tortured myself that something terrible had happened to you. It made me half-mad." His teeth gleamed, bright against his tan. "I punched FitzRoy in the nose."

A laugh burst from her. "Gods, I wish I'd been there to see that."

"I do, too. Although if you'd been there, I'd probably just have left you to do the hitting." He shrugged. "You owe it to him more than I do."

She inclined her head. "Very chivalrous of you."

"I try." He gave her a long look, biting his lip in a way that made her have to clench her hands against the need to grab him. With a sigh, his gaze slid away. "I owe you apologies, too. Those things I said to Perry and then to you the night you disappeared—I meant them, but I should've spoken to you properly about it all ages ago."

That wasn't his fault. "You tried, but I—"

"But I was a coward. I let you stop me every damn time." The corner of his mouth twisted in a sardonic smile. "I bottled it up until it all spewed out. Ugly and hurtful. And for that, I'm sorry."

She swallowed, her throat suddenly thick. Painful as talking had been, not talking had been stupid. But then, could she have had this conversation with him back then? She'd been too raw, too hurt. This time apart, despite not being her choice —maybe it was exactly what she'd needed, what *they'd* needed.

Nodding, she touched his arm. She couldn't get the words out, but hopefully he'd understand what that gesture meant. *You're forgiven for that, too.*

He leaned into her hand, then pulled away until it dropped, his arm pulling tighter to himself. "And the bigger apology." He bowed his head, eyes screwing shut for a moment. "My anger. It gets—*I* get out of control. You shouldn't need to mind me or wake me up from it. You should be able to rely on me if I'm going to be your—to be in your boarding party. So, I am sorry for losing myself, for hurting you, for scaring you—for any and all of it. I've been talking to Perry and although I was frantic while you were gone, I've been managing a lot better."

The look he gave her was wide-eyed, intense. His vulnerability squeezed her chest.

For all the times she'd seen true emotion from him, rather than the controlled mask, it still struck her. These were the moments she'd been reminded of when she'd seen George pull a Knigh-like expression. These were the moments she felt close to him. These were the moments that thundered in her heart the hardest.

"I missed you, you know," she blurted, underside of her fist tapping his chest. It was a stupid admission, but she'd resolved to be open this one time, and that meant saying stupid things. At least she'd managed to stop herself grabbing him at the last moment, though her fist still rested against the solid curve of his muscles, no matter how much she told it to get back to her side. Traitorous thing.

She shook her head to clear it of his dizzying proximity. She still had more to say. "Much as I sniped and poked at you on the *Swallow* and avoided you on the *Respair*, I... I suppose I've grown used to having you around. You're part of my life now. I don't know what your plans are, whether you're going to leave or—"

"I'm afraid you're stuck with me." A grin lifted one corner of his mouth. "You see, no one else will have me. And"—he bit his lip again, the lopsided smile gone—"I missed *you.*"

His hand rose and for a second she thought he was going to plunge it into her hair and kiss her like he'd done dozens of times. But instead, it went to her collar. With a small frown, his gaze followed the movement of his fingertips along her collar's edge as he straightened it.

"Vee," he said, "no matter how nasty you managed to be, you stood by me all the times that mattered—you got me to speak to Billy, you saved me from the rest of the crew, and you've talked me down from berserking twice now."

Watching him, she barely breathed. Any sudden movement or sound might break the spell that had woven around them, that had brought them an inch apart, allowing his warmth and scent to flood her, all cinnamon and soap and old leather.

He still fiddled with her collar, leaving her far too aware of the way it made the shirt's fabric brush against her shoulder and chest, a delicious tease. "You missed me," he murmured, voice dropping as he met her gaze. "I missed you. I'm not sure what that means."

Vice swallowed, unable to tear her eyes away from his. They glistened with the sunset's fiery colours, a million miles from dull grey.

What *did* this thing between them mean? That was such a heavy question, it blocked her throat.

Was he making an offer? Did he, somehow, despite all of it, still want her?

Because she sure as hells still wanted him. In this gorgeous moment where it was just them and the sea and the setting sun, Lords and Ladies, she wanted him.

She bit her lip.

But...

Of course there was a damn *but*.

This gorgeous moment was the problem. *She* didn't want to snap at him. *He* wasn't feeling guilty over what he'd done to her. They'd managed to have a genuine, civil conversation without resorting to ripping chunks out of each other or tearing any clothes off. And that was an achievement.

This peace had been hard-won.

It had taken rescue from a gibbet, fleeing a country and its Navy, fighting their way through a ship-killer of a storm, battling warships, kidnapping, *and* escaping the kraken—*twice*.

They couldn't go through all that again.

Besides, following her body's wants had got them in trouble before, back on the *Swallow*. Now was the time to listen to her brain and it said, *Keep this, don't ruin it.*

Gods damn it. Her brain was right.

She couldn't take what she wanted, however much she ached to reach across the inches between them and pull him to her lips.

Instead, she could help him. Together, they'd find Drake's treasure and he'd get his cut, and then he could start his new life. A big house on some pretty island out of the Navy's reach. He could even bring his family across from Albion.

Stability, comfort, structure—they were the things he needed and the things treasure could buy.

Because although he'd cleaned up, there were still circles

under his eyes and he looked damn tired. He clearly wasn't coping well with pirate life—it couldn't give him what he needed.

She forced a smile in place. It wasn't entirely fake—after all, they were bound to have a great adventure in the meantime. "It means... we're friends."

Friends. Somehow she pushed that word out, despite it being painful, despite her lips wanting nothing more than to cover his, taste him, tell him to take her over the damn rail, even if the whole crew could see.

His eyebrows rose slowly, then he nodded. "I suppose it's an improvement on *no friend of mine.* I'll take it."

She winced at the reference. Lords, sometimes she said some horrible things. But it had been right at the time —necessary.

The corner of his mouth twitched in a lopsided grin as he backed off a step. "Friends?" He held out his hand.

"Friends," she said, shaking it.

He squeezed before he let go and went to the taffrail. His gaze roved over their glittering wake. "Well, I have some news for my *friend.*" Again, that lopsided grin as he eyed her sidelong. "I just had an interesting chat with Munroe."

"Oh?" She arched an eyebrow, folding her arms and leaning her hip against the taffrail.

"He's... concerned after seeing Mercia send the kraken after us. And although his men weren't entirely thrilled at the prospect of helping pirates, they were even less impressed that their Admiral was willing to sacrifice the *Venatrix* and her crew just to get to us."

She growled, frowning. She'd been so wrapped up in getting rid of the kraken, she hadn't stopped to think about it that way. "Can't say I blame them."

"So Munroe made a proposal. We put him and the crew ashore somewhere not too far from a friendly port with food and water. And we keep the *Venatrix.*"

Vice froze. She blinked. "We keep...?" She didn't have enough breath to finish the sentence.

"She's the Navy's newest design: small, fast, well-armed for her size, copper-sheathed with a shallow draught." Knigh cocked his head, eyebrow rising at the same time. "Munroe thinks we might make better use of the ship than Mercia."

She dragged in a breath. "We keep the *Venatrix?*"

He chuckled and grabbed her shoulder, giving her a little shake. "Yes."

"Huh," she exhaled.

"Munroe and his men get a little revenge on Mercia and as they're all in on it, all culpable, they'll keep the secret."

A laugh of disbelief came out as she rubbed her face. This ship. She'd wanted it since the moment she'd laid eyes on it. And even if Perry was captain, rather than her, she'd still be sailing this huntress of the seas.

"Oh, and I think you might be right—about there being some sort of treasure, at least." He said it casually, but Vice jerked upright. "That clue isn't nonsense. I've worked out where it leads."

She grabbed his cheek, so close to pressing her mouth to his, she could feel his breath on her face. But—*friends.* Instead, she kissed his cheek, his neat beard rasping her lips. "You bloody genius." Her hands tingled and despite the weariness cloaking her, a thrill buzzed through her veins. "Because *I* have the cipher key."

His brows shot up. "But—*how?*"

"I'll tell you later." She pulled away and leant over the rail, grinning. "My brain is fried after"—she gestured at the sky, then him, then her chest—"can we just be quiet a while?"

"Of course," he said, inclining his head. He crossed his arms and rested on the rail, jerking his chin at the sliver of red sun on the horizon. "We have some sunset left."

"We do," she murmured, mirroring him.

They sank into silence, although her mind refused to be still.

Her friends were safe, and they'd come for her. They had the *Venatrix*. She had the Copper Drake and its cipher. Knigh had worked out FitzRoy's clue. Hells, he was actually entertaining the possibility that there was such a thing as Drake's treasure—that was a victory in itself.

Considering a few months ago she'd been locked in an iron gibbet waiting to hang, this was progress.

"I know I said I'd be quiet," he said after a few minutes, "but... some might consider it an ill omen, losing a ship called the *Respair*. Recovery after despair felt apt after Portsmouth."

She'd been a fine ship, true. And it was a shame to lose her, but...

Smiling, she watched him sidelong as he frowned at their wake. "Knigh Blackwood, worried about ill omens—there's a turn up for the books." When he shot her a scowl, she gentled the tease in her expression. "It was the right ship for that time.

But now we've recovered from despair." Her chest filled with the truth of that, and it stopped her voice for a moment. "We're friends, we've got the clues, and we have this ship."

His eyebrows rose, and the scowl disappeared. After all that had happened today, it might've only been a small victory, but it warmed her all the same.

She bumped her hip into his and gestured to the deepening night and the wide sky. "Let's see where it takes us."

Vice & Knigh's adventures continue in
UNDER BLACK SKIES, out now.
Read on for the author's note with behind the scenes details
about ADT and a sneak preview of *Under Black Skies*.

If you enjoyed *Against Dark Tides*, please leave a review on
Amazon and/or Goodreads.
And if you're over "just friends," remember you can get *Hissing
Hellcats*, a short story set just after events in *that* glow-worm
cave as a free gift for joining my newsletter crew.

AUTHOR NOTE

Caution: Here be Spoilers!
Read After _Against Dark Tides_.

So there we have it – Vice and Knigh are and will continue to be 'just friends'. (And I type that with aaall the side-eye in the world!)

I mean, come on, you've seen these two together... Like that's going to last! (Remember, you can enjoy a short story while Vice and Knigh are together (set during book 1's timeline) by signing up to my newsletter – _Hissing Hellcats_ is a thank you gift for joining: https://www.claresager.com/bbsback/)

But, yes, for now, our favourite pirate and former pirate hunter are friends. And, as Vice realises in that last scene – it's an achievement to get to that point, a hard-won victory. I think they've earned a bit of a breather to just enjoy that sunset.

Maybe the same could be said for me (and perhaps you, too), because this book was a challenge to write on a few levels. As a clue, I'm writing this author note in September 2020, just 5 months after writing the author note for *Beneath Black Sails*. **What** a 5 months they've been.

If you're reading this, you know all about 2020, so I'm not going to drag you through a list of all the s**t that's gone down, but I know you know. If you've lived through 2020, you've seeeeeen stuff.

I started writing *Against Dark Tides* (ADT) in February/March 2020, then of course Covid-19 hit the UK, followed by lockdown, etc, etc. No surprise, then, this book took a lot longer to write than I'd planned.

But the challenge isn't necessarily the important thing – it's how we deal with it. Coping mechanisms feel like the theme for 2020 (and we still have the last quarter to go!). The gods and the fair folk (and maybe even the Wild Hunt) must've been smiling on me because I somehow lucked into discovering my 2020 life raft.

Not meditation. Not binge-watching Tiger King. Not long baths filled with Lush's bubble bars (although that is a new pleasure I discovered this year). And not even eating my own body weight in chocolate or building a home gym to make up for gyms being closed (I did one of those two things – I'll let you guess which.).

It was a friend. I met Lasairiona McMaster at an author conference two weeks before lockdown hit the UK. Somehow, as the world condensed around us, she and I became account-ability buddies, unofficial self-care coaches, and close friends.

She kicked my butt when I was being flakey, and she bullied me (in the nicest possible way) into being kinder to myself when I was impatient at my slow progress.

I won't go into every single way she helped me, but I will say these two things:

1. This book wouldn't have come out in September if not for her.

2. You might need to hear this – just surviving 2020 is an achievement. Well done! And if you made **any** progress on **anything** in 2020, that is not to be sniffed at. You are a Pirate Queen/King and Vice and I are both proud of you.

When I asked my reader group for help naming ships in ADT (particularly the re-named *Covadonga*), Clare Dix shared a word that was just perfect: *Respair*, which British institution and lexicographer Susie Dent had shared the disused word in a tweet, meaning "fresh hope and a recovery from despair".

It felt like a perfect word both for this stage of Vice and Knigh's story... and for this year.

It's a shame that we still use the word *despair* and yet have forgotten *respair*, when surely *respair* is an all-the-more important concept to cling to.

I think that word lingered in my mind as I wrote, seeping out in little moments, like the celebration of Yule, as Knigh says in his toast: "The light in the night of the year. The sun returns. Winter is won. To surviving the dark."

Of course, the circumstances of 2020 weren't the only challenge of this book... After *that betrayal* in *Beneath Black Sails*, this next part of Vice and Knigh's story was always going to be tricky to execute. How the hells do you get a couple from enemies to lovers to enemies again and *then* turn them into friends convincingly?

That was my biggest concern with writing this book, and I put a lot of time and planning into pulling it off. This book was always going to be the most angsty out of the series, with that constant push and pull between Vice and Knigh of wanting and yet hurting and wanting and hurting...

It could never be as simple as "Oh, you apologised? Oh, OK! Kissing time!" So, although ADT is kind of agonising at times and it's hard leaving them as 'just friends' (*Mmm-hmm!*), I hope you enjoyed that back and forth and found their path to friendship satisfying and truthful.

I mean, it only took a bloody KRAKEN!!!

I've always loved the sea – as a kid, I wanted to be a marine biologist, and I was particularly interested in the creatures that lurk in the deepest parts of the ocean. But there's also that trepidation about the sea – it gives life and takes it, conditions change with deceptive speed, and that crucial element of the unknown... What lies beneath the surface?

No surprise, then, when I decided to write a pirate series, I knew there needed to be a sea 'monster' (or not monster...) and, for me, those old etchings showing a ship battling a giant octopus are **so** iconic, it had to be a kraken-inspired creature.

(Although the legends vary between the kraken being a giant squid or an octopus, for me squid have a certain delicacy to their bodies – I can't picture them crushing ships in their slender tentacles. On the other hand, the octopus could be more threatening, with its muscular arms and robust body. Plus, octopuses are incredibly clever, albeit in a very different way to mammals.)

If you'd like to read more about my inspiration and be the first to get news about my books, you can sign up for my newsletter if you haven't already, right here: https://www.claresager.com/bbsback

I tend to email a couple of times a month (plus an extra if I have a new release) and members get some gifts for joining.

One gift you might be particularly interested to get your hands on is the free ebook of the full-length prequel *Across Dark Seas*. ADS tells the story of **how Lady Avice Ferrers, hciress, became Lady Vice, notorious pirate** and is *only* available when you join my newsletter.

I also share articles and book-related goodness on my social media: I'm most active on Instagram (@claresager), in my reader group on Facebook, where I sometimes ask for help with things like what to call ships (https://www.facebook.com/groups/HiddenCourt), and on my Discord channel (https://discord.gg/tKpdxPwJQ8).

As with BBS, you can get some fun extras, including playlists for the books in the series, deleted scenes, and a Pinterest board here: https://www.claresager.com/bbssecret. I'm adding to the page all the time, so keep your eye out for more goodies!

There you go – that's enough from me until the author note for *Under Black Skies* where Vice and Knigh encounter fiendish puzzles, a stolen map, and a betrayal that will shake pirate-kind. Dun, dun, duuuuunnnn!

In the meantime, happy reading and here's **to surviving the dark**.

All the very best,

Clare Sager, September 2020

x

[Edited May 2021 – Read on for a sneak peek of Under Black Skies...]

UNDER BLACK SKIES – SNEAK PEEK

IMPATIENCE

Despite the sea breeze, the air was already thick with heat and sweat. The low morning sun forced Vice to shield her eyes as she left the quarterdeck's cabins. Even the cries and clatter of work were quieter than usual, as if the weather had dulled everyone's energy, leaving only lacklustre shanties ghosting the air.

A cheer broke the muffled quiet. Then laughter... clapping... a gruff shout.

Vice stalked towards the noise. Men and women had grouped together, backs to her.

Crowding wasn't so unusual—with Munroe's Navy crew still aboard, space was at even more of a premium than normal. But to see a couple of dozen pirates *and* Navy sailors gathered...

Trouble—had to be.

"Come on," someone shouted.

"Hit him!"

She groaned. This would be the fourth fight she'd broken up in as many days. Surprise, surprise, the Royal Navy mixed with pirates about as well as oil with water.

"Not this again." Rolling her eyes, she pushed through the crowd. "Out of the way, you bloodthirsty—"

A flash of white hair. *Knigh.* Her body coiled, ready to spring forward.

She blinked, stopping short. He and Aedan wore brown leather practice gloves. Not a fight, just sparring.

Something in her chest remained tight, her heart thrumming against it.

The pair circled, eyes locked together. Their bare torsos gleamed with sweat, highlighting each ripple of movement, each tensed sinew, each shift in stance.

Not sparing her a glance, Knigh passed, broad shoulders squared. The shadows of his muscles merged into the dark lines tattooed over his upper back—the moon and stars of the Blackwood family crest.

Aedan's frown deepened, leaving a look intense for a man normally so carefree. As he moved, she caught glimpses of the twin swallows inked across his chest in blue and black.

Two men both over six feet tall, muscular, skilled fighters— no wonder they'd drawn an audience.

A jab, a dodge. Vice twitched as if she were in the ring, as if her actions would keep Knigh from Aedan's strikes.

A right hook, the slap of leather on flesh, a whoosh of air forced from lungs.

She rocked on the balls of her feet and had to catch herself before she ran forward and pulled Knigh away to safety.

Sparring, not danger.

Aedan backed off a step and waited for Knigh to catch his breath.

Although that strike must've been hard, it was only a moment before Knigh looked up, teeth flashing in a fierce grin.

Uh-oh, Aedan was in trouble now. Vice swallowed, the sweet taste of victory already on her tongue.

Knigh sprung at him, jabbed for his belly, but at the last instant he pulled the blow.

Aedan had already taken the bait, defence low and ready for a strike that never came.

That left his cheek open as Knigh connected, the punch so fast Vice would've missed it if she'd blinked.

But watching this fight, blinking was out of the question. Her heart thundered, and the grunt that came from Aedan was as bright in her bones as if it were her own victory.

Hands fisted at her side, she exhaled, long and low, trying to expel some of the energy that had her twitching and tensing over a fight that wasn't hers.

They circled again, bringing Knigh almost in arm's reach. Tanned... tall... hair a little scruffy in contrast with the close-trimmed beard emphasising the angle of his jaw and the perfect lines of his cheekbones...

Wild Hunt take her if he wasn't good to look at.

And that was the problem—she was looking at him too much. Far, far too much for *just friends*.

She straightened, clearing her throat. She had things to do —primarily *not* loitering to stare at Knigh Blackwood.

Get a grip. She pressed through the crowd, heading fore again.

She'd just checked on Barnacle in the captain's cabin, which, thanks to the presence of two crews, she was sharing with Perry. Unsurprisingly, the little grey cat was in the sea chest she'd claimed as they'd fled the sinking *Respair*. Her cushion had survived. Its declaration of *non obsequiorum—we do not submit*—somewhat at odds with her position lying with half-shut eyes.

All four kittens were tucked against her, a row of wriggling fluffy bodies. They let out the occasional mew or squeak as they fought over the best spot. Vice, Knigh, and Perry had named the kittens now. The girl who looked like a miniature version of Barnacle was Flotsam. Her sister was a pale silvery tabby, and they'd called her Jetsam. The two boys were Anchor and Cable, the former all black and the latter a dark smoky tabby like their father.

Barnacle had accepted the fuss and chin scratches and hadn't so much as miaowed as Vice grumbled at the delay to their plans. Saba and Perry had been less understanding of, as Perry put it, her *bloody impatience.*

Five nights ago, as they'd sailed away from the *Sovereign*, Knigh had shown her the shape of Hewanorra's twin mountains in the jagged edge of Drake's poetry. And she'd been itching to get there ever since.

If not for this diversion to Redland, they'd already *be* in Hewanorra. She'd be uncovering the next clue to Drake's treasure this very second.

But they'd agreed to leave Munroe and his crew in a safe place. And Ichirouganaim fit the bill.

She nodded to Wynn and Effie as she passed. The sisters waved, then went back to inspecting the port cannons's gunlocks and side arms.

Called Redland by most Albionic folk, Ichirouganaim was also Saba's homeland. Munroe and his men would have no concerns about food, water, or survival, and Saba's mother would welcome them. Once the *Venatrix* and its new pirate crew were far away, she'd get a message to the Royal Navy saying their crew were there and in need of assistance.

At least Hewanorra was only a day's sail from—

"Vee," Knigh's voice carried over the deck, "hold on!"

JUST FRIENDS

Vice's stomach fluttered. Ridiculous thing—it didn't seem to understand they were just friends.

Steeling herself, she slowed and let him catch up.

Still shirtless.

Bollocks.

Her heart beat harder, faster, a distant thudding in her ears.

"I have a proposal for you." His smile dazzled in the low morning sun as he dropped into step beside her. "Good gods, it's hot." He squeezed a soaking towel over himself, sending water trickling down the taut lines of his shoulders and chest. A low sigh escaped his lips, and he wrung the towel out over his head, plastering his hair around his face in a way that simply *begged* her to smooth it back.

Stop staring.

Grimacing, she scrubbed her eyes to hide the expression

and shield herself from him. Double-bollocks. She *had* been staring. *Hard.*

She clenched her hands against the want—the want to grab his arm and make him face her. The want to slide up over that chest and into his thick hair, to try to squash that white streak that refused to be tamed.

In short, the desperate want for Knigh Blackwood.

Gods damn it.

This was ridiculous. *She* was ridiculous.

She'd been with plenty of attractive lovers—Aedan was handsome and drew looks wherever he went. And although dark-haired, intense FitzRoy was his opposite in almost every way, he won his fair share of admiring glances. So why the hells did the mere proximity of Knigh Blackwood have this power over her?

As further excuse to avoid looking at him, she checked over her shoulder. The crowd had dispersed, and Aedan stood alone, wiping himself down. *He* was still shirtless and gleaming, and yet she didn't itch to grab him. There was something wrong with her.

In control of herself again, she cleared her throat and chanced raising an eyebrow at Knigh. "You two really bonded while I was gone."

"*Because* you were gone, and we were both losing our minds over it." He shook his head, grin fading below a brief frown as he looked aft. "Though I must confess I'm puzzled, considering he was ready to shoot me when we returned from Albion and then I almost…"

Cut his arm off on the Sovereign.

She inclined her head, wincing. That was her fault. And the sudden change that came over him tied a knot in her gut.

Instead of sinking into gloom, Knigh exhaled, and the corner of his mouth lifted. "But I'm trying not to question it too much. I'm just glad to have a friend on board."

Somehow, *his* relief eased *her* belly. "Don't you mean *another* friend?" She cocked her head and flashed him a smile. "You've got Me, Perry, Aedan, Barnacle..."

His mouth twisted, but amusement sparked in his narrowed eyes. "We're having to count the cat now?"

"Hey, she's a very discerning cat."

He scoffed, fingers scraping against the trimmed beard at his jaw. "This is true."

"But seriously—you also saved Aedan's life that day, and you've more than proved yourself to the crew. You came after me"—her stomach flipped to say it, so close to his words *I'll always come for you*—"even though that meant attacking the Navy's flagship *and* her division. And you saved them all when the *Respair* sank."

"*You* saved—"

"There wouldn't have been anyone *to* save, if you hadn't evacuated so quickly. Just accept it, Knigh"—she grinned up at him—"you're one of us now."

"*One of us.*" He said it like it was a cause for wonder—his mouth softening, no longer sardonic. His gaze roved over her face as though he might find the hint of a lie there.

Maybe he believed it at last. Maybe he felt like he belonged here.

Maybe he'd want to stay, even once they had Drake's treasure.

With a single nod, she wiped the grin from her face, aiming for something more earnest. Maybe, just *maybe*, despite all the horrible things she'd said and done to him, she could make him feel better and not only worse.

Gods only knew if her expression *was* earnest, but as they moved fore, his grey eyes were still on her—on her mouth, specifically.

Her heart pounded against her ribs, loud in her ears.

Perhaps she wasn't the only one who felt this *thing* that still hung between them.

But it was out of the question. Off limits.

They were *friends*. Not so long ago that had seemed impossible, and it had been a tough battle to get here. But here they were.

No way was she going to ruin that.

When they'd discussed taking Munroe and his crew to Redland, he'd asked, "What about getting back to the Navy?"

But she'd heard the unsaid words in his question: *What about getting back to the Navy, like I cannot?* And they were a dagger in her gut.

So she cocked her head, the picture of light-heartedness, certainly not affected by his presence or intensity. Not in the slightest. "You have a proposal?"

"Oh, er, yes." He shuddered as if ridding himself of confusion—or perhaps of that moment that had stretched out between them.

Ahead, the low, green mass of Redland rose from the glittering sea. The breeze ruffled her hair, briny and fresh, tinged with distant smoke. They'd dock within half an hour, and it would take maybe an hour to drop off Munroe and his crew.

Then they could finally set sail for Hewanorra.

They stopped at the bow—she with a smile, he with a preoccupied frown.

His knuckles turned white as he gripped the rail and leant back against it. "The thing is, I can't spar with Aedan all the time."

"Aedan?" She frowned back towards where they'd been sparring, but there was no sign of their blond friend. What did this have to do with—?

"And this is how whittling went." He held out a lumpy piece of sun-bleached wood. Jagged lines scored their way across the surface, splinters jutting out.

She squinted at the... *thing*. What *was* that?

Face screwed up, he turned it over. "I'm not sure I have Saba's knack for it."

"I wouldn't say that." She tensed her cheeks, attempting an encouraging smile. "It's... it's..."

It was a shape. And it was wood. That was all she had. She willed something recognisable to appear.

An elongated blob with splintery gouges and twisting woodworm holes.

She swallowed. "It's... nice?"

"Don't patronise me." His fingers folded over the *thing* and he shoved it in his pocket. "It's meant to be a whale shark—you know, like at the reef?"

"Oh? Oh. Oh!" She forced her mouth into a bright smile,

rather than the confused grimace she'd given the alleged 'whale shark.' "Well, it's—erm—kind of—"

A low chuckle rumbled through him and raised his eyebrows at her. "Seriously, Vee, don't worry. I've already given up my whittling ambitions—I'll leave that to Saba. Too many splinters, anyway. And frustration is the exact opposite of what I was aiming for."

"So, sparring. Whittling. I must be missing something, because I'm not connecting the dots."

"Ah, yes." His hands opened and closed into loose fists. "Perry said I needed a distraction for my hands and my mind. An activity to focus on and keep me calm."

A pang hit Vice in the chest. Small but definitely sharp, like one of those splinters from his whittling. He was still talking to Perry about the reasons behind his anger—the darkness that made him lose control sometimes.

Since Vice had returned to the crew, she and Knigh had spent every night chatting over rum after the others had drifted to their bunks, catching up on their time apart. He'd told her how talking to Perry was helping make sense of the feelings that plagued him—feelings about his father in particular.

Talking to Perry. Not to her.

And why should he have come to her? Yes, they were friends, but as she'd just said, she wasn't his *only* friend.

If that pang was jealousy, it was stupid. Whoever helped Knigh with his anger, it could only be a good thing. It wasn't like she had any claim over him.

She coughed, as if she could get rid of the troublesome splinter. "An activity?"

"Well." He eyed her sidelong. "I was hoping you'd let me help decipher the Copper Drake. Perry mentioned it was going slowly."

"More like Perry said I'd been moaning about it being utterly glacial."

He cleared his throat, but the twitch at the edge of his mouth betrayed that he was covering a laugh. "The words *grousing* and *bellyaching* might've been uttered. I didn't have the heart to point out the irony that *she* was complaining about *you* complaining."

She chuckled, using it as an excuse to look away from him and delay answering. Working together on the clues would make it quicker.

But it also meant her and him together in a little cabin. Alone. All the time in the world to drink up those little expressions of his—the ones she'd seen echoed on his brother George's face back on the *Sovereign*. Far too much time with the constant warmth of cinnamon, soap, and worn leather in the air.

She caught it now, just lightly, before the breeze swept away all but briny air. It made her suck in a sharp breath, but that only drove the scent of him deeper until she was swimming in it, drowning in it, sweet and spiced and clean.

It would be unbearable. Impossible.

But he was the only other person in the crew who spoke Latium, so it wasn't as though she had a lot of options.

They said 'familiarity breeds contempt.' Maybe time cooped up together was exactly what she needed to get rid of any lingering feelings for him.

"The help would be..."

Ahead, in the open bay, three black-sailed ships cut through the glittering water, not yet at dock. Something about them had stilled the words in her throat. Something was wrong.

A second later, she realised. Black sails. *Full* sails, like voids against the brightly painted buildings beyond.

The ships weren't prepared for docking.

It twitched in her belly.

Still leaning against the rail, Knigh glanced over his shoulder and stiffened. "What's wrong?"

Whose ships were they? And why were they sailing through the bay rather than slowing ready to dock? "Can you see a flag?" She craned to glimpse one.

Now standing to attention, the alertness practically rolled off him. "There." He bent close and pointed.

On the nearest ship—a black flag with a white spear piercing a crimson heart. Whose flag was that? A new captain, perhaps, allying with more experienced crews.

"They're all flying the same," he muttered. "Anyone you—?"

Cannons boomed.

Discover who's attacking and why, as well as how well Vice and Knigh's attempt at being 'just friends' goes in *UNDER BLACK SKIES*, available now.

ACKNOWLEDGMENTS

As this book was written in 2020 during the Covid-19 pandemic, it requires more thanks than usual.

First off, this book might not have made it past the finish line if not for one person (and it certainly would've been considerably later if not for her): Lasairiona McMaster. She is my accountability buddy who stood by me all through lock-down and knows exactly when to kick my arse into working and when to tell me to STEP AWAY FROM THE KEYBOARD! Selfless, thoughtful, and hilarious, she's quite a woman. *Thank you* doesn't quite cover it, but THANK YOU, my friend.

More thanks and love to my GLORF and RFS admin friends for all the advice, support, and friendship. Big love to Tameri and Josie – thank you for checking in with me, keeping me sane(ish), and just for being your awesome selves. I feel so lucky to have such great author-friends.

Big practical thanks to Clare Dix for suggesting some **fantastic** ship names, especially the *Respair* – a stroke of genius. Thanks also to May Sage, Anne-Mhairi Simpson, and Sandrine for help with the Latin – all that's right is because of them, any errors are mine.

Massive thanks to my advance team for reading and giving

feedback and early reviews, to Catharine, Jennifer, Beth, and Las for reading and picking up errors – and thanks to all for loving Vice and Knigh and their story.

The amazing covers you see on this series are thanks to the crew at Deranged Doctor Designs. Love your work, as always!

Big love and thanks to all you wonderful readers for the amazing response to these characters and their stories – I'm thrilled to be sharing this with you and am so grateful for your support.

Finally, thanks to my partner in crime and cat-wrangling, my partner in life and lockdown, my best friend – my husband Russ. Thank you for the walks, the podcasts, and *whispers* making me go running. Most of all, thanks for your support and thoughtfulness, including by building an incredible study.

ALSO BY CLARE SAGER – SET IN THE SABREVERSE

Beneath Black Sails – Piracy, magic, and betrayal all tied up in a steamy romantic fantasy bow. Complete series.

Book 0 – *Across Dark Seas* – *Free Book*

Book 1 – *Beneath Black Sails*

Book 2 – *Against Dark Tides*

Book 3 – *Under Black Skies*

Book 4 – *Through Dark Storms*

Bound by a Fae Bargain – Steamy fantasy romance stories where you can learn more about the elusive fae.

Stolen Threadwitch Bride

These Gentle Wolves – Available in Flirting With Darkness, a fantasy romance & paranormal romance anthology

The Prince & the Thief – Quin cons from the rich to give to the poor. Fantasy adventure with darker themes and steamy romance.

Book 0 – *The Thief's Gambit*

Book 1 – *The Prince & the Thief* – Forthcoming, join the newsletter crew to be the first to know when it's released.

ABOUT THE AUTHOR

Clare Sager writes fantasy adventures full of action, intrigue, and romance. She lives in Nottingham, Robin Hood country, so it's no surprise she writes about characters who don't always play by the rules.

You can find her online home at www.claresager.com or connect with her on social media at the links below or by email at clare@claresager.com.

- instagram.com/claresager
- tiktok.com/@claresager
- bookbub.com/authors/clare-sager
- facebook.com/claresagerauthor
- amazon.com/author/claresager
- twitter.com/ClareSAuthor

Made in United States
Troutdale, OR
07/08/2023